ITP:
Book Two

Joshua and Aaron

by David Gelber

RUFFIANPRESS

Ruffian Press
150 FM 1959
Houston, TX 77034
www.ruffianpress.com
www.itpfuturehope.com

Library of Congress Catalog Number: 2010906750

ISBN-13: 978-0-9820763-4-7
ISBN-10: 0-9820763-4-7

First Edition – 2010

Cover Design:
Duncan Long
www.duncanlong.com

Typesetting/Book Layout Design:
Gianna Carini
www.brighteyes.org

Printed in the United States of America.

Dedication

This novel is dedicated to my parents, Julius and Elisabeth Gelber, married 63 years and still in love.

ITP:
Book Two

Joshua and Aaron

You may surely eat of every tree of the garden, but of the tree of knowledge of good and evil you shall not eat, for in the day that you eat of it you shall surely die.

—God

You will not surely die. For God knows that when you eat of it your eyes will be opened, and you will be like God.

—Satan

When you pass through the waters, I will be with you; and through the rivers, they shall not overwhelm you; when you walk through fire you shall not be burned, and the flame shall not consume you.

—Isaiah 43:2

Blessed are those who are persecuted for righteousness' sake, for theirs is the kingdom of heaven.

—Matthew 5:10

৵৹৻

I. Beginning

JOSHUA SMITH WALKED UP THE STAIRS TO HIS APART-
ment, his mind wandering off in every direction. The day had been
typically successful; three winners and several thousand dollars richer.
It never really mattered, the money that is. It went into the bank or was
spent on the rare luxury item. The simple, anonymous life he had chosen for himself was all he needed. No commitments, obligations, or
deadlines encumbered him and he was content.

He walked through his front door, greeted by the room immediately coming to life. Sensors in the door established his identity and the
lights came on, the music of Bach started to play, and news and messages flashed on the several monitors around the apartment. *What's for
dinner*, he thought. Unlike most of the apartments and homes of the
day, he had disabled the food synthesizer; he preferred preparing his
own fresh food, a task he thoroughly enjoyed. The extra cost was not
an issue, but the superior taste certainly was.

"Let's see what we've got in the pantry," he said to himself as he
rummaged through the refrigerator. He pulled out some fresh cheese,
a bottle of fresh spring water, an apple, and some carrots. He went to
work, peeling the carrot and slicing the cheese, and laid it all out on
the table in front of one of the monitors. As soon as he sat down, his
messages started to appear. As they flashed across the screen he gave a
light tap on the table deleting each. "Free . . ." delete, "Win . . ." delete,
"for a good time . . ." delete, and on and on. The fifty-first message
caught his eye. "G. O'Donnel is asking you to call him."

Anyone that carries a moniker G. O'D really wants attention, he thought.
He said, "open," and the complete message appeared on the screen.

"Greetings, Joshua Smith.

Allow me to introduce myself. My name is Geoffrey O'Donnel and
I represent Solar Concern, a charitable organization that is focused on
improving the lives of the numerous displaced and forgotten people

that live among us. You are cordially invited to join our organization as we carry out the work that our Lord asked of us over two thousand years ago. Your unique and special talents would be of great service to our organization. If you are interested or would like more information, please reply to this message or call the number below. Thank you for your consideration.

Sincerely, Geoffrey O'Donnel"

Very unusual, Joshua thought, *and a good way to get noticed. I'll need to research that organization someday.* He picked up a slice of cheese, deleted the rest of his messages, and pulled up the past performances and recordings of the entries for the following day at Monmouth Park.

❧∘❧

II. At the Track

JOSHUA STOOD AT BAR#23 WITH THE EVER-CHANGING members of the group that gathered regularly to share their thoughts and insights on the day's horses. They were at Monmouth Park trying their skills at what had been called the Sport of Kings in the past. Today their collective attentions were focused on the fifth race, an offering for $40,000 claimers, restricted to fillies and mares. The field was full and Joshua saw it as the best opportunity of the day. None of the contestants really stood out and he had zeroed in on Slow Beat. She looked ordinary on paper, her last race had been anything but outstanding, but she was trained by the Master, Judd Herschel. Joshua had seen her last race in person; the jockey never moved, his hands remained perfectly still throughout the race and she still had closed three lengths in the last eighth of a mile. Today she was dropping slightly in class and stretching out by a sixteenth of a mile. She was ready to run her best and she was 7/2, which promised a reasonably healthy payoff.

The others had varying opinions, some voicing them loudly, others guarding their thoughts as if they were the entrance to King Solomon's lost treasure. Joshua never cared who knew what or how he bet. Some would ask for his thoughts and he always clearly gave his complete analysis. "One minute to Post," blared the announcer overhead. He moved to his seat to watch the race, his impassive face shielding the butterflies from his companions.

"They're in the gate . . . and they're off. Misty Snow takes the early lead, followed by Slow Beat on the rail . . . on the turn Slow Beat takes the lead and draws off by three lengths, Hard Annie moves into second . . . Slow Beat leads by three, but has bolted." The filly had taken a right turn and was heading to the outside rail as the jockey desperately tried to return her to a straight path and Hard Annie closed the gap. In a few strides Slow Beat had righted herself and the two fillies raced as a team to the wire. "As they approach the wire it's too close to call between Slow Beat and Hard Annie."

Joshua and the others waited an eternity as the photo was processed and examined by the judges. The patrons at the bar watched the slow motion, magnified replay, but it was too close to call. "Dead Heat," someone yelled out, but there were still no numbers posted on the board. Finally, the results went up. Slow Beat had prevailed by the slimmest of noses. Joshua's hand shook slightly as he slowly walked to the kiosk and redeemed his winner, $500 to win and $200 on the exacta made for a good day's work. He would leave several thousand dollars richer for the day; thinking that no matter how good one could be it was always nice to be lucky once in a while.

The remaining races were uneventful, nothing worthy of a serious wager and no horses of interest. He left after seven races, walking around the outside of the track toward his home. As he passed the backstretch he ducked through a hole in the fence, taking a shortcut through the stable area. As he walked past the barns and the dilapidated hovels that served as shelter for the grooms and hotwalkers, he heard his name called.

"Hello, Joshua, hello." It was Ray, one of the grooms. The unofficial boss of the oft neglected backstretch personnel.

"Hey there, Ray," Joshua said to the old man. Ray was about ninety years old, thick white hair and tanned skin that had been beaten by the sun into a thick leathery covering. He had been a groom for sixty years. He loved horses, scotch, and cigars, in that order.

"How did you do today?" Ray asked.

"Slow Beat was good to me, although she made it exciting."

"Funny about that, you know. That is the most steady horse I know. It's weird for her to get spooked like that. Just racing luck, I guess. I'm glad I saw you, by the way. Can you take a look at Bessie?"

"What's up with her?" Joshua asked.

"She don't look right, that's all, won't eat, feels warm, has done nothing but lay in bed for two days. Me and some of the others had to cover for her, you know, so they wouldn't put her out."

"It's really not my place, you should call a real doctor."

"I don't want to cause trouble, can't you just eyeball her a bit? If you say she needs a doctor, then we'll get her to the hospital. Come on," he pleaded, "follow me."

Joshua agreed and followed the elderly man to an old shack adjacent to Barn 41, a solid brick structure that housed the valuable thoroughbreds. He found Bessie laying on a cot, covered by a worn sheet, shivering, her eyes a deep yellow and her belly swollen and tight.

"Hey, Bessie, how are you doing?" he asked, although he could see that it was anything but good.

"OK, I guess, just a little weak," she answered in a croaky whisper.

"How long have you felt weak. Joshua gently pushed on her tense belly as he tried to get some history. She winced in pain.

"A few days, but I feel better today."

"Uh huh . . . able to eat?" She just stared at him. "Been drinking much?"

"Not a drop, I swear."

"OK, Bessie. I'm going to talk to Ray. We'll be back in a minute." The two men walked outside. "It's not good, Ray," Joshua said. "She needs to be in a hospital. Has she really not been drinking?"

Ray answered, "I'm not going to lie to you, Joshua. She used to drink a lot, but ever since she went to the meeting last year she hasn't touched a drop. She just took sick, that's all."

"Well, her liver is shot. If you get her to the hospital they can give her some Hepatic Rejuvinin and she'll probably recover, but she needs to go now. I'll help you if you want. Get some of the boys to cover for you. Do you have a car or should we call an ambulance?"

"I can borrow Mr. Mac's truck. He's gone until tomorrow. Let me talk to Andy and Paul and then we'll go."

Joshua sat with Bessie until Ray came back, shaking his head. "What's wrong?"Joshua asked.

"Truck's broke down," Ray said matter-of-factly.

"Wait here with Bessie; I'll call a taxi."

Ray shook his head again. "Good luck, no taxicab is gonna come to us here. We'd be better off carryin' her."

Joshua made the call anyway. "They said they'd be here as soon as possible."

"Saying is one thing, but doing is another," Ray said, shaking his head again. The sun was starting to settle in the sky as they sat and waited. Ray looked up at Joshua and said, "Why do you do it?"

"Do what?"

"You know, come around, bring food, take care of our problems. We aren't anything to you and you don't owe us nothin'. Most of our troubles are caused by our own selves anyway, drinking or carrying on or fighting. Like I said, you don't owe us a thing."

Joshua was still for a minute. Then he stared into Ray's eyes intently. "Ray, you couldn't be more wrong. You people are of great importance. I make my living by counting on you to do your jobs, to care for these helpless beasts and keep them in tip top shape and running as true to form as possible. It may seem crass, but if Bessie is sick, then Bold Thunder over there is going to suffer, and tomorrow in the third race he won't be up to snuff. Likewise, if you are off the sauce, then your "children" will be all the better for it and if one of them looks ready to win I know that you'll have him ready to run his best. So, you see, when I come around and see all of you, it's really for my own selfish reasons."

Ray nodded as if in agreement, but muttered under his breath, "that don't explain the money."

"What?"

"I said, 'That don't explain the money.' All the money that you spend out of your own pocket, bringing us medicine and food and books. You say what you want, but I think you are an angel from God, sent to look over us. That's what I think and that's what all the others think."

"I wish I was an angel," Joshua replied. "Then I could just waive my hands or flap my wings and poor Bessie would have a new liver and we wouldn't have to figure out how to get her to the hospital. It's obvious that no taxi is coming."

A full moon filled up the night sky as the two men sat with the sleeping Bessie. Joshua got up suddenly. "Wait here," he said. "I'm going to the hospital to see if I can find help. I'll be back as quick as Ruth's Rising." Before Ray could say a word, Joshua was gone.

At that moment, kilometers away, UN Representative Dennis McCally walked out the main entrance of the Diblonski Building and quickly climbed into the waiting limousine. He loosened his tie and wiped his brow, relieved that the meeting was finished. He hated to be the bearer of bad news, but it was better than having one of Mr. Diblonski's executives tell the big man first or, even worse, having the old man find out for himself. "My Georgetown townhouse, please," he said.

Although Mr. Diblonski had seemed disappointed, McCally was sure that in the end he agreed with the representative's position. The church organization in Brooklyn was doing society a great service with its attention to the underprivileged in that area. There was no question in his mind that they should be allowed to keep the property that the church stood on, along with the surrounding structures. The new Diblonski facility could be built anywhere; he had even found a superior and less expensive location in Queens. In the end McCally was sure that his colleague agreed. Besides, as a UN Representative he believed he had some obligation to the people he represented; he was sure that ultimately Mr. Diblonski understood.

The driver nodded at McCally's command and started on his way. McCally touched behind his ear and the little green dot started to glow as a hologram of notes appeared. He started to study them as the driver sped away toward the ocean and away from Washington DC.

"You're going the wrong way," McCally said with a note of apprehension in his voice.

"Mr. Diblonski's orders, sir. He thought you might need some rest. He's instructed me to take you to his beach house in Oceanside."

Very thoughtful of the big man, McCally thought, but, for some reason, he still felt uneasy. The driver nodded his head and a clear partition came down between the front and back seats. The driver checked his surveillance sensors, saw that there was no one within visual range and no long range monitoring in the area, and then flipped a switch. Before long McCally was unconscious and after a few more minutes his breathing had completely stopped. As the limousine sped along, he was deposited on the side of the road; he rolled into the ditch and lay motionless.

Ten minutes later, Joshua Smith walked along the same road; the lights of the hospital were finally in sight; he started a slow trot, but suddenly stopped as he saw the body lying along the side of the road. *I don't have time for this,* he thought as he climbed down into the shallow gully and turned the body over. The face looked familiar as he felt for a carotid pulse. The body was warm, but cyanosis was indicated by the bluish-purple lips and black tongue.

"Maybe there's still time," he said out loud as he hoisted the body over his shoulders and continued on his way to the hospital which was still about a kilometer away. The extra burden made the walk seem long and slow. He finally saw a sign that said, "EMERGENCY SER-VICES," with an arrow pointing to the back of the building. No one came to help as he walked through the sliding doors into the Emergency Department. A handwritten sign was on the reception desk, "Out to Dinner. Self Service Available."

Just great, he thought. He waved his ID card in front of the scanner and walked into the ED. There were long lines of homogenous people at the various self-service kiosks, putting on monitoring devices, running through the therapeutic devices, receiving computer prescribed medications, entering private therapy cubicles to receive their pre-scribed interventions; all fully automated without a doctor or nurse in sight. The "patients" all looked the same to Joshua, buxom women with perfect skin and perfect features alternating with muscular men sporting their own clear complexions surrounding their perfectly bland personas. He looked around until he found the red "L&D" but-ton (Life and Death). He deposited the dead body on the floor, hit the red button, and walked out.

He waived his ID card again and hopped into one of the ambulances that was parked at the entrance and input the address to the barns at the track. The ambulance sped away.

He arrived back at the track to find Bessie gasping for breath, her tense, swollen abdomen pushing against her chest, her legs as big as tree trunks. He loaded her into the back of the ambulance and it raced back to the hospital. En route, Joshua hooked her up to the diagnostic monitor. The findings were as he expected: liver function only 6%, renal function 12%, hyperdynamic cardiac activity, tissue perfusion normal, but oxygen utilization only 41%. Therapeutics were initiated with toxin specific immunoglobulin and exogenous hepatic and renal support. As the ambulance pulled into the hospital emergency receiving dock her breathing had slowed, her heart rate had decreased, and she was awake and talking comfortably.

An automated stretcher met them and she was carted into the ED as her therapeutics continued. Joshua walked alongside and stayed with her as she was brought to a treatment room. He expected she would stay as the process of hepatic regeneration usually took about one week to complete. He noted that the body he had delivered was gone. There still was no attendant around. He inquired at the shiny aluminum and glass patient information kiosk, searching for resuscitations within the last hour; none were found. He altered his search to include unsuccessful resuscitations; once again there were none.

Now he was more than curious. The body couldn't have been dead for more than twenty minutes when he found it and he had delivered it only about ten minutes later, plenty of time for initiation of degeneration suspension and reversal. The man should have been good as new. Joshua picked up the emergency line and called the operator, trying to get a hold of the ED director.

"I'm sorry, sir, but all the physicians are tied up."

"But, I brought a person and left him for resuscitation not more than thirty minutes ago."

"We have no record of any post mortem resuscitations today, sir. Have a nice day."

Joshua was perplexed and confused by the mystery, but decided that there was nothing more that he could do. He checked on Bessie, who was looking much better, and then started for home.

છ≫⊙

III. Meeting at Home

IT WAS LATE WHEN JOSHUA REACHED THE TOP OF THE two flights of stairs and stood outside the door to his apartment. There was a light shining from beneath the door, unusual because the lights were designed to automatically be off if Joshua was out. It had been years since the sordid affair with Richard Cosby and Senator Leavitt, but Joshua was still looking over his shoulder. An uninvited guest waiting in his apartment left him more than a little uncomfortable, but, anyone who took so little pain to hide his presence probably was not any immediate danger. He went in trying to maintain an attitude of calm indifference.

Sitting on his couch was an elderly man with long white hair, dark glasses. He was impeccably dressed in a charcoal gray suit with a red and black tie. The man stood up as soon as the door opened.

"Good evening, Mr. Smith. You don't seem very surprised to see me here."

"Oh, I'm surprised, alright, but you didn't bother to conceal your presence. Do I know you?"

"Certainly not, but I do know you, in a sense, as I have been watching you for years. Allow me to introduce myself. My name is Geoffrey O'Donnel; here is my card."

Joshua took the card, which was black with white lettering:

GEOFFREY O'DONNEL
SOLAR CONCERN
NEW YORK, NEW YORK

"Glad to meet you, Mr. O'Donnel. I read your message yesterday. What can I do for you?" Joshua put the card in his pocket as both men sat down.

"I've forgotten my manners. May I offer you something to drink?" Joshua asked. "I'm sure there's something in the fridge."

"No thank you, I'm fine. But, I have something to offer you; something that you desperately need although you don't realize it. In fact, you've needed my help for years. It's only by luck that you are still here."

"I'm listening."

"First, turn on your monitor and bring up the current news."

"OK, I'll play along; monitor on." The news came up, and there on the screen was a picture of the same man Joshua had deposited, dead, at the hospital.

"UN Representative, Dennis McCally, was found dead in his Georgetown apartment this evening, victim of an apparent drug overdose. Representative McCally had been in the UN for two years. The death comes as a complete surprise . . ."

O'Donnel turned the monitor off and sat down facing Joshua.

"McCally reached his political position with the help of Aaron Diblonski. You had some dealings years ago with another Diblonski protégé, Adrian Leavitt. Both these men are now dead and, like it or not, you are involved with both. You were lucky with Leavitt; Diblonski never figured out that you were with Richard Cosby or that it was your idea to break into Leavitt's office, although he has been looking for you for years. But, they do know that you are the one that left McCally at the hospital and that you know that he didn't die of an overdose at his apartment. They don't know that it is the same individual involved in both these deaths, but it's only a matter of time before they learn that little fact. The truth is, Joshua Smith, Aaron Diblonski is looking for you and you are about to be found. Your luck is about to run out."

Joshua sat silently for a moment contemplating everything O'Donnel said. He knew that he was in trouble, big trouble. He shuddered to think about what waited for him at the hands of Aaron Diblonski.

"You're right, Mr. O'Donnel, I'm in big trouble. I'm open to suggestions; I'm also curious as to how you know so much."

O'Donnel ignored Joshua's inquisitiveness and said, "Come with me tonight, to New York. You have some remarkable talents that could be of great help to me. You've helped a great many people for someone so young, always very quietly, but also very effectively. I am offering you a chance to continue to do such work, but now in the public eye."

"This will keep me safe?"

"Hiding in plain sight is often the best way to be inconspicuous. I've found that people are far more apt to search under rocks than in a crowd when something or someone is missing. And, you will help a great many people who are in need, the same as you helped Bessie tonight. She is recovering quite nicely, by the way. I thought you'd want to know."

Joshua looked around his small apartment and thought about the life he lead and about the last seven years waiting for the long arm of Aaron Diblonski to reach out and crush him. "Let me think about it until morning," he said.

"If you truly believe that is the best course of action for you then you are not nearly as perceptive as I thought."

Joshua closed his eyes for a brief moment. "You're right; if I wait until morning there won't be any decision to make, knowing the way Diblonski works. OK, let's go; time is wasting. Let me get a few things."

"Certainly, but please hurry."

Joshua packed a few clothes and his personal hygiene kit. He looked at all the books, feeling like he was leaving his best friends behind. He packed his picture of Ruth Rising, the complete works of Dostoyevsky, some fresh fruit and, as an afterthought, the Bible he had "borrowed" from Richard Cosby years ago.

"This Book has helped me out of jams in the past," he commented. "Anyway, I'm ready to go."

The two quickly descended the staircase and climbed into O'Donnel's black limousine, which was waiting in front. Two minutes after they left, a plain black vehicle pulled up in front of Joshua's apartment.

৯৯৯

IV. Diblonski and Company

AARON DIBLONSKI SAT IN THE BOARD ROOM OF HIS washington office building, leaning back in his tall leather chair, his eyes closed, lost in thought. As was his custom, he was early for the board meeting. Today's session of the Executive Board was especially important; he had arrived almost an hour early. Most of the Board members knew of this habit and made it a point never to arrive early; rather they always were careful to arrive exactly at the appointed time. Randy Peskew was the newest member of the Executive Board and had not been informed of Mr. Diblonski's idiosyncrasies, intentionally it seemed. Mr. Diblonski briefly opened his eyes when Peskew sat down, but remained silent. Peskew started to squirm, but maintained enough composure to not address the chairman without being addressed first. Finally, five minutes before the scheduled start, Mr. Diblonski opened his mouth.

"Good afternoon, Mister . . ."

"P-Peskew, sir. Th-This is my first Executive Board meeting. I'm sorry I disturbed you."

"Don't apologize, Mr. Peskew, particularly when you really are not sincere. You may be sorry, but only because you arrived separately from the pack of yes men that will descend en masse in exactly four minutes."

"Y-You're right sir . . . You'll have to excuse me. I didn't plan to be alone with you. My full name is Randy Peskew, Vice president in charge of Research and Development . . . R and D."

"A very important position. I shall be anxious to hear your report. Our last Vice President for Research and Development preferred to spend his days playing games and was a great disappointment. I'm sure that you will greatly surpass his feeble accomplishments. But, enough small talk; it's 1:00 p.m., the sheep will be arriving any second."

As soon as the words left his mouth, the double doors flew open and the remaining Board members walked in and silently took their seats.

Seated on Diblonski's immediate left was President for External Affairs, Peter Simmons, and on Diblonski's right was Abe Masur, President for Global Operations. These two were Diblonski's main executives, running day-to-day operations of all of the many divisions of Diblonski Ltd.

This multi-planet conglomerate was involved in manufacturing, entertainment, media production and distribution, mining and energy production, and extensive retail distribution. The company pioneered the joint venture model between industry and government which had proved incredibly profitable for both parties. Diblonski Ltd. was founded in 2052 and Aaron Diblonski had chaired the company all those years. No one knew exactly how old Mr. Diblonski was and no one had ever had the courage to ask him. For his part, Diblonski was always impeccably dressed, youthful in appearance and energetic in every facet of his life. In an age where people routinely lived to over one hundred and twenty, Diblonski seemed to be well over one hundred and fifty.

As everyone took their assigned seats Mr. Diblonski stood up and addressed the membership.

"The meeting is called to order at 1:03 p.m. It is noted that everyone is in attendance. We will start with Mr. Simmons' report."

Peter Simmons stood up. "Our model of expansion by partnering with the governments of nations continues to be a great success. The table projected to each of you shows the governments that currently partner with us; out of 182 UN members, 165 are equal partners with us in at least one venture. In all of these joint ventures our executives are the principal managers, with the governments delegating control to our management team. Profitability is depicted on this graph, as you can see we have achieved over twenty-five percent growth across the board over the last six months. Any questions?"

Simmons moved toward his seat, but was interrupted by Mr. Diblonski.

"Before you finish, Peter, could you explain the flattening of growth in the eastern United States?"

"I wasn't aware of any flattening of growth," Simmons replied.

"I've looked at the data you provided and in New Jersey, New York, Pennsylvania, and Virginia the profits of our casinos are growing at a rate of only sixteen percent. This is definitely diminished from the historical growth of twenty-five percent."

"I hadn't considered that change to be anything other than a statistical aberration. I am confident that the growth will return to historical levels before the fiscal year is completed."

"I do not share your confidence, Mr. Simmons," Diblonski answered, a slight note of disgust in his voice, "and if I were in your position, I would be investigating this trend to be sure it is not the start of a prolonged decline in our position in these areas and to be sure that it is contained to only these areas."

"Yes, sir; I will have my team look into it today," Simmons stammered.

"If I were in your place I would be sure to investigate it myself," Diblonski said without any emotion or change in his voice. "Our competition has begun to reemerge in this part of the United States and the negative effect on growth is apparent. The rebirth of religion in these areas is a great potential threat and must be crushed."

"Yes, sir, it will be tended to today." Simmons sat down and seemed to fade into his leather chair.

"Mr. Masur," Diblonski continued, "what is new in Global Operations?"

Masur stood up and activated the hologram of his presentation. A globe appeared above the conference table and began to rotate, going faster and faster, the moon appeared and gradually the globe shrank as it took its place within the solar system.

"Global Operations should rightly be called Interplanetary Solar Operations as our influence now reaches to the ends of our solar system. Our mining facilities on Titan are producing a steady stream of iron, copper, platinum, and silver. Carbon mines on Orion are processing at 99% capacity and new sources of essential raw materials are being cataloged daily."

"There has been predictable steady growth of food synthesizer raw materials paralleling population growth as one would expect."

The holograms danced and spun as the presentation seemed to dazzle even Mr. Diblonski. The remaining divisions made their respective reports and the meeting started to wind down with only Research and Development left to report. This came from Mr. Peskew, the newest Vice President. Diblonski turned to him.

"Allow me to introduce Randy Peskew, newly appointed Vice President for Research and Development. Mr. Peskew made quite an impression on me today; arriving early for the meeting which allowed the two of us to have quite an engrossing and interesting conversation prior to the arrival of the rest of you. Mr. Peskew."

Peskew wasn't sure what to think as he stood up.

"R-R and D is pursuing the continued integration of the G-Green Dot in series to produce . . . a, an autonomous solution to artificial intelligence."

His voice wavered more than usual as he spoke and there were a few snickers from other committee members, but Mr. Diblonski was silent, never taking his eyes off the junior executive.

Peskew continued, "Th-The p-production of robots capable of independent thought has been an obstacle that we are on the brink of overcoming. The p-picotechnology utilized in the Green Dot product linked as a series of integrated processors is very powerful. This should give any robot the ability to effectively learn and develop independent reasoning that will eliminate the need for repetitive human input. In other words we will have robots that can think for themselves, freeing us and our customers from almost all routine day-to-day tasks. M-My department anticipates a working prototype within eighteen months. Are there any questions?"

Peskew took his seat as Mr. Diblonski stood up and addressed the board members.

"Diblonski Ltd. is built on the premise that we can provide for the majority, if not all, of the population of this world, every item and facet of their existence to keep them comfortable, safe and productive. We are partnered with nearly every government on this globe in a business model that has been beneficial to our customers, that is the people and their elected representatives. We have achieved this success through innovation and anticipation of the wants and needs of our customers. Those of you that embrace this model and grow with us will see unlimited potential in earnings, rank, and power. Anyone of you has the ability to rise to the highest echelons within this corporation, even to usurp my role as CEO and Chairman of the Board. I have been in this position for ages and look forward to the day that one of you or someone as yet unknown shows the fortitude and ingenuity that will allow me to confidently hand the reins over and ease into a much deserved retirement. I charge you to take this as a challenge and dazzle me with innovation and creativity. That's it; meeting adjourned."

Diblonski and Masur remained seated as the other committee members hastily exited.

"What are the latest figures on lifetime partnerships?" Diblonski asked.

"One hundred percent members number 2,697,323,101; yearly renewable members have reached 6,899,004,765, trial members are 5,098,454,888. Overall totals are up thirteen percent, while population growth is at seven percent. At this rate, complete conversion will take at least twenty more years."

"Well, we've worked for all these years, we can afford a few more years. What about the recent security breech?"

"Our recent mishap is in the process of being sanitized. The media have been effectively controlled, official investigation and findings have all been within our guidelines, but there is one loose end."

"I heard; I hope it will be quickly tied up with a minimum of company input."

"We are working toward that end, but we have lost the individual. We know who he is, but so far the where has eluded us. Don't worry; this will be cleared up within twenty-four hours."

"I hope so; I don't want another "simple inconvenience" dragged out and unsolved for years and years."

Masur winced at the reference to the Cosby affair that still gnawed at both of them, seven years later.

"I will keep you posted; you can expect a clean resolution to the current dilemma by tomorrow."

ॐ

V. Law Enforcement 2163

THE LAW ENFORCEMENT SYSTEM EVOLVED OVER THE years to accommodate the shrinking world; a world where the rapid expansion of technology allowed workers to easily commute between cities and towns that were hundreds of kilometers apart. A lawyer in New York City could easily wake up at seven, play racquet ball with the local judge, shower, have breakfast, and arrive in court in Washington DC by ten. Rapid travel by modern automobiles and mass transit made such commutes simple and ordinary.

Local law enforcement, responding to such changes, morphed into the Global Criminal Prevention and Law Enforcement System. Under the auspices of the United Nations, national justice systems administered regional law enforcement agencies. Within the United States, the old time local police department and Federal Bureau of Investigation merged into the various regional police departments, officially called the Regional Law Enforcement Departments. There were seven regional departments under the direction of the US Justice Department. They were the Northeast, Southeast, Midwest, Southwest, West Coast, Pacific, and Alaskan Law Enforcement Departments.

Each functioned autonomously from local government, reporting to the regional offices and investigating criminal activity within that particular region. Despite the great advances humanity had made, human frailty was unchanged. Crimes of passion, domestic violence, theft, kidnapping, and all the other acts that one individual can perpetrate on another still plagued society. The regional law enforcement systems allowed for coordinated investigative efforts over the large geographic areas made smaller by modern technology.

In addition to this new police system, medical research into the criminal mind provided exciting insight into the motivations that led an individual to pursue criminal activity. Specific genes on chromosomes eighteen and twenty-three were discovered to be permissive to allow criminal persuasion. The landmark study by Trent and Goodwin in 2124 found that fifty-five percent of habitual criminals had these genes. The UN Council of 2130 was convened and a consensus statement issued that all violent criminals would undergo complete genetic screening and comprehensive neurophysiologic mapping and analysis. This would allow genetic predisposition to be revealed and manipulated; with the result being prevention of any return to antisocial behavior.

Overall, seventy-two percent of violent criminals had been rehabilitated and returned to productive society utilizing the available neurologic manipulations. By the year 2150 the UN had hailed the law enforcement system as one of the great successes of modern society.

๑๛๑

VI. David Sanders

DAVID SANDERS, FORMERLY OF THE ASTROPILOT CORPS but now a messenger of God, sat in his study with his daughter, Little Debbie, on his lap. Across the room a wall filled with shiny plaques and trophies stared at them; reminders of a past life filled with victorious competitions and complete emptiness. He was trying to get his travel papers together, but the young girl insisted that she was more important.

"Why do you have to leave, Daddy? You just got home a few days ago and I want to play with you," she pleaded.

David smiled at her and held her close to his chest. "This will be the last time for a while. I'll be gone for a few weeks and then I'll be home for a whole month and we can do everything."

"That will be wonderful," she said with a hint of anticipation in her voice.

"While I'm gone you have to watch after your mommy. Make sure that she eats properly and that she doesn't get too wrapped up in her work. You know how she can be."

"Oh, I know, Daddy, but don't worry David and I will take good care of her."

At the mention of his name Little Debbie's older brother came in. He was short for his age, with the jet black hair of his father, but his mother's eyes and her remarkable intellectual gifts. Fortunately, both he and his sister had been spared her frustrating reading disability. Debbie seemed to favor the father and certainly had his athletic prowess, already capable of running eight hundred meters in less than two minutes; really remarkable for a five year old.

David Jr. sat in the chair next to his father and sister. "Can't I go with you this time? I'm sure that I can help out."

"Your mother and sister need you here. While I'm gone you have to take care of them. Besides, Little Bit will be with me."

Oh, Daddy," Debbie observed, "Little Bit is so old he can barely get himself up on that worn out chair he likes."

"He may be old, but he has taken care of me for years and I'd be lost without him."

At the mention of his name, the little white dog picked his head up and one ear stood up. He crawled out of his bed in the corner and, despite what the little girl said, deftly jumped into her lap, as if trying to prove that he was just as nimble as ever.

David put both the dog and his daughter on the floor. "I need to finish packing now. Go tell your mother that we can go out in a few minutes. I'm sure that she'll want to finish whatever she's working on before we leave."

The two children ran out of the room, while Little Bit stayed behind. David picked up the old westie and held him in his lap. "It must be a little rough for you, old fella. It's not like the old days, no intrigue, no evil senators; still the message of hope we bring is more important than anything," David said as he stroked the dog's rough fur.

His companion looked up with his big black eyes and one ear drooping and gave a little bark as if to say that he understood and agreed with everything David had said. David, actually, was positive that his diminutive friend did understand.

They got up and David put on his shorts and running shoes as the kids returned with their mother. The five went out and started on their afternoon run, Little Bit given the luxury of riding in a cart, pushed along by David Sr.

૭ઌન્ડ

VII. Lieutenant Ryan

LIEUTENANT MICHAEL RYAN LOOKED AT THE REPORT ON the monitor at his desk.

"The findings and conclusions concerning the death of UN Representative Dennis McCally are that this is an accidental overdose of Euphoricin resulting in asphyxiation. The body was found with an empty container of Euphoricin in the home and typical physical findings of overdose . . . physiologic scans confirm . . . no evidence of foul play . . ."

Signed by Sergeant Theodore Moore, May 12, 2163.

Seems to be in order, Ryan thought, *just a few other details to confirm.* He read through the entire report, but he didn't find it mentioned anywhere.

"Forensic Pathology," he said and a call was placed to Dr. Evelyn Wall, Chief Forensic Pathologist of the Washington DC Crime Lab.

"Hello, Michael," she answered. "What can I do for you?"

"Hello, Eve. I was given this report on the investigation into Representative McCally's death. The COD is listed as Euphoricin overdose, but I don't see any mention of discoloration of fingers and toes. I've never seen an overdose from Eupho without it. I wasn't actually in the apartment; Sergeant Moore was the investigating detective. I'm only signing off on the report. Can you look into this for me?"

"Of course; let me pull the file and I'll get back to you. Give me an hour or two."

Ryan turned back to the report. This is very unusual. Sergeant Moore is usually very thorough and would never miss something so basic; probably just an oversight. I'll just have him fix it before I sign off he thought and went back to his other work.

છે∼૭

VIII. New Jersey to New York

JOSHUA AND O'DONNEL SPED AWAY FROM JOSHUA'S apartment heading north. The night seemed especially dark and Joshua noticed that the black limousine was navigating by instrument control, without lights and was staying away from the main roads. He reached into his bag and took out two apples, offering one to his companion.

"No, thank you, I'm not hungry," O'Donnel said.

"Are you sure? This is a real apple, freshly picked from a real orchard."

The older man gave a faint smile and said, "Are you so sure of that? Did you pick it yourself? You have this aversion to synthesized food, but is it really as bad as you think? Let me show you something; give me your apple."

Joshua gave him a funny look.

"OK, I'll play along." Joshua handed O'Donnel the apple.

He put the apple into a metal bin that opened up from the floor, closed the metal door, and pushed a button. There were a few flashing lights and then a dinging signal and the door popped open. O'Donnel took out two identical apples and handed them to Joshua.

"Tell me, which is your real apple and which is the synthesized duplicate?"

Joshua took each one, turned them over and over, studying each one, sniffing them, and finally took a bite of each.

"This is the real one," he said, keeping the real one for himself and handing the copy to his companion.

"How can you be so sure?"

"I just am. I don't think that you really know which is which."

"On that you are wrong. I do know, but you are correct. You are eating the real apple. It is this uncanny ability of yours that has brought me to you. You have some remarkable traits that my organization wishes to utilize for what I'm sure you will agree is a most noble goal. There is a government task force that the State of New York has formed to investigate the problem of the "displaced" persons that exist within our society. You had encounters with some of these lost souls years ago during the ITP affair and you encounter them on the backstretch at Monmouth Park. You delivered one to the hospital today. They are called a plague on our "modern" civilization and they are shunned as if they were lepers."

A blinking light appeared on the console and O'Donnel stopped.

"Excuse me for a moment."

He held his finger to his ear and then returned to Joshua, who felt the limo slow and stop, pulling over well off the road.

"Hurry, get out," O'Donnell said calmly.

"What's up?" Joshua asked as the floor of the limousine popped open, exposing the ground underneath. Deciding that it was no time to ask questions, Joshua grabbed his bag and they quickly climbed out and crawled along the ground toward a grove of trees about fifteen meters away.

As they reached the cover of the trees, Joshua heard a whistling noise that gradually grew louder until it abruptly stopped and the limousine exploded, almost silently.

"That was close," O'Donnel remarked, still incredibly calm.

Joshua grabbed him by the shoulders and pulled him around, a wild look in his eyes.

"Would you please tell me what's going on? Who's trying to kill me and just who are you? Why should "Solar Concern" be wrapped up in murder and bombs and what have I got to do with any of it?"

"Calm down, Mr. Smith. You are safe for the moment and I'm sure these would be assassins now assume that you are dead. So . . . we can relax. Diblonski's minions will not return; at least not for a long time. We can proceed with our plan. Now, follow me, that is, if you wish, or you may stay here; just be aware that the author of that little present will be very thorough and will be here shortly to verify that you are dead. Oh, that reminds me, I need some of your hair. Quickly, quickly."

O'Donnel gave him some tweezers and Joshua pulled out several hairs, which were put into a little gold container. After five minutes the contents were spread out over the wreckage.

"Your DNA, which will prove to the assailants that you were obliterated by the blast. Now let's go; our transport is about four kilometers from here. The two hurried away, with Joshua feeling more than a little apprehensive, but also seeing no alternative but to trust this strange man who had thrust himself into Joshua's previously simple, uncomplicated life.

As they started, Joshua almost immediately walked into a large bush and then tripped over a large tree root. He got up and brushed the dirt from his hands.

"Put these on," O'Donnel said. "They'll help you see."

"What are they; night vision goggles?"

"That's right, but especially powerful and sensitive. You will see things in a way that you've never seen before."

Joshua put on the black eyewear and immediately was filled with awe. The pitch black night became illuminated with bright light and every detail of the forest, from the bark of the trees to the lichen on the rocks came alive. Insects crawled along branches, butterflies were sleeping, hidden by leaves, even the wind took on new and brilliant detail. Joshua made his way easily, almost enjoying the walk as his troubles faded into the background for the moment. He noticed that his companion hadn't donned any goggles, but still seemed to walk effortlessly through the forest. *Strange,* Joshua thought, but he didn't say a word.

"I don't need them; the goggles, I can see perfectly fine on my own."

"How is that?" Joshua asked. "You don't look like a cat."

"We see and hear what we've been trained to see and hear. You walk down a noisy street and hear cars whiz by, people talking, or an occasional barking dog. I hear a bird singing in a tree after feeding its babies. Those goggles free you to see the world apart from society's limits. I have already learned to see where others are blind. If you work at it, you also can free your mind to see the hidden world that exists in plain sight all around."

They reached a clearing and Joshua could see a dirt road running along the edge. An old truck pulled up alongside them from amongst the trees on the opposite side and they climbed into the front seat. There was a real person driving.

"This is Larson; he works for me," O'Donnel said.

"Pleased to meet you, Mr. Larson." Joshua put out his hand and Larson shook it but didn't say a word. He turned to O'Donnel.

"We'd better hurry if you want to catch that train into the city, sir."

Joshua noticed the obvious respect that Larson gave O'Donnel, filing it away in his head for future use. He yawned and realized it was nearly morning. As the truck bounced along the rough roads he fell asleep, just as they passed a big neon sign:

WELCOME TO NEW YORK
THE EMPIRE STATE

As they were passing the sign, a nondescript black car stopped alongside the remains of O'Donnel's vehicle back in New Jersey. A man dressed in a black coat stepped out and surveyed the wreckage, scanning the remains and running a thorough spectral analysis. He put his finger to his ear and reported, "Sanitizing complete." He departed as suddenly as he had appeared. Many kilometers away Aaron Diblonski opened a book and started to read as the huge fire in his study blazed hotter than ever.

ॐ‑ॐ

IX. Looking for Joshua

ERNIE CORYLLOS SLAMMED HIS FIST DOWN HARD ON THE table. the apartment appeared deserted and Coryllos noticed that all the personal hygiene implements were missing, but several appliances were still running, suggesting that someone had left in a hurry. He rummaged around but found very little of use, nothing that clearly identified his quarry and no usable personal data. There was a holographic imager by the bed, the type that repeatedly projected a series of photos.

"Damn, he was here and I just missed him. Nobody knew I was coming, but somehow he was tipped off. Well, it's not a complete waste; this picture file may help."

He activated the imager and holograms began to appear one after the other. There were several racehorses, a man in an astropilot uniform, a woman in a white coat, a white dog, several people gathered around a bar, another lone man.

"Analyzing these may give some clues," he said out loud. "Maybe one will be the one I'm looking for."

He took the faded dot from his pocket and activated his amplifier. A holographic message danced in front of him:

"Find one responsible for RC elimination. Bring to me. No limit."

It was dated 1/2/2157 and unsigned, but he knew that such a missive came from the big boss, who had been very patient, but had never cancelled the work order. *He must really want this guy,* he thought. Nearly seven years of searching had brought him to this apartment, at least it wasn't another dead end. Now, he had one more clue. He took the picture file with him as he returned to his room to run an analysis.

❧

X. David Sanders

DAVID SANDERS LOOKED AT HIS ITINERARY, A SCHEDULE which was a far cry from jetting around the solar system or blasting between dimensions. His current travels were taking him to various venues along the Jersey coast and ended in a rally in Brooklyn. In seven years of bringing the word of God to the lost people of this world, he had experienced triumph as well as frustration. The lost souls who had been shunned by mainstream society were more than receptive to the word, and many followed him from town to town, and many more heard the Truth on numerous broadcasts. Still, most of the 99.99% of people who lived, worked, and played within what was called "proper society" remained lost. There was an occasional convert, but there was far more ridicule and derision. David was never discouraged, however; his faith remained unshakeable and he had long ago learned to shake the dust from his clothes and move to the next town.

He looked at the holograms of Deborah, David Jr., and Little Debbie; he missed them terribly. This mission trip would be over soon and he would be back with them for at least one month before his next trip. He looked at his rose gold watch. It was too early to call; Deborah would be wrapped up in her latest project and the kids would be deep into their studies. He had three hours to kill so he put on his shorts and running shoes and headed out to get some exercise. Little Bit was fast asleep on the bed; he let the old dog sleep, although the little westie really enjoyed being pushed in his little cart.

Running was the best way David knew to prepare for an evening of bringing God's word to the people. It helped him clear away unimportant thoughts and allowed him to focus on his upcoming message. As he ran along the streets he felt uneasy; he thought about Joshua Smith. He hadn't heard from his friend since Little Debbie's first birthday, nearly four years ago. *I really should call him when I get back to my room*, he thought, and he continued on his run spending the remainder of the time reflecting on his life before the ITP had transformed him.

Old memories of profound emptiness and brief, meaningless pleasures raced through his brain. These memories mixed with recollection of the frequent vigorous training that was required of an Astropilot; all these jumbled thoughts sent the steady pace of his running, the thud of each footfall, fading into the background. He recalled the powerful feeling of elation he would feel as he rocketed through open space and his pace quickened. As his speed increased he thought about Ruth and he slowed as a few tears filled his eyes. He saw so much of her in Deborah; they both were gifts from God, but the brief time in Eden remained tucked away in a special part of his soul. He always felt guilty when such thoughts crept in, as if he were unfaithful to Deborah. He shook his head and continued on his way.

As he ran past a rare grove thick with trees and bushes, a figure shrouded in black, hiding in the shadows, watched his progress. After David passed, the observer made a call and then disappeared.

❧❧

XI. Gideon

JOSHUA AND O'DONNEL CLIMBED ABOARD THE RAPID transit that would take them into Manhattan. The car was empty as they took their seats. Joshua was studying the goggles that he had worn walking through the woods. They were plain, glass goggles with a rubber strap; no built in mechanics, no evidence of any nano or pico processor, nothing to say that they were anything but cheap toy goggles.

"How do these work?" he asked. "I don't see anything that would give them any special visionary power."

O'Donnel looked up and smiled. "Oh, they are powered, alright. The mechanism is hidden. Those goggles are specially tuned to the wearer, in this case you. You may keep them. They may come in handy if you get into a jam."

Joshua continued to examine them as the transport pulled into the station.

"We'll take a taxi from here."

As they got into the cab Joshua's phone buzzed. He looked at the ID and saw that it was David Sanders. *What a surprise,* he thought.

"Don't answer it," O'Donnel said. "Even though it seems to be a friend, from now on you must be very careful. The enemy believe Joshua Smith is dead and he must remain dead, at least for now. That reminds me; you need a new name." The older man scratched his chin and then announced, "From now on you will be Gideon . . . Gideon Jones. What do you think?"

"Gideon, Joshua, a name's a name, it doesn't matter. Now that I'm dead no one will be looking for me, " Joshua said with an air of indifference.

"A very healthy attitude." O'Donnel pushed a few buttons and a disc appeared. "Here are your ID documents, everything that you will need to get started." O'Donnel also waved what appeared to be a scanning device over "Gideon" and in thirty seconds Joshua's looks were converted to Gideon's; black hair, brown eyes, fuller face, and broader shoulders.

The cab stopped in front of a large apartment complex and O'Donnel opened the door.

"Apartment 5B and please take the elevator."

The taxi sped away leaving Joshua standing alone in front of the massive apartment complex.

"What do I do . . ." Joshua started, but the cab was gone before he could finish the question.

Apartment 5B, he thought. I hope the front door is open. He went to the entrance, which opened automatically. There was an automated doorman which greeted him by name as he walked into the foyer. He saw the stairs to the right, but heeded O'Donnel's words and took the elevator. As he approached the elevator, the door opened as soon as he came within 10 meters and he walked in. The fifth floor light was already on and before he could think he was on the fifth floor. 5B was to the right, and as soon as he reached the door, it opened automatically.

The apartment was lavish compared to his Oceanside home. It was a double quad configuration with two bedrooms, central computer console, and, apparently, all the latest conveniences. Joshua checked out the kitchen first. Thankfully, it was truly functional with a refrigerator stocked with real food, fruits and vegetables, cheese, and pure spring water. Joshua sat down in the large chair in the central room. It immediately conformed to his body as soft jazz started to play. *This O'Donnel really knows his stuff*, he thought, although he still wasn't quite comfortable; the feeling of apprehension remained. Joshua took out the disc that he had been given and started to read about himself, rather his new self, and the Stolts Commission, which he learned he was to testify before.

He started with the biographical information of Gideon Jones. The photograph was of him a few years ago, doctored to conform to his new appearance. He had gone to Johns Hopkins University, graduated with a BA in Social and Behavioral Science, worked for a time as a social worker in Philadelphia, returned to school and received a Master's in Sociology. Single, never married, no bad habits; all in all a boring, nondescript life that perfectly qualified him for the appointed task. He reflected on the day's events and gave a deep sigh as he realized the life he had come to love was gone, probably forever. *Oh, well,* he thought, *better to be a living sociologist than a dead horseplayer. Now,* he thought, *let me see what I'm supposed to be doing.*

෨ஂஂஂஂ෯

XII. The Stolts Commission

THE STOLTS COMMISSION, NAMED FOR GOVERNOR HAR-
ris T. Stolts of New York, was formed to investigate and bring solu-
tions to the growing problem of the displaced people that lived on
the fringes of the urban areas. The problem was particularly acute in
New York State, where accusations had been leveled against supposed
marauding gangs of youths; accusations of violence and theft that society would not tolerate. It was a story Gideon had heard many times
and one that he knew was not entirely true. His experience years ago
with the demonic Richard Cosby, and more recently his friendship
with backstretch workers at the track, definitely gave him a unique
perspective.

The Stolts Commission had generated annual reports every year
for the last three, each of which was as vacuous as it was voluminous.
There was plenty of second hand testimony from witnesses who had
heard of this or that, interviews with social workers who had never
left the cozy confines of their offices on Central Park, and overhead
surveillance depicting some sort of activity outside the "civilized"
areas which was reported as criminal gangs plotting who knows what.
Gideon read through the specifics, that is, the few that were there.

Police reports for five years had catalogued two hundred separate
episodes of gang activity. However, closer inspection revealed that all
but twenty of these were public disturbance, disorderly conduct or
defacement of public property. The other twenty were more violent,
armed robbery, assault, one sexual assault, and one murder. None of
these more serious arrests had led to a conviction. Reports of social
workers were universally unsubstantiated generalizations. There were
no direct interviews, no field work of any kind, and no attempt to
quantify the true extent of this presumed social problem.

All of this was neatly packaged with the greatest solemnity as
proof of society's failings and reason to continue funding for this

highly important project. From Gideon's perspective, nothing of any value was contained in any of the reports, and he could see that he would need to start from scratch with direct contact with the cities underprivileged if anything truly meaningful was to be forthcoming. Exploring such new territory, particularly potentially dangerous parts of cities was best done in the light of day, preferably early in the morning. Tomorrow he would start his research on the outskirts of the city.

He turned on Vivaldi, but thought for a moment and changed it to Billie Holliday, found the complete works of Dickens on the shelf, and lay down to read, *A Tale of Two Cities,* again.

పోంం

XIII. Modern Mental Health

EXTRAORDINARY ADVANCES IN HEALTH CARE WERE A hallmark of the twenty second century. Detailed scanning and imaging to the cellular and even the molecular level allowed incredibly precise diagnostic accuracy and led to the development of the cellular based therapeutic systems that were extremely specific and almost devoid of harmful side effects. The drugs developed led to new therapies for a great spectrum of diseases that were very effective. In addition, new recreational drugs were discovered that were safe and nonaddictive. The government encouraged the distribution of such drugs at various controlled venues; actively discouraged the intake of alcoholic beverages as being a less controlled recreational vehicle, with greater potential for abuse and addiction. However, alcoholic beverages still were legal and available from most casinos and taverns, the lessons of Prohibition never being forgotten.

The problem of mental health disorders, however, was a persistent plague on society. The intricacies and mysteries of the human brain defied all attempts to accurately study and categorize such maladies as depression, schizophrenia, manic disorders, deviant behaviors, and numerous other mental health conditions. Science could not explain why a person with a perfectly normal cellular brain scan, normal intrathecal chemical and transmitter analysis, and normal neuroelectrical activity should be depressed to the point of suicide. Similarly, individuals with astronomically high serotonin levels and nonexistent gamma butyrnin levels which would lead one to predict an uncontrollable manic state could actually be perfectly normal. Medications that specifically targeted such chemicals and neurotransmitters were notoriously inconsistent in their efficacy. Thus, the "science" of mental health was more of an art form than any other aspect of medicine.

The government dealt with the difficulties inherent to mental health therapeutics in a very special, truly sympathetic and caring approach. Every individual diagnosed with a serious mental health disorder that failed simple therapeutic intervention was guaranteed intensive inpatient treatment at a government sanctioned facility. Such institutions were staffed by professionally trained therapists, educated and experienced in the latest medical and behavioral modalities optimized to allow the mentally infirm individual to become a productive member of society. The media widely reported on the incredible success these sanitoriums, as they were called, achieved. The occasional negative reports, cynically referring to sanitoriums as sanitation centers, were denounced by the mainstream media as irresponsible and inaccurate. Indeed, the incredible success of modern mental health facilities was one of the shining lights of the latter half of the twenty-second century.

ॐ

XIV. Outside Town

GIDEON LEFT HIS FANCY APARTMENT AT 7:00 A.M. THE street was shrouded in fog as he hailed a taxi which drove him to the south end of the city, over the bridge, and into Brooklyn. This area was an amalgam of old warehouses, empty lofts, and silent factories. As expected there were very few people about, making the rough, worn down neighborhood relatively safe, but perhaps making his task much more difficult. Unfortunately, it wouldn't work just to go knock on someone's door and say, "Excuse me, I'm from the government and I'd like to ask you some questions." That would be a good way to get his throat slit or his nose broken. *I wish Little Bit were here,* he thought; that little dog would find a way in two seconds. The last time he had made such a venture, that westie had been invaluable, scouting out the way and saving Gideon's life.

"I'll just wander around and I'm sure I'll fine something," he said to himself. He walked past a silent brick building checkered with broken windows and turned down a narrow alley. The contrast between the lights and holography that lit up streets around his new home in midtown Manhattan and the stark emptiness of these dilapidated buildings was striking. As he neared the end of the alley he heard a crash from behind and turned to see a tall heavyset man standing over a fallen wooden crate. Gideon quickly ran back to the man, who was pressing his hands against the sides of his head visibly agitated and upset.

"Here, let me help," Gideon said calmly. He bent over and righted the crate and put some smaller boxes that had fallen back inside. "This looks too heavy for one man, even someone as big as you. You take that end and I'll take the front. Just tell me which way to go."

The man was silent, but picked up the end of the crate and softly mumbled, "Through that door and up the stairs and then to the left."

Gideon picked up the lead end and the two carried the large crate up to the man's room at the top of the stairs.

"I can get it from here," the man stated as they reached the door. "Thank you for your help."

"You're welcome." Gideon held out his hand and the other man took and shook it. Gideon turned and started down the stairs.

"Would you like a cup of coffee?" the man asked in a low voice.

"Sure, thank you," Gideon said as he went back up the stairs and helped push the crate into the apartment.

The room was small, maybe eight by six meters, but fairly neat. There was a small computer console and food synthesizer, a bed, a table with two straight back chairs, and a small personal hygiene center near the bed. The walls looked old and worn, but everything was clean. Gideon turned and faced the man. "Gideon Jones," he said and held out his hand again.

"Ed," the man replied. He was about two meters tall, bulky, with thick black hair, eyes that were slightly prominent, and clean shaven. He was neatly dressed in a green work shirt and black pants.

"This is a very nice place you've got here. This is not a part of town that gets much attention from the government, but you seem to have made it very livable."

"Thank you; I do the best that I can with what I have. Oh, I almost forgot, coffee. How do you like it?"

"Just a glass of water will be fine."

"OK." He poured a glass from the dispenser and then turned to the synthesizer. "Coffee, black. That's for me," he explained.

"So I gathered."

They sat down at the table and silently sipped on their drinks.

"Have you lived here long?" Gideon asked.

"Long enough," Ed answered warily.

Gideon looked around the room; there wasn't much to see, but tucked in the corner he saw a small bookshelf. He got up and looked at the collection. There was the complete works of Charles Dickens, Les

Miserables, F. Scott Fitzgerald, Sinclair Lewis, City of God, and many others; all classic works of literature.

"Very impressive. I love to read real books, also. I've read everything that you've got here. There's nothing better than a good book, especially one that you can actually hold and has real pages."

"Books are my only true passion," Ed replied. "Of course, I could find them on the computer, but I also prefer to turn the page myself."

"You are missing one of the greatest classics," Gideon observed. He reached into his back pocket. "This is really essential to any collection of classic literature." He handed Ed the Bible.

Ed's eyes widened as he took the leather-bound volume and quickly opened it, flipping the pages rapidly and then he quickly closed it, looking around to see if there was anyone else watching.

"This is amazing," he exclaimed. "These are very difficult to find and just as hard to keep once found. You're lucky to have it."

"It's yours. Just don't try to copy it; I was once told that trying to reproduce the Bible is a sure way to make it and possibly you disappear."

"I can't take something so rare and precious. Even though it's all mythology, it still is great literature"

"I want you to have it, and I'm pretty sure I can find another. Now, can you tell me about living in these parts; do you have friends; how many people would you say live in this area; is it dangerous; anything would be helpful."

"What are you, a government pollster? Anyway, someone carrying a Bible is no government official. I've lived in this room for about eight years. I used to work as an accountant, mostly monitoring the work of the automated computers; pretty mundane. Eight years ago I started to have trouble sleeping, lost interest in just about everything and then I just didn't have the energy to go to work. Oh, they carried me along for a while, but then I stopped caring and I lost my job, my home and my family. I wandered out here and some of the street people felt sorry for me. They set me up in this room, brought me food and even those books. After a while I was a little better. I take these pills and they give me the energy to get up and face each day."

Ed held up a container with blue pills; Gideon recognized them as one of the more potent antidepressants.

"Do you ever think of trying to go back; that is back to your old home and family?" Gideon asked.

"Never; I'll never go back, because if I did I would end up right back here or worse, pills or no pills."

Gideon didn't press the issue and changed the subject. "Where are the people that helped you? Are they around here? I'd like to meet them."

"Oh, they're all around. The people living in these parts all look out for each other."

"Could you take me to meet some of them."

Ed studied the cover of the Bible, turning it over and over and thumbing through the pages. "Yes, I guess it would be OK. Let me get my coat and I'll see who we can find."

The door automatically locked behind them as they headed out to the street.

❧

XV. On the Street

THE SUN WAS SHINING AND IT HAD WARMED CONSIDER-
ably as they walked between the ramshackle buildings. A few people were walking down the street, most staying away from the two
men. Ed walked with some purpose, as if he had a definite destination
already selected.

"I'm going to find Aldous; he'd be the best person for you to talk
with. He's been on the streets all his life and now he looks out for all
of us. He's a preacher of sorts; always talking about God and Jesus.
Personally, I don't believe any of it and I don't go to his services, but,
if you want to find out about what it's like living outside 'proper' society, he's your man. I'm sure he's at the church."

"You read that Bible I gave you and then you can judge for yourself what is true," Gideon said.

They came to an old church, standing tall and proud among all the
rundown buildings, its grimy yellow bricks leading to a steeple with a
shiny cross at the top. The door was made of faded wood with black,
slightly rusted hinges that creaked as they were opened. The entrance
way was dark and led to a dark sanctuary with broken stained glass
windows and a mixture of pews, benches, and chairs. In the front
Gideon saw a young man, probably in his twenties, dressed in a black
shirt and pants with long black hair. When he heard the noise from the
back of the sanctuary he turned and walked quickly to greet them.

"Welcome to the Lord's house," he said loudly as he shook Ed's
and Gideon's hands. He stared at Gideon for a long time before he
bade them to sit. A young woman emerged from behind the altar and
Aldous spoke softly to her and she disappeared.

"This is Gideon Jones," Ed said. "He says he's part of some government committee studying the outcasts of society. I thought that you
could help."

"Thank you, Ed," Aldous replied. "I will try to help. Mr. Jones, you said?"

Gideon answered, "That's right, Gideon Jones; I represent the Stolts Commission, a committee charged with studying and aiding society's outcasts. I thought it would be a good idea to get some first-hand knowledge. I was fortunate enough to meet Ed here and now I have had the good fortune to meet you."

Ed stood up and said, "If you'll excuse me, I have to leave. Nice seeing you again, Aldous. Thanks for the book, Mr. Jones." He left through a side door, leaving the two men alone in the huge dark sanctuary, a huge cross casting a shadow over them as they sat in a pew near the back.

Aldous started to talk softly, "You can try to change your look, but I'd recognize you anywhere. Where's Little Bit?"

"I was hoping you didn't remember and please don't talk much about it. It's safer for me to let the past stay buried."

"I never found out what happened, except that you and Mr. Cosby and Jameson went into that office building and only you came out. I suspected that the others are in jail or dead or something. I do know that I am thankful for those few words you read to me that started me on the road to salvation."

"Let's just say that Richard Cosby was not the man you thought him to be and that both he and Miss Jameson are gone. I am sure, however, that Jameson is in a much better place."

"As I think about all that Mr. Cosby preached and what I've learned since, I realize that he was leading all of us on a path straight to hell. I have tried to undo the damage, but it takes time. David Sanders has been a great help. We are bringing God's word back into this world; believe me it is something that is desperately needed, at least among those that are lost and unfulfilled.

"The lost and unfulfilled, I think that's everybody; anyway, that's why I'm here. I'm part of this commission that is supposed to be examining the very souls that you are trying to mend. Can you help me?"

"There are so many of them, thousands just here in New York. Stay with me today and you'll surely have the opportunity to meet and talk with some. However, now," he looked at his watch, "it is time for tea."

The young woman returned with a tray loaded with a silver tea-pot, cups, saucers, cream, sugar, and what looked like real lemons, all expertly balanced. Gideon saw that the girl used only her left arm. Along with the tea, there were a variety of pastries that also looked real.

"I know that you have a passion for fresh, unsynthesized fare. Martha prepared this while we were talking. Let's see, we have English Breakfast, Earl Grey, Black Zinger, and Dynamite tea; apple scones, cinnamon rolls, and cream cheese Danish. Take your pick."

"One of each, I think, and English Breakfast. Who knows the next time I'll find real food such as this."

The two men sat down in the small alcove behind the altar, while Martha stood by, poised to refill their cups or take away an empty plate. She was plainly dressed, in a long blue and white skirt and white blouse, her blonde hair tied into a bun. She had smooth white skin and the bloom of youth that made her beautiful without glamour. Gideon smiled at her and she returned a slight smile and quickly turned away, disappearing into the adjacent room. He noticed that she kept her right arm folded tightly against her waist.

"She's shy," he commented as he raised the cup to his lips. After a moment, sweet strains of music appeared, piano music by Chopin.

"Martha has lived a hard life and only now is learning to trust people. You noticed her right arm; the result of an unfortunate accident she suffered as a young child. She has amazing talent for one who only has one and a half arms. The piano gives her a sense of purpose and allows her some escape from the demons that torment her." The sweet melody continued as Aldous went on. "She was caught up in the moral decay that pervades our society, decay that is graciously administered by our 'benevolent' government and the industries that it partners with. In particular, Diblonski Ltd."

At the name, Diblonski, Gideon stiffened slightly and spilled his tea on his shirt as his cup crashed to the floor. The playing stopped and Martha rushed to his side with a towel and gently cleaned the stain as best she could.

"I'm afraid that shirt will be ruined," she said softly. "Let me take it and wash it for you."

"That's very kind of you, but I don't have anything to put on while it is being cleaned."

"It only takes a minute." Gideon pulled off the shirt and she left.

"You seemed startled when I mentioned Diblonski. You've had some dealings with them?"

"Are we safe here? I mean really secure?" Gideon asked.

"I think so. What's all this about?" Aldous asked, perplexed.

"Let's go for a walk outside and I'll tell you."

Martha returned with his shirt and the two men got up and started for the door. Aldous told Martha to watch over things until he returned. As they walked down the empty streets, Gideon recounted all the details of his encounter with Richard Cosby.

"Cosby worked for Aaron Diblonski. His 'street ministry' was an elaborate setup that put him in contact with people such as you; vulnerable people, searching for some meaning. He gave you 'meaning' which kept you in your place, gave society something to be afraid of, and kept order; order that was orchestrated by Aaron Diblonski. Cosby was truly a demon; poor Jameson gave her life stopping him. She was the real hero and, of all people, she was saved in the end, and now I'm sure she is in the best place."

Aldous thought about all Gideon said. "Are you sure that you can trust me? Here I am doing exactly the same thing Cosby did."

"I thought about that, but Ed convinced me that you are the real thing. His reluctance to accept your preaching tells me that you are not delivering watered down homilies that could come from the government as easily as from the Bible. Plus, you remembered me, which means our brief encounter made some sort of impression. No, I think you're safe."

They walked by endless nearly identical old, ramshackle town-houses, all in need of painting or washing, but each one slightly different from its neighbor. They all had similar heavy green wiring running along the front windows and on top of each set of four was a large dish. The old buildings variously had flowers in the windows or a potted plant on the front porch; many had prominent crosses on the doors. Aldous turned to go into one of the townhomes, a brown brick building, a large cross on the door, and an Amish hex sign above the door. He didn't knock, but went right in as if he were expected. An elderly gray-haired man neatly dressed in a plaid shirt, brown slacks, and sandals greeted them.

"Welcome to my home, Mr. Jones, and so nice to see you again so soon, Aldous," he greeted them. "Martha called and said that you'd probably stop by to see me. My name is Barnabas, but most people around here call me Doc. What can I do for you?" He asked, staring directly at Gideon.

"You come straight to the point, Doc. You probably know that I'm from the Stolts Commission; doing research of a sort on people like you. I guess Aldous, rather Martha told you about me. Of course, I already know a great deal about you."

"What could you possibly know; we've only just met."

"Let's see, you are called Doc, not because you are a medical doctor, rather you have a Ph.D. in electrical engineering; you live with a dog, a golden retriever, I suspect; you graduated from the University of Texas in 2140; you were married once, but your wife is deceased, I'm sorry; you are vegetarian and you are prone to sleep walking."

"Amazing, how could you know so much?"

"Oh, just by looking around, looking at you, at your walls and furnishings."

"You should be a detective."

"I used to do similar work, but now I work for the state of New York. Tell me why you live here, rather than within mainstream society?"

Barnabas sighed and invited the two men to sit. He brought some bottles of cold water and started to relate his saga.

৶৽৻

XVI. Barnabas

"WHERE SHOULD I START; I GUESS THE BEGINNING IS always best." He stopped and stared into space for a few seconds and then began speaking again. "You are one hundred percent correct in every observation that you have made. I graduated from UT and went to work for Austin Electronics and Engineering designing home systems and doing quite well. We had a number of patents and improved home energy efficiency, productivity and such by about fifty percent. Our products and designs were in great demand and all was well. After two years of hard work, I married Rachel and we started to live the global dream. And, Rachel and I, we had a lifetime marriage contract, which was actually fairly common in those days. We talked about children, but neither one of us thought it wise to bring new life into such a crazy, mixed up world. Times being what they were, with the exploding population and all, no one thought it odd that we didn't want children; we were happy as we were, just the two of us." He stopped again, stared into space for about ten seconds, shook his head, briefly, and then started again.

Work was going along smoothly and we were very comfortable, living in a double quad home with any luxury we wanted, fancy car, expensive vacations; Rachel was free to stay home and pursue her hobbies, painting and poetry. She published several volumes, perhaps you've read her work; the last was *Poems and Echos* by Rachel Dixon."

"Poetry has never been my thing, I'm sorry, I much prefer fiction," Gideon said.

Barnabas looked at him up and down more closely. "Yes, you don't look like the poetry type. No matter, where was I; oh yes, anyway, we were living an idyllic life and then he came."

"Who came?"

"Diblonski, the evil empire. Our success had spawned several attempts to take us over, but all were politely rebuffed. But Diblonski

Ltd., if there is a devil it is that conglomerate. First their representative came to meet with our board. By this time I was Vice President for Research and Development. They made an extremely generous offer, large amounts of cash, stock, guarantee of high positions in the new company which would be a subsidiary of Diblonski, but maintain some independence. All of us were tempted and we had nearly decided to sell when they started."

"The voices," Gideon said calmly.

"Yes, the voices, but how did you know?"

"Never mind, go on."

"Anyway, at night I would hear this rumbling voice telling me that we shouldn't sell, that Diblonski was evil and would use the knowledge and engineering that we provided for the ultimate destruction of the very people we were trying to serve. I would wake up in cold sweats, shaking. At first I dared tell no one, or else they'd think that I was crazy. I wasn't sure myself, really. I was a man of science, confident in the order that existed in the universe and now I was hearing voices. Well, something told me that the voices may be telling the truth and I started to stall the deal, ask for more information, make up questions, anything to put off the final sale. I managed to postpone the merger for about eight months, but finally I'd run out of tricks and the final vote was scheduled for a Monday. I'd have the weekend to figure something out. For months I'd been listening to this voice; Rachel never heard it and I didn't dare to tell her or else she'd think that I was crazy. I was already almost sure that I was. Anyway, I decided that the only thing that I could do was to talk back to it. For all these months I lay there listening to this voice and thought that as long as I never said anything it meant that I was still sane."

He stopped again and stared to his right and then to his left, got up and walked around the room, and then sat back down.

"Sorry, where was I? Oh, yes, the final vote . . ."

Gideon interrupted. "The voice is still coming, I see. It must be very hard."

Barnabas raised his hand as if to say not to worry. "I'm OK. I know what it is and I've learned to live with it, in fact I welcome it. Anyway,

Sunday night came and I heard the voice again, calling me by name, 'Barnabas, Barnabas . . . you have the power within you to stop this evil empire from consuming all that you have built that is good. You alone can make a stand and keep evil in its place.'

"With a soft voice, trembling, I spoke up, 'Who are you to torment me so? I am only one man. Show yourself and help me understand what you want from me.'

"There was silence for a long time and I really thought that I was free of the voice, but then it came again, louder. 'Only you can stop him. Tell the truth about him, tell the world that he is evil and only wants destruction. Do this for me and you will receive the greatest reward.'

"There was a smell of in the room, like fresh baked goods, but sweet, and then I was overcome with revelation; this was the Lord. I was never one for Bible mythology, but I couldn't deny a truth that was so obvious. The next day I awoke with a sense of peace and tranquility. I went to the meeting and told my story. There was much laughter and the representatives from Diblonski all smiled and I was cast as much the fool. Only, one of the Diblonski people, a Mr. Masur, didn't seem amused. He placed a call and five minutes later I was carried out of the room. I was brought to a local hospital and then put into an ambulance and taken to another place. They locked me in a room, more like a prison cell, really. They ran brain scans looking for the typical chemical imbalances seen in those that are mentally ill; all normal, normal dopamine, serotonin, synaptic polypeptide gamma butyrate, everything. Synaptic transmission and reception, all normal. Total body hormonal assay and distribution, normal. With everything normal, I thought that they would let me go. But they kept me locked away for months. Finally, I was released, but only on a short pass, to visit Rachel and put my affairs in order; I was to report back and undergo 'rehabilitation.' I wasn't sure what that meant, but I didn't want any part of it. Rachel and I put what we could into the car and started driving, as far away from Austin as we could get. That was the end of my career. Rachel and I lost everything but each other and we drifted from place to place until we settled here and we lived together happily for years. The misfits we found needed some help. When we arrived most of the people living around here didn't have power or any amenities, really. There were plenty of old, outdated solar generators around; it didn't take much for me to rig them up to provide some heat and electricity to all these old buildings. So, I continued the work that I had started in Austin, helping to provide for the physical needs of our little community. Then a few years ago Aldous showed up and provided for our spiritual needs. We were happy here for years. Poor Rachel became ill last year and now she is gone." Barnabas voice halted and he started to cry. Gideon went and sat next to him, putting his arm around the older man.

"You were given a great honor, to be God's messenger. And, God did not forget you. He brought you to these people and you have done great things for them. I've been in other cities, in places like this, and the work you've done is amazing. You have truly served the least of his people and He is surely pleased and you can be sure that Rachel is waiting for you and there will be a place reserved for you, just as is promised in His Word."

Barnabas' tears stopped and he smiled. "I know what you say is true, but I don't know why I know. Thank you . . . Thank you so much. I hope that I will see you again."

Aldous and Gideon left. "I think that I have everything that I need," Gideon said. "I'm going to be leaving now. Tomorrow I have to give a speech to the Commission and to the state legislature. I need to go home and figure out what I'm going to say. Thank you for all your help."

The two walked together until they reached a point where Gideon could get a cab home, shook hands, and promised to get together again soon. The sun was high in the sky and the day had warmed up considerably. Gideon changed his mind and decided to walk home. He put his hands in his pockets and headed for the tall buildings of Manhattan humming Vivaldi as he walked.

⌘

XVII. The Speech

GIDEON SPENT THE REST OF THE DAY REFLECTING ON what he had seen, thinking about what the Stolts Commission was supposed to be doing and what he would say the next day. He mulled over a great many things in his mind and that evening committed all his thoughts to paper.

The next day he waited in the front row of the legislature while a number of routine tasks were carried out. Finally, the president of the body, vice governor, Herbert Hanover, stood to introduce him.

"Ladies and gentlemen of the Legislature and members of the Stolts Commission, I have the great pleasure to present to you a newcomer to this important body. This man comes with the highest recommendations, by way of Baltimore, graduated at the top of his class from the Johns Hopkins University with a Master's degree in Social and Behavioral Sciences and a wealth of knowledge on the social ills that plague our society. He has published numerous scholarly articles in academic and popular journals and we now have the good fortune to have his expertise on our own Stolts Commission. Without further delay, I present to you, Gideon Jones."

There was a smattering of applause as Gideon made his way to the podium. He felt a little uncomfortable dressed in a black suit with a tie. He carried no papers and there was no prompting device. He was au naturel so to speak. He looked cool and calm as he moved behind the podium. The thin filaments that projected from the podium automatically adjusted to his height as he addressed the audience.

"Members of the Stolts Commission, Senators, and Assemblymen, thank you for the opportunity to stand before you today. It is indeed a great honor to be a part of such an important social endeavor, one that has yielded such outstanding results during its years of existence. I congratulate Chairman Bernard Metzger on his management of such a disparate group and would applaud the Commission's many accomplishments if I could easily think of them or even one." Gideon made his presentation without any assistance; no audio, video, or holographic enhancement. It was only his voice and his words, but this was enough to hold the audience captive.

"This Commission as it is today exists only to perpetuate itself, to bring a series of worthless and unfounded fears and platitudes that serve to stoke a fire that was started by the media and is perpetuated by the collective minds of our media moguls and, in particular, the conglomerate, Diblonski Ltd. I've reached this conclusion after thorough review of every Stolts Commission report since its inception years ago. These reports seem built on an unsubstantiated mountain of hearsay evidence, second- and third-hand reports and prejudices voiced by officials and media whose sole purpose is to provide a common enemy for the people to fear and the government to battle. On the other hand, I have, over the years, had the opportunity to spend time with the inhabitants of these "slums" as the less fortunate parts of our cities are called. It's true that those people who live in such places differ in many ways from the 99.9% of us who live in what I call, 'polite society,' although I'm beginning to think that even this term is truly an oxymoron.

"These outcasts from the mainstream are mostly there by choice. For a variety of reasons they have chosen to build an underground culture on their own, with their own sense of social order. Many are there because our legitimate social circles have let them down or threatened them with incarceration or worse. Some have belief in religion and consequently are shunned or have suffered unmerciful ridicule; there are also the mentally infirm who gravitate away from polite society and find refuge among a group of people that actually care about them and accept them as they are. All in all these rundown, forgotten neighborhoods are populated by a motley group of misfits, who refuse to be round pegs forced to fit into square holes.

"But, they are criminals you say; dangerous gangs of violent youths, preying on productive members of the mainstream. You've all seen them arrested, held up as shining examples of the effectiveness and efficiency of our government, keeping us safe and allowing us the freedom to take another pill or look for the next high. This is what we are fed on a daily basis and it is our government and its business partners, such as Diblonski Ltd. that foment this lie.

"Yesterday, I was privileged to spend time with some extraordinary people, all living in the southwest corner of Brooklyn, an area long forgotten by our benevolent government. They live in old, somewhat rundown, but orderly, functional apartments, have all the basic necessities, and live life as they choose. They are free; free to spend their days reading or helping their neighbors or worshipping; free from any worry that the government authorities may disapprove. They struck me as extremely happy, productive individuals. One had become depressed and was forced to drop out of productive society and find his way on the streets. He was accepted by this underground world and now is safe and happy, taking his medication and putting his life back together.

"Another was unjustly incarcerated by some sort of authority, branded a risk to himself and others. From what I could see, the only risk that this man posed was to the existing social order. There was a young woman, cast off by everyone, abused, forced to fend for herself, taken in by the local religious leader and now finding the soul that she had lost. Her redemption came through religion and her own beautiful music, which free her from the demons of her past. These and others are not any danger to us, themselves, or anyone. They are better than the lot of us and we would do well to study and learn from such social outcasts.

"But, I am here to support the Stolts Commission, to provide you with a recommendation for its future role within this government. I can tell you that there is one role that it can adopt that will make it functional and well worth the millions of dollars it receives every year to justify its existence. Send the members of the Commission out into these so-called less fortunate areas on the outskirts of our cities. Let them see how a truly cooperative society can function and then let them report back to you so that our civilization can learn from them and become truly civilized. Thank you."

Gideon stood silently for a few moments and then spoke again. "I hope I haven't shocked you with my report. I am ready to answer any questions you may have." The room was silent, initially, and then erupted with shouts of outrage and anger. Mr. Hanover did his best to try to restore order, and after about five minutes quiet was restored.

Several senators and assemblymen jumped to their feet hoping to get their chance to respond to Gideon's scathing comments. The media present vigorously pounded their reports into their nanopods or sent them via green dots to their various outlets. Gideon stood calmly at the podium, ready to field all of the questions and derogatory comments that he knew were forthcoming. The first came from the front row, Senator Peter Fulbean, a mountain of a man with pale skin usually accented with perspiration.

"Mr. Jones, you have great temerity to come before this august forum, a newcomer, unknown to us, and hurl such vicious and, to my mind, unfounded accusations. I cannot believe that years studying the deep and disturbing social issues that face our society have all been a huge sham. Do you have anything more than your anecdotal experience to justify your wild accusations?"

"Thank you, Senator," Gideon replied. "I admit that I am a newcomer and perhaps could have been more delicate in my presentation, but I firmly believe that sugarcoating such a serious issue and perpetuating misleading reports serves no one. There is a network of pastoral leaders throughout the entire globe that regularly report to an international database on their constituents. I realize that our government and mainstream society have no interest in the observations of a group of religious leaders, but I know that their reports are true, at least to the extent that one can rely on human perception. This information is readily available and verifiable. It was this database that served as the basis for my conclusions. It is accessible at the number you have in your agenda. This database is well referenced and is corroborated by my own observations."

Senator Sylvia Silver stood up and started to address Gideon, "Mr. Jones, I have no doubt that you believe your report to be valid. I think you have much to learn about diplomacy, but let's put that aside for now. All that I see here is a he said, she said situation. I ask you who are we to believe and what is it that makes you so sure that your point of view is the correct one?"

"Senator," Gideon started calmly, "I have spent my life looking at various situations, assessing the pros and cons, looking for every little nuance that could possibly lead me to the correct conclusion, and I state with the greatest certainty the words that I have spoken today are true. I would never have been chosen for this position if it were any other way. All my life I have made it my purpose to look at a given situation and find the right answer; the one that leads to the truth. I am telling you that without any doubt that the Stolts Commission has been a sham and its lack of action nearly criminal. This lie has been perpetuated for the advancement of our government and its private partners. However, now it is time to seek the truth."

Senator Fulbean rose again, his face redder; he wiped his brow with his handkerchief. "Mr. Jones, I must protest the singling out of one of our governments' partners as the focus of your unfounded accusations. Diblonski Ltd. has been a champion of individual rights and has done mountains of charitable works among the very people you now profess need no such help. This is the same company that has made the wonderful 'Green Dot' available free of charge to the entire solar system. How is it that they are responsible for such devious behavior as you describe?"

Gideon stood silently for a moment before answering and then chose his words carefully. "Senator, I do not speak out of haste or without proper documentation. There is no doubt that government, private industry, and the population as a whole benefit greatly from such alliances. However, it is those media outlets controlled by Diblonski that have been most persistent and definitive in their portrayal of these outcasts as dangerous to polite society. I would love to be found wrong on this or any of the other issues that I have raised today. If factual proof can be produced demonstrating the fallacy of my position, I would be overjoyed to publicly recant my testimony. In all of my research, such facts have not been evident."

Gideon continued to present outward calm, but inside he worried that the words he spoke gave away too much and threatened to expose his true identity. Thankfully, the remaining questions were simple and evaded the central issue; strictly politicians desiring to hear themselves speak. The session was adjourned once he was finished and he quickly exited to await the media fallout. He snuck out the back of the chamber and avoided the initial media onslaught. He fully expected to be removed from his present position and hoped that he would be able to return to his private life and find his way back to the track. The uproar that did result was totally unexpected and something he was unprepared to face.

ॐ

XVIII. Working on the File

CORYLLOS PLANNED TO START WORK AS SOON AS HE arrived at his apartment. He settled into his most comfortable chair and activated the computer console. The monitor immediately sprang to life and he was greeted by hologram, TOP PRIORITY, in bright red letters, accompanied by an alarm that was designed to hold his attention until he reviewed the waiting message.

"Open priority message," he said.

You are urgently requested to confirm the elimination of this unknown man who was witness to the death of UN Representative, Dennis McCally. This man's identity is unknown. We thought he was eliminated in southern New Jersey, but we cannot 100% confirm; if he survived our initial intervention, we suspect he has headed north. Subject is to be permanently silenced. We have no information beyond this image taken from hospital video surveillance.

The image revealed Joshua/Gideon. It was poor quality, but in a flash, Coryllos isolated it, cleaned it up, and was greeted by a high resolution photo of his new quarry. With this new priority missive, he put the other file away as he continued to analyze the surveillance video and data from the "elimination" in south Jersey. The blast analysis revealed typical debris after a hyposonic combustion: metallic fragments, synthetic leather shards, organic materials. DNA mass analysis seemed in order except the volume seemed low, although still within acceptable limits. He read the report again. The subject was inside the vehicle at impact; when this fact was added to the blast analysis, DNA mass was just outside the expected value. This was enough to cast doubt on the success of the "elimination."

He ran the surveillance disc through the computer image analysis, hoping to pick up additional clues that would point to location or help with identifying the man. He already knew the name and location of the hospital and he knew that although the man had logged in with his ID card, this information had been mysteriously purged from the records. He amplified the clothes the man wore; they were nondescript, size and the manufacturers were not apparent. There was a white object sticking out of the man's shirt pocket. He zeroed in on this, sharpened and enhanced to see that it was a disc from Monmouth Park. The man had been to the track that day. Nothing else of interest was obtained from the record; but at least he had somewhere to start. Tomorrow he would go to the track.

He went back to the other file, opened it up, and plugged it into his computer. "Identify figures in the file," he commanded. The computer dutifully started to name the images. Some came rather quickly: Major David Sanders, Dr. Deborah Tennyson, Little Bit. The horses were Ruffian, Ruth Rising, Job's Pleasure, and Son of War. The people at the bar were not as quickly identified, but the location was Bar #23 at Monmouth Park. The lone man's image came up and he immediately recognized it as the same man that appeared in the image from the hospital.

Now that was an unexpected bit of information he thought. The same man that was involved with the death of Richard Cosby was also witness to Rep. McCally. He was sure that the boss would want to be informed of this very unusual finding; an encrypted report was sent immediately. Finally, he asked the computer to continue to search as he lay down to relax. Bar #23 at Monmouth track, that was the place he would start. He was convinced that his quarry was still alive and that this man was more resourceful than most. It seemed that his target liked to go to the track; an excellent venue for anonymity. He decided he had done enough work for the day; it was time to relax. He took a pill, closed his eyes, and fell back onto his bed, a smile creeping on to his face as the pill started to work its magic. Years of sorrow mixed with triumphant success faded to the recesses of his brain as his mind blanked out, becoming empty of everything but pure feelings of pleasure.

৯৽ঌ

XIX. Media Response

THE MEDIA WERE QUICK TO PUT OUT THE NEWS OF GIDE-on's speech. The smell of scandal and controversy permeated the air-waves as the reports started to appear. Gideon fully expected to be vilified for such blatant and raw criticism of what had been considered a noble and important state committee. The reports surprised him and he wasn't sure if he was pleased.

William Jennings of the IBS network filed these words:

"Today, at the state capitol in Albany, a newcomer to the political scene spoke before a joint session of the New York State Legislature on the issue of society's outcasts, long studied by the much ballyhooed Stolts Commission. For years this Commission has portrayed such outcasts as a drain and menace to the mainstream, a source of violence and crime that plagued all good law abiding citizens. Today, Mr. Gideon Jones descended upon the capitol and put this commission and its members to shame. Citing well documented personal observation and extensive research he demonstrated to this reporter that these so-called outcasts are happy and productive members of an alternative society that they have built for themselves. This underground exists outside the purview of our ever watchful government, enjoying a freedom most of us only dream about. He suggested that the gangs and crime that we have all come to fear are figments of the collective imaginations of yours truly; reporting on false and misleading news coming straight from government officials. If this is true the scandal could shake up the entire political scene for years to come. So far, I have heard not a peep from any government officials, although vehement denials immediately were issued by our government's private industry partners, particularly Diblonski Ltd. I ask you now, where are you, Governor Stolts; what do you say, Attorney General Paulson? WE are waiting. But for now, I applaud the courage and honesty of Mr.

Jones. I'm sure we will hear much more from this remarkable man in the days to come."

Most of the other reports were similar, praising Gideon and vilifying the government. Gideon came home to find his apartment building surrounded by a swarm of media types. He managed to sneak past them using a side entrance. He entered his apartment and was greeted by a multitude of bright lights indicating messages waiting.

"Collate and organize by source, " he said and the monitor became an orderly mix, arranged by source and time each message was sent. "File media," he said. That left only three messages, one from his boss on the Committee, one from Mr. O'Donnel, and the last from one Aaron Diblonski. He ignored the one from his boss.

The message from O'Donnel was brief: "A fine job, but be very careful. See you soon."

The one from Diblonski was equally brief: "Come to meet me tomorrow at three o'clock p.m. Transportation will be arranged. AD."

Gideon sat down after reading this message. He had really struck a nerve. He worried a bit; he knew a great deal about Aaron Diblonski, enough to be concerned for his own safety. He would need a shield. He looked at all the media messages. There was one from Brian Sivestre of ABS, a fair and somewhat impartial journalist; he would make an adequate defender. He highlighted that message and sent a response. Afterward, he made himself dinner: cantaloupe, cheese and ice water, shut down his computer system, and lay back to listen to Berlioz. In ten minutes, he was fast asleep.

کی

XX. Waiting for Gideon

ABE MASUR WAITED FOR THE DOOR TO OPEN. TRIPS TO the Diblonski homestead were rare and he was only summoned for the most dire crises. The call today did not surprise him, however. This Gideon Jones was promising to be much more than an annoyance; upsetting the established order and potentially ruining years of carefully laid plans. This had the potential to far overshadow all recent setbacks, even more than that Cosby affair of years past.

The door opened and Masur made his way straight to the master study where he found Mr. Diblonski waiting. As always, Diblonski was impeccably dressed in a gray suit with a large polished black gold watch glittering with diamonds on the face and bezel. Masur felt a little uneasy, casually dressed as he was in jeans and shirt without a collar. He hadn't thought to change, given the urgency of the message and it being Saturday. No comment was made however as he walked into the study and sat down in the large leather chair opposite his boss. There were no greetings or small talk.

"This is a big mess, Mr. Masur," Diblonski started. "This Gideon Jones has upset decades of careful planning and could potentially undermine our entire operation. So, tell me what you know about him."

Masur wiped a few beads of sweat from his brow and activated the Green Dot that he sported behind his left ear. A hologram materialized with the image of Gideon Jones at the podium, recreating his recent presentation. Biographical data appeared beside the hologram and a woman's voice started the presentation.

"Gideon Jones was born in Baltimore, Maryland; February 19, 2131, an only child. Both parents were killed in a lunar shuttle accident when Gideon was ten years old. He was raised by the state, attended Dunbar High School, graduated number three in his class in 2147, attended Johns Hopkins University 2148-2152, graduated with a BA in Social and Behavioral Science and received a Master's in the same area in 2153. He went to work for the city of Baltimore studying the activities of the underclass, instituted reforms that led to a decrease in reported criminal activity by seventy-three percent. Served as consultant to the UN committee on displaced persons and helped integrate over one million such people into mainstream society and then came to the Stolts Commission just recently. He made a report to this commission yesterday, the details of which can be replayed at your request. He has no known family; he has no significant other, he likes jazz music, he has never been known to frequent any casinos. His blood type is O positive; genetic makeup is unremarkable. He has black hair and brown eyes; he is 180 centimeters tall; his weight is sixty kilograms." The presentation stopped at this point.

"Nothing much to go on here, sir."

"Just wait, Mr. Masur, let me think for a moment." Mr. Diblonski was silent for about thirty seconds, his face passive, without any emotion. "This totally bland person must have some sort of weakness. This lack of apparent vice may be just the point that we can exploit and use to discredit this annoying gnat that is upsetting our business."

"Can we exploit a vice that does not exist?"

"Every man has a flaw, an Achilles' heel that can be utilized to bring him under our control or, if he resists, destroy him. I have sent him an invitation to meet me here tomorrow; I'm sure he will grace us with his presence. Please be sure that Mr. Simmons is also available." Diblonski sat down in the large chair by the fire and opened a book, the cue for Masur that it was time to leave.

Masur wasn't so sure that this Gideon Jones was such a huge threat, but he wasn't about to doubt Mr. Diblonski. Diblonski Ltd. had become the largest, most powerful entity in the solar system under his guidance and Masur had never known the boss to be mistaken about anything. As he left he put the call through to Simmons and then spent the rest of the day studying every aspect of the record of Jones speech and every other record available on this new nemesis that he knew was destined for oblivion."

৯৹৽

XXI. Scanners

ONE OF THE POWERFUL TOOLS THAT FACILITATED THE incredible technological advances of the twenty-second century was the laser driven nanoscanner. The quest to know more and more about the unseen world throughout human history has led to the development of devices to see the very small and the very distant. The microscope allowed direct examination of cells and the telescope allowed viewing of distant heavenly bodies.

The light microscope gave way to the electron microscope which allowed the study of cellular detail on a remarkably fine scale. Various electron microscopes allowed direct observation in a variety of ways. The big leap forward came with the highly focused laser driven nanoscanner. This incredible device was first used to give extremely detailed images of cell surfaces, revealing them to be a sea of structures composed of variably charged and shaped molecules and proteins.

The nanoscanner was directly responsible for the modern approach to medical pharmaceuticals which were designed to either augment or block individual membrane structures with exceptionally accurate and specific compounds. This allowed development of medications that were highly effective and specific with very minimal side effects. In addition, the treatment of most tumors became nearly one hundred per cent successful as direct scanning of tumor cells provided a map that could be used to build antibodies specific to only the tumor, while leaving normal cells untouched. Cancers, which were routinely detected at very early stages, melted away without any significant morbidity.

Only recently have these powerful scanning devices been utilized for non-medical purposes, The most powerful new scanner was built by Randy Peskew while in the employ of Diblonski Ltd. This scanner, called the picoscope, could be used to elucidate and magnify the precise structure of individual molecules. Thus, combining the easily measurable surface charges with molecular shape new molecules could be created, some which would never have been predicted by traditional chemistry.

These powerful scanners offered the hope for future applications which would allow more powerful computing devices and expansion of picotechnology to previously unimaginable levels.

In addition to scanning on the molecular level, powerful and compact medical scanners allowed medical diagnostics to achieve unparalleled accuracy. The vagaries of medical histories and physical exam were replaced by the extreme precision of these scanners. The role of physicians changed greatly as individuals often were diagnosed and treatment initiated by fully automated and portable diagnostic and therapeutic modules. Medical personnel assumed a more advisory role, as well as becoming responsible for the proper functioning of these medical devices. Medical errors became rare while therapeutic success increased dramatically.

❧❧

XXII. Randy Peskew

RANDY PESKEW WAS ALONE IN THE LAB STUDYING THE picomatrix on the original Green Dot design. The Dot had been developed by Amos Pierson in the year 2148 after Pierson had invented the picomatrix, which allowed vast amounts of data to be stored on a chip that was only ten microns in diameter. Pierson had mysteriously disappeared shortly after his company had been sold to Diblonski Ltd. He had embarked on a round the world cruise on a Diblonski luxury yacht and just vanished from the ship one evening. He left his marvelous creation behind and over the years an army of microelectrical engineers, scientists, systems designers, and curious hobbyists had studied the ingenious picomatrix. New facets of the matrix had been unlocked allowing ever smaller and more powerful "Dots" to be designed. Pierson had encoded such a vast array of variable processors within the matrix that most of the engineers believed that only about ten percent of the matrix potential had been tapped. Most were sure that there was an interlocking mechanism that could be utilized to allow the matrix to be made into a series of parallel circuits that would increase the memory and processing capability exponentially, which would create endless possibilities, including processing and data manipulation that would rival the creativity of the human brain.

Peskew was trying to access a segment of the matrix that had previously been protected by a wall of encryption that had defied the most brilliant minds' attempts to penetrate. He was utilizing his newly designed linear scanning electron photon picoscope, which allowed for magnification of the matrix by a factor of ten to the twelfth power. This made the matrix visible in remarkable detail. What he saw excited him, as the wall appeared as a simple keyhole, rather than the complex picoprocessor board he had expected. All he had to do was find the key. He focused his picoscope into the keyhole and scanned the locking mechanism. The results were fed into his computer. He sat back to see what he would find. Most of the time these doors led to complete meltdown of the computing mechanism, pico-sized jokes left by Amos Pierson. On rare occasions a true breakthrough was discovered and technology lurched forward.

While the computer did its analysis, Peskew sat back and read the latest company newsletter.

"Diblonski Ltd. has great plans for you and all its employees. The management strives to create an environment that is conducive to maintaining a happy, efficient, productive workforce. The latest and most exciting program is the Diblonski membership awards program. Anyone in our solar system can become a partner with our great company, enjoying the many perks of membership, such as discounts on merchandise and entertainment, free executive level health care, enhanced food synthesizers, and many others.

"As an employee of Diblonski Ltd. you can see rapid job advancement by signing up new members. Those that join at the highest level will bring the referring employee D points. Accumulation of D points leads to greater employee benefits. See your HR representative for all the details."

The monitor lit up and the key appeared. He generated the necessary code that modified the lock and the hidden matrix became visible. The newly found sequences were unique and very elegant. The key had unlocked a series of commands that created a startling change in the "Dot" matrix. A microelectrical field was generated around the dot, one that looked very familiar and, if his suspicions were true had tremendous potential for a totally fresh and innovative use for the ubiquitous Green Dot.

❧

XXIII. Lieutenant Ryan

LIEUTENANT RYAN CAREFULLY READ THROUGH THE pathologists findings from the autopsy on Rep. McCally. All the pathological findings confirmed death by asphyxiation, no obvious external trauma and no definite evidence of foul play. Toxicology confirmed Euphoricin at lethal doses, but no discoloration of the digits. He made one more call to Dr. Wall.

"Hello Eve, I'm just reading your findings on Rep. McCally." The hologram of the attractive pathogist materialized sitting across from Ryan. "Can you do one more thing for me? Run a tox screen for any potentially lethal compounds that would be masked by toxic levels of Euphoricin in the blood stream and pay particular attention to any that would be affected by peri- or postmortem administration of Eupho. Thanks." Without a word the image next to him disappeared.

Ryan sat back in his chair and closed his eyes; something wasn't right and it was becoming apparent that Sgt. Moore's report was at best incomplete. Someone had gone to very great lengths to make Rep. McCally's death look like an accidental overdose. He realized that something involving such an important official could involve the highest echelons of the government and he needed to be very careful. He decided to keep his doubts to himself for now, but he held off on signing off on Moore's report. When the Captain called he would think of some excuse for the delay. He left the office and drove to McCally's apartment.

๕๛๛

XIV. Coryllos

CORYLLOS' CAR PARKED ITSELF AT MONMOUTH PARK and he took the short walk to the clubhouse entrance. In all his years he had never been to the track, but he had done some research into the world of thoroughbred racing and wagering. He bought a program and a small disc that carried holographic records of all that day's contestants' previous races. He dressed as inconspicuously as he thought possible, blue jean shirt, dark pants, and dark glasses. He was unshaven, assuming that people that frequented the track were down on their luck, desperate and indifferent about their personal appearance. He wandered around the cavernous structure that was the clubhouse, still with an hour to kill before the first race. People milled about looking busy and purposeful, staring at holograms of past races, looking at times and numbers, all focusing intently on the upcoming races.

Such a bore he thought; but he had to at least appear to be interested if he was to have any chance at success. After about fifteen minutes he wandered over to Bar #23 and asked for a scotch on the rocks. He stood at the bar as a crowd of people began to gather; they seemed to recognize each other, but also kept to themselves as they studied their numbers and holograms.

"Cold Rick is a lock . . . go with Shady Pop . . . one six double . . ." The chatter of the track wafted through the air as he nursed his drink. An older man, white haired and wrinkled, came up to the bar.

"My usual, Jack," he said. The bartender nodded and a drink appeared almost immediately. The white-haired man looked up at one of the myriad of monitors and down at his figures which were on a sheet of paper.

"Who do you like?" Coryllos asked, trying his best to catch the man's interest.

The man slowly turned away from his studying and looked at Coryllos. "You're new around here," he said as a statement of fact. "Let me give you a word of advice. This race ain't worth more than a two buck interest bet. Most of these sorry excuses for racehorses couldn't pull a milk wagon. Wait for the fourth race, that is, if you want to make any money."

Coryllos smiled and feigned interest by looking at the contestants for the fourth race. "Thanks for the tip. Who's good in the fourth." He stared at the names of the horses and the numbers by each name, but it was just a jumble to him.

"You really are new at this." He held out his hand and shook Coryllos'. "Obadiah," he said introducing himself. "Let me give you some pointers. Look for the horse that is ready to run their best, not the one that has just run their best. You get the difference. These trainers like nothing better than to play games; keep the horses true condition hidden until they can spring a surprise. Look at everything and then look again. If you really try, you can beat them."

Several other people started to gather around and offer their advice. Coryllos was sure that some of them knew of the unnamed man. The talk continued, most of it meaningless chatter until he heard them start talking about a particular person.

"It's too bad Joshua isn't here, he'd really help you get started. Haven't seen him for a while, but there was a man with some sort of ESP."

Coryllos sensed that he may have found the name that was eluding him, but he needed to be careful. He correctly sensed that if he seemed too eager to find information he would be met by a stone wall. He decided to play along for a while longer.

"What's so great about this Joshua," he asked innocently.

Obadiah answered him. "Joshua Smith, true horseplaying legend. It seemed like he never lost. He used to stand right where you are, lean up against the bar, real quiet like, but inside that head the wheels certainly were turning. He had a way about him, looked at things in a different way. If any of us looked from the top down, he looked from the bottom up; however, he looked like he was special. He picked the best races to bet and he always knew the right thing to do. Real polite, too. Never failed to help somebody or give advice if he was asked. Don't know where he's been these last few weeks. Of course he's disappeared like this before, but then he just shows up one day like he was never gone, never says a word about where he was or what he was doing."

Some of the others gathered around told their stories about Joshua and Coryllos was convinced that this Joshua Smith was the man he was seeking. He decided to play it cool for the rest of the day; he would return tomorrow and ask a few more questions. He relaxed and stayed to watch the races with his new found companions.

❧❦

XV. Gideon and Aaron

GIDEON WOKE WITH THE RISING SUN, ROLLED OUT OF bed into his waiting hygiene center which provided a hot shower, shave, and every other necessity, after which he sat down at the table in his kitchen for breakfast; fresh strawberries with cream, hot tea, and a toasted bagel with butter. The day's itinerary projected over his food: "MEETING WITH AARON DIBLONSKI, 3:00 P.M." in bold red letters; otherwise the day was free. Gideon knew that although nothing was scheduled, he wasn't free. The morning would be spent reviewing every scrap of information available on Aaron Diblonski, Diblonski Ltd., and anything connected with either entity.

As soon as he finished he turned on the music of Gillespie and sat down at his monitor and began studying everything he could find on Diblonski. There was a wealth of data on the financial aspects of the company, founded in 2052, astounding growth averaging twenty-five percent annually, development of the government/industry model, philanthropic ventures, and corporate structure. Aaron Diblonski had been at the helm since the beginning, starting it as a manufacturer of personal entertainment systems, pioneering holographic imaging on a wide scale. From this beginning he had grown the company into everything: manufacturing, entertainment, media, mining, financial, and personal health services until he had reached the behemoth status it now enjoyed. *Truly a ten thousand kilo gorilla,* he thought as he turned to the available personal data on Aaron Diblonski.

This was much sketchier. His birth was presumed to be in 2013, location not known, education was listed as MBA University of Pennsylvania granted in 2033. He had never married, had no children, and no known family. He currently resided in Washington DC, but also maintained homes in New York City, Chicago, Honolulu, Beijing, Moscow, London, and Jerusalem. He had a pet cat named Lucipher, presumably named for the cat featured in an animated production of Cinderella from years past. He was rarely seen in public, but when he did appear he was invariably surrounded by three or four beautiful young women, a bevy of bodyguards and personal secretaries shielding him from all prying by the media. The only images available were those supplied by his official photographer and these always showed him as a tall, thin, tanned man, clean shaven, usually dressed in a dark suit, wearing dark glasses.

Nothing much here, Gideon thought. There was more in the shadows, Gideon knew. His encounter with Richard Cosby suggested that Diblonski was more than a fabulously successful entrepreneur; there was a sinister side that perhaps crossed over into a supernatural realm. This made Diblonski much more dangerous, but perhaps more predictable. Years before, after his encounter with Richard Cosby he studied the characteristics of demons and devils. He was sure that there was something Satanic about Diblonski and that this man's ultimate purpose was the eventual conversion of every living soul to the side of Satan. Gideon wasn't entirely sure what was to be believed, but he couldn't deny the events surrounding the destruction of Richard Cosby and there was no explanation for what he had seen except for the hand of Satan reaching out of Hell, trying to swat him away like an annoying gnat.

After finishing his study of Diblonski he quickly scanned through all the available data on the Diblonski Ltd. corporate structure. He paid particular attention to the executive board and the second in command, Abraham Masur. He made mental notes of the unusual background and experience Masur brought to his job and his mercurial rise from obscurity to number two man. Gideon finished his preparation and lay back to relax. Fireworks were sure to come and he needed to be well rested.

At 2:00 Brian Sivestre walked through the front door and rode the elevator to Gideon's apartment. He was met at the door before he had a chance to ring the bell. Sivestre was medium height, a little heavy set, particularly for the times, sporting a dark brown moustache and a conspicuous Green Dot.

"Hello, Mr. Sivestre," Gideon greeted the reporter. "I'm glad you could come."

"The pleasure's all mine, Mr. Jones. Thank you for this opportunity; I'm sure that you had hundreds of requests."

Gideon ignored that comment and the two sat down. A wet bar popped out of the coffee table. "Would either of you care for a bit of refreshment?" the bar asked with an impeccable British accent.

"Scotch, single blend," Sivestre said.

"Ice water," Gideon added. The drinks appeared and the two men started with some idle chatter about nothing before Sivestre began more serious questioning.

"You tossed propriety to the wind with your little speech yesterday; either you have a desire to be out of public service or you have designs on climbing to a higher level within the government."

"Wrong on both counts, Mr. Sivestre. That's what I like about you media types. Quick to make inappropriate assumptions with little regard for the truth. I hope you are different, because you are about to get much more than you bargained for."

"How's that?"

"You'll know in about ten seconds." A call came through announcing that his transportation to the Diblonski residence had arrived. "We are adding another party to this little get together. One Aaron Diblonski; you are about to get the exclusive of the year, that is if you wish to go with me."

"Of course!" he exclaimed with proper enthusiasm. "Any opportunity to get close to Diblonski is a chance at the Pulitzer. Let's go."

The two men quickly left the apartment, the security system automatically activating as they walked out the door. Gideon hit a switch inside his jacket as they left, activating a second layer of security, just in case. They entered a long black limousine and were whisked away to the appointed rendezvous. As soon as the limousine pulled away a white sports car pulled up and a woman got out and casually walked into the building and up to Gideon's apartment. She stood outside the door, ran a quick scan, made note of the number, and quickly left.

The ride to Diblonski's midtown apartment was quiet and uneventful. The two men said very little, both a little fearful that they were being monitored; a point on which they were correct. The limo pulled up in front of a tall glass and concrete building and they were instructed to take elevator #1. They weren't told which floor, but they soon realized that this elevator only had one destination, the top floor penthouse apartment on the 78th floor. They exited and were immediately ushered into a grand foyer where they were greeted by Abe Masur.

"Welcome, Mr. Jones, we are delighted that you could come on such short notice," he said as he eyed both men up and down. "And you are . . . ?" he questioned staring at Sivestre.

"Brian Sivestre, ABS Media Services. Mr. Jones was kind enough to ask me to join him."

"Are you a friend of Mr. Jones?"

"Oh yes, we've known each other for years. I just happened to be in town and Gideon didn't feel right leaving me alone, since I'm here for such a short visit. You don't mind, do you? Because if it's a problem I can wait in the limo."

"Oh no, it's no problem. Follow me, Mr. Diblonski is expecting you in the study."

The three men walked down a short hallway to a tall, very solid double door, deep mahogany in color with gold trim. The "apartment" was huge with tall ceilings, gold crown molding and fixtures, with paintings and sculptures adorning the walls. The art collection reminded Gideon of Adrian Leavitt and he shook his head briefly as if to shake that unpleasant memory from his consciousness. The double doors opened automatically as they approached and they were greeted by an impeccably dressed man who appeared about forty, with jet black hair, tanned, clean shaven, and thin. Mr. Diblonski extended his hand and shook Gideon's hand. Gideon felt a cold shiver run up his back as he took the thin long fingers into his own strong hand.

"Hello, Mr. Jones," Diblonski said as they shook hands. "Mr. Sivestre, I didn't know that you were acquainted with Mr. Jones."

"Yes, we're very old friends."

"I'm so glad you could join us. Won't you sit down? Can I offer either of you some refreshment?"

"Nothing for me," Gideon replied. He noticed a striking watch on Diblonski's wrist, completely black with bright red markers.

"Single blend Scotch, if it's not too much trouble," Sivestre answered. The drink appeared as they both sank into the most luxurious, comfortable chairs either had ever seen.

"That's an impressive antique watch your wearing," Gideon remarked. "Are you a connoisseur of antique mechanical watches?"

"How kind of you to notice. Yes, I have a soft spot for true marvels of human ingenuity, unique items that demonstrate the human ability to rise above mediocrity; such a rare trait these days. The complicated mechanical wristwatch is truly the epitome of such ingenuity; it is a pity that they have mostly disappeared into antique shops and journals of technical history."

"You and I have one thing in common, then." Gideon held out his wrist displaying his blue and silver watch with the name DeBethune on the dial. This is an antique I found a few years ago; I reconditioned it myself."

"Very nice indeed," Diblonski said. "Mine is an Hublot; an Hublot Big Bang Red Devil to be exact. It is one of several dozen fine antique watches I have in my collection. Let me show you one of my favorites. He opened a wooden case and removed a shiny gray watch with a black dial and gold hands.

"This is a very rare minute repeater. Listen." He pushed a button and Joshua heard a song, specifically, 'the Danse Macabre.' "

"Very unusual choice of music for such a watch."

"Yes, I had it reconditioned to my own specifications. Such mechanical marvels truly demonstrate the creativity of the human mind, don't you think, Mr. Jones?"

"I think that such genius as creates these 'mechanical marvels' as you so aptly call them is a gift from God." Joshua glanced at Masur and saw a brief wince at the mention of deity, a response he wholly expected. Mr. Diblonski, he noted, remained composed.

"From what I know of God, He would have been content to keep humanity naked and ignorant. The serpent did Adam and Eve a favor; freeing them from such servitude and allowing mankind to flourish and surpass their keeper."

"Do you truly believe that we are better off today, struggling for a few brief moments of happiness before we leave this forlorn world?"

"This world is all we have and mankind has rightly learned that it's best to make the most of what we have here and now, because, Mr. Jones, as I said, what we have today is all there is."

Gideon decided not to argue the point and responded, "Enough of philosophy; as enjoyable as it is, I'm sure that you did not invite me to this wonderful home to debate God and his influence on humanity. I must say that you have quite an impressive home."

"You are very observant, Mr. Jones. Truly inspired creations of human genius are my great passion. Besides my unique watches, I also have a very extensive collection of rare paintings I'm sure you noticed and some very rare, one of a kind flowers that I developed myself; including some that are here," he pointed to a very striking plant with the brightest red and orange flowers Gideon had ever seen, "and some more that are in the greenhouse at my home in Washington. You might say that I have a fondness for rare things of beauty and grace. This particular plant is unique, only two exist in the solar system; this one here and its sister, which is at my home outside Washington. But, enough of such idle conversation. We could talk about such a fascinating topic for days, but then we would miss the primary purpose of this meeting."

"Of course; now, what can I do for you, Mr. Diblonski?" Gideon asked, as he bent to sniff the sweet aroma emanating from the beautiful plant. He looked up and wiped some white pollen from his nose and shirt as he turned and faced Mr. Diblonski.

"You have made quite a name for yourself, Mr. Jones, in a very short time. Your resume is very impressive, although I must disagree with some of the comments you made in your speech the other day."

"I thought that you might, otherwise I wouldn't be here enjoying your gracious hospitality. I do, however, stand by every word."

"As you should, Mr. Jones, or else there would have been no point in uttering them. I believe that you have done my company a bit of an injustice, however. Our goal has always been to help the downtrodden of society; to lift people out of the gutter, so to speak, and bring them to loftier levels within our society. Do you find this to be an unworthy pursuit, Mr. Jones?"

Gideon sat silently for a moment. "I will have a drink, after all; a glass of ice water," he said, before answering Diblonski's question. "I don't deny that the charitable work you have performed has been admirable and as a whole has been a boon to many of the less fortunate people on this great planet. I was merely saying that our government and its many partners, such as you, do not necessarily have all the answers. If you did, there would be no social outcasts."

It was Diblonski's turn to pause, but he continued to look directly into Gideon's eyes. Finally, he responded, "Mr. Jones, your own words particularly singled out Diblonski Ltd as the entity perpetrating a vast ruse upon our great society as a means to maintain control of the population by instilling a fear that you say is unfounded. Do you at this time stand by these words or are you willing to recant this slander." Mr. Diblonski maintained an outward appearance of calm that belied the force of his words.

Gideon tried to present just as calm a demeanor, but there was a slight wavering of his voice. He had definitely struck a nerve, but he also realized that he had entered treacherous waters and he needed to be very careful. He replied, "I am more than willing to recant, as you call it, if I can be convinced that I was in any way in error. Thus far I have heard only semi-righteous outrage without substance. If you are able to prove to me that my own observations are mere false apparitions I will gladly tell Mr. Sivestre here that I am wrong and then, I am sure, he will tell the world. I would then cheerfully leave this brief foray into public life behind and return to the private social work that I truly love."

Diblonski sat silently for what seemed to be hours before he spoke, "I can see that our discussion is finished. I am disappointed, Mr. Jones. Mr. Masur will show you out. Good day."

Diblonski disappeared through a second door as Masur showed Gideon and Sivestre to the waiting limousine. When he returned, Diblonski was waiting.

Diblonski was pruning the leaves from one of his rare plants and without looking up addressed his underling, "This Gideon Jones is trouble; I think he should be invited to a party."

Masur smiled, nodded his head, and responded: "Yes sir. I suspected a party would be in Mr. Jones' future, so I took the liberty of sending one of our people to his apartment to do some preliminary fact finding. Unfortunately, this Jones has some supplementary security and she wasn't able to get in. We will however continue our surveillance at the party and afterward."

Diblonski nodded his head slightly, then put the plant down, sat by the huge fire, opening a book as Mr. Masur quickly departed.

❧❦

XVI. Back at the Track

CORYLLOS ARRIVED AT MONMOUTH PARK JUST BEFORE the first race. As he walked up to Bar #23, the first raced went off. The familiar crowd was gathered around the high definition hologram as the horses sprang from the starting gate. About a minute and a half later it was over and everyone gathered around the bar.

"Hello, Mister, excuse me, what was your name?" one of the patrons asked Coryllos.

"A great race . . . love that Santos," someone yelled referring to the jockey, Angel Santos, who had just piloted Storm Kat to victory; *a victory which seemed very popular with everyone around him,* Coryllos thought.

"It looks like Storm Kat was the people's choice," Coryllos commented to no one in particular.

"Three to one, top speed ratings, drop in class . . . the best bet of the week, that's for sure," one of the men said. "I'm surprised you missed it," he added.

"Had a late start and then ran into traffic," Coryllos lied, trying to explain how someone who was trying to become a serious horseplayer could miss such a golden opportunity. *Careful,* he thought, *don't blow it.* He continued, "I wasn't so sure he was such a sure thing. He looked too good. I thought they were just trying to set him up for his next race."

The others nodded and he realized he was OK. "Do you think Joshua Smith would have bet on him?"

A pale-skinned man with a short stubbly beard stared at him when he asked this question and then remarked, "You sure want to know about this Joshua Smith. What are you, his mother?"

Coryllos laughed and tried to play it down. "Oh, no; it's just that yesterday you all were going on about what a legend he is. I'm just curious, that's all."

"Well, he's not here," the man said. "So, it doesn't really matter." The man brushed up against Coryllos and jammed something into his hand.

"Watch it," Coryllos said loudly.

"Sue me," the other man said and he walked away.

Coryllos opened up his program and snuck the note that he had received inside. He went to the bar and ordered a gin and tonic, took a short sip and then excused himself. He stepped into a hygiene center and looked at the message. "Stairwell 18 after the next race." He finished up and walked back to the bar.

"I don't like anything in this race," Coryllos said and he left to find the stairwell as the race was going off. He walked away from the grandstand and found the numerous doors that opened into the stairs and quickly found number eighteen. He looked around and made sure he was not seen and also did a quick scan to check for surveillance. Seeing the coast was clear, he ducked inside and waited, for what he hoped would be some sort of break.

"Your early," a voice said from above him. The pale-faced man came down the stairs. "You seem to be awfully interested in Joshua Smith; too interested, in my opinion. Of course, I don't really care. This whole crowd ain't worth much, bunch of losers if you ask me."

Coryllos ignored these comments. "What do you know about this man, Joshua Smith. I'd like to find him."

"So anxious; you need to relax. He either owes you money, which I doubt, or he ran off with your girl; whatever, I may be able to help you. Of course, I assume you would be very grateful."

"How grateful?"

"Oh, about a thousand bucks grateful."

Coryllos tried to play it cool. He put his hand to his chin and scratched his nose. "I'll tell you what; I'll give you two thousand if your information is useful."

"Let me see the cash."

Coryllos slowly reached into his pocket and pulled out a wad of bills and peeled off twenty one-hundred-dollar bills and held them out. The other man reached to grab them, but Coryllos pulled them back.

"Not so fast, first tell me."

The pale man stared at the money and his hands started to shake. "Alright, the last time anyone saw Joshua Smith around here was the night that UN Representative, what was his name, McCally, committed suicide. Smith was at the track, as usual; but instead of leaving and going home afterward, he snuck into the backstretch. Some of the backstretch workers would have been the last people he saw. He used to go see them a lot at the end of the day. I think he got some tips from them or something. Anyway, there's an opening in the fence on the way out to the lot; that's where he used to sneak in. You talk to them and I bet you'll find him." As he finished these words, he snatched the money from Coryllos' hand and started to count it.

"Very helpful, sir; well worth your fee," and he put out his hand. The other man reluctantly grasped it. Coryllos squeezed tightly and then whirled the man around and grabbed him around the neck. There was a sharp twist and a loud "snap" and Coryllos, with a tear rolling down one cheek, whispered, "I'm sorry," and gently laid the lifeless figure on the stairs, took back his two thousand dollars, did another quick scan, and quietly exited. He disappeared into the crowd on the ground floor; staying as inconspicuous as possible until after the last race and left the track with the exiting throng. As he passed the backstretch he ducked inside, going through the same opening in the fence that Joshua had passed through weeks before. He took a quick look around and recorded images of the buildings and the personnel. He ducked back out through the same opening in the fence after about ten minutes. His research would continue on another day.

ॐ

XVII. At the Party

THE DOOR OPENED AUTOMATICALLY AS JOSHUA approached; the ride up the elevator to the 130th floor had taken barely ten seconds. The room was a huge open circle with all the walls replaced by tall, almost invisible windows that provided an uninterrupted view of the Manhattan skyline. The rotating colored lights that bathed the room mingled intimately with the lights of the city creating a stunning, surreal appearance. The room was full of people wandering about and, to Gideon's eye, feigning a sense of interest in each other. He did not see any of his fellow commission members. He had tried to dress as inconspicuously as possible, black sweater and gray slacks, but noticed that his conservative dress stood out amidst the garish and revealing outfits that surrounded him. All around the room trays of food and bowls of pills were stationed strategically guarding against any potential complaints regarding inaccessible food or stimulants. Scantily clad waiters and waitresses moved effortlessly through and between the small groups of guests mingling in their best partygoer style.

Gideon wandered about the room. He sampled some of the hors d'ouvres and wrinkled his nose at the synthesized fare. Such a fancy place should have real food, he thought. The pills he recognized as the latest fad stimulants, Nirvana and Ambrosia. One heightened senses, while the other was a hormone stimulator and mood disinhibitor. Both were considered innocuous and completely safe; they had become favorites of the social elite, lacking the harsh aftereffects of some of their older cousins. He walked up to a group of four people carrying on a passionate conversation, at least by outward appearance. No one gave him any notice as he stood by.

" . . . do you believe he wore a blue open collar with those tight, red slacks . . . mauve is definitely in this year for men and women and everything in between . . . all the rave is the astrocruise . . . look at this brochure . . ."

He wandered past another group. ". . . Diblonski is up thirty points . . . precious metals are where you need to be . . ."

Gideon couldn't see any world issues being solved by either group. As he wandered around he heard someone shouting, "GIDEON," but he didn't respond. He heard it again, only closer, slapped himself on the forehead and turned to see Rudy, another member of the Stolts Commission, striding toward him.

"I'm so glad you decided to come," Rudy said. "This place would be so boring without you."

"With me or without, I can tell that this is where all the great decisions of society are made," Gideon responded with more than a touch of sarcasm. "Who's wearing what, what the stock market is going to do, the best getaways. If this is the elite of the New York social set, send me back to Baltimore."

They looked around the room. There were a number of people sitting on large cushions staring off into space. "Green Dots" of every color lightly glowing; at the far end of the room, under the glass ceiling, partygoers paired off, "dancing" to the loud boomer music, gyrating and grinding back and forth as a prelude to more intimate, physical interaction.

"Rudy, I don't belong with these people. I can't mix and mingle, talking about nothing and pretend that the Earth's future depends on it."

"OK, just hang around until the media types get here. It would do our commission some good to get some free positive publicity. Excuse me, but I see someone that I need to talk to. I'll be back as soon as I can."

Rudy left to talk to a buxom blonde, her prominent breasts barely constrained by her skimpy dress. Gideon wandered around the room making no attempt to hide his boredom. As he walked by the end of the room opposite the dance floor there, was a closed door. A very attractive brunette bumped into him as he approached the door.

"Excuse me," she said in a very comely voice. Gideon smiled at her as she passed by and stared at her as she walked to the far end of the room.

He turned back to the closed door, opened it, and peeked inside where he found four men and two women sitting around a table. They were holding playing cards and there were some cards and chips in the middle of the table.

"Raise three hundred," one of the women said.

"Call," said another.

"I'm out," said a third.

"Full house, jacks and threes," the woman said and she pulled the money toward her.

The poker game piqued Gideon's interest. He had only played for fun when he was younger, always preferring horses to cards; he considered the ponies to be more cerebral and much less given to random chance. He watched them play for a few hands. The game was New York Cross 'Em. Each player received two cards face down. Seven other cards were dealt face down in the middle of the table. These cards were exposed in sequence, First the cross of the "t" was exposed, which was three cards, then the stem, which was an additional three, and the point of the "cross" was the last to be turned over. A final card was dealt face down to any players still participating. The players could make their best hand using either the vertical stem or the "horizontal" of the "cross," along with the top point and their three down cards. Bets were taken after the initial deal, as each set of cards was exposed and after the final deal. The limit typically increased in a progressive fashion with each round of wagering.

"Can you use another sacrificial lamb?" Joshua asked after he had observed enough to understand the play.

They looked him over, up and down. "Sure, pull up a chair," one of them said. He was heavy set with a stubbly beard. "Ante is fifty, minimum bet is twenty, and progressive limit to two hundred."

Gideon sat down between the woman, who was middle-aged, probably no more than sixty-five, blonde, slightly heavy set and elegantly dressed in a red silk dress and white scarf, a dazzling diamond necklace hanging down between her exposed cleavage, and another youngish man who was burly with a black moustache, dressed in casual nondescript attire and smoking one of the popular thin cigars. He introduced himself as Crash and then introduced the other players.

"On your right is Ruby, next to her is Tony," he said, pointing to the man with the stubbly beard. Then Angie, seated next to Tony, who was dressed in a simple black dress with pale complexion and jet black hair. Then there was Dan, who was dressed in jeans and a work shirt and distinguished by his shaved head and large bright gold earrings in each ear. And finally, Stanley, who was next to Crash and was blonde with smooth dark brown skin, dressed completely in white, wearing a shirt without a collar.

"It's Ruby's deal," said Crash.

The blonde picked up the deck and shuffled the cards, demonstrating her skills with aplomb; two cards down to each player as each tossed in his ante. Joshua pulled a thousand dollars from his pocket.

"Keep your money for now. If you're here we assume you are good for your debts," Dan said. "Just tell me how much you want to start with."

"One thousand, please."

"Ooh, a polite man for a change. Honey, we need to get together after the game," Ruby said as she peaked at her hole cards. "It's your bet, honey," nodding towards Gideon.

Gideon pulled up the corner of his cards and saw Ace/King of diamonds. "Twenty dollars," he said softly.

"You're going to have to talk louder, young man," interjected Crash. "Call," he said.

"I'm out."

"Call and raise forty."

"Out."

"Call."

"I'll call," Tony said loudly.

Number one, as the first flop was called, was done and the queen of diamonds, ten of diamonds, and two of clubs was exposed.

Gideon started again. "Check," he said

The betting went around the table as Crash bet fifty, the next four folded, and Tony raised to one hundred. Gideon called.

Number two flop revealed the king of spades, seven of clubs, and nine of clubs.

Gideon checked again, Crash bet one hundred, Tony called, and Gideon called.

The point card was turned over exposing the five of spades.

Gideon paused and studied his cards and the faces of his two remaining opponents. Both appeared impassive as Crash stared into space, then turned his head suddenly to the left and then stared straight ahead. Tony, on the other hand, smiled, exposing his very white teeth.

"Two hundred," Gideon said.

Crash paused for a moment and studied Gideon's face, looking for any expression that would give an edge. Gideon sat still as Crash saw a slight waver of his hands.

"Call and raise two hundred," Crash said loudly.

Tony's smile faded away as he stared at his cards and the other players. "Call," he finally said.

Without hesitation Gideon stated, "Call and raise two hundred."

Crash studied his cards and finally said, "call."

Tony folded.

The final down card was dealt.

"Two hundred," Gideon started.

"Call," replied Crash.

Gideon flipped over his cards revealing the ace, king, and four of diamonds. Crash threw down his cards in disgust. "Beginner's luck," he said. Gideon agreed with him.

The game continued with Gideon winning a little more than he lost as the friendly mood started to fade. Time dragged on until he looked up to see that it was approaching five.

"One more hand, fellows, and then I've got to go," Gideon said.

"Shall we raise the stakes, perhaps to one hundred minimum and two thousand maximum?" Crash asked.

Tony, Dan, Stanley, and Angie bowed out, leaving Ruby, Crash, and Gideon to play. Gideon dealt as they each threw in their ante; two down cards to each player. Gideon carefully peeled back the corners of the two cards and two kings stared back at him, spades and clubs. Crash started the betting, after studying his cards, the queen of diamonds and queen of clubs.

"Five hundred," he said.

Ruby threw her cards away.

Gideon looked at his cards again. "Your five and five more," he said quietly.

Crash paused, thinking, once again turned his head to the left, and then shook it violently as if he were disagreeing with an unseen kibitzer. He had noted that the better his hand the quieter Gideon became, but maybe it was a trick to throw everyone off and make a big score on the last hand.

"Call," he said.

Number one was revealed, the ace of spades, the two of diamonds, and the ace of hearts.

"Five hundred," Crash said feigning indifference.

"Fifteen hundred," Gideon said, now even quieter.

"I'll see your raise and raise another thousand," Crash said, convinced that Gideon was bluffing.

"I'll call," Gideon said a little more forcefully.

Number two was revealed, the eight of spades, jack of clubs, and the ten of spades.

"I'll go for a thousand," Crash stated.

"Your thousand and two thousand more," Gideon almost whispered.

Crash turned his head again and called without comment.

The point card was revealed, the queen of spades.

'Two thousand," Crash said, maintaining the air of indifference.

"I'll see your two and raise two," Gideon said in a loud voice.

"Your two and two more."

"Call."

The final down card came. Joshua picked up all three of his cards and looked at them, shielding them from his competitors.

"Two thousand," Crash said, his hand shaking slightly.

"Call and raise two thousand," Gideon said, once again becoming quiet.

"Your two and two more."

"Call."

Crash flipped over his cards exposing his full house, queens over aces, and started to take the pot.

"I think that kings are higher than queens, at least these enlightened times haven't changed that yet," Gideon said as he turned over three kings.

Crash collapsed in the chair as the reality hit. Seventeen thousand dollars was a bit steep and he certainly didn't have the cash with him. Gideon sensed that Crash was troubled and sat down next to him.

"It was just for fun. I wouldn't take that much money from anyone. I just wanted the challenge." Gideon threw a bundle of bills on the table, leaving his chips and his money and walked away. The other players stared in disbelief as he walked into the main room.

What he saw made him sick. There were partygoers scattered about the room, some paired off, some solitary, unconscious, passed out on one of many large pillows; many more were off in private rooms. All were in various states of intoxication and it was obvious that any sense of shame had long been abandoned. He walked toward the door, anxious to escape this foray into elite society as quickly as possible. As he reached the elevator a young woman with long brunette hair and beauty that would have put Helen of Troy to shame stopped him. Gideon remembered her from earlier in the evening when she had bumped onto him.

"That was a noble thing you did," she remarked, positioning herself between him and his chance for escape.

"Perhaps, but the money is of no consequence to me. Over the years I've learned that a healthy contempt for the almighty dollar helps keep things in proper perspective and sometimes keeps me out of trouble."

"Still, Crash would have been in hot water with the owners of this place. He's won millions of dollars playing poker over the last year, but Crash holds on to money as well as you can hold water in your fist; most of his winnings are long gone. He never would have been able to pay and that would not have been looked upon very favorably by hotel officials. You would have seen him with a broken arm tomorrow or two broken legs if you had complained."

"Well, he should be safe then, Miss . . ."

"Beauty; that is, my friends call me Beauty."

"Your friends are very perceptive, Beauty. Now if you'll excuse me, I really need to be going." He gently moved her aside as the elevator arrived. He quickly entered and made his way down to a waiting taxi. As he rode back to his apartment he had a feeling of exhilaration. Certainly it wasn't the party or the people, who seemed to be incredible bores. He realized it was the poker game; the competition against other people and the extreme and rapid gambling decisions that had pumped out the excess adrenalin. This was so much more gambling than the racetrack, which was more pedestrian, but considerably more analytical than the impulsive action that cards offered. The brief encounter with Beauty had added an extra helping of hormones to those already coursing through his veins. He decided to take a walk before going up to his apartment. The streets were ablaze with lights and holograms sending their false promises to the early birds and nighthawks out and about in the early morning haze.

Gideon pulled the goggles from his pocket. He carried them at all times, believing them too valuable to be left unattended. As he cruised between the towering buildings, he thought that it would be impossible for much out of the ordinary to live in this jungle of concrete and electricity. He put them on and once again was amazed. Numerous insects in shades of green, yellow, and orange immediately appeared. Dogs foraging among piles of garbage competed with cats and rats for the prize of humanities' refuse. The rats were about everywhere; all shapes and sizes crawled along buildings down the "modern" storm sewers that were modern in name only. Gideon was not surprised to see these creatures amidst the urban blight, however, there was much more to be seen. Snakes slithered about the drainage system, occasionally emerging in the street to capture any particularly slothful rodents. Birds flitted about and perched high above the street, keeping a watchful vigil over the city below or attending to nests expertly constructed on ledges and rafters all over the city.

Alive in spite of humanity, Gideon thought as he approached his apartment. Exhaustion overwhelmed him as he eschewed the stairs and rode the elevator up to his apartment on the fifth floor. The door immediately opened as he approached and the monitoring system announced that his invited guest was waiting within. He stopped and activated the security system record in the foyer. The shadowy figure of a woman was shown entering the apartment, going straight to his bedroom where he could see her shower and climb into his bed where she now lay sleeping. *Goldilocks looking for Papa Bear,* he thought as he made his way to the bedroom as silently as possible.

Curiosity overwhelmed reason as he opened the door and turned on the light to see Beauty raise her head up sleepily from his pillow, exposing her bare shoulders and her perfectly shaped breasts. Gideon turned his head and handed her a robe that was draped over the chair. She pulled the covers over herself silently and put the robe on.

"I'm sorry, really. I know I shouldn't have done it, but I lifted your key at the party, had it copied, and slipped it back in your pocket before you got on the elevator," she explained.

"You could have just asked, you know," Gideon replied.

"And you would have said no. I know what you are like and I also know the best ways to quickly break the ice. Waiting naked in someone's bed usually works pretty well."

"You are right about that. I can see that you have nothing to hide. Well, since you're here, can I make you some breakfast?"

"That would be very nice, thank you."

"Give me a minute to clean up and change and I'll whip up some real eggs and toast." Gideon disappeared into the bathroom and Beauty lay back down on the bed. After a few minutes she came out wearing his robe and found him at the stove, scrambling some fresh eggs, squeezing some fresh oranges, and toasting real bread.

"Smells good," she said as she yawned and leaned against the counter, her long brown hair looking disheveled and her bare leg extending out from beneath the robe, a perfectly enticing picture of sensuality. Gideon glanced at her briefly and then returned to his cooking.

"Have a seat," he said. "Everything will be ready in a minute." He put the eggs and toast on a plate, poured the juice into two glasses; rummaged around in the refrigerator until he found some butter and blackberry preserves, and then sat down with her to enjoy breakfast.

෧ඁ෧

XVIII. Gideon and Beauty

THEY FINISHED BREAKFAST TOGETHER AND GIDEON walked down to the street with her and called a taxi, which pulled up to the curb in less than one minute. He helped her into the cab and, as an afterthought, climbed in with her.

"Where to?" he asked.

"Fifty-eight Central Park South, apt 6B," she answered."You know, you really don't need to ride home with me. I've ridden in thousands of taxis, always without any mishap."

"I'm sure, but I just want to show you that chivalry is not dead," Gideon answered as he looked out the window at the same New York streets he had seen dozens of times before. The cab sped along, expertly finding its way through the relatively light early morning traffic. In less than ten minutes they stopped in front of Beauty's apartment. Gideon got out first and gave her his hand as he walked her to the door.

"Good bye, Beauty, you've made this one of the more interesting and pleasant evenings and mornings that I've ever had. I wish you well in your future life." His voice was slightly hesitant.

She smiled at him and walked slowly through the foyer as the door started to close. Gideon stared at the empty cab and then at Beauty as she walked away, then back at the waiting cab, and once more at Beauty. He thought about his empty apartment as he watched Beauty call for the elevator. The door seemed to be waiting for him to make up his mind before it closed completely. He waved the taxi away and ducked inside as the door snapped shut behind him.

"May I call you sometime?" he asked plaintively. She turned and looked at the abject figure standing in the lobby, turned around, and slowly walked back to him. She took his hand in hers and kissed him lightly on his closed mouth. Gideon stood motionless for a moment and then wrapped his arms tightly around her waist and gave her a long deep kiss on her open mouth. He took her hand in his and they walked together through the waiting elevator doors and rode up to her apartment. From that moment, they were together.

Gideon's electrifying speech and natural charm made him the new media darling. He was named chairman of the Stolts Comission and began to work tirelessly to lighten the burden of society's outcasts, doing his best to not upset the delicate balance that existed between mainstream society and this underground world. Programs were set up throughout the state to monitor and assist community leaders and provide government services to these underprivileged souls. His efforts were well received and with each success the media trumpeted his virtues and ignored any deficiencies, which were few.

When he was not working, he could be seen around town with Beauty on his arm. She became as much a media darling as Gideon and it was a rare day when their images did not grace one of the daily news reports. Little was known about Beauty and rumors were rampant; stories began to pop up of a sordid background, broken marriage contracts, unsanctioned children, and any other misdeed that the gossip "reporters" could dream up. No one knew anything about the beautiful, charming young woman, and she made no effort to dispel any of the reports. After a particularly cruel article which portrayed her as a the moral equivalent of Jack the Ripper, she and Gideon decided that it was time to clear the air and put an end to all the speculation that had been swirling about the couple.

Gideon called Brian Sivestre, one reporter that he thought could be trusted to file an accurate and unbiased report, and offered him an exclusive interview. The following morning at 11:00, Mr. Sivestre rang the bell to Gideon's apartment and was immediately ushered in to meet a very anxious Beauty.

꙳

XIX. The Backstretch

CORYLLOS, AT HIS NEXT AVAILABLE OPPORTUNITY, FOUND his way back to the barns on the backstretch of Monmouth Park. He had to use a few accumulated favors to get passage into the usually restricted area. He decided it was best not to repeat his entry using the surreptitious method he and Joshua used previously. He walked among the backstretch personnel in the late morning. Most of the trainers were gone leaving grooms and hotwalkers milling about; some were cooling out their charges, while others were relaxing around the barns and sheds.

He was dressed in a neat plaid shirt and nondescript black trousers as he walked along the paths between the long barns. His fingers were adorned with two large gold and diamond rings and he was wearing black leather shoes. As he walked along, breathing in the sweet scent of freshly cut hay mixed with the more pungent aroma of horse manure, he began to appreciate how out of place he appeared; it would not be easy to get these people to open up to him. Horses peered up from their stalls offering the occasional whinny at his passing before they returned to their feed or playing with the dogs, goats, and cats that populated the backstretch. The numerous workers mostly ignored him, although he sensed that there were a few wary eyes cast his way, particularly if he ventured too close to one of the horses.

After about twenty minutes of walking about he stopped to talk to one of the more orderly appearing workers.

"Excuse me, do you think you could help me? Do you know a man named Joshua Smith?"

The man walked on and Coryllos asked again, more forcefully, "I said, do you know a Joshua Smith?"

This time the man stopped and turned around. He was older, with deep wrinkles in his tanned skin and white hair. "I've seen him around," the man said cautiously, "but I don't know him much; talk to Ray."

"Where do I find Ray?"

"Barn fifty-one." And the man walked away quickly.

Coryllos looked at each barn and noticed a large number painted on the end. He was standing next to number forty. He walked on until he came to a long brick barn, next to a weather beaten shed. The stalls were full of horses and he saw an elderly man sitting on a bench at the opposite end.

"You Ray?" Coryllos asked.

Ray glanced up at the visitor then looked at the ground and muttered a few incomprehensible words.

Coryllos was more insistent. "I'm looking for Ray; I'm a friend of Joshua Smith and I was told he sometimes comes around here."

At the mention of Joshua's name Ray looked up and his face seemed to brighten. Still wary, however, he asked cautiously, "You know Joshua Smith?"

"Yes, yes; I've been looking all over for him. He's a good friend."

"How do you know him?"

"Why, he helped find me when I was lost. My name is David Sanders," Coryllos answered coolly. "It seems he's disappeared and now I'm trying to pay him back for all he did for me."

At the mention of Sanders name Ray smiled and relaxed."Well," Ray said, "I ain't seen Joshua for weeks. Not since that night he took Bessie to the hospital, practically carried her there hisself. I'm sure I don't have to tell you, but that Joshua, he's like a angel from heaven, sent to watch over us."

"When was Bessie sick?"

"A few weeks ago. Yep, that Joshua he went to the hospital and brought back an ambulance and took her hisself. They fixed her up and now she's good as new. Hey, Bessie," he called to a middle-aged woman dressed in a dirty sweat shirt and jeans.

"What is it, Ray? Old Homicide there needs to be watered," she answered.

"Just give me a minute, old woman," Ray said. "Do you remember when you were so sick? And we thought you was a goner?"

"Oh, yeah, a few weeks ago; it's lucky Joshua come around when he did, otherwise Old Homicide would be on his own. They gave me some medicine at the hospital and it made my old wore out liver just like new."

Coryllos found all this conversation very informative. If his suspicions were correct, this Joshua Smith was definitely involved in both Richard Cosby's death and the liquidation of Rep. McCally. He asked one more question.

"Which hospital were you in, Bessie?"

"The one that's closest to here, what's it called . . . Ocean something . . . Oceanside Memorial. That's the one. A fine place . . . fixed me up perfect."

"Thanks, Bessie, and thanks, Ray. When I see him I'll tell Joshua what a help you were." He turned and left through the main entrance and headed to the hospital. It would be simple to confirm that Bessie was there the same night as McCally's death and bring his quarry one step closer.

❧❧

XXX. Interview

"GOOD MORNING, MR. SIVESTRE," GIDEON STARTED. "I'M pleased to see you again so soon." The two men shook hands and then the door to the bedroom opened and Gideon said, "This fair young maiden is Beauty."

"She certainly is all that," Sivestre commented. Beauty was dressed in a simple white dress that was sleeveless, hung to just above her knees and had a very flattering v-neck. She had her hair put back and wore simple diamond stud earrings. All in all she was a picture of perfect feminine form that would have rivaled Aphrodite.

"Good morning, Mr. Sivestre; won't you sit down," she said, her voice soft and a little enticing. "Can we offer anything for you to drink?"

"Thank you, a glass of water would be nice." Before his back hit the soft leather of his chair, a mechanical server was at his side dispensing his drink. Gideon and Beauty sat opposite him on the red leather love seat.

"Shall we start?" Gideon asked.

"Ok . . . first, tell me, is Beauty your real name?"

"Why, yes; it's my legal name."

"Surely, your parents didn't name you just 'Beauty,' and don't you have a last name?"

"I've only known myself as Beauty; after all, what parent doesn't consider their child beautiful, no matter how he or she may appear? However, I don't know much about my parents. They were killed when I was a baby and I was raised by the government."

"Where did you grow up?"

""Here in New York, Fifty-eighth and Madison, in a government-run communal home. It was really a lovely place; there were seven of us with our 'Mother,' Mrs. Switts. She was a very nice lady with gray hair. She's gone now, I think."

"What about school?"

"I went to public elementary and high school; PS 135 and HS 42. I started at CCNY, but dropped out and went to work modeling and then as assistant to Mr. James Mctavish. He's a lawyer. I quit a few years ago and have lived doing odd jobs ever since."

"All very mundane, it seems. Have you heard of any of the scandalous reports that are circulating through the various media outlets? Will you comment on them?"

"Gossip is just that, unfounded and untrue. My life has been a perfect bore, really, that is until I met this wonderful man. He has shown me so many new things and is far more interesting than me. You really should be interviewing him."

"Leave me out of this," Gideon interjected. "There are plenty of lies out there about me."

"Well, Beauty, you certainly are charming and I have to say that I don't see any hint of scandal here. Just one more thing; how is it that you two came to meet?"

"I saw him at a party and I thought that he was cute. I lifted his key and copied it and was waiting for him in his apartment when he arrived home. I guess he liked what he saw and we have been together ever since."

"One other thing; do you remember the names of the other six girls that lived with Mrs. Switts?"

"Let's see, there was Barbara, we called her Babs, Francine, Pinky, Susan, Martha, and Sonia. I don't know where any of them are now. We all sort of went our separate ways when we left."

At the name Martha, Gideon's ears perked up. He wondered if there was any connection.

"Well, thank you for your time," Sivestre said as he got up. "I can't think of anything else to ask, so I'll be on my way. Thank you again." He stood up and Gideon walked him to the door, which opened automatically as he approached.

"Good day, Mr Sivestre."

"Good day, Mr. Jones. Thank you for your time and hospitality."

Sivestre approached the waiting elevator, but changed his mind and decided to take the stairs. The extra exercise wouldn't hurt and the solitude of the stairwell helped him think. The interview was enlightening for sure, more by what wasn't said than by the brief words that were actually related. At least he had a starting point; that is unless it was all a lie.

Gideon turned around to see Beauty with a smile running from ear to ear; as soon as she saw his face she burst into laughter that she couldn't stop. Gideon didn't see any humor as he sat next to her.

"That was quite a story you told," he stated.

"It was all true."

"I know it was true to the extent that you told it, but you left a great deal out. I know it and I'm sure that Sivestre knows it. I am positive that at this very moment he is checking out Fifty-eighth and Madison, Mrs. Switts, Babs, and all the rest. It won't take him very long to learn the truth and then we could be in trouble."

Beauty stopped laughing, a slight scowl replacing her mirthful expression. "What do you or that reporter know about what's true? What is truth anyway? What really happened or what everyone believes? The real truth is that I grew up in a hellhole, cold and hungry while 'Mother' told every case worker, social worker, and government official what a wonderful job she was doing, cleaned us up for every inspection so that the world believed we were treated with kindness and benevolence. Let Mr. Sivestre investigate; all he'll find is glowing reports about what a wonderful foster parent dear 'Mother' was. The strange men, the abuse, the cruelty never existed in the eyes of the government; so I ask you again, what is truth?"

"The truth is what really happened, what you and Martha and Babs and all the others have buried in the depths of your soul."

"I know what's true and I'd just as soon forget and move on with my life. Mrs. Switts used all of us. She kept everything that was meant for us, sold it, traded it for who knows what. She kept us locked in a tiny room on the seventieth floor. She paraded the strangest men in and out; men that were mean and dirty. Finally, she was planning to sell us to these men. Once we reached sixteen, we were gone. I was always called Beauty; I don't even know if I have a real name. Well, Beauty was going to fetch top dollar; only I tricked her. A month before my sixteenth birthday I climbed out of the window, walked along the ledge, and climbed up to the roof, then down the stairs to freedom."

"What about the others?"

"I don't know, sold probably. Poor Martha once had the nerve to complain to the inspectors that she was hungry. 'Mother' just said it was childish prattle and nothing to be concerned about. Of course, they believed 'dear Mother' and left. After that, Martha was beaten terribly and afterward we always called her 'lefty' because they broke all the bones in her right arm and hand."

"What happened to her?"

"I don't know. I left."

"What happened after you left?"

"I found my way, OK. I kicked around here and there. Being Beauty opens some doors; that's for sure. Various men and women took care of me, some nice, some not so nice. Then, I met Crash one day. He was like me; lost, aimless, just kicking around. He liked to play cards, but lost most of the time; he was always in and out of trouble, little things usually. One day we went to this meeting; we thought it was a government meeting where we might get some good food. What we heard was a man talking about being successful in this lifetime, but he wasn't from the government. He promised that our lives would change and all we had to do was become members of the Diblonski team. It sounded too good to be true, but at that point what did we have to lose? Oh, there were a bunch of papers to sign, but nothing else and right away things changed. Crash started winning at poker all the time. As a matter of fact that game against you was the first time he's lost in more than a year. That's one reason he didn't have any money that night; he was so used to winning he never felt the need to have to carry any cash. And for me; why respectable people started to call and then I met some people that made me really beautiful and I always seemed to know the right thing to say and those Diblonski people wanted so little in return."

Gideon had become much more interested when the name Diblonski came up. "What did they ask you to do in return?"

"Nothing much, meet some people once in a while, date a man or woman, always meaningless stuff. Most of the time I was just free to do as I pleased."

Gideon was quiet for a time, thinking about what she said, the automated waiter marching by every so often offering drinks. Finally, he asked, "Can you remember any of the names of the people you met?"

"Let's see, George, Danny, Sandy . . . I never learned their last names."

"Did the Diblonski people ask you to meet me?"

"Oh no, that was my idea. I thought you were cute. Someone from Diblonski did tell me that you were going to be at that party and also where you lived. And they helped me sneak in so that I could meet you."

Gideon became quiet again; he put his arm around Beauty and held her closely. "Well, I for one am very happy that you decided to crash that party. And, I don't think that whatever comes out of the pen of Mr. Sivestre is going to be any problem for you," he said. *No, you have much bigger problems,* he thought, but he didn't say anything else.

కోళ్ళ

XXXI. The World of Poker

GIDEON CONTINUED WITH HIS WORK, ACTUALLY GET-
ting some positive results from the Stolts Commission. Social workers by the dozen descended upon the now rediscovered community,
bringing welcome government assistance with minimal bureaucracy.
Certainly Aldous welcomed the help and, although wary, most of the
forgotten outcasts were happy to be remembered. Still, old habits are
not easily shed and often those determined to help were greeted with
blank stares, unanswered calls and empty apartments.

There were weekly meetings by the members of the Commission
and all in all the reports revealed favorable progress. Gideon continued to be very active, usually in concert with Aldous, overseeing the
government efforts and ensuring that government aid did not add any
burden. After a few weeks it was apparent that the field work was on
track and Gideon was able to get some rest. He had been spending
twelve to sixteen hours a day at work and he was starting to find it
difficult to concentrate. Each day was a repetition of waking, eating,
working, eating, and sleeping, leaving little time to devote to Beauty
or any activities outside work.

When he finally took a break, he and Beauty were invited to
another affair; only this one was centered around a major poker tournament. Gideon's interest was raised and he was curious to see if he
could repeat his previous success. He spent the night before the event
studying up on proper strategy for the various types of poker. The
tournament was New York Cross 'Em, the same game he had played
at the previous party. Gideon soon learned that this was the game that
was played at all the tournaments. He, as always, was a quick study
and in a short time all the probabilities and strategies were committed
to memory. He sat down with a deck of cards and began to practice
the various moves, his manual dexterity shining as the cards danced
around his fingertips.

Beauty called into the room for him. "Gideon, it's way past time to eat and I want some of that fresh food that you make; can't you stop for a while?"

Gideon looked at his watch: 9:30; it was late. "OK. I'll be there in a minute," he yelled. He fanned out the cards, practiced hiding the aces and one-handed cuts, and then put them away. He started dinner, preparing a vegetable soup with carrots, celery, potatoes, onions, and spinach, with pasta. He was thankful for the rapid cookers that had been developed, as the meal was ready in about ten minutes. He added some Italian bread and a bottle of white wine, and the two lovebirds sat down to the meal which served as a prelude to a very entertaining evening at home, filled with the finest jazz, the finest wine, and the most beautiful woman.

Poker had been a popular card game for hundreds of years. During the early twenty-first century it had become elevated to the status of professional athletics and the best players came to be revered with awe that was usually reserved for movie stars and football players. The game had evolved over the years. Five card draw gave way to five card stud which was followed by Texas Hold 'Em and later by Seven Card Cuban. The game now was New York Cross 'Em, but the strategy was still the same. Know the odds, maintain a calm unchanging demeanor, study your opponent, and be lucky. The highest level tournaments routinely distributed prizes over ten million dollars to the winner. Crash, Gideon's previous opponent, was one of the top players on the circuit having won four tournaments in the previous year. He had burst on the poker scene only eighteen months before and quickly established himself as a player to be respected, with a cool, but unusual demeanor at the table, and a short temper in public. No one knew how he had risen to the top of the poker world so quickly, but he was the reigning champ and he was straining at the bit for an official match with the upstart, Gideon Jones.

Time and again, Crash was asked how he had evolved from a two-bit gambler to the pinnacle of the poker world. His standard answer was that hard work, perseverance, and a little luck paid off in the end. He never mentioned that joining the Diblonski team may have also helped. For the time being he was living the high life; fame, money, women, he had them all. Still, he lacked the woman and it gnawed at him constantly. He had been great friends with Beauty, before he was famous and before she had been swept off her feet by Gideon, and he was devastated that she was not his girl. Every time he saw Gideon and Beauty together his heart rate went up, the hairs on his neck stood up and he had to turn his head away. When he learned that Gideon was playing in the New York tournament he became a last minute entry, hoping for the chance to avenge his earlier humiliation and earnestly believing that a victory would bring Beauty back into his life forever.

The evening of the New York World Series of Poker began with a cocktail party attended by all the finest people; Gideon recognized many from the previous party. Crash arrived with three very attractive women in tow, a dark-skinned brunette, a pale redhead, and a tanned blonde, as well as an entourage of bodyguards and lackeys. Crash looked like a caricature of an old time celebrity with a bold, flashy suit and an attitude to match. As soon as he walked in he was surrounded by the media and a barrage of questions were hurled his way: ". . . are you afraid of Jones . . . was the last game a fluke . . . who are you most worried about . . ." He tried to ignore them, but stopped to make a statement.

"Ladies and gentlemen, tonight we are playing in the real thing. I have no qualms or fears about facing any of my worthy opponents, professional or amateur. New York has been my town for most of my life and after tonight I will be its king. I guarantee it."

He left them pounding their nanopods and transmitting via Green Dots his comments along with those of the other contestants as Crash disappeared into a private room to prepare for the tournament with a private banquet and some alone time with his girls.

కోౡ

XXXII. The Match

SIXTY-FOUR PLAYERS SAT DOWN AT EIGHT TABLES TO begin the tournament which was scheduled to run over two nights. The victors from each of the tables would meet the following night for the World Series Championship and first prize of $15 million dollars. Crash started at the table farthest from Gideon, the largest crowds surrounding those two tables. The other players were some of the finest in the world and there was a slight odor of resentment aimed at Gideon being allowed to play with so little experience. The sponsors, sensing a media bonanza, had made the final decision. Gideon's presence nearly doubled their advertising revenue, guaranteeing a sizable profit.

The cards were the standard hoyle class five, red and blue. Each table had a professional dealer and the stakes were unlimited. Gideon's normally cool impassive demeanor seemed to have disappeared as he paced nervously waiting for the tournament to start. Crash, for his part, was cool and unflappable as he laughed with his ladies before the start. At eight o'clock sharp they all took their seats and the games began.

The antes flew back and forth as Gideon's pregame jitters vanished and he sat motionless as the cards were dealt. His opponents were seasoned veterans and they mostly ignored the newcomer, each donning his or her best poker demeanor.

The first deal presented Gideon with a pair of aces, a strong hand which he bet rather conservatively. He was called by New York Jack, a player known for putting pressure on inexperienced players, often bringing home victory with little or nothing. The first turn revealed another ace, the ace of diamonds, along with the five of clubs and four of diamonds, leaving Gideon in the driver's seat. He checked to his opponent, who placed a very large wager as the other players folded. Gideon calmly called. As cards were revealed, the betting went back and forth. Gideon still felt confident with his three aces, but his opponent's aggressive play had him slightly worried. The pot had reached over three million dollars; very high for the first hand. The exposed cards revealed possibilities of a straight or a flush. The point card was turned revealing the five of diamonds which left Gideon with a full house. He bet five hundred thousand, his face never changing expression and he was called. His final down card came, the two of diamonds. He bet another five hundred thousand and Jack raised him five hundred thousand. The pot had reached over five million dollars as each player had nearly exhausted their starting chip allotment.

Gideon called. New York Jack was very methodical as he revealed the two of clubs and three of spades; a baby straight. He smiled, thinking he had taught the neophyte a lesson. Gideon flipped over his two aces and was amused to see Jack's smile fade as Gideon pulled in the stack of chips. The large pot put him in the driver's seat and the next three hours passed with Gideon proving he was no amateur.

Crash, at the other end of the room, proved to be just as successful. He started in a less spectacular fashion, but he won pot after pot, playing with a cool abandon that was described as devilish and cold-blooded by the numerous media commentators in attendance. The rivals' victories set up the prospect for a very entertaining final the following evening.

The media speculated in its usual fashion, calling the upcoming event a rematch of David and Goliath and the greatest poker shootout since the OK Corral. Gideon ignored all the hoopla, while Crash thrust himself into the limelight, guaranteeing that he would carry the trophy and the $15 million dollar first prize home and adding that the lovely Beauty would finally see what a real man could do.

The hint of a romantic triangle fueled the media hysteria and speculation became even wilder and increasingly bizarre. Entertainment editor, Lee Lacey, of the UBS network field a typical report:

"Today the famed poker star known as Crash came out and bluntly stated that Gideon Jones, Chairman of the Stolts Commission and well known face about town, had no right participating in the big tournament today. Crash added that Mr. Jones had bribed tournament officials to allow him in solely for the purpose of bringing unwarranted publicity to himself and that the only way Jones could win was by holding up the armored truck delivering the prize money. This Crash then predicted that Jones' companion, Miss Beauty, would be leaving the Casino on his arm after the night's events and that Jones had drugged her to get her to be his escort . . ."

As the report was aired an image of Crash was broadcast; a wild-eyed, disheveled hologram of the reigning champ; apparently it was an old police hologram from the past days. All things considered, the stage was set for a very exciting match the following night.

❧❦

XXXIII. A Perfect Future

RANDY PESKEW COULDN'T STAND TO KEEP HIS DISCOVERY to himself. He called his colleagues, Drs. Michael Nathan and Ansom Carroll. Those two were immediately beneath him in the department; brilliant researchers who shared Peskew's belief that there was an ultimate good that only science could eventually achieve. That discovery would usher in a utopian society; one where there was no hatred, envy, sadness, or want.

"Look at this key I've uncovered and tell me what you think," Dr. Peskew said nonchalantly, hiding his great excitement.

His two co-workers studied the matrix and the computations and derivations that Peskew had already performed. They went through all the equations, shook their heads, went back through the equations a second time, and then both smiled as they looked up.

"Can this be true?" Dr. Nathan asked. "The possibilities are endless."

"It is amazing isn't it," Peskew added. "If this is implemented in the proper way, I foresee a society where there is no enmity or hatred between men. No more taunting and ridicule of young boys by their peers, perfect harmony between all mankind; in short, a return to the perfect world dreamed about and written about in countless fantasies but never realized."

"Have you done any live testing yet?" Dr. Carroll inquired.

"No, I think it best to work out a precise mechanism of action and a method of introduction. The matrix will only properly function in humans. I believe it is possible to utilize a universal signal that will allow simultaneous activation once we have all the proper parameters worked out. Once activated, I calculate that one could have complete control within a few hours. After that all that would be needed would be a simple command computer. Behavior modification could be sent over existing networks."

"Surely you would never consider implementing something like this?" Nathan asked. "This is something to be left alone; no individual could properly control such power."

Peskew saw the look of shock on his colleague's face. "Of course this new key represents amazing power. I certainly wouldn't trust any of it in the hands of Aaron Diblonski, or that Abe Masur and politicians are nothing more than Diblonski lackeys. No, gentlemen, this is something to be studied by us scientists; the new knowledge we glean from this discovery must be kept secret until mankind has the wisdom to utilize it in a way that is best for everyone. We alone truly know what is best for the masses." The three men solemnly reflected on the power of this newly discovered aspect of the picomatrix. Peskew believed that his two colleagues shared his ideals and that they were the only men to be trusted with the knowledge of such potential power. But, to be on the safe side, he kept the second key he had discovered to himself. If either of them proved to be unreliable, its implementation would keep things under his control alone.

"Now, doctors," he said, "we must be very careful approaching the exposition of the integration sequence and even more careful with any potential implementation commands. This must never fall into the wrong hands. I have encrypted it here and here." He pointed to two separate files on his system. "Only the three of us have access and anyone monitoring us will see us working on legitimate projects, as long as it is accessed from one of these terminals." He pointed to the terminals, which were the ones they used most frequently.

Dr. Carroll spoke up. "No question, but a comment. I realize , and I'm sure that you both also are aware, that we are taking a huge risk. If this research is discovered by anyone that is a 'member' of the Diblonski 'team,' we must be prepared to immediately destroy our data. Such a thing falling into the hands of the evil empire would spell doom, not only for us, but for all of mankind."

The other two nodded in agreement. None of them realized just how wrong they were.

૭∽๑

XXXIV. David Comes to Town

THE NEXT MORNING, GIDEON ATE BREAKFAST ALONE; Beauty was still asleep. As he sipped a cup of tea and ate his grapes and wheat toast, he perused the local news. *Nothing new under the sun,* he thought. The typical mundane reports on government productivity, UN activities, sporting events, and the economy.

Let's see what's happening around town," he said out loud. The usual casino events, concerts, virtual vacations, and such. But then he saw something that caught his eye. David Sanders was scheduled to speak in two days at the Brooklyn Forum. The announcement read:

"David Sanders, former major in the Astropilot Corps and legendary ITP pilot, will bring his evangelical crusade to the Brooklyn Forum on July 4th. His message will be, 'Bringing God Back into Your Life.' Admission is free and no advance reservation is necessary. There will be music beginning at 1:00 p.m. and Sanders is due to speak at 2:30. Refreshments will be available . . ."

Very interesting, Gideon thought. I wonder if Aldous will be there with Martha. The crusade was in Aldous' part of town. *This could be very enlightening,* he thought, *and probably beneficial to Beauty. And, perhaps I can safely talk to David.* July 4th was a Friday and Gideon didn't have any urgent work to do.

"Put on my schedule," he told the computer as he finished his breakfast. He pulled out a deck of playing cards and began to shuffle them and fan them out, practicing a myriad of tricks he was learning from an old book on card play and card tricks. There was palming cards, shuffling tricks that allowed him to keep a certain card on top or on the bottom. The cards danced at the tips of his fingers and in the palms of his hands like a Balanchine ballet. If I'm going to play anymore poker, at least I'll look like I know what I'm doing.

As he practiced, Beauty walked in wearing a short nightgown and gave him a kiss. "Good morning," she said softly, then added, "number two." The synthesizer went to work and in less than two minutes, white toast, orange juice, and a bowl of grape jelly appeared. She sat down to eat as Gideon was about to get up.

"There's a David Sanders Crusade in Brooklyn on Friday that I think would be worth going to," he stated. "You know about him, don't you?"

"Never heard of him," she answered. "Is he someone important?"

"He talks about God and such; years ago he was supposed to be mankind's salvation by going through the ITP, but that didn't work out and afterwards he became this big preacher or prophet. He travels around the world talking about God to anyone that will listen. I think it will be worthwhile to attend as it ties in with my work. I'd like you go with me; I'll even buy you a new dress."

Beauty's face lit up at the prospect of shopping. "A new dress and earrings," she stated emphatically. "Let's go today, to the real store, not the home mall."

"The real store it is, then. Why don't you get dressed and come with me downtown; I'll do a little work and then we'll hit Fifth Avenue."

Beauty giggled with delight as she raced into the bedroom. "Oh Gideon," she called, "could you come in here for a second. I need some help."

"What help could you possibly need," he said as he casually made his way into the bedroom. A soon as he walked through the door, the now naked Beauty grabbed him about the waist and pulled him down onto the bed. An hour later they were on their way downtown.

૱

XXXV. Final Match

THE DAY WAS UNEVENTFUL AS THE POKER WORLD reached a feverish buzz in anticipation of the evening's match. Gideon cut his work day short and dined in the late afternoon with Beauty in their apartment. He donned a black shirt and pants for the big event and Beauty wore her new, sleek black dress adorned with a platinum and diamond necklace and a matching bracelet.

The media commentary described them as New York royalty as they arrived at the New York Regency; the first of the contestants to arrive. They were ushered into a private room to wait for the start, scheduled for eight o'clock. Gideon continued practicing with his cards displaying an outward calm that belied the butterflies dancing in his stomach. All the years at the track had not prepared him for such a competition. He did have the one essential that all gamblers needed; a healthy contempt for money and overall indifference to the outcome of the proceedings.

Beauty, for her part, played the role of the staunch supporter perfectly. She radiated warmth and charm as she dazzled the media. When asked if she was nervous, she answered, "All I have to do is watch and pray, of course, not that we'll win, but pray that Gideon will be gentle with the other players and not beat them too quickly."

She gave her most comely smile as she talked and all the men in attendance seemed to melt as she and Gideon passed through the hotel lobby. In their private room, Gideon sipped a glass of water as Beauty lay on the bed for a moment, then jumped up to sit next to him and then walked around the room.

"Relax," he said. "The key to any successful wagering is to realize that none of it really matters. Win or lose, there's always another chance, another game, and the option to give it all up and walk away is always on the table."

Despite these words, Beauty continued her nervous pacing. There was still about thirty five minutes until the start so he took her hand and they went up to the roof to look at the early evening sky before the big event.

On the roof they were away from crowds and the media, staring out at the sun settling low in the sky as clouds rolled past. Gideon held Beauty's hand as he tried to make the formless clouds become more familiar images. A gentle breeze blew in from the east bringing the faint scent of saltwater and Gideon thought he heard the cry of seagulls. His mind wandered away as he thought about Gerald O'Donnel and he put his hand into his pocket and felt the glasses that he always carried. *Maybe I'm learning,* he thought as the cries of the gulls became louder.

He felt a squeeze of his hand as he heard Beauty say, "That looks like a ship."

He looked up and saw a cloud blowing by and nodded his head in agreement. *At least she was distracted,* he thought. He looked at the sky and saw a very distinct image of a man seated at a desk, white against the deep blue evening sky. From the west he saw another cloud, with a reddish hue, that he thought looked like a caricature of the devil. He felt a chill run down his spine, and then the two clouds seemed to attack each other. He felt a pull on his arm as he watched and Beauty said, "I'm cold, let's go in."

He put his arm around her waist and turned to go in, but glanced over his shoulder and saw the red cloud overshadowing the white one. He felt the chill again as they went inside and boarded the waiting elevator.

They made a quick stop at their room and then rode the elevator together to the Grand Royal Ballroom, the venue for the big event. Beauty was ushered to her seat in the third row while Gideon waited just out of sight. The ballroom quickly filled to capacity as the other players arrived. Crash was the last to appear; two young ladies disengaged from his arms and were seated in the same row as Beauty.

Eight players gathered in the small room off the ballroom. In addition to Gideon and Crash, there was Pete Smooth from Atlanta; Ruby

King who Gideon had played with at his previous engagement; Jack Snow from LA; William Holtz, aka Bronx Billy; the legendary Lou Driscoll, champion for nine straight years in the 2150's but considered past his prime by most poker experts; Angie from Omaha; and finally, Queen Lucia from the Bahamas. A colorful bunch, the cream of the poker world vying for the $15 million top prize. All save Gideon were seasoned professionals, but after his exploits in the preliminary round, no one, save Crash, begrudged the newcomer his spot at the table.

In the anteroom there were introductions all around, and then the ballroom lights dimmed and the light over the impressive oak and green felt table slowly brightened as the players were introduced and took their seats. Gideon sensed how a boxing champion must feel before a big bout as he took his seat which, it turned out was opposite Crash.

Once they were all seated, Gideon examined each of his competitors and had the feeling that they were examining him. Ruby was dressed in a black dress, sequined once again exposing ample cleavage accented by a glittering diamond pendant on a yellow gold chain. Pete Smooth wore dark black glasses adorning his clean shaven head and clean white collarless shirt and pants; he smiled as Gideon looked his way exposing bright white teeth with the latest gold accents. Gideon smiled back. Bronx Billy had a faux cowboy look all the way down to the wooden toothpick perched between his teeth. Lou Driscoll was impeccably dressed in a gray suit and also sported dark glasses accented by a cigar. Angie eschewed any glitz, had a hair pinned up and wore a tight black sweater and jeans which showed off a very attractively curved figure. Then there was the Queen, Queen Lucia, very dark skin, mirrored glasses, dressed in a simple wraparound skirt and halter. Finally there was Crash fidgeting in his seat, sweat already forming on his brow under the hot lights, dressed in an open shirt with a gold chain about his neck. Gideon thought of all the contestants, Crash seemed out of place.

He had studied Crash's previous tournaments and realized that the uneasiness he noticed was usual for the current champ. Gideon had also learned that Crash's victories usually depended more on luck and bravado; his poker skills were amateurish at best. Luck courtesy of Diblonski Gideon thought as the dealer came in and the first deck of cards was shuffled. But, luck or skill, Crash had been very successful over the last several months and remained the favorite to walk away with the first place trophy and the money.

All the antes were thrown in, the first hand was dealt, and the play began. Gideon sat quietly at first, studying his opponents and giving only a casual glance to his cards, the two of clubs and five of diamonds which he quickly folded. Ruby started the wagering with fifty thousand as only Crash stayed in. The Cross was revealed in the usual three steps as Ruby and Crash went back and forth. The final down card brought a slight smile from Crash who then suddenly turned his head to the right and opened his mouth as if he were about to address someone. He then turned back to the game and bet three hundred thousand. Ruby stared at her cards and then called. Crash flipped over a full house, tens over fives. Ruby threw her cards down as Crash pulled in the pot of over $1.5 million. A very auspicious start for the champ which left Ruby in dire straits.

Play continued with a series of small pots and poor hands for Gideon. He was starting to think that he should jump in just to stir the cauldron a bit, but luck intervened first. On the eighth hand, he was dealt a pair of kings as his two hole cards. He looked around the table at the various poker faces, finally stopping at Crash who turned his head quickly from right to left as he started the betting. He peaked at his cards a second time, shook his head and then threw in $250,000, very aggressive for the first two cards. Players folded until Ruby called and Gideon followed with a call and then raised $200,000, called by both Ruby and Crash.

The stem was revealed, king of hearts, two of diamonds, and jack of spades. Crash bet $500,000; Ruby and Gideon called. Next came the cross, ace of spades, ten of spades, and four of clubs. Crash checked, Ruby checked, and Gideon bet $500,000. Crash quickly called and Ruby hesitated. She peaked at her cards and at the table. Her stack of chips was very low and to call would exhaust them and finish her evening if she lost. She looked around at the other players sitting impassively. Gideon smiled at her, the others ignored her and Crash continued to shake his head at an unseen companion that appeared to be tormenting him from his shoulder. Finally, Ruby called. With her being out of chips the betting ceased as the cards were turned face up and the hand dealt out with enough hesitating flare that built to a climax. The cards were turned up. Ruby displayed a pair of jacks, while Crash had the queen of clubs and the ten of clubs. The point card was turned over: the ten of hearts.

Finally, the final cards were dealt to each player. Gideon with his three kings was in the driver's seat, while Crash hoped for any card that would give him the win; Ruby closed her eyes, sensing her night was about to end. The final cards dealt out: Ruby, the two of spades; Gideon, the seven of clubs; and Crash, the ten of diamonds.

Ruby smiled as she stood up, the first to go as the game heated up. She waved to the crowd as she took her bag and walked off to a polite applause. Crash grinned from ear to ear, and the shaking of his head stopped for the moment as he raked in his winnings; the large pot gave him a sizable lead and a tactical advantage over the rest of the players. Gideon offered polite words of congratulations as the dealer shuffled the cards for the next hand.

The next hand brought Gideon a pair of jacks and he started with a sizable wager which knocked everyone but Bronx Billy who called Gideon's $350,000 bet and raised another $250,000. The stem revealed another jack and Gideon threw in half a million, which was called. The cross didn't help Gideon, but he stayed aggressive and went with another half a million. Bronx Billy matched him as the point card was flipped, the seven of spades which paired with the seven of clubs on the stem and gave Gideon a full house. He bet a million and was promptly raised another million. Gideon stared at his opponents impassive face and saw the toothpick receive a couple of extra chews. Gideon called and raised $1.5 million. Billy stared at the cards on the table and looked at his hole cards again. He had only $1.5 million left and if he lost, it would be the end.

"What the Hell," he said with a slight hissing through his toothpick. He called and the final card was dealt face down.

Gideon peaked at the final hole card which was the two of clubs, which gave him no help. With his competitor tapped out, there was no wager, and Gideon, being last called, flipped over his cards revealing his full house, jacks over sevens. Bronx Billy flipped over his cards revealing three twos, another full house.

"That sucks," Billy snarled when he noticed that Gideon's final card had been the fourth two. He stood up and shook each player's hands and left the table. The large pot boosted Gideon into a close second behind Crash as the stage was quickly becoming set for a showdown. One by one, the other players bowed out until only Crash and Gideon remained. It was approaching midnight, but no one had left the ballroom in anticipation of the final clash. The media had all that it had hoped for as the final two took a thirty-minute break before the conclusion.

Back in his room Gideon sat on the bed with Beauty, his eyes closed, deep in thought. He turned to Beauty and asked, "What was Crash like before the two of you 'joined' the Diblonski team? He acts in a rather bizarre way during these events, not just today, but in every tournament. It looks like there is someone on his shoulder coaching him or something like that. Does that make any sense to you?"

Beauty's bright smile faded, replaced by a scowl. She stood up and walked away and stood looking out the window. Finally, she answered him.

"Crash was, I guess you'd call it unstable in the old days. He was always OK with me; I think he really loves me and I sort of felt sorry for him. He could be a lot of fun, but there were times when he was scary. He seemed to hear a voice and then he would go off by himself, away from other people. A few times he asked me to lock him away so that he wouldn't 'cause anybody any trouble,' I believe is what he said. I think he had hurt a lot of people before I met him. He's a pretty strong guy and a lot of the others on the street seemed to be afraid of him. After we signed up with Diblonski he was better. He was almost always calm and he had most everything he wanted. After all, he's been very successful."

Gideon stood up and walked to the window. He put his arms around Beauty's waist and kissed the back of her neck. "Thanks, you've been a big help. Now, I've got to be very careful how I play this final match. It seems that besides playing Crash, I'm also playing against Aaron Diblonski, or at least one of his servants."

Gideon looked at his watch and said, "Let's head back, the final starts in five minutes." He took her hand and they headed to the elevator.

Beauty took her seat as Gideon returned to the table, followed shortly by Crash. Gideon offered a brief grin, but Crash only stared back and then looked down at the table. With great fanfare, a basket of money was brought in, held high by two buxom, scantily clad ladies who dumped the cash at the end of the table: $15 million dollars to be given to the victor.

After all the ceremony the dealer sat down between the two adversaries, shuffled the cards, and offered them to Crash to cut. He did so without looking up, continuing to stare at his large pile of chips, which added up to $9,235,000. Gideon wasn't far behind with a stack of $8,765,000. The crowd became quiet as the antes were tossed into the center of the table and the first down cards were dealt.

Gideon glanced at his first two hole cards, the five and six of spades. He looked up to see Crash still staring at the table; the usual head turning gyrations were absent. Gideon started with $200,000 and Crash called. The change in Crash's demeanor was apparent to everyone and Gideon wondered if his unseen "coach" had abandoned him. The stem and cross left Gideon with a chance at either a flush or a straight and he continued his conservative wagering of $200,000 each time called by Crash. The point didn't help, but Crash still was content to follow Gideon's lead. The final down card left Gideon with a baby straight and he started with wagering $500,000. Crash looked at his cards and threw them away. Gideon's win put him ahead for the moment as the dealer shuffled a new deck of cards.

As the cards were dealt Gideon looked across the table and saw Crash look up and then turn his head as if responding to an unseen poker coach perched on his right shoulder. A smile returned to Crash's face and Gideon realized the real game was about to commence.

Gideon looked at his hole cards and then across the table at his now grinning adversary. From that moment, the crowds, the lights, even the dealer disappeared from Gideon's thoughts. All he saw were the cards and the stacks of chips. He began to play with the same cool abandon and skill that made him a legend at the track. Even Crash's presence faded away as pairs rolled into straights, flushes, timely bluffs, and a sixth sense that he hadn't felt within himself for weeks. Crash played valiantly, but with each hand thousands of dollars were transferred to the growing stack of chips in front of Gideon.

Commentators were awed by the display of prowess that was demonstrated over that ninety-minute period that brought Gideon to the brink of triumph. As the end seemed to approach, Gideon looked up and appeared to become aware of his surroundings for the first time. He looked at Crash, hair awry from running his hands through it, face red, and wet with beads of sweat, silently arguing with some unseen entity. Crash was down to $300,000.00 while Gideon had well over $17 million. Everyone believed that this was to be the final hand. Gideon revealed a bit of emotion for the first time since play had started. He closed his eyes and put his head back as if to say it's finally going to be over, but as Beauty looked on, she saw only pity and compassion, the same expression she had seen when Gideon talked about the many lost and aimless people he tried to help every day. What followed shocked everyone but Beauty.

The next hand was dealt and Gideon looked at his hole cards, a pair of threes. As Crash started to bet, Gideon threw his cards down. Over the next hour, utilizing all the skills that had brought him so close to victory, Gideon proceeded to methodically lose every chip in front of him. The final hand played out with Gideon losing his final $500,000 leaving Crash exultant in victory. Gideon stood up and quickly shook the victor's hand and left to meet Beauty who was waiting in their room.

❧⚓❧

XXXVI. Media

AFTER A FEW MINUTES ALONE WITH BEAUTY, GIDEON went back to the ballroom to meet with members of the media who were anxiously awaiting any words. He sat at the makeshift podium, sipping a glass of ice water, and offered a brief statement.

"I came to play my best and, for a few moments, I thought that my feeble skills would carry me to victory. Unfortunately, the experience my worthy opponent brought to the table was more than I could overcome. It was a good match, but now I'm ready to return to the truly important work of salvaging the lives of many of the lost souls shunned by our society. I'm sure that Crash will have much more to say. Thank you." He left the table, refusing to answer any more questions.

A few minutes later Crash appeared carrying a broad smile and a large glass of scotch. He was surrounded by his entourage including his customary two gorgeous women in tow. He sat at the podium and fielded questions.

"Were you ever worried?"

He answered, "I knew that my skills are more than a match for any upstart amateur, although I have to say that it was pretty close."

"Do you think Gideon Jones, if he were more experienced, could eventually dethrone you?"

Crash grimaced and answered, "No."

"When is your next tournament?"

"I'm still savoring this sweet prize. I can't plan that far in the future."

"You seemed almost lost in the beginning; lacking your usual confident demeanor; was this on purpose?"

"It was all part of the master plan to lull Mr. Jones into a state of false security and then deliver a final crushing death blow. As you saw, my plan worked perfectly."

The questions went on for several more minutes with nothing of consequence revealed. After the press conference, many of the poker experts began to publicly question the whole series of events. Whispers that Gideon had deliberately squandered his lead and allowed Crash to win became frequent and fodder for much media speculation.

Expert analysis of the play, although finding no definitive proof of deceit, still raised many questions. Gideon refused any comment on the events, calling it ancient history, while Crash vehemently defended what he came to believe was his own skillful play. In the end, public opinion declared Gideon the victor while Crash was regarded as the recipient of Gideon's largesse, again.

⪻⪼

XXXVII. David's Sermon

DAVID SANDERS STOOD AT THE PULPIT OF THE OVERFLOW-ing Forum in South Brooklyn. He was dressed in a gray shirt with no collar, black trousers, and shoes. His jet black hair complemented his deep, tan-surrounded eyes that were piercing as black jewels. As the crowd took their seats and extra chairs were brought from the annex, he stood as a solitary figure in the front of the room. From the first sermon seven years before he had maintained the same style; a lone figure standing in God's place, bringing words of hope to a lost world; a world searching for guidance.

Once the people had settled down and Vivaldi finished, he began to speak. He never employed any preliminary speakers or introduction. They came for the word of God preached by David Sanders and he always delivered. He looked over the people with a sense of satisfaction. There were the expected disheveled, slightly unclean folks that he knew to be the displaced of society, along the side aisles and in back were the members of the media, obvious in their mixture of disdain and anticipation.

In the front row were the church personnel, and conspicuous in the second row were two very well dressed and handsome young adults. *I guess anyone can be curious,* he thought as he prepared to speak. Unnoticed in the back of the church was another unexpected attendee, Randy Peskew.

"Good afternoon," he started. "My name is David Sanders, previously of the Astropilot Corps, but now a member of the army of Our Lord God and his Son, Jesus Christ. Thank you all for coming today; I hope that I will be worthy of the great confidence in me that is demonstrated by your presence here today. Let me open our service with a word of prayer.

"Dear Heavenly Father, thank You for the opportunity to bring Your message to the people that are gathered here today. Please bless this venue and everyone here, and show them that You are with us and a part of their lives, and that this world You have created for us is only a brief stop on our journey through space and time; one that will ultimately bring us into Your presence. We ask that You be merciful when we stand before You, and that instead of seeing us for the sinners that we are, we be covered with the righteousness of Your Son. Please guide my speech so that the words I deliver today will shed the light of Your love to all those here today and that Your words will be carried to the streets, to the city, and to all the world. We ask this in Jesus' name, Amen.

"Today, my friends, I want to talk to you about pain. We all live our lives with some degree of pain, whether it be now, tomorrow, or next year. Pain comes in many forms; the physical pain we feel when we drop a heavy weight on our foot, emotional pain of a lost love, mental pain of plans gone awry, and spiritual pain of a life without God. It is hard to believe, but all these pains are a special gift from our God, for in their own ways they each bring us closer to Him.

"Years ago I was privileged to journey to a world light years away from our Earth; God's world, perfect, wonderful, and holy. His chosen people, created in His image, lived there in perfect harmony with God, their Creator. I arrived there suffering great physical pain; the consequences of my ill-fated journey. These pains however, told me several things. First and most obvious was that I was injured and in need of medical attention, something God lovingly bestowed upon me. But, there was also the mental anguish of being lost; lost from my world, truly a stranger in a strange land. The physical pain waned as it usually does, the mental anguish also faded as I came to know the inhabitants of this paradise. In time, I came to love the people of this new world, only to be deceived and ultimately I became the tool of Satan, leaving that perfect world in ruin and becoming a curse on the lips of all its people. The mental pain I suffered is still with me today.

"Finally, there is the spiritual pain of separation from our God. The last is the most merciless, leaving an empty shell where a man once stood. Our world suffers most from this spiritual pain; we have left God behind, choosing to go through our lives following the Great Deceiver, Satan. We worship our idols, sex, drugs, hedonistic pleasures, ignore our Creator and for what? A few moments of guilty pleasure, followed by emptiness and solitude."

Gideon looked over at Beauty; she was staring intently at David, mesmerized by every word that came from his lips. *There may be hope for her after all,* he thought. He turned his attention back to the sermon.

"The Bible tells us a great deal about pain, in fact an entire book is devoted to suffering and pain. The Book of Job begins with a cosmic wager between God and Satan. Satan comes into God's presence and tells Him of his travels to and fro upon the Earth. The two place a wager of sorts on God's noble servant Job, upright and faithful. 'Take away his riches and God's protection and surely he will curse his God,' Satan says. God puts Job into Satan's hand, first taking his possessions and then his health. We follow the Book as Job's friends try to explain his suffering and find the cause for his affliction. Throughout the ordeal, Job steadfastly maintains his belief in God, although he expresses his anger and even poses questions to God. God never answers Job, however, choosing instead to question Job. In the end, we are left with Job being restored, the cosmic wager won by God. We are never told the consequences of this wager. I can tell you truly, however, that God has a purpose in everything that He does and all His actions are to the ultimate good. The pain that Job suffered and the pain that we suffer must, ultimately, be considered gifts from God.

"But, how can pain be a gift? We live in a world of constant screening and surveillance, warnings ring out at the slightest danger. We listen to these external warnings, heeding them and taking measures to avoid all the potential threats. All the while, we ignore the warnings that emanate from the center of our soul. The pain in our back, the throbbing of our head, the ache in our heart; all telling us that something is not right, be it physical, mental, emotional, or spiritual. We can fill our lives with empty pleasures and never escape the great pain. We are in need of a physician, a doctor who can bind our wounds and relieve our pain.

"But, who is this doctor?" David's voice began to rise, growing louder as his passion filled the sanctuary. "I tell you now that it is not our government, not the Diblonski's of this world, not a night at the casinos that can ease our suffering. No, it is the Great Physician, God, and his son, Jesus Christ, that can bring true relief from such deep, intense pain. How can He do this, you ask? How does He know anything about suffering? He knows because He came to this world, He became a man and suffered all the humiliation and degradation that we face every day. He was challenged with great temptation, offered the world by Satan, but chose obedience to God as the greater reward.

"And what was His reward? He suffered for you and for me. He saw this sinful world and took pity on us, choosing to drink the cup of sorrow and be obedient to His Father. And so He suffered; nailed to a cross, our sins heaped upon Him, His helpless soul tormented by demons, forsaken by His Father, and finally overcome by death. How Satan exulted as he sensed triumph over his great adversary, but his sense of triumph and elation soon faded away. Jesus, dead and buried, rose from the grave, crushed the head of Satan and gave us hope. And it is because of this hope that I can stand before you today. I can promise you that faith in God and His Son is not in vain. For the words of John 3:16 are as true today as they were thousands of years ago. 'For God so loved the world that He sent His only begotten Son that whoever believes in Him shall not die, but will have everlasting life.'

"I have lived through the suffering and triumph of our Lord in a way that no person has ever been privileged before, and I have seen the glory of God, and I tell you today that truer words have never been uttered. Trust in our Lord, put your faith in God and His Son and you shall know everlasting life, glory and eternity with your God.

"In the name of the Father, Son, and Holy Spirit, Amen." David sat down, those present sat in silence contemplating the power and truth of his words. The silence was replaced by music as the powerful strains of Vivaldi filled the church. Aldous, accompanied by Martha, went to the podium.

"Thank you all for being here today. We have a number of Bibles available for anyone who wishes one, and if you wish to hear David speak again, his schedule is available at the table outside or can be downloaded to your Green Dot. Our regular service will be in two days at our church. The address is listed with David's schedule and David will be in attendance. Thank you for coming. We will conclude our worship with hymn #465, 'How Firm a Foundation.' Miss Martha here will lead us."

He stood aside as Martha started the hymn; the audience slowly joined in on the singing. Randy Peskew, who had maintained a mild interest throughout, was suddenly spellbound by the angelic Martha as the service closed with the sound of her sweet soprano voice leading the congregation.

As the listeners started to file out, Aldous, Martha, and David stood at the door and greeted each of them. As Gideon and Beauty walked out and shook their hands, David saw something very familiar in Gideon's eyes. After he shook Gideon's hands, he looked at his palm where a message had neatly been deposited. "Meet me for Dinner at the Great White Way, 7:00 p.m. -Gideon."

David shook his hand and the message was gone. He turned and looked at the handsome couple as they climbed into their long black limousine, and then he turned back to his guests to see a long line building up and resumed greeting each as they left the Forum.

Randy Peskew raced through the line, past David and Aldous, and lingered when he came to Martha. He stared into her eyes for a moment and she smiled at him. He found the courage to speak.

"You h-have a l-lovely voice," he started. "L-l-like an angel," he stammered.

"Thank you," she replied as she turned her head away, embarrassed by his praise.

Peskew noticed her shyness and felt a little more at ease. "What's your name?"

"Martha," she replied, her voice no more than a whisper.

"A beautiful name for a beautiful girl," Peskew said, not sure where he was finding the courage to talk to such a lovely woman. "W-where do you live?"

"Here in Brooklyn, in the church. I help out with the people who live around here."

Peskew shook her hand again and said, "It w-was wo-wonderful to meet you and to hear you sing. Perhaps I'll see you again," he said, his voice breaking up again, and he hurried out and disappeared into the crowd.

৯৽৹

XXXVIII. Dinner with David

GIDEON WAS WAITING OUTSIDE THE GREAT WHITE WAY Casino for David to arrive. They were supposed to meet at 7:00 p.m. and it was now 7:45. *Some things never change,* Gideon thought. He had kept himself amused by studying the variety of people as they passed by the entrance to the restaurant. He had seen it all before, the exotic outfits designed to impress an as yet unknown companion, the look of casual indifference on everyone's face that was just a step away from desperation; perhaps out of every fifty people that passed he would see one couple or small group of people that actually seemed happy. They were usually younger and Gideon was sure it was their innocence (or ignorance) or lack of cynicism that allowed them the luxury to be truly carefree. Of course it was all speculation by Gideon, but he wasn't far from the truth.

Finally, he saw David Sanders arrive; he walked toward the preacher/pilot and extended his hand when the two met.

"Mr. Sanders; Gideon Jones, a great admirer," Gideon welcomed him.

"Thank you for asking me, Mr. Jones. I'm not sure why you wish to dine with me; I certainly don't travel in the same social circle as you," David answered, slightly wary of this stranger that had almost commanded him to come for dinner. David had maintained some sense of control by arriving late, and it was apparent that Mr. Jones didn't mind. "I'm sorry that I'm late, that seems to be a chronic problem of mine."

"I know, but no matter, I had a grand time studying the faces of the people as they passed by."

David was startled by this comment, so familiar as if words that he had heard before. He looked into the eyes of Mr. Jones, they were deep brown, but very bright; the black hair and freshly grown beard were unfamiliar, but the overall appearance grew more and more recognizable.

"May I see your watch?" David asked. He looked at the striking mechanical watch on Gideon's left wrist and saw the name DeBethune and then he smiled. Gideon held his finger to his lips and David didn't say a word as the two entered the restaurant and were quickly shown to their table.

As Gideon was about to speak, it was David's turn to signal for silence as he activated a device on his wrist.

"OK, now we can talk. You remember this little thing that Deborah had; well it certainly comes in handy when I want to talk without any prying ears to worry about. So, tell me, what's going on? How did Joshua Smith become Gideon Jones?"

"Well, it's a long story and I'm not sure I believe it yet myself, but it started . . ." Gideon recounted everything that had happened, leaving no detail out.

"Amazing," David said when he was through. "You know that there are some media types that are touting you as the next governor or senator? That's quite a change from the degenerate horseplayer you used to be."

"You're right and I'm not sure that it's such a change for the better. I think I prefer Monmouth to the Big Apple and Bar #23 to Philly's Club. Still, there are some perks that I can't complain about."

"I know, I've seen her picture; she lives up to her name, that's for sure."

"Well . . . you know, I'm trying to introduce her to the finer things in life. Of course, for my safety, I've had to change my taste in music a bit. I can live with jazz, I suppose, although it is a weak substitute for Bach. How goes your work? You drew quite a crowd today."

"It goes, sometimes good, more times not so good. I thought my words would shine like a beacon through a pitch black night, but it seems to be more of a flashlight with batteries running down. I'd always thought that the people's lives were so empty, just as mine was empty; that I would fill some void and the whole world would embrace the truth. The actual truth is that I've had to learn to be happy with frequent questions and inquiry, but only occasional converts. I have to remind myself that God does the work, that He chooses and that I am only a messenger."

"Well, don't be discouraged. I seem to recall that you said that if one person heard your words and was saved, that would be enough and would make it all worthwhile. I'm sure there have been many more than one."

"Of course you're right, as always, but it is still painful to look around and see so many people doomed to an eternity of suffering."

Gideon was silent for a moment, his face displaying a bit of a scowl before he replied. "Do we know that to be fact, the existence of Hell, that is; do you really believe that's what awaits most of us?"

"You've read the Bible and I've lived through it. I have to believe that everything that comes from God is to be believed and I think that deep in your heart you also know this is true."

"Well, I know the Bible; I've read it at least five times, but I still think there is an out that will keep me and Beauty and all the others out of Hell. That is what I am searching for."

"Of course, you know, there is an out as you call it. It screams at you from the pages throughout the Bible, you just don't want to believe that something so simple can be the answer; you think that being 'good' will do just fine. I think that deep down inside, you know the truth. I just pray that someday what is deep down inside will find its way into that brilliant mind and you will find some peace."

Gideon answered, "I appreciate your concern; perhaps you're right. I don't really know myself. I do wonder about Hell sometimes. For instance, if someone is sent to Hell, who decides that individual's punishment, God or Satan? And if Satan decides, does he reward someone like Hitler; that is, does he give a lighter, less painful sentence to those that are more evil in this life. If you think about it, Satan hates God's creation, particularly man. So, if someone is especially cruel to mankind, i.e. Hitler or anyone else that history has called evil, would they be given a place of favor by Satan or does God render judgment and send them to greater torment based on the severity of their sin? And are some sins worse than others? If my only sin is that I didn't love God with all my heart mind and soul, does that make me better or worse than a mass murderer who tortured his victims before killing them, but went to church every Sunday?"

David thought about Gideon's comments and then said, "I think that you think too much and it is time to order dinner." The waiter approached the table as the two men opened their menus.

"What do you have that's fresh?" Gideon asked.

"The fresh special of the day is Broiled Snapper with Crabmeat, asparagus, and new potatoes, three hundred dollars. The other specials are listed on the side of your menu."

"The fresh special for me," Gideon said, "with some fresh fruit and a glass of ice water."

"Grilled rib-eye steak, baked potato, and asparagus. For me, skip the fruit, but bring me a Caesar Salad and whatever beer you have on tap. I may have changed my occupation, but my tastes haven't changed." These words caused Gideon to look up into the eyes of his companion, half expecting to see them roving about the room looking for willing female companionship. He was reassured to see the big brown eyes only staring back at him.

"How's your family?" Gideon asked, changing the subject.

"They're all great. The kids exceed every expectation and have, luckily, inherited each of our best qualities. Deborah hasn't changed a bit; she has plenty of work as an independent contractor and consultant, besides raising two extraordinary kids. And you, tell me about this 'Beauty.' I never expected you to go for such a woman. I always figured you'd meet someone at the track and spend your days figuring the daily double together and your nights being serenaded by Berlioz or Bach."

"Well. let's just say that Beauty popped into my life one night and I thought it would be nice to have some companionship. She is like an unwritten story bound up in a perfectly stylized package. She seems open to anything new and I have to say I enjoy having her around."

"Sounds like love to me. When you just like being around someone and can relax and let down your guard, without worry or fear; that is the beginning of love and friendship. I hope she makes you happy."

The dinners arrived and their attention shifted to the food. Gideon sat quietly, pushing his food around the plate, while David attacked his steak. He looked up and saw that Gideon wasn't eating and a look of despair on his face.

"What's wrong?" David asked, although he had an idea already.

"I'm worried; for the first time in my life there is someone that I care so much about that I'm scared for her. I've spent the last seven years looking over my shoulder, never seeing anyone, but still always aware that one day I would get a tap on the shoulder and be taken away to who knows where. Although I would think about it now and then, I just accepted that someday the past would catch up with me and it would all be over. In a way that's why we became friends in the first place. Before the ITP you were just the same, wild, a bit more ambitious, but ultimately sharing the same sense of nihilism that I felt. I always knew that was why you did the crazy things that you did; you didn't care; live . . . die, it didn't matter, it was all nothingness and emptiness. But, you had an experience that most people couldn't even dream about and I don't blame you for seeing things in a different light. I see things differently now, but not for the same reason. I guess that's what love can do, only . . ."

"Only what? Oh, I know, it won't last."

"That's it; if history tells us nothing else, the one truth that I see is that love doesn't last. This thought is killing me. It's a good thing I'm not going to the track these days, because I don't think I could think straight enough to pick an odds on favorite to show."

"You'll survive; men have managed to survive worse through the ages. Now. Let's see what they have for dessert."

The rest of dinner was devoted to small talk about nothing in particular and they parted, promising to try to communicate more regularly.

After dinner Gideon went to the King of Jazz Club which was within the same casino. Beauty was waiting for him, looking radiant in a sleek, yellow sequined dress. She was seated at the bar sipping a club soda when Gideon came in. He tried to be as inconspicuous as possible; the media attention was becoming overwhelming. However, as soon as the two sat down, they were interrupted by the faint whirring of surreptitious recorders capturing every movement and whisper to be reported almost instantaneously in all the usual gossip media outlets.

"Let's go," Gideon whispered to her. "I need to be alone with just you, no cameras, recorders, or anything." They got up before even ordering and walked out, being trailed indiscreetly by a mob of media types hoping for a scoop. Gideon saw David leaving another club, two beautiful blondes in tow. He felt the hairs on the back of his neck stand up and a previously unknown feeling of righteous indignation well up from within.

He pulled Beauty by the arm and met David as he was about to enter an empty elevator. "I see that some things never change," he exclaimed loudly, his voice rising with each word. "Here you are, God's supposed chosen messenger, with a companion who loves you, two small children and you are back to old tricks. You have some nerve, Major Sanders, speaking of God, yet breaking all his rules."

David was startled by this interruption and started to explain, "this is not what you think . . ." Before he could say another word, Gideon shouted, "Don't give me any sorry explanations. I've seen it before." And he pushed David against the closed elevator. David, almost by reflex, whirled around and struck Gideon on the side of the head, knocking him to the floor, before regaining his composure. He bent down and helped Gideon up, but he was pushed away.

"Leave me be . . . just go on with your playthings. I should have known that all your preaching was just for show." He grabbed Beauty by the arm and marched out to a waiting taxi. David, a little confused, stood motionless for a moment, then ran after him, but just missed the couple as they sped away. David went back inside, ignoring the crowd of people that was following him. He pushed his way through the mass of onlookers, escaped into the first elevator that arrived, and went up to his room, alone.

ॐ

XXXIX. Media Exultation

IN LESS THAN ONE MINUTE, IT SEEMED, REPORTS OF THE altercation filled every media outlet. Gideon Jones was the darling of the moment, while David Sanders had never completely fallen away from media scrutiny. Their dining together had been of lukewarm interest to the various reporters, but now the story brought visions of Glamour Awards and dollar signs. The accounts ran the gamut from Sanders starting the argument without provocation or justification to the two men arguing over the three women who were peripherally involved. Not one of the reports was completely accurate.

Wayne Bryson of the IBS network filed this:

"A stunning display of hypocrisy and chutzpah transpired at the Great White Way Casino just a few minutes ago. Former Astropilot and modern day 'prophet,' David Sanders, accosted our own respected Gideon Jones today. Apparently without provocation, Mr. Sanders struck Mr. Jones on the jaw, knocking him to the ground and causing serious injury. Jones was quickly ushered out of the casino and taken to an unknown hospital for treatment where we have reports that he is stable and expected to make a complete recovery.

"Mr. Sanders immediately disappeared and quickly vacated the casino's hotel, evading police inquiry and refusing to answer any questions from this or any other reporter. This so-called messenger of God proves that hypocrisy reigns supreme. Eyewitness accounts relate how Sanders was in the company of two buxom beauties when Mr. Jones approached him with his own Beauty at his side. Apparently two women are not enough for Sanders and the very one-sided brief altercation transpired.

"Here we have another example of religion fostering violence; demonstrating that humanity must police itself utilizing the rule of law rather than the very flawed voice of God. This is Wayne Bryson, live from the Great White Way."

A second report came from Maggie Tryce:

"Live from the Great White Way Casino; Hello everyone; Maggie Tryce here, your girl on the go, with the latest scoop on the Jones / Sanders brouhaha. Former Major David Sanders and social celebrity Gideon Jones had a knock down drag out fight in the casino lobby, apparently over a very enticing young brunette. Eyewitnesses report that Jones was carried out on a stretcher to a waiting ambulance, while the young lady remained in the company of Major Sanders. Here with the legal perspective is the personal attorney to the Great White Way Casino, Earl 'Big Jack' Scott. Mr. Scott, what are the legal implications of such a public altercation?"

Scott was a big man sporting a huge white cowboy hat. His card said that he hailed from Wichita Falls, Texas, but in reality he grew up in Elmira, New York.

"Howdy, Ms. Tryce; I want to thank y'all for askin' such a poor public servant's opinion on sech a messy legal matter. From what these here bystanders told me, I'da have to say that this Major Sanders is in a heap o' trouble. I'd say he's lookin' at charges of assault and battery and possible kidnappin'. I even think that my client, Mr. Francis, over yonder was assaulted by this loco space cowboy and we intend to file suit just as soon as the courts open in the a.m."

"Thank you, Mr. Scott."

"Call me Big Jack."

"Thank you, Big Jack, for that very interesting perspective."

Thus the media maintained their usual accurate, even handed reporting, presenting every aspect from every possible angle.

☙❧

XL. Escape

GIDEON AND BEAUTY RACED AWAY FROM THE CASINO as fast as the taxi could carry them. Beauty had never seen such a wild expression on her companion's usually serene, calm face. Gideon didn't say a word as the cab pulled up in front of his apartment building. There was already a mob in front.

"Drive on," Gideon said and the taxi took off. "Saratoga, Excelsior," he added and started to calm down.

"What's wrong?" Beauty asked, innocently. "He shouldn't have hit you like that, but what's he to you anyway?"

"You don't understand," he cried. "You can't understand, nobody will. It's like a person I used to know, my best friend, someone I had great faith in is gone." He looked at the deep black eyes staring at him and realized that he was right about her confusion. But, she should be confused. She never knew Joshua, only Gideon; hip, superficial, and disposable Gideon. This way of life that he had chosen was beginning to unravel and for the first time in all his years he was scared.

The two sat silently for the rest of the drive to Saratoga. Over the years, Saratoga, New York had been a personal sanctuary for Joshua and now he hoped it would also serve Gideon. His favorite stop was the stately and very comfortable Excelsior Hotel. It was tucked safely within the confines of the Saratoga Spa Park, the rooms were luxurious and the restaurant had a vast menu of fresh food. As Gideon he hadn't visited yet; this was his first trip up north from the city. He needed some time to unwind, think about what he had become and what had just happened with David. It was mid-August and the season was in full swing. He called ahead and was relieved that they would be able to find a room for such a well-respected patron.

Beauty lay with her head against his chest as he turned on some music: Berlioz, instead of the jazz he had recently become accustomed to. As he sat thinking about David, he was overcome with a revelation that everything that he did, everything David did, indeed everything the whole universe did was for naught. The Diblonski's of the world always triumphed in the end. Oh, he might have a brief moment in the sun, the proverbial fifteen minutes of fame, but in the end there was nothing but emptiness. At this moment he was beginning to believe that Hemingway had gotten it right. All one can truly do is choose his own time and manner of death. As this revelation came over him he looked down at the now sleeping Beauty and realized that there was only one thing in this world that made these thoughts false; the love of one person for another. His moment of despair passed and he quickly fell asleep for the remainder of the trip.

౷

XLI. David's Thoughts

WHEN DAVID ENTERED HIS HOTEL ROOM HE NOTICED that the communication system was flashing from every angle and there was a hologram stating that he had over two thousand messages waiting for him. Little Bit was barking and standing on his hind legs as if asking what all the excitement was about. David saw that all the messages were from various media types and he deleted every one of them. He lay down on the bed staring at the ceiling, thinking about the colossal misunderstanding that had just transpired and he tried to think of a way to undo the damage. Of course he didn't care about the media response; they would think what they wanted anyway. The believers probably would understand and accept the truth when he told them, but Joshua/Gideon was important to him and he knew that he would have to find a way to explain. Still it would be tricky for several reasons, primarily Joshua's safety. Too much contact risked exposing Joshua to Diblonski's minions. And, with his current notoriety, Joshua was always followed by the media; it would be very hard to contact him. No, it would have to be up to Joshua. There was nothing David could do but wait; wait for the visit that he was sure would be coming.

He got up from the bed and changed into his robe and called Deborah, activating his security to prevent any unwanted intrusions or eavesdropping. He wasn't worried what she would think. She knew the truth and would be supportive of anything that he did.

"Hello, beautiful," he started when she answered. Her image appeared to be sitting right next to him as he recounted the events of the day. "I guess you heard the news; I'm sure that you can guess what happened . . ." They talked for a time before David said he needed to go. He climbed into a cold shower, always his preference since his ITP adventure, and then fell into bed and was asleep in five minutes, Little Bit at his side.

፨

XLII. Further Response

AARON DIBLONSKI CALLED MR. MASUR AS SOON AS HE saw the reports. "I need you now," he said calmly. Masur knew that such a request meant immediately. He left his solitary bed, hopped into his personal sanitizer and valet, emerging refreshed and dressed in less than one minute, and jumped into the waiting car which sped away, depositing him at Mr. Diblonski's front door in less than ten minutes. He went straight in through the open door to find his boss sitting in front of the large fire reading an old book.

Without looking up Mr. Diblonski started to speak, "The events of today present an excellent opportunity. These two men have been more than a nuisance, our growth has suffered due to their interference. This fortunate encounter provides us with a window that we need to exploit. If this is handled properly both parties can be eliminated and the company's growth can then resume unhindered. Indeed, if managed appropriately, this opportunity will allow us to flourish on an even greater scale and our great enemy eliminated forever. I think you know what to do. We have some of our operatives already in place. They can be utilized to some degree, but I don't want any mistakes. Put our best men on it, also, but strike now. Mr. Jones will try to contact Major Sanders very soon and our people need to be ready and in position." He went back to his book and Masur departed through a side door to a smaller anteroom. He sat down at the monitor and started to make calls. In ten minutes the work was done and he left. He returned home to his empty bed, and in less than five minutes was fast asleep.

৯৽৽৶

XLIII. Randy and Martha

RANDY PESKEW FELT A JOY THAT WAS UTTERLY NEW. OF course, he was completely oblivious to all that had transpired between Gideon and David and wouldn't have cared in the least, anyway. All his thoughts centered around Martha, sweet angel Martha, who had touched his heart and soul with her simple charm and carried him to a place he had never been before.

The next day he went back to the church and stood across the street, watching the entrance, waiting for her to come or go, just to catch a brief glimpse. He paced back and forth for hours and finally he saw the door open and she came out, but only for a moment to water the plants out front. She turned and looked at him from the steps of the church and he saw her smile. He smiled back and, for a moment, thought he should go over to her, but he wasn't sure as she turned and went inside. But, the faint smile that he was sure he saw left a smile on his face and a fluttering in his stomach. He went home for the day, whistling and humming quietly, forgot all about work, and looked forward to tomorrow.

෨∘ᡈ

XLIV. Saratoga

GIDEON AND BEAUTY FELL BACK ON THE SOFT KING BED in the Palace Suite of the Excelsior Hotel. They had arrived at 2:00 a.m. and even though they had rested on the trip north they were both exhausted from the night's events. After about twenty minutes Beauty got up and was ushered into the luxurious Personal Care Center for a personalized rejuvenation session. The hotel had the latest in personal technology, and as she walked into the Care Center she was greeted by lights that dimmed, light rays scanned her body and mind and she was gently lowered into a soft, warm chair. She set the system to seductive and then relaxed as she was enveloped by soft padding from neck to toes and gently massaged over every individual muscle group, with extra attention paid to any that seemed overly tense. Her skin tingled as the massage continued with an extra dermal charge, washing away dead skin cells, moisturizing and caressing every square centimeter of her body, then gently carrying her through a multi-head, perfumed shower, that was set to the perfect temperature, with special jets to massage her scalp and feet. She emerged to the final phase of gentle anointing of her body with a mixture of perfumed body oils and pheromones as she was wrapped in a soft pink robe and returned to the bedroom.

Gideon smiled as she sat on the bed and he put his arm around her waist and kissed her lightly on the cheek.

"Your turn," she said, jumping up from the bed and grabbing his hand. She pushed him into the care center and waited for him to finish. While she waited she saw her Green Dot start to glow. Someone was trying to reach her and she could tell by the color that it was from the Diblonski organization. They had told her they would only call if it was something very important, but she also knew that Gideon didn't like her association with the Diblonski group. Still, they had done so much for her, she felt an obligation to at least listen to them; besides, Gideon wouldn't be out for several minutes. The message was brief. "Be at the Great White Way Casino with Gideon within the next seventy-two hours." She wasn't sure what it meant, but it seemed like an innocent request. Gideon emerged in a deep blue robe as she put the "Dot" away; he took her in his arms, kissed her, and they fell back on the bed.

৶৽৻৾

XLV. Crash

CRASH DEACTIVATED THE GREEN DOT THAT SAT BEHIND his left ear and sat down. He had thought that his old life was gone forever, but the past had just suddenly caught up with him. A middle of the night call from the number two man in the Diblonski conglomerate had a way of complicating one's plans. *There's always a price to pay*, he thought as he activated the global positioning function on his "Dot." There it is, 3350 West Mayberry, in the Bronx. Membership in the Diblonski organization apparently had its responsibilities to go along with the many perks. Still, if this worked out, nobody would be permanently damaged and perhaps he could get her back.

The hatred that had been simmering inside was now surfacing as a full boil. Of course he didn't mind losing, he was more than used to that, even when he thought he had won. It was the charity that he hated; he didn't need it and he didn't want to feel indebted to such a man. This job would be enjoyable, and after it was done the slate would be wiped clean and he would be done with Diblonski Ltd.

He took a very roundabout route to Mayberry, being very careful that he was not followed and found the package inside the doorway of #3350, a nondescript quad complex. He tucked the small box under his coat and took a different route to the Great White Way Casino, where he checked in under the name of William Harrison, a room already reserved in that name. Now all he'd have to do was to wait for the next call. He was sure it would be at least a day or two, so he went down to the casino to kill time; looking for some action, which he quickly found. He sat down at the table, his face obscured by large dark glasses; he put his money down and started to play, taking care to keep his Green Dot activated.

꙰

XLVI. Saratoga

BEAUTY AWOKE TO THE SMELL OF FRESHLY SCRAMBLED eggs, toasted English muffin, melon and berries, and fresh squeezed orange juice. She saw Gideon reading the reports from the previous day; he was shaking his head.

"This is bad for David Sanders," he stated, a slight hint of remorse in his voice. "The media are vilifying him, painting him as a supreme hypocrite, preaching love and acceptance and God's mercy one day, and then violently lashing out at anyone who crosses him. This could really damage his cause."

"What does it matter? He hit you didn't he; he deserves whatever he gets," Beauty replied as she sat down to eat, wearing only a short nightshirt.

"You don't get it. His cause is my cause. Oh, he may approach things differently, but ultimately we're working for the same thing; for the underdogs in this world. He wants to enlighten them and give them hope. This isn't much different from what I'm trying to do, except, he has been doing it for years with some very real results. I'm afraid I may have done irreparable harm to his work."

"Then go to him; make it right. If he is such a noble person, he'll forgive you in a minute. He's probably waiting for you right now."

Gideon considered her words for a few seconds and smiled. "Of course, you're right. I really had already decided to try to see him. As a matter of fact, I'm sure he's waiting for me to make the first move. Things being what they are, there's no way he could safely come to me, even if he knew where we were. No, tomorrow we'll head back to the city and I'll make things right and by next week it will all be forgotten." He sat down and joined her, eating only the fruit with cream, washing it down with the juice and some ice water.

"When you're ready I'll show you the highlights of Saratoga," he said as he got up to dress. Beauty disappeared into the care center, emerging looking stunning in a yellow sundress and white hat. Gideon took her hand and they quickly descended to the ground level as he led her out the rear entrance. A short walk away was a beautiful rose garden in full bloom, trails meandering between the bright red, pink and yellow flowers. The young couple strolled slowly saying nothing at first, admiring the beauty surrounding them.

"This used to be an artists' retreat, a hundred and fifty years ago, give or take a decade. It was called Yaddo, although I'm not sure how it got that name. They used to let visitors walk through the gardens, but you had to be a struggling artist to be allowed in the house. About fifty years ago it was renovated and converted into the Excelsior Hotel, very exclusive and very luxurious," Gideon explained.

"It's wonderful, just like you," Beauty remarked as she wrapped her arm around him.

"Saratoga has always been an oasis for me. The beauty of this garden, the fabled racetrack, the music and the whole atmosphere. It carries me back to a time I never was a part of. Years ago, before I was anybody I used to come up here in the springtime, walk through the track; watch the occasional horse workout. I always came early in the morning. The air would be cool and misty and the horses would have steam flaring from their nostrils as they raced by. Those were simpler times," he sighed, "no worries, no media snooping, but no Beauty either. It is definitely better with you."

Beauty became lost in thought as they walked around the vast garden. They reached the end where there was a large field of grass. She dropped her arm and ran across the grass, laughing.

"I'll bet you can't catch me", she screamed as she sprinted away, a picture of youthful loveliness, holding her hat as she bounded across the grass. Gideon laughed as he raced after her. Within a hundred meters he reached her and pulled her to the ground, wrapped his arms around her waist and gently kissed her. The two rolled on to their backs and looked up at the summer sky.

"I've never been so happy", she sighed. "All my life has been a struggle, but now I finally feel like I've found my place."

"I know", Gideon replied. "I never want this moment to end." He leaned over and kissed her gently on her moist red lips. They lay there looking at the clouds, oblivious to everything around them and, for the moment, at peace.

The remainder of the day was spent uneventfully, shopping, dinner at Siro's, a live performance by the Symphony and room service for dessert. Gideon decided to return to New York the following day and try to patch things up with David. He looked up David's schedule, confirming that he hadn't left the city and reserved a car to take them downstate. He had the concierge reserve the vehicle in the name of Mr. Smith, so as not to alert the media. The following morning he and Beauty left unnoticed for what Gideon hoped would be an uneventful meeting with his old friend.

೫%

XLVII. Randy and Martha

RANDY PESKEW BEGAN TAKING THE SHORT RIDE INTO Brooklyn each day to stand outside the old church, anticipating any brief moment that let him gaze at the beautiful angel that had touched his soul. Like clockwork, Martha would appear and water the plants and smile at the nervous man who stared at her each day. Peskew usually would walk up and down the street, pretending to belong there, but he didn't fool anyone.

This went on daily for almost a week until the big day with the big wind. On that day Martha appeared as usual to water the plants only on this day there was a strong wind, so strong it blew her hat away down the street. Peskew, who had been staring at her, as usual, ran off after it. The hat was an old white bonnet and as he ran he saw it come to rest on the ledge of a tall building. He waited for a while, but it seemed to have taken up permanent residence, so he turned to go back to the church and was met by Martha about one block from the front door.

"Thank you so much, but don't worry. It was just an old bonnet, nearly worn out," she said in her sweet, soft voice.

"I'm sorry that I couldn't rescue it for you, Miss Martha," he answered, using up all his courage.

"Walk back to the church with me Mr . . ."

"P-Peskew, Randy Peskew. You probably don't remember, but we met at the meeting a few weeks ago."

"Oh, I do remember you; you were so sweet." She took his arm and held it with her one good arm.

Peskew was embarrassed at first, but finally relaxed and the two walked slowly back to the church. Peskew noticed her crooked arm.

"Wh-What happened to your arm, if you don't mind my asking?"

"Oh, it's nothing, just a childhood accident. I don't even notice that it's any different most of the time." They arrived at the entrance to the church and stood outside the door awkwardly, as if they were just returning from their first date.

"Th-Thank you for the walk, Martha, it was a great pleasure."

Martha smiled at him. "You are so sweet and so polite. Come inside with me and we can sit and talk for a while." She took his hand and they went inside and sat down at the back of the sanctuary.

They talked for hours, mostly Peskew spoke about himself, his past and his work. Martha listened very attentively, fascinated by this very important man who seemed so smitten. She revealed very little about her personal life or her past, preferring to focus on him and on her work for the church. The church grew dim as night fell and she realized how late it was.

"Oh, I really need to let you go. I have so much to do and you have a long ride back into Manhattan."

"M-May I see you tomorrow?"

"I'd like that. We can go to the park."

"Very w-well, it's a date. I-I'll meet you here tomorrow at the same time." And, she gave him a light kiss on the cheek as he got up to leave.

She stood in the door and watched him as he walked away, until he was out of sight and then she slowly closed the doors and went to tell Aldous about all that had happened.

Peskew walked away smiling, feeling like he was being swept away on a cloud. He skipped the subway and walked to the bridge and sat down by the river. He had never felt so happy and, for the moment, all thoughts of Green Dots, pico matrices and chips faded into the background, replaced by a lovely vision named Martha.

❧

XLVIII. Waiting for Gideon

"HANG UP," DAVID SAID AND THE COMPUTER SHUTOFF the phone system and Gideon's image faded away. He was glad Gideon had called; now they would be able to clear up this dreadful misunderstanding. David hadn't slept at all the previous night, which was extremely unusual. He sat on the deep comfortable chair in his hotel room and Little Bit jumped into his lap. "You've still got some spring in your step for an old dog," he said, staring into the little Westie's eyes. The deep black eyes stared right back and Little Bit gave a short yap as if to say, "I know what you're feeling."

"Nothing to do for the next couple of hours, little guy. I'm sure you'll recognize 'Gideon' as soon as he walks through the door. No disguise or altered appearance is going to fool that Westie nose."

David put on his running clothes and put Little Bit in his cart and went out to the elevator. He had at least two hours until Gideon arrived and running a few kilometers would help him pass the time. In the old days, Little Bit would have run along with him, but at fourteen it was too much strain for his long-time companion. They left the hotel and headed up Broadway towards Central Park. As he turned to the right out of the hotel entrance, Crash slipped in from the left and made his way to the room next to David's, which he had reserved the previous day, and waited. The morning run usually lasted about an hour and the maid always came during that time. While the door was propped open, he would have his opportunity.

An hour later David and Little Bit returned to the freshly cleaned room. Little Bit plopped down on the bed and David turned on the shower and closed the door to the bathroom. As he was showering, he heard a brief yelp from the dog and stuck his head out.

"Little Bit, is someone there?" He didn't get any reply. He walked out of the shower and was met by a stranger, aiming a weapon of some sort at him. Before he could say a word he saw a flash and then he was enveloped by a string of lights, which led to intense burning pain for a brief moment followed by total numbness and then collapse. He was enveloped within utter and absolute blackness as he crashed to the floor, conscious for a moment, and then still and seemingly lifeless.

His assailant sat down on the personal hygiene center and stared at his handiwork, then let out a deep sigh. *I've done my part for the last time,* he thought as he waited in the room to finish the task. In the other room, Little Bit lay unconscious but breathing. The neural disrupter was programmed for human nervous systems and had only rendered the dog unconscious. The little Westie lay on the bed, his breathing shallow, but very much alive.

෨ඁ

XLIX. At the Park

THAT SAME DAY, RANDY PESKEW AND MARTHA MET AT the usual time and walked the short distance to Prospect Park. They held hands lovingly as Martha pointed out the sites and distinguishing features of the neighborhood. They walked past the old brewery which Aldous and members of the church had converted to a recreation center; there was an abandoned jail, still with barbed wire crowning its wall, a statue of George Washington stood at the entrance to the park, the nose worn away by the years and the hair now sporting a greenish hue.

The park, however, was magnificent. It was the unofficial border separating the misfits from proper society and the government kept it pristine. The two walked to the lake that formed the nucleus of the green oasis. They sat on two large, artificial boulders at the edge of the water, holding hands and looking out at a few live ducks that had stumbled upon the waters in the midst of the big city. There were children on the other side enticing the already plump mallards to join them for lunch. Randy gazed into Martha's eyes and saw a sparkle of love that he had never experienced before.

"W-Why do you care?" he asked.

"Care?" she responded innocently. "Care for what?"

"F-For me. W-Why out of all the people in this world did you take pity on someone like me and actually care?"

"Oh; I don't know. You did look so pitiful, but it wasn't out of pity. No, you looked like you needed a friend. And you are kind of cute and certainly intelligent. Really, the more I'm with you the more intriguing I find you." She gave him a kiss on his cheek. He put his arms around her and gave her a long, loving kiss on her lips.

"I've been so lonely for so long. You're such an angel to have such feelings for someone so wretched. You don't know, but I'm really evil.

Anyone that works for the Prince of Evil like I do can't help but be s-stained by his iniquity, at least that's how it seems to me."

"You don't work for Satan, do you? I thought you worked for Diblonski."

Peskew looked down at his feet. "There's not much difference between the two. Oh, I know that Diblonski's not really the devil, but what he does, the way he manipulates everything for his own purpose. He seems to want the best for everyone, but it really is just for Diblonski."

"He can't be that bad," Martha remarked.

Peskew just shook his head."P-Probably not, but I sat alone with him one day and I had this feeling of evil that still makes me shudder. That's why I like being with you. You fill me with happiness and peace. Why do you think that is?"

Martha smiled and said, "It's the love that God has for us that you sense. Before I was taken in by Mr. Aldous I was lost, in despair, aimlessly wandering on the streets; I probably would have been dead soon. But, he taught me about God and Jesus and now I have found peace. If you come to our church, I'm sure that you can find this peace, too."

"Just being with you gives me peace. Of course it's not very good for my work, but I'm sure Mr. Diblonski can survive without a day or two of research."

The two lovebirds stood up and walked along the path, they stopped and bought some synthesized ice cream and watched a hologram of some clowns and acrobats in the park arena.

"I'll bet the real thing is much more exciting," Peskew said when the show was finished. He looked at the time hologram which suddenly projected in front of his eyes. "Six o'clock; we should be heading back."

They turned and walked back to the church, their arms wrapped around each other. They reached the entrance to the church and Martha asked him to come inside with her. They walked through the sanctuary and went through one of the rear doors to a hallway with a number of rooms. The hall was dimly lit and there was a low grunting noise coming from one of the rooms.

"Come on," Martha said. "There's someone I want you to meet."

She took him by the hand and led him to the source of the grunting noises. When she opened the door, Peskew saw a young man, probably about seventeen, in an old mechanical wheelchair, propped up by a pillow and a strap around his waist. There was a contortion to his face, which had prominent acne, and there was drool running from the corner of his mouth and forming a dark wet spot on his blue shirt. The boy's arms were also twisted and he seemed to writhe around in the chair, unable to find a comfortable position.

"This is Adam, at least that's what Aldous and I named him," Martha explained. "We found him in the back of the church one morning, about three years ago. We didn't know who he was or where he came from. He was dressed in old ragged clothes; wasted and dirty, with sores all over his body. We've taken care of him ever since. I'm not sure if he understands me, but everyday I talk to him, clean him, read the Bible to him."

"He l-looks like he needs a lot of work and attention, but I can see that he likes you and that you have certainly been a wonderful caregiver. I'm sure that in his own way he is thankful for all that you've done," Peskew observed.

"You are right when you say that he needs attention, but, truthfully, I am the one that is thankful. He has taught me more about giving and love than anyone. I really thought that I could never be so loved by anyone else, that is, until I met you."

Peskew felt warm and was sure that his face was red. "I would love to learn to care for him, and you, forever," he said softly as he put his arm around her and gave her a gentle kiss on her cheek.

She gave him a hug and then said, "Come with me now and you can help me get him ready for bed."

And so they shared the task of bathing and cleaning Martha's special charge. Peskew marveled at Martha's skill, despite her one useless arm. Together they put him into bed and then walked hand-in-hand to the front of the church.

When they reached the entrance they embraced and Martha gave her shy lover a long goodnight kiss. She slowly went inside as Peskew turned towards home and walked away with a sprightly spring in his step and a promise that he would see her the next day.

৵৽৵

L. Second Assault

THE TAXI DEPOSITED GIDEON AND BEAUTY AT A SIDE entrance to the Great White Way Casino. Gideon had called before they left and let David know that they were coming; both parties were contrite and Gideon was sure that they would patch things up. The more he thought about the incident, the more he realized that he may have been wrong and there was some alternative explanation.

As the taxi pulled up to the side entrance, Gideon checked the surrounding area for any surveillance apparatus before disembarking. He and Beauty quickly exited the cab and darted through the open side entrance. The elevators were right inside the doors and they rode alone up to the twentieth floor and David's room. As they approached the door, Gideon realized that he had left his coat in the taxi.

"Go on ahead, I'm going to try to catch that cab," he said. "David's expecting us, so there shouldn't be any problem." He raced back to the elevator, hoping that the cabs did the expected and lined up at the hotel queue. He called the taxi company and asked for Micah Davies, the name he had seen on the taxi ID. He was told that the driver had waited at the hotel and that they would gladly instruct him to pull around to the side. Gideon waited for what seemed to be an hour, but what was really only about five minutes before he saw the yellow cab pull around the corner. He thanked the driver profusely and gave him a hundred dollar tip before quickly walking inside and back up the elevator. This time there was an elderly couple riding with him. They exchanged courteous hellos before Gideon reached the twentieth floor. He worried about leaving Beauty alone for too long; not about David, who he really trusted, but there were so many media types floating around looking for anything the least bit sordid.

After Gideon had left to retrieve his coat, Beauty rang the hotel room buzzer, but no one answered. *Strange,* she thought. She knew that they were expected. She tried the door and, surprisingly, found it open. *He must have left it unlocked for us,* she thought and went inside.

The room was a large suite. She heard the shower running. *That must be why he left the door open,* she thought. She sat down on the very comfortable sofa and looked around the room. *I wish Gideon would get here,* she said to herself.

She peered over at the bathroom and saw the door slightly ajar, in the mirror she saw the bare feet of a person lying on the floor. *What's going on?* She got up and peeked into the bathroom and saw David, unconscious, sprawled on the floor, in a pool of water, covered by a wet towel. Before she could scream, she looked up to see Crash standing in the shower holding a neural disrupter. His face reddened when he saw her and he jumped and grabbed her by the waist and put his hand over her mouth.

"So this is what you're up to," he hissed through clenched teeth. "Taking up with that upstart Gideon was bad enough, but now throwing yourself at this hypocritical Jesus freak is too much. With everything we've been through together, you never noticed anything, but this is too much . . ."

"Crash, you've got it all wrong, let me . . ." she tried to explain.

He clapped his hand over her mouth and she bit him. "You little tramp; you're going to pay for that." He pushed her down to the ground next to David and aimed his weapon at her.

"Crash, no!" But he pulled the trigger and she slumped down next to David. Crash looked at her motionless body and threw the disrupter to the floor, and started to run out. However, he stopped and regained his composure. His hatred of Gideon boiled to the surface and he took the special container out and released its contents, then placed the weapon underneath Beauty. He stopped to look at the monitors and saw Gideon entering the elevator in the lobby. He left one more item on the door to the room and then quickly made his way down the stairs.

Gideon walked quickly from the elevator to David's room. He knocked on the door but there was no response; he tried the door and found it open. His hand felt wet after he turned the old style door knob and went inside. He heard the shower running and called out, "Beauty . . . David, anybody here?" His call was answered by the running water of the shower and he hurried to investigate. He found the still bodies on the bathroom floor, fully-clothed Beauty draped across David. His hands shook as he rolled Beauty over and on to her back. She was limp and, although he felt a pulse, she wasn't breathing. He called out 911 and the room's computer system sprang to life. He was immediately connected to Emergency Services.

"Emergency, Great White Way Hotel Casino, room 2056, David Sanders' room."

"Response team is en route," the operator replied.

Gideon saw the weapon on the floor, but left it untouched; he bent over David and saw that he also was not breathing, but also still had a pulse. He started old fashioned mouth-to-mouth respiration, alternating between the two. In less than two minutes, emergency personnel arrived and each of the victims was expertly placed on portable ventilators and taken away. Despite his protests, Gideon was forced to stay in the room until the police showed up two minutes later.

First the uniformed patrolmen and then a lieutenant in plain clothes arrived. He was Lt. Scott Rosales, the most experienced homicide detective in the New York division. He was carrying a scanning device and as he walked into the room he did a quick probe. He also did a scan of Gideon. What he found surprised him. All over the hotel room was evidence of Gideon's presence, his DNA, blood, his prints on the weapon and disrupter oil on his hand, something that could only be deposited by firing the weapon.

He turned to Gideon. "You been in this room before, Mr.?" he queried.

"Jones, Gideon Jones. No, sir. I had to leave Beauty, that is the young lady, alone and came back to this . . ." Gideon answered, but he was interrupted before he could finish.

"Why'd you do it? What, did you catch your girl with him?" he asked facetiously, pointing to David. "It's always the same story these days, two men fighting over a cheap whore. Mr. Jones, I'm afraid you are under arrest for the attempted murder of David Sanders and Miss Beauty. Boys, take him away." The detective shook his head. "Almost too simple," he said to himself. *But caution is usually the first thing forgotten in these domestic disputes,* he thought.

He took another look around the room and ran another scan. There was nothing else to suggest that it could be anything but two guys fighting over a woman. *Sad,* he thought; *it's just never worth it.* He carefully put the weapon in an evidence bag noticing some yellowish powder on the grip and trigger. This was recorded and he took a swab for analysis. The room was carefully recorded in every detail, date and time marked on the encrypted recordings to prevent tampering. A more detailed spectral analysis was then made of every aspect of the hotel room, the hallway, elevators and the hotel lobby, and all entrances. All surveillance and security data was obtained; once again care taking to ensure there was no tampering. The crime scene evaluation completed he released all of the hotel except for the actual room. He left to go downtown to interview his suspect.

As he walked out of the front entrance he was greeted by the biggest throng of media representatives he had ever encountered in his thirty years as a police lieutenant.

"Why do you think he did . . . have you questioned Gideon Jones . . . are Sanders and Beauty going to be OK?"

The questions came fast and furious and were all answered with the same response: "No comment." He climbed into his waiting police cruiser and sat back for the short ride to the station.

Gideon was thrown into the back seat of a different police cruiser which then sped away. A uniformed officer read him his rights as the windows blackened to prevent any unwanted intrusion. The officer whispered into the air as instructions were received through his communicator. He tapped on the partition and whispered to the driver. Gideon could make out the words "change in instructions . . . psychological evaluation."

The police car turned around and the siren stopped. The police cruiser took on the plain black appearance of a million cars on the road as it sped away to the Westchester Rehabilitation Center. *I'm definitely not crazy*, Gideon thought as the officer placed a blindfold over his eyes and covered his mouth with a thick adhesive pad. *Something's not right*, Gideon thought, but at that moment he was helpless to protest.

ഏഏ

LI. Resuscitation

DAVID AND BEAUTY WERE LOADED INTO THE WAITING ambulance and immediately connected to devices that monitored all their body functions. Each had complete absence of respiratory effort, the result of the neural disruption. Small tubes were inserted in their mouths which intuitively snaked their way into each victim's trachea and inflated to allow for artificial ventilation. Each body system was monitored and physiologic optimization was begun. In a very short time both David and Beauty were stabilized, their trauma assessed and therapeutic regimens initiated.

The ambulance arrived at New York Bellevue Hospital in less than fifteen minutes and they were quickly transported to the waiting trauma intensive care unit. Each had already been scanned, properly identified and dispatches sent to notify next of kin. On arrival to the trauma ward, criminal scientists were waiting to complete the victim assessment and nurses expertly began necessary life support measures. The physicians remained in their offices receiving telemetry and directing care from distant sites.

The principal injury they had suffered was complete neural disruption resulting in synaptic dysjunction. Essentially, every neural connection was disrupted leaving living organisms whose cells were existing in isolation. Generally, the neural disruptor devices caused temporary incapacitation, usually unconsciousness that lasted anywhere from thirty seconds to several hours. The weapons used in this attack had apparently been modified to be more lethal.

In a remote office Dr. Byron Greenway, a neurologist, was consulting with the Chief of Trauma, Dr. Lillian Trestco.

"It looks like they each took a full blast from an extremely modified weapon. There's no way to predict the duration of the disruption, but I'd wager it's going to be permanent," Dr. Greenway explained. "I suggest that you begin to make plans to keep them for a long time."

"Do you think there is any benefit to examining either of them in person?" Dr. Trestco asked. "I know we can see everything on telemetry here, but it just seems so impersonal. In medical school they used to tell us that the act of touching a patient, the personal contact, was therapeutic."

"Mumbo jumbo from the 1950's, Doctor. We can see everything about those poor souls on the monitors, and in far greater detail and specificity than from seeing them in person. And, maintaining the impartial and impersonal approach promotes far superior outcomes. You know this, surely they taught you about Dr. Repost's work during all that training you've had."

"Yes, yes, I know the study. 'Personal contact leads to personal bias and clouds reasoning leading to substandard outcomes.' His results have never been reproduced."

"His study design was flawless. It would be nearly criminal to knowingly submit patients to another study; we already know that the modern approach is superior."

Dr. Trestco sat silently for a few minutes, studying the monitors and the physiologic data. "I'm going to lunch," she announced. "I'll talk to you later."

"Ok, see you later." Dr. Greenway turned back to the monitors and stared at the two motionless patients, as a cacophony of beeps and bings filled the room.

෨ᢀᡧᠥ

LII. Peskew

RANDY PESKEW RETURNED TO HIS APARTMENT AND found a red light flashing across the room, signifying a very important message. He activated his home security as he had been instructed during the Diblonski orientation sessions. Once the red light turned green he opened the message and read a memo from Abe Masur.

"To: Randy Peskew, Director of Research and Development

A situation has arisen that demands your immediate attention in our west coast office. Please be ready to depart by 2000 on August 20. Transportation will be sent for you. Please tell no one and be prepared to assimilate the duties of our west coast research operation. —AM"

Of all the nuisances, Peskew thought. This job is more trouble than it's worth. I can't see how anything could be of such importance. Even worse, I won't see Martha tomorrow; that was the greatest annoyance. I better send her a note, but then he remembered the missive not to tell anyone.

"I'll just be vague," he said to himself. He commanded his computer, "Send message tomorrow; had to leave on business, be back soon, love Randy. Please send this after ten in the morning."

With that important task finished he threw some essentials into a bag and waited for his ride. Promptly at ten PM a black limousine pulled up. He activated his home security system, standard issue for all Diblonski executives and also activated his personal system, one he had designed that he used to shield his most private research.

He raced down the automated stairs to the waiting car and was whisked away to the airport. Two hours later he landed in San Diego and was immediately taken to Diblonski's west coast office complex.

He was put into an office where he sat and waited for another two hours. He called out and was told that his meeting would start shortly. He sat down and continued to wait.

A few minutes later Mr. Masur came in.

"Sorry to have kept you waiting, Mr. Peskew. I was tied up straightening out a few details pertaining to your visit, but he, rather they, are all in order now. So, let's get down to business. We have had a problem with R&D out here. You are new to the organization, so we don't hold you responsible, but we do need your help to assess and minimize the damage, so to speak. What we had was a spy; an individual selling Diblonski secrets to our competition. We have plugged the leak, if you'll pardon the expression, but we need your expertise to undo what has been done." Masur stopped for a moment.

Peskew sunk a bit in his large overstuffed chair as Masur was speaking, but asked, "Couldn't I have done this from New York?"

Masur's voice rose a notch. "We needed you here," he said with some force and then his voice returned to normal. Long distance evaluation of the data is not possible. Some of it is very sensitive and there were some security concerns requiring us to limit transmissions. This is all the data that needs to be reviewed. We have made a room for you here in our complex with all necessary comforts. Please go through this research and confirm its validity and any possible breaches of security."

"I think trained security personnel would do a better job," Peskew observed.

Masur's face turned a shade of red and his voice rose again. "This is assigned to you as Vice President of R&D. Your participation has been requested personally by Mr. Diblonski. It seems you made quite an impression on him at the last board meeting. You would be wise to not let the boss down. If you are diligent it shouldn't take you more than two weeks." Masur stopped and a young blonde woman came in. "This is Miss Long; she will show you to your quarters. I'll check in with you tomorrow." He left via a door opposite the one Miss Long had entered.

"Follow me," the pretty young woman said.

They walked down a long corridor and then up a private elevator to a very spacious, luxurious apartment where Peskew deposited his bag.

"I'll be available for anything you might need, just call. My number is built in to the system; just ask for Miss Long." And she left. Peskew quickly noticed that the doors only opened from the outside. *I guess I'm stuck until I finish,* he thought. He popped the file into the computer and started to work.

༂

LIII. Lieutenant Ryan

THE REPORT FROM THE SANDERS/BEAUTY ASSAULT SAT on Lieutenant Ryan's desk as he conferred with Lt. Rosales. Such a high profile assault was immediately brought to Ryan's attention and he was planning to interview the primary suspect personally. He assumed that Gideon Jones was being held at Police Central in Manhattan and he was about to leave to take the short drive up north.

"We can't find him or the driver," Rosales explained. "They never made it to Central and our last satellite location has them heading towards the West Side Expressway and then they disappeared. From there they could have gone anywhere."

Lt. Ryan felt his hands start to shake as Rosales' words started to sink in. "Are you telling me that the primary suspect in a double attempted murder just up and vanished? And, not just any murder, but one involving two of the most high profile media figures in the solar system? Please tell me it's April first."

"Sorry, Ryan, but it seems that this Jones is one slippery character. Everything, car, driver, and suspect have fallen off the face of the earth."

Ryan calmed down and said with a very even voice, "Leave everything in place, Lieutenant. That is, the crime scene, all the evidence, surveillance, everything. I'll be there in an hour. Oh, and tell the vultures from the media, 'No comment.' Tell them the investigation is ongoing and we'll have a statement as soon as all the evidence has been examined. Tell them Jones was taken into custody for questioning as a person of interest."

"And if they ask any more questions?"

"Tell them to buzz off . . . no, tell them an official statement will be issued when all the facts have been corroborated; that we don't want anyone jumping to any unfounded conclusions and that this case will not be tried in the media."

The usual tripe, Ryan thought; nobody believed it and it didn't matter. The media would say whatever they wanted, truth being a secondary consideration. Rating and sales was what mattered. He glanced at the report on his desk as his car was brought around. Nothing seemed out of the ordinary, except the presence of some unusual powder, identified as pollen from an unknown plant. *More than coincidence,* he thought as he called the crime lab.

ক্ষ

LIV. Out of Body

DAVID HAD A SENSE OF DÉJÀ VU. HIS CONSCIOUSNESS floated above his motionless body within a black void. It all seemed very familiar. He felt for his pulse but there was none. He put his hand in front of his face and saw nothing except total blackness. He decided there was nothing to do but wait for the arrival he was sure to come. Time stood still until he saw a faint light. He remained motionless as the light grew brighter and seemed to move closer. He became aware of the scent of freshly baked cookies and the man appeared, the same man he had met years ago, one whom he knew was there to save him from doom.

"Wait here," the man said. "I'm not sure you are ready."

So, David waited, minutes, hours, years, it didn't matter. He felt like he was close to home and a sense of joy welled up from inside. Out of the light he saw a figure walking towards him; he could tell it was a woman by the silhouette. As she emerged from the light he saw a pink dress and the face of his darling Deborah. As she walked closer, she changed. The beauty of Deborah altered in subtle ways, the eyes grew deeper and bluer, almond shaped, the figure rounder, the hair shiny and full and he found himself standing next to Ruth. He took her hand in his and then embraced her and they were soon surrounded by sunlight, plants, and animals; back in Eden, at least for the time being. They sat silently at the edge of the water, holding each other, not knowing if this would be forever or for only a moment.

Finally, David found the strength to speak. "Is it forever or only for a short while?"

"I do not know, but does it matter? We have this moment and that is enough," Ruth answered.

"You are right; it is enough." And he was still, holding her as the sun set and a full moon bathed them in pale light.

❧✺❧

LV. Martha and Aldous

MARTHA READ THE SHORT NOTE FROM RANDY AND GAVE a short sigh of disappointment. Aldous was sitting nearby and sensed her distress and asked her to come sit next to him.

"This man is special," he said as a statement of fact.

Martha's face turned red and she turned her head away. "In all my years I've never met someone that liked me just for me. He doesn't have any meanness and doesn't say things to try to trick me and he's just such a lonely man. I'm sorry he had to go away."

"I'm sure it's just for a short time," Aldous reassured her. "I'll bet he's thinking about you right now and counting the seconds until he comes home."

Martha just sat and smiled as Aldous stood up and retired to his room. After a few minutes she dimmed the lights in the sanctuary and went to her quarters, washed, and lay down to try to sleep, visions of Randy Peskew filling her head.

About an hour later Aldous was sitting at his desk staring at the monitor wishing the sermon he was working on would write itself when he heard a scream followed by crying from Martha's room. He quickly stood up and made his way to her room. She was on the bed drenched in sweat; she had thrown off her blanket and had a wild expression on her face, one of fear and pain. Aldous sat on the edge of the bed and held her. As she moved, she winced in pain.

"What's wrong?" he asked.

"My stomach hurts, especially when I move," she whispered her voice barely audible.

Aldous lay her back down and he saw that her sheets were drenched in blood. "We need to get you to a hospital," he stated.

Martha screamed, "NO . . . NO! I won't go. Leave me be. If God wants to take me home now, please let him; but I won't go to any hospital ever again."

"At least let me call a doctor or nurse."

At this suggestion, Martha remained silent and Aldous took that to mean that it would be OK. The church caretaker, Samuel, came in from outside where his quarters were and Aldous spoke quietly to the elderly man who turned and walked out.

As he was leaving Aldous called out to him. "Take Jasmine with you, she'll be a big help if you have any problem." The minister then put a cool towel on Martha's forehead, not really sure what to do next.

Samuel and Jasmine climbed into the church van and took the road through the park to the nearest hospital. Jasmine served as church secretary, cook, maid, and anything else that needed to be done. She had wandered in to one of Aldous services three years before after a long night at one of the casinos in Queens. She was never quite sure how she had found her way in to Brooklyn, but the sermon touched her heart and she never returned to the empty life she left behind. She did, however, retain a certain streetwise charm that often served her well when dealing with reticent donors to the church.

The two pulled into the parking lot at South Brooklyn Hospital and entered the emergency entrance. The hospital was nearly empty; only two patients were standing at self-serve kiosks; experiencing the usual scans prior to being administered the proper shot or pill.

"Looks like a quiet night," Samuel observed.

"Yeah," Jaz said. "Not a creature's stirring except for a mouse." She pointed to a corner where a gray mouse scampered along the wall and then disappeared. She stood at the counter and started to shout, "ANYBODY HOME, HEY,WE NEED SOME HELP!" She climbed over the counter into a back room, but still didn't find a soul. "What kind of hospital is this; where is everybody? Hey, anybody, we need some H-E-L-P."

Finally, a young man dressed in white got off the elevator and was immediately accosted by the brash woman.

"Hey, you . . . you a doctor," Jaz yelled.

The man was startled and looked over his shoulder.

"Yeah, I'm talking to you. What kind of place you running here? A body could be dead a week and no one would even notice." She grabbed the man by the arm.

"Excuse me, Miss, I'm just checking on the kiosks. Do you need some assistance?"

"Deaf and Dumb," Jaz said. "What do you think I've been screaming about for the last five minutes? What I need is someone to come help a sick friend. Are you a doctor, Albert Schweitzer?"

"No, a nurse. I'm Mr. Hobart; the night shift nurse. I'm afraid there's no one here but me. If your friend is sick, bring him in and I'll be happy to look him over."

"Now listen to me, Hogan," she exclaimed.

"Hobart."

"OK, Holster. My friend, a young lady named Martha, is too sick to come into this tower of quackery. Why don't you be a good little nurse and write a little sign that says 'OUT TO LUNCH' and climb into the back of our van out there and come take a look." She held his arm tightly and dragged him toward the door. Hobart felt like he had been trapped in the unrelenting jaws of a pit bull and decided he had no choice but to cooperate.

Samuel quickly wrote a message that said, "Back in Five Minutes," and the three left for the short drive to the church. Hobart grabbed a portable Diagnostic and Therapeutic system on his way out.

Jaz talked nonstop during the ride. "You know, Holstein, you're really cute; do you have a steady girlfriend or is it a different bimbo every night. One club after another, waking up at 4:00 a.m. to find some strange butt staring you in the face. I used to be like that, but now I got religion and, well, I just can't say enough . . . do you live at the hospital 'cause you can stay with me. I certainly wouldn't kick you out of bed . . ."

"Are we almost there?" he whispered to Samuel, somewhat exasperated. A few moments later he saw the cross on the church. Samuel pulled around the back and parked the van. With a short sigh, Hobart took his equipment and followed Samuel inside.

"I'll be waiting for you, honey; when you finish, you come on over and see me."

Hobart walked a little faster.

❧

LVI. Martha's Future

HOBART WAS USHERED INTO MARTHA'S ROOM. HE GAVE a short gasp as he saw the young woman lying on the bed, blood soaked sheets rolled up on the floor next to her. He quickly unpacked the medical equipment and knelt down beside her.

The Diagnostic scanner made a soft whir as it probed her from head to foot. Data started to appear almost instantly:

Pulse, 140
Blood Pressure, 60/20
Respirations, 38
Temperature, 34 C
Oxygen Saturation, 82 %
Tissue Oxygen Delivery, 12%
Cardiac Output, 9.6 liters/minute
CNS Oxygen Delivery, 48%

The scanning continued; the whirring becoming louder. Hobart studied his patient more closely as the machine did its work. Her eyes were a shade of yellow, there were black and blue patches on her arms and legs, the abdomen was distended and tense and she winced in pain if he even stroked it lightly. As she lay on the bed there was passage of bright red blood, from her rectum, he presumed.

More data appeared from the diagnostic scanner:

Liver Function, 10%
Renal Function, 2%
GI Perfusion, 11%
Etiology of organ failure: advanced disseminated adenocarcinoma of the colon.
Prognosis, poor

Hobart stood up and talked quietly with Aldous, who had remained at the door. "There you have it, sir. She has widespread cancer; probably been growing for years."

"Can't you treat her?" Aldous asked.

"Why, yes, but I can't do much here. At the hospital we can synthesize a tumor specific immunokiller; sort of a hit man for cancer. It's possible that we can wipe all this away, but we have to take her now. She doesn't have much time . . ."

"No," came a weak voice. "Let me be."

Aldous sat down beside her and gently stroked her cheek. "Don't you want to be saved?"

"I was saved long ago when you took me in. I'm ready to end all the suffering. But, please, leave me alone for a few minutes."

Aldous whispered, "Alright," and he and Hobart left the room and closed the door. They waited outside for about ten minutes and then Aldous peaked inside. A street lamp suffused the room in pale light and Martha lay on the bed, dressed in her finest Sunday dress, her arms across her chest, and a look of peace and serenity that Aldous almost envied. The fetid smell of death was gone and he was sure there was a faint odor of fresh baking. He realized she was gone and knelt at her bedside and cried. Hobart stood in the doorway, not sure if he should come in or simply leave when he heard a voice from behind. The distinct sound of Jaz.

"He cries, not because she is dead, rather they are tears of joy, because she has gone to be with the God she loved; and, he cries because of his own loss and the loss we all feel. But, for Martha there is a celebration in Heaven. Look at her, finally at peace with a world which treated her so cruelly." She put her arm around the nurse, who was only beginning to sense all that had happened. They walked away together.

☙❧

LVII. Peskew Returns

RANDY PESKEW FLEW IN FROM THE WEST COAST AFTER A week of purposeless meetings, shuffling paper, and pointless review of research that had been obsolete for six months. Excitement and anticipation overwhelmed him as he thought of Martha and the prospect of their being together the next day. He hadn't had a chance to inform her of his early return, but he was confident that she would be outside watering the plants in the afternoon tomorrow. The words and warnings from Mr. Masur were only faint echoes, rapidly fading into the remote areas of his brain.

He unpacked his small bag and put his few belongings away and lay down to sleep, his room bathed in the light of a full moon. Restlessness overcame exhaustion and he got up and stared out his window at the full moon illuminating the night sky. He almost thought that he could see all the activity; thousands of workers gathering the endless supply of photons from the sun and transmitting them through numerous relay stations until they found their way to food synthesizers, automobiles, lights, and every other pointless machine created for this wondrous thing called humanity.

And, it was wondrous; that two people, total strangers, totally different in every way should find a spark that ignites and sends them soaring to unfathomable heights of happiness. He looked up and, in a cloud that passed in front of the full moon, he saw a vision of his dear Martha smiling down at him. He stood up and felt like he should climb out the window to join her, but the image faded and he was overcome with exhaustion. He laid on his bed and slowly fell into a deep sleep; feeling as though his lovely Martha was there with him caressing his head.

The next morning he awoke refreshed and started out early towards Brooklyn. He arrived at the church much earlier than usual and, feeling bold, went inside to find her. What he saw left him confused and with a sense of foreboding. The large cross in the sanctuary was draped with a black cloth. A funeral dirge played and there was a closed coffin in the front. Numerous worshippers dressed in black passed by the casket as Aldous stood by, his head bowed in prayer.

Aldous looked up and saw Peskew at the back of the worship center; he stopped his prayers and walked towards the back slowly shaking his head. The actions of the pastor left him worried, but one thing left him even more concerned; Martha was not there. He started to shake and turned as if to run out, but instead stopped and sat in the pew in the last row. After a few seconds, he knelt down in front of the pew as Aldous reached the back and knelt beside him.

"We didn't know how to find you and it happened so fast. I'm sorry." Aldous tried to console the shattered soul, who had grasped the tragedy without the need for any explanation.

"Wh-What happened?" Peskew asked, his voice wavering and his upper lip trembling.

"She became very ill, very suddenly. We did all we could, but it didn't matter. She is with the God she loved so and she's at peace."

"Peace . . . peace, you say; empty words from a decaying humanity," Peskew murmured as he started to get up, clenching his hands into fists. "If this is God's mercy and love, then I curse God and I curse Satan and all mankind. No person or thing deserves to exist."

The distraught man quickly stood up and kicked the pew, ripping it from the floor with a loud crack. He threw the Bible and hymnal to the ground and stormed out of the church. Aldous stood up, stunned for a moment, then ran after Peskew, but outside the front entrance all he saw were crowds of nameless people. He slowly turned and returned to the very heartrending task that awaited him inside.

࿊

LVIII. Gideon

GIDEON RODE IN SILENCE FOR ANOTHER THIRTY MINUTES, his hands bound with the latest magnetic cuffs, his eyes shielded and his mouth covered with a thick gag. He heard the guard move and murmur, in a barely audible voice, "Time for a nap." There was a slight popping noise and Gideon was rendered unconscious.

When he awoke, he was in a dark room; the floor and walls were soft and cushioned and Gideon could barely see anything. There was no light, only faint illumination from a window about six meters from the floor. As his eyes grew accustomed to the darkness he saw that there was nothing to see. Except for the padding on the floor and walls, the room was empty; no furniture, no bed, no hygiene facilities. His clothes and personal belongings were gone and he was dressed in loose fitting jumpsuit and slip-on shoes without socks.

This isn't police headquarters, Gideon thought; *no, I'm in a mental rehabilitation facility in an isolation room. There must be some mistake; this can't be right.* For the first time in a very long time Gideon was worried. Rumors of dangerous individuals abounded, rumors of them being locked away without hearings, trials, or chance for release. Such persons were left alone to contemplate their private hell, eventually going irreversibly insane, permanently caged with no hope for salvation or redemption.

Gideon decided, if nothing else, he would make his presence known. He stood up and felt around the room, finding a slight depression that he presumed was a door. He stood and started to pound with his fists, yelling, "I'm here . . . I'm here . . . I need the toilet . . . I'm hungry." As loud as he could, over and over again he kept it up. As his voice was starting to grow hoarse he heard a clicking sound and then an alarm.

"Stand back from the door," said a booming voice. In a flash the door slid open, disappearing into the wall and he was face to face with three uniformed guards, dressed in white, their faces obscured by helmets with dark visors. Each brandished a neural disrupter and a club. Gideon stood well back from the door as two came into the room and the other stayed outside the door. Gideon decided a touch of boldness would serve him well.

"Where have you been, I've been calling for hours. I don't like being ignored like that."

His audacity was met by a rap on his shins by the club and he crumpled to the ground. "Silence," said one of the guards. They didn't utter another sound. A hygiene center was wheeled in. "You've got three minutes."

Seeing that discussion or argument would be fruitless, Gideon was practical and stepped in. He finished quickly and the center was removed. A tray of what they called food and water was left as the guards disappeared. Gideon realized he was famished, only briefly smelled what was offered and ate it quickly. The plate dissolved away as soon as he finished as did the glass. The night grew darker as he lay down, falling into a fitful sleep, all the time very conscious of the fact that he was in deep trouble.

☙❧

LIX. Crash Escapes

CRASH EMERGED FROM THE SIDE ENTRANCE OF THE hotel and hurried down Broadway to Fifty-Eighth Street and into Central Park. He carefully looked around in all directions and checked his personal surveillance, doing his best to be sure that the coast was clear. He tried to be inconspicuous as he quickly blended in with the crowds enjoying the sun in the park, the sweat on his forehead certainly was appropriate for such a warm day. He slipped away from the crowd and quickly walked to a more wooded, secluded area of the park, and when he was sure he was alone leaned against a tree and started to cry. He crumbled to the ground against the tree, his face buried in his hands.

"What have I done," he cried, shaking his head back and forth.

"You shouldn't be so upset." He heard a low voice. "You have served very well, been a very good team player, and you are due a very special reward."

Crash looked up, but the voice seemed to be coming all around, from the trees, the bushes, the sky, but he didn't see anyone.

"What could I have possibly earned; I've all but killed the woman I love, my career is gone. What do I have now?"

"Look what you've done." A hologram appeared that revealed the recent events in remarkable detail, starting with the neural disruption of David and Beauty, then the arrest of Gideon. Images followed that revealed the future that Gideon faced and Crash smiled as he was privileged to see the torment and suffering his adversary was to experience. *Justice will be served*, he thought.

But, then, he saw himself, sitting by the tree and his future began to unfold. A flash appeared and he saw himself slumped over, his face contorted with fear, his body surrounded by whooping figures, shrouded in black, seeming to hover above the ground. He watched them pick up his lifeless body and carry it to a hideous place where he was judged and sentenced. The pain and suffering that followed was too horrible to watch. Fear gripped him; *I've got to get away now,* he thought and he started to get up.

At that instant there was a real flash and this vision of the future began to unfold. "Time to pay up," the voice said and a lone figure dressed in black emerged and dropped his weapon next to the now lifeless Crash. "Nothing's ever for free," he said out loud as he walked away.

Crash was found the following day, his pockets turned inside out, wallet and all valuables gone. The detectives chalked it up to another robbery in the park as they went through the formalities of investigating. Such robberies had become all too commonplace and the perpetrators were rarely found. As they were gathering and recording the evidence, no one noticed the white powder on the victim's shirtsleeve. Crash was packed up and carted away to a morgue that had become very busy in the last few days.

❧❧

LX. Beauty

BEAUTY LAY ON THE HOSPITAL BED WITH SUCH A SERENE look on her face that her nurse shook her to see if she was truly in a state of neural disconnection. Receiving no response, the nurse went on with her business as Beauty remained motionless, the room silent except for the steady beep of the monitors indicating that there was life behind her motionless, vacant eyes.

The mind behind those eyes was carried far away, as David had been. But, while David was sitting with his beloved Ruth, Beauty found herself in a small room. The room was filled with the most opulent riches; priceless jewels, gold, platinum, fancy silk dresses; the finest of everything. She reclined on a huge round bed, with fur-lined quilts and enclosed by a sheer white curtain.

She was awakened by a light shining down from the ceiling and took delight in all that she found. There was a tray of food, a sumptuous banquet with the freshest fruit, juice, breads, and pastries.

"This is simply wonderful," she said out loud as she rose from her bed and sampled a grape from the banquet table. She stretched her arms and ran to the wardrobe, pulling each item off and holding it to her body as she stood in front of the large mirror at the end of the room. She ate some more and decided it was time to go out. She looked around the room, but she couldn't see a door or window.

What is this place she asked herself and she heard a sweet gentle voice. "You are home, my dear. You have been given everything you have ever asked for; yours forever and ever. So, try the food, put on the finery and the jewels; all of this is yours forever."

"What is this place? Why am I here?"

"It's your final destination, your reward for services well done. We thank you for your good work."

"Who are you?"

With this question the veil was pulled back and Beauty could see where she was. A curtain covering one of the walls rose very slowly and behind it was a window, as large as the whole wall, revealing black emptiness outside her opulent cage. She went up close to the window and pressed her nose against it and, as she stared outside, she saw children playing, their parents sitting nearby keeping a steady vigil. She stared for a long time and then went back to her many things and sat down and cried, uncontrollable tears that flowed and flowed. She went back to the window; the children were gone and there was only black emptiness until a faint light appeared.

The light quickly brightened and she gasped as a huge hideous beast appeared outside the window and banged on the glass trying to get in. The monster was at least three meters tall with a face of greenish brown slime, crooked with a mouth pulled up on one side into permanent sneer. The eyes were uneven and red with pinpoint pupils, the nose pointed. There was no hair on its head and the body was long and snakelike, with short scaly arms and legs. She saw it scream silently revealing yellow teeth, sharp with a bright red tongue.

She jumped back from the window as the hideous beast stood there, staring. Despite its ugliness she saw something familiar in it and she was overwhelmed by a sense of pity. The two stared at each other for a long time before the monster finally slinked away, shaking its massive head as the curtain closed.

Beauty turned to her opulent prison, lay down on the bed and started to cry. In her sorrow she longed for only one thing; that the gruesome creature would return.

၆ႜၜၐ

LXI. Deborah Arrives

"COMPUTER OFF," DEBORAH WHISPERED AS THE CALLER from the hospital finished a very formal notification of next of kin. She sat motionless and speechless for a minute before jumping up to find her kids.

"There's been some sort of terrible accident in New York and your father has been badly injured. We need to go to New York City."

David Jr. and Little Debbie stopped their playing and tears welled up in their eyes. "Is Daddy going to be OK?" the little girl asked.

"I don't know, baby girl," Deborah answered softly. "We need to go right away." She turned to the home computer system. "Pack bags, please. We're going to New York City, length of stay unknown."

Immediately there was some rumbling and whirring as the home went to work packing everything necessary for a trip to New York in late August. In less than ten minutes they were packed and ready to go as a taxi pulled up in front.

They carried the bags down to the street and climbed into the sleek cab.

"This is neat," David Jr. said. "This is one of those new aerotaxis that can do five hundred fifty km/hr. We should be there in no time."

Indeed, once they were on their way the trip from Wildwood to New York, which was about three hundred kilometers, lasted less than an hour and the family was let off at the hospital while their bags were delivered to the Great White Way and safely deposited in their suite.

The family entered the hospital lobby and was greeted by a voice from inside a shiny metallic pillar just inside the main entrance. "Welcome to New York Bellevue Hospital; please choose from the following menu and I will guide you to the proper department."

The monitor built into the pillar lit up and Deborah was faced with a list of choices that made no sense to her. "Come over here, Junior, and help your mother," she commanded.

"Gee, Mom, it's so simple; someday I'll figure out a way for you to read such things. Now, let's see." He looked through the choices, reading each to his dyslexic mother until he got to, "Visit a Patient," and Deborah told him to pick that option. Next, he read, "Input Patient's Name." The boy did as requested and was told that David Sanders was on the third floor in the Intensive Care Unit.

Deborah and the kids raced up to the ICU. Deborah asked the kids to stay in the waiting area while she went into his room. She found David on life support, surprisingly attended by a doctor at the bedside. David was motionless, a breathing device supporting his respirations, his heart beating regularly, a faint smile seemed to be on his lips. Little Bit was curled up at the foot of the bed. The little dog stood up slowly as Deborah arrived and stood by David's head as if to say, "The problem is here."

Deborah smiled at the little Westie and turned to the doctor. "This must be serious for you to be here," Deborah said to Dr. Trestco.

"Not all physicians shun attending to their patients in person. I guess I'm old fashioned, but I wanted to examine these two patients up close."

"What 'two' patients?" Deborah asked.

"Why, Mr. Sanders, here, and the woman they call Beauty in the next bed. They were found together."

"Please, Dr . . ."

"Trestco."

"Dr. Trestco; Mr. Sanders, David, is my husband. Could you please tell me what has happened?"

Dr. Trestco recounted the entire story and the extent of David's injuries. Finally, he told Deborah his prognosis. "Most neural disruptor injuries are transient, the effects lasting for a few seconds to a few minutes. The disruptor field at the usual available levels effects only the higher neurologic functions, rendering the victim unconscious, but leaving the basic brain functions intact. David and Ms. Beauty have been hit with a blast of a very high magnitude. All their neural functions have been disrupted and may take years to recover, if they recover at all. It's like every circuit in a building has been turned off and melted. For now, these two are in a state of living death. Their hearts still work, their organs continue on, and there may be some brain function and perception. But, one cell cannot talk to another and, to use an old phrase, they are locked in. He may be able to hear you, maybe even have some comprehension, but he can't move or respond, and he may be like this forever."

Deborah was silent as she sat down on the bed next to David. She closed her eyes and, for the first time she could remember, she cried, burying her head in David's chest. Dr. Trestco stepped back into the doorway, not knowing what to do or say. Finally, Deborah looked up, her eyes red and swollen.

"Thank you, Doctor. I'm sure that you are doing all that you can and will continue to do so. If you will excuse me now, I need to go talk to my children. I'm sure that they are worried. Thank you."

As she walked out of the room, the doctor grabbed her arm. "They did arrest a suspect, in case you didn't know; a Gideon Jones. They are questioning him now, I think."

"Thank you again, Doctor," said Deborah as she hurried out of the room.

She found David Jr. and Little Debbie sitting in the visitor's area, quietly awaiting their mother's return. Deborah found a nurse who guided them to a private room where Deborah could explain to her two small children all that had happened.

She sat them down and kneeled on the floor next to them, looked into their eyes, and as calmly as she was able started to explain what had occurred.

"Debbie, David, there has been a very bad tragedy. Your father is sick; someone who is very bad hurt him. This person, who is in jail now, tried to kill your father and now Daddy will need to stay in the hospital for a while."

"Should we pray for Daddy?" Debbie asked.

"Oh, yes, my dear baby girl. Most definitely we need to pray for Daddy and for the woman that was with him; and even for the man that hurt them. We need to pray for all of them."

David Jr. had been sitting silently, looking glum, but also determined. "Mommy, I think that we should go right now; go where Daddy went before I was born. He told me that he went right up and talked to God. Wouldn't that be best, to talk to God in person?"

Deborah closed her eyes and shook her head. "God is everywhere; if we pray right here it's just as if we were standing in front of Him and talking right into His ear. So, don't worry about where He is. He will hear us and take care of Daddy. And if He doesn't do it right away, you still must keep believing and trying, because He always hears us when we pray."

"Where's Little Bit, Mommy? Is he hurt, too?" Debbie asked.

"He was hurt just a little, dear. He's in the room with Daddy. He's doing his job, making sure that the nurses do theirs. As a matter of fact, I think that it's time for us to go see Daddy."

Deborah stood up and took her children's hands and led them to David's room.

೭ францу

LXII. Peskew Responds

RANDY PESKEW ENTERED HIS LAB AND SLAMMED THE door as hard as he could. The built-in curbing system only allowed it to close lightly. He started to punch the wall, but thought twice and decided that a broken hand would only add to his sorrow. Instead he picked up a small computer from the first table he found and threw it against the wall. He was careful, however, not to destroy his own computer.

He sat down at his monitor and stared at the blank screen, oblivious to the passage of time. When he finally hit the startup button the room lights had automatically turned on as the sun became a faint pink hew in the western sky. As the console sprang to life, the first icon he saw was the encrypted symbol for the picomatrix system that would permit biological assimilation. Wretched humanity was responsible for his suffering and it was time to stop all such useless sorrow. It would be for the good of all mankind. No more bowing to an amoral deity, no more Diblonski's exploiting human weakness for personal profit. It was time to bring perfect order into the galaxy.

In quick order he downloaded all the data on the biological assimilation program and key that he had discovered. He erased the data from all the other lab computers; his and his coworkers'. He substituted the previously devised dummy "key" that would keep his coworkers unaware of his actions until it was too late and he loaded the powerful scanner into his bag. The key, the scanner, and a portable transmitter were all he needed to carry out his plan.

I don't need the help of the others, he thought. This is simple enough, a couple of weeks creating a program that will allow simultaneous uploading of the "key" and universal implementation and the world would be a better place; a true utopia. No more hatred, no more jealousy or envy, no violence, no ridicule, no ridicule. He thought for a moment and then sat down at the console and created a message, something to be delivered in forty eight hours:

"To A. Diblonski
From R. Peskew, VP for R&D

This letter tenders my resignation from Diblonski Ltd. I have discovered that my particular skills are not suitable for such a sophisticated operation as Diblonski Ltd. In particular, the promotion of and exultation of human weaknesses by your organization cannot be condoned and should not be promulgated. To be part of such an organization is more than I can bear. I am sorry that I cannot continue in such a well-equipped facility. I will continue my research as a private consultant and I will be happy to assist you in such a capacity once I have established myself. I will contact you about such a possibility. Thank you.
    --Randy Peskew"

He set it to be delivered only to Diblonski himself. He checked around the lab one more time and left, closing the door quietly.

෯෨

LXIII. More Powder

LIEUTENANT RYAN GLANCED AT THE NEW REPORT THAT had appeared on his desk. Another murder in the park, probably attempted robbery. He was about to sign off when he saw mention of some unusual pollen found in the trace analysis from the victim. He took a closer look at the name; all it said was Crash.

So this thug, Crash, finally received justice, he thought. Some big celebrity; wins a few hands of poker and all of a sudden he's a big sensation. Ryan remembered a few run-ins with Crash before he achieved his recent notoriety, mostly minor stuff, petty theft, assaults and such, but now it looked like he was somehow in the thick of some very high profile criminal activity. The lieutenant wondered whether Crash was an innocent victim or more deeply involved.

He read the report more closely. He was found alone in a secluded area of Central Park. Analysis suggested that he had recently fired a neural disrupter, although there were obvious attempts to clear away this evidence. The chemical analysis of the pollen found on him was pending, but Ryan was willing to bet a week's pay that it would match that from Sanders, Beauty, and McCally. These cases were beginning to get interesting. *There must be a common thread,* he thought; something other than pollen; find that and he was sure he'd find his murderer. However, pollen was not much to go on.

He called the lab to find out when the analysis of the pollen would be completed and was pleased when he was told that they had just finished and it matched the findings from the other cases. *Fascinating,* he mused. *Our murderer has an interest in horticulture.* He called for his car and took a short ride to City College where he hoped to find an expert in botany that could help him.

෨෧

LIV. Gideon

GIDEON AWOKE TO FAINT LIGHT COMING THROUGH THE window high above the floor. He looked around his room, three by three, padded walls and floor, and nothing else. He screamed at the door and this time the three attendants arrived in only a few minutes. The same routine ensued as he was allowed to use the hygiene center, eat, and he was left alone. As the day passed he was visited on regular basis, every six hours on the dot with food, water, and hygienic facilities. Gideon was becoming discouraged at the prospect of a future filled with nothing else.

Surely something is wrong, he thought. He was suspect in two attempted murders; shouldn't the authorities want to question him? Shouldn't he be allowed to speak in his own defense? Didn't he have any rights? The monotony went on until the fourth day when a new visitor appeared. A man in a white coat, with dark hair and pale skin, came with the three attendants. He motioned to them after Gideon had finished his morning routine and the tallest guard aimed a small pointer at Gideon, pushed a button, and Gideon was rendered unconscious. He awoke perhaps fifteen minutes later in the office of the man in the white coat.

The man sat opposite Gideon in a tall chair; the two separated by his large wooden desk and a plaque that bore his name, Dr. Samson. Gideon sat on a hard chair, his arms bound behind him and to the chair.

The doctor addressed him. "Good morning, Mr. Jones; my name is Dr. Samson. You are here to undergo a preliminary psychiatric evaluation prior to questioning for the attempted murder of two people. Unlike the world outside these walls, in here you are considered guilty until you can demonstrate to me and the authorities here that you are innocent and not a danger to yourself, our staff, and society as a whole. Do you understand what I have said? Please nod yes or no."

Gideon nodded yes.

"Very good, you are a fast learner. This should proceed very quickly and smoothly. Now, then, tell me your name."

"Gideon Jones."

"Your age."

"Thirty-six."

"And, what were you doing at the hotel of David Sanders?"

"I was to meet him to discuss the minor altercation he and I had experienced several days before. I wanted to apologize."

"Did you find your significant other, one Miss Beauty, in a compromising position with Mr. Sanders, thus compelling you, in a fit of anger, to assault both of them?"

"No."

Dr. Samson's voice started to rise. "Am I to believe that you have the self control and sense of calm to stand by when you discover that your woman, who could easily rival Aphrodite's beauty, has shared her affections with another man, and not just any man; one whom you had just a few days before had a serious altercation? Do you expect me to believe that?" He was screaming now, with his face only a few centimeters from Gideon's.

"Yes," Gideon answered calmly. "However, I must add that your assumptions are incorrect."

Dr. Samson's face was bright red and Gideon heard a faint wheezing as the doctor returned to his chair and fumbled through his drawer. He took a green pill and then a blue one.

"That Valusil is not good to mix with Methamine. Your blood pressure will go way up," Gideon said in a matter of fact, informative way.

The doctor laughed. "You seem very perceptive, 'Doctor,' but I've taken these for years. I know what I'm doing."

"I hope you're right. They recently changed Valusil's chemical structure and the new formulation is more rapidly converted to epinephrine in your body; especially when mixed with a monoamine compound, which, I'm sure you know, Methamine is."

"Quiet; you are here to be interviewed, not to give a lecture in pharmacology." The doctor rubbed his temples as he stared down at the desk drawer.

"The chemical structure is usually listed on the insert disc, which should be in the original bottle."

"I don't need an inmate to preach to me about . . ." The doctor's voice trailed off as he sat back in his chair and then slumped forward.

Dr. Samson looked up slowly, his face was flushed and beads of perspiration formed on his forehead. Gideon saw the doctor's eyes roll back; he tried to jump up and catch him as the doctor suddenly stood up and then fell forward, crashing onto the desk, and then to the floor where he lay motionless. Gideon, still bound to his chair, felt helpless. He saw a red button on the desk, a panic button, perhaps. With great effort he stood up and bent forward to hit the button with his head. An alarm sounded as he lost his balance and crashed to the floor, landing on top of the unconscious doctor.

More trouble, he thought as his three attendants raced into the room. They roughly pulled Gideon off the doctor, knocking his shoulder out of its socket as one of them bent down over Dr. Samson. "He's dead, I think. Emergency medical team to room 128. You're in big trouble," he screamed at Gideon, who was very aware of the obvious.

❧⚬❧

LV. In David's Room

DEBORAH, DAVID JR., AND DEBBIE QUIETLY WENT INTO David's room. Deborah stood back as the two young children went up to their father's bedside. David Jr. stood at the side as Debbie climbed onto the bed and knelt next to her injured father. She saw that slight appearance of a smile and exclaimed, "Oh Mommy, he's just sleeping. Daddy, you need to get up because you promised to teach me how to fly in outer space." She reached out and shook him, but he didn't move.

David Jr. was silent and bent his head down and started to cry.

Little Debbie looked over at her brother and smiled. "Don't cry, David; Daddy's just asleep and he'll be up and home to play with us real soon. I'm sure of it. God loves him and he does so much work for Him that I'm sure Daddy will be all better before we know it."

Deborah moved closer to the hospital bed. "That's right, baby girl. He'll be home soon. We all just have to pray and God will bring him home to us." She managed a faint smile through the tears that filled her eyes.

"Mommy, Daddy always said that God hears all our prayers and answers them when the time is right. If we all pray really hard won't God answer us sooner?"

"Yes, baby girl, that's right. If anyone in this universe knows about God, it's Daddy. We just have to believe that this is another way that God is using Daddy for his work." Deborah turned to her son, who remained silent. "David, your sister is right. We must put our faith in God and believe that He will bring your father back to us."

The boy climbed up on the hospital bed and stared into his father's eyes and held his hand. He thought he felt a light squeeze and the smile on David Sr.'s face seemed to grow bigger. "He knows we're here, Mommy, I'm sure of it." The sadness left the boy's eyes and he held the injured man's hand tighter. His reticence departed with the sadness and the boy started talking to his father, nonstop about everything that had happened to him and the family in the past several days.

Deborah felt more hopeful as the boy continued his monologue. Maybe he can hear us in there somewhere. She smiled at her two children and wished she had as much faith. She closed her eyes and said a silent prayer, not a prayer asking for healing, for she had prayed this constantly since she had been informed of the tragedy. She prayed for strength; strength of faith that would help her believe that everything that had transpired was part of God's plan and, ultimately, for good.

కావం

LVI. Ryan

LT. RYAN LEFT THE BIOLOGY CENTER AT CITY COLLEGE shaking his head at the so-called experts. "Plant DNA isn't important . . . no one ever took the time . . . hopeless task" was all he had found out. He was back to square one; the same pollen found on the victims of four murders or attempted murders. The break he had hoped for never materialized and he was left with nothing.

Gideon Jones was the key and he was gone, who knows where. The Northeast region chief was not going to be happy and someone was going to be made the scapegoat. *I guess I'll need to get my hands dirty on this case*, he thought. He pulled into Central and headed for the morgue; the post mortem on Crash had been completed and he ran over to the lab to get the results. The report was just coming up on the monitors when he sat down to review everything. COD was a single shot from a light gun, pierced the heart with death almost instantaneous. Unusually high epinephrine levels in the bloodstream, high levels of euphoricin consistent with recreational use. This caught his eye and he pulled up the report of Rep. McCally's death.

Both had euphoricin in their systems and analysis revealed that the purity levels were exact matches and the impurity analysis also was an exact match. The wheels in Ryan's head began to turn as it became apparent that there were now two pieces of evidence that tied these murders together, the pollen and the drug. Time to dig a little deeper. "Background profiles on the victims, please," he politely asked the computer and then he added, "side by side correlation with all intersections highlighted."

In less than ten seconds, profiles of the two were displayed with yellow highlights over everything they had in common. "Both Pisces . . . both male . . . single . . . euphoricin . . . pollen." *Nothing*, Ryan thought, *another dead end.* He shut off the monitor and looked out the window and shouted, "Gideon Jones where are you?" The buzzing of cars from the street drowned out his words as he returned to his office to pursue a more solvable crime.

ॐॐ

LVII. Beauty

BEAUTY SAT ON HER HUGE ROUND BED, HER BODY caressed by soft silky sheets. The sights she had witnessed were branded on her mind and she was afraid the images would return, but also afraid that they wouldn't. She found another sumptuous banquet waiting for her and she picked at the finest crab, caviar, and fresh fruits and vegetables, more out of habit than hunger. She sipped a glass of white wine and, as soon as she finished, sat down near the curtain as the display resumed.

Once again she saw the children playing in a handsome park while their parents sat nearby chatting, keeping a watchful eye on their young offspring. Beauty could see that there were eleven children, five boys and six girls. They were happily playing with a jump rope, then running and laughing; all very attractive and neatly dressed. As they ran, one of the girls fell and skinned her knee, and Beauty could see a large dirty spot on her pretty pink dress. The little girl lay on the ground crying.

Beauty expected her mother to go and scoop the injured child up into her arms and console her, but the parents all just sat and continued talking. The other children, however, gathered around the poor girl, each carrying a large stick. Beauty watched and then tried to turn away as the ten playmates raised their sticks above their heads and with perfect choreography brought their weapons crashing down on the poor defenseless child. As they did this the parents looked on with very approving looks on their faces, even the girl's own mother did nothing to help. The beating went on for an eternity, and when it was over the children and parents once again left, leaving the beaten child behind, blood running out of her ears and mouth as she lay motionless on the ground.

After several minutes the light appeared again in the distance and the hideous beast shuffled into the park. He slowed as he approached, looking directly at Beauty with the saddest eyes that she had ever seen. Instead of coming to the window, he stopped at the side of the helpless child, bent down and gently lifted her into his short scaly arms. Beauty thought she saw the girl take a breath as the beast slowly slinked away, gently cradling the injured babe. Beauty saw a tear fall from the beast's eye as his light faded away in the distance.

When he had disappeared, the curtain closed and Beauty ran to her bed, threw herself down and wept uncontrollably, until her sorrow was replaced by deep dreamless sleep.

৵৶

LVIII. Dr. Trestco

DR. TRESTCO SAT IN THE HOSPITAL CAFETERIA NIBBLING on a synthesized muffin, reading the morning news on the table monitor. She looked up as Deborah came in and sat down next to her. She had a plate of fruit and a cup of tea and a very exhausted look as her large glasses failed to hide the deep, dark circles under her eyes.

"You look tired," Dr. Trestco remarked, stating the obvious. "You look like I used to look when I was an intern. All this modern medicine and technology that almost makes doctors an unnecessary luxury and they still make us go through these archaic internships; some progress."

Deborah looked at the young physician and yawned. "Excuse me, Doctor; I was up most of the night; part of the time sitting at David's bedside, but also doing some work. It's funny, though, I'm always up until three or four working on something. I don't know why I'm so tired today."

"It's different if you're worrying while you're up, but, no matter. I'm going to see him when I'm finished; I'm sure I'll get the same dirty looks from the nurses," Trestco replied.

"I don't see what's wrong with doctors examining their patients. The whole concept seems silly to me and somewhat cold."

"That's why I'm going to see him and Beauty. I know the books say it's contraindicated, but seeing a patient in person, talking to him, examining him, just doesn't seem wrong to me. I'll either get kicked off the staff or start a whole new trend. The rebirth of traditional medicine; doctors talking to their patients and actually showing some concern."

Deborah looked down at her food and then said, "I'm transferring David to a hospital closer to home. I know it's not that far from Wildwood to New York, but I'd rather be home and the kids would rather be home and I'm sure it won't make a difference to David. He can be 'locked in' at Monmouth Hospital the same as here."

"I can't say that I blame you. We've done all that we can; he's stable and you still have your life to live."

Deborah looked at Trestco and stared into her eyes; she saw strength and compassion, a look that reminded her of Joshua. "You know, Doctor," she noted, "you remind me of a friend, actually. He was going to be a doctor, but quit before he finished medical school. Despite an outward appearance of indifference and cynicism, he is the most compassionate person I ever met. He actually delivered my son at my home; unfortunately, he got mixed up with some very dangerous people and, for his own safety, I haven't seen him for years. Anyway, you have some of his qualities; you care, far more than other doctors that I've met."

"Thank you for the compliment." Trestco thought for a moment and then added, "So many doctors I know seem to go through the motions. They put their Green Dots on auto, go out to casinos night after night, partying, and leave actual patient care to all the monitors and therapeutic units and the nurses. If you question them, they hide behind that 'landmark' study that says physicians need to be detached. It's so easy to fall into such a trap, and the sad thing is nobody knows or cares. I guess that's why I went into trauma. Trauma is one of the few specialties where being hands-on can make a difference. And I'm lucky to be so talented. I would have been sent off to the hinterlands years ago if I wasn't good at what I do. Unfortunately, it takes more than one person to rewrite the medical journals."

"Any other people in your life?"

"Not really; just the usual occasional fling after a night at the Casino. I used to go frequently, but after a while it becomes tiring; the feeling of being on display. I'd rather stay home and go to a virtual casino; just as much fun without having to deal with an eighty kilo headache, if you know what I mean."

"Oh, I know exactly what you're saying. I tried that scene once, but then I got caught up in the ITP and all that notoriety, and now kids and

David and still lots of work. But believe me, Doctor, I wouldn't trade my life for anything."

"Even with David as he is?"

"Yes, even with all that has happened. I have one thing that you lack, Doctor. Belief. Belief that God chose David for a very special task; a task that has only started. At first I despaired; I was angry and felt lost, but my kids showed me what true faith is. You see, they believe that their father has been given the most important job in the solar system. God will not abandon David until the job is done; if he can do the job while in this coma, then let it be done. We all do our best, which may not be very good, but God has nothing but His best. Even if we don't comprehend His purpose now, someday we will. Through all these trials, all He asks of us is to remain faithful, just as He remains faithful to us. Does this make any sense?'

"A little. I've never believed in any sort of God; Science has been my God."

"As it was mine."

"But, I've seen things in this hospital that defy scientific explanation. Perhaps I need to open my eyes and see." Trestco looked at the time projection and jumped up. "I'm sorry, but I really need to go. It was so nice chatting with you. Good luck with David. I'm sure we'll see each other again. In the meantime, feel free to call anytime."

"Thank you. Please, take care of Beauty. I have the feeling that you are all she has in the world at the moment."

Dr. Trestco hurried out and Deborah went back to her breakfast, her thoughts turning to her kids and arranging transport for David.

৵৽৽

LIX. Really Big Trouble

GIDEON WAS ROUGHLY PICKED UP BY THE THREE GUARDS as the emergency medical team arrived. Of course, Gideon knew that the doctor was permanently dead and that no amount of resuscitation could revive him. Even though the time was short, the combination of drugs over such a long time created an irreversible condition. He started to protest to his "attendants" that he could not be held responsible for the doctor's death.

"Surely you three know that I could not have done a thing to the doctor. I was chained to the chair and only a herculean effort on my part allowed me to call you. Think about it, why would I have called if I had killed the poor man. I would have sat quietly in my chair and waited."

"Quiet," one of the guards yelled as they threw Gideon into his cell, only this time they didn't slam the door. They each pulled out a new device; a new method of punishment. They stood back and fired the modified disrupters at Gideon, taking turns aiming at different parts of his body. Gideon did his best to cover up, but each sent a wave of burning, intense pain through his body. The assault seemed to go on and on, lasting for an eternity, which was in reality about thirty minutes. When it was over, Gideon lay prostrate on the floor of his cell. There was not an external mark on his body, and the pain had stopped except for aching in every muscle and joint of his body.

He lay silent as his assailants left him and darkness fell. It was hours before Gideon felt able to move; *they'll be back,* he thought, *and next time may be worse.* Unfortunately he didn't see any options. I hope someone figures out that I had nothing to do with that doctor's death or else mine will be next.

❧

LXX. CNS Probe

ONE OF THE GREATEST ADVANCES IN MENTAL HEALTH IS the CNS Probe, which holds the promise of accurately characterizing and diagnosing the myriad psychiatric disorders. Generic schizophrenia was discovered via CNS Probe to be a wide spectrum of disorders, each requiring specific and varying therapy. The basic principle of the CNS Probe is that under identical circumstances of external stimulation and sensory input the Central Nervous Systems should respond in a predictable manner. Variations from the predicted norm are interpreted with incredible accuracy and catalogued to provide extremely precise diagnoses and therapeutic guidelines.

The Probe, although still experimental, has been widely utilized and has been credited with returning a majority of the mentally ill to mainstream, productive society. Resistance by a small faction of mental health professionals, who cite flawed anectodal studies that suggest the probe can be harmful, has been denounced by mainstream psychiatry as irresponsible and detrimental to society as a whole.

The probing process consists of placing the subject in a standardized environment devoid of any stimulation or sensory input. A uniform assimilation period of forty minutes is initiated and then probing of the entire CNS system by sector, then by neural pathway, followed by neurotransmitter levels provides a roadmap of the brain that can be correlated with standardized databases allowing extremely accurate diagnosis. Success has been achieved at a remarkable ninety percent; accurate diagnoses consistently leading to subsequent return to functional mainstream society.

The ten percent that are deemed unreliable were usually due to the subject's idiosyncracies and/or anomalies. It has been discovered that there are individuals that have paradoxical responses to the controlled environment that lead to false positive and false negative results. Such individuals usually have an innate or learned ability to block the probe even in the sensory deprived environment. It also has been learned that subjects known to be pathologic liars, who are able to influence physiologic functions and mask emotions often give false readings when probed. More traditional methods of diagnosis are required in such individuals and accuracy is at best fifty percent.

Very recently the CNS Probe has been coupled with the Gamma Beam manipulation of CNS receptors and neurotransmitters. This newly devised therapeutic manipulation grew out of research into old style ECT or Electro Convulsive Therapy. This medieval, barbaric treatment for depression, also called electroshock therapy, induced a generalized seizure, under sedation or anesthesia, often improving the depressive symptoms in the patient, but at the price of memory loss and with considerable variability in results.

The new controlled Gamma Beams allowed the introduction of small charges at very specific sites within the brain. This refinement has shown great promise towards permanently altering electrochemical imbalances within the CNS of the mentally ill, facilitating their return to functional society. The mechanism is described as setting off a microscopic shock within a specific series of synapses which alters neurotransmitter levels, usually permanently. The Gamma Beam precisely localizes the target and a photon carrying a burst of energy is released in that locale. The level of energy delivered and released can be very accurately controlled and the response is predictable with an error margin of less than ten percent. Final testing has begun in this extremely exciting area with widespread implementation expected within the next two years.

భువ

LXXI. David and Ruth

DAVID AND RUTH SAT BY THE WATER'S EDGE, HOLDING hands, oblivious to everything around them. They stared into each other's eyes and savored the moments that they were sharing together. The water was like glass and their reflections looked back at them with smiling approval.

"I hope this moment never ends," Ruth said as she turned and kissed David lightly on his lips.

"You are so beautiful, God has truly blessed me," David answered, but in his bliss a sense of trouble came to him. He looked out over the crystal clear water and saw the image of Joshua beneath the surface, as if he were watching his friend through a window. What he saw was troubling as Joshua was isolated, suffocating and his life was fading away. Demons circled around ready to escort him to a place that David couldn't see, but left him feeling troubled and worried for his friend. He jumped to his feet and almost dove in the water to try to reach the dying image, but Ruth grabbed him.

"There's nothing you can do, all we can do is have faith and believe that it is all for the best and that in the end it will be for good," Ruth counseled, displaying the wisdom David should have had.

David threw a pebble into the water and the image faded away with the ripples in the water. David sat down again and held Ruth tightly. *Paradise lost again,* he thought.

৵৵৶

LXXII. Locked Away

GIDEON STAYED ALONE IN HIS CELL FOR DAYS. THE REGU-
lar delivery of food and facilities continued with only the briefest visits
by his guards. He had no time outside his cell, no contact of any sort.
His thoughts wandered towards the most hideous possibilities ranging from an eternity of isolation in his tiny cell to eventual insanity, his
mind ravaged by his own unbridled thoughts turned inward by utter
hopelessness. He started counting the days, although he found it difficult to keep track. He sat and recounted the multitude of books and
scholarly works he had read, some of them he recited out loud, doing
his best to not make a single error.

He thought about God and the Bible, David, Deborah, and mostly
Beauty. Finally, he had nearly resigned himself to eventual madness
when the door opened and he was taken, with his eyes shielded and
hands immobilized to meet another "therapist." He remembered
thinking that he felt like a lamb being led to the slaughter.

He was seated in a large comfortable chair, unbound, the room
bright and warm. First a rolling table was brought to him laden with
fresh food, water and a monitor carrying the latest news. His initial
wariness gave way to hunger and he gorged himself. He paid little
attention to the news that was broadcast until an item came on that
stated that David Sanders and the woman he had been assaulted with,
one called Beauty, remained in hospital suffering from complete neural disruption. Hope for their recovery was slim; Sanders' wife, Dr.
Deborah Tennyson, remained at his bedside at Monmouth General
Hospital where he had been transported once he was stabilized. Miss
Beauty remained in New York Hospital.

The alleged perpetrator, Mr. Gideon Jones, was being held at an
unnamed facility under suspicion of attempted murder. As soon as
this report was finished the cart automatically rolled away and the

door opposite him opened and a woman in a white coat entered and sat down across from him.

"Mr. Jones, my name is Dr. Sela Corwyn. I'm a psychiatrist specializing in the criminal mind. I'd like to ask you some questions, if you don't mind."

"Go ahead, Doctor; I'll certainly do my best to answer whatever I can," Gideon said with a cautious voice.

"Thank you. Now, can you tell me what exactly happened on the day of the alleged assault against Mr. Sanders and Miss Beauty, as she is called?"

Gideon recounted all the events leading up to his current dilemma, including his attendance at David's sermon, their dinner together, the altercation, trip to Saratoga and return; everything up to the present interview. He did not reveal his true identity. When he finished, Dr. Corwyn shook her head slowly.

"Something doesn't add up. Why should you care one bit about Sanders' romantic escapades, someone that you barely knew?"

Gideon realized that this doctor was bright and perceptive and would not be easily fooled. "I guess I have an over-developed sense of morality. It did not seem proper to me that a man who, only a short time before, had been preaching the word of God was now breaking some of God's basic rules."

The doctor stared at Gideon for a moment, apparently contemplating the veracity of Gideon's response. "Mr. Jones, I'm not sure exactly what to think. The reports I've reviewed suggest that you are a danger to society. That you had two serious outbreaks in a very short time and that while confined in this facility your actions led to the death of one of our finest counselors. I think that a CNS Probe is the only answer to this paradox; the contradiction presented by your apparent rationality now and the considerable irrational behavior you previously demonstrated."

☙❧

LXXIII. In the Box

THE CNS PROBE WAS SET IN AN OPEN COURTYARD; IT appeared to be a large concrete box with elaborate carvings in the side and top. Gideon thought it was unusual to have that appearance, rather than a sleek high tech look so common everywhere else. They walked him through the control room which had windows that looked out into the yard, past an impressive array of machinery with flashing lights and luminous dials. As he walked past, one of the technicians pushed a button and the front and top of the Probe opened.

"The Probe is very safe, Mr. Jones," Dr. Corwyn explained. "All that is intended for today is synaptic and transmitter mapping. You will be placed inside, given time to assimilate and reach the appropriate steady state and then the probe will commence. It is perfectly painless and shouldn't take more than one hour from start to finish. Are you ready?"

"Why is it set apart; in the middle of that courtyard? It looks like an ornamental statue, rather than a highly sensitive medical device."

"It is vital for proper neurophysiologic readings that there be no electromagnetic interference from surrounding structures. We can compensate for the static fields emanating from the planet surfaces and atmosphere, but modern buildings exhibit too much variability. That is why the probe stands alone. You can thank our benefactor, Diblonski Ltd., for this elaborate machine. They donated the money for its purchase only six months ago. Now, in you go,"

Gideon slowly shook his head, hesitating for a moment; but he saw the guards with their heavy clubs and decided that he would do well to go along with them. They took him to a small room where he removed his clothes and donned very light, almost weightless gown. They had him lay down on a very soft mat which slowly moved into the Probe and the covers closed.

He was engulfed by darkness, his arms were at his side and he had almost no room to move. His head lay on a very comfortable pillow and he felt the chamber around his body fill with water which apparently was set at a temperature for optimum comfort. All in all, he had the sense of floating freely, comfortable and serene. He relaxed, hoping to achieve "steady state" quickly so as to be finished quickly. Although it was perfectly painless and, in a sense, very relaxing, he didn't trust anyone in this place; thus far all he had experienced was pain and misery. These thoughts started to fade as he grew more comfortable in the sensory deprivation chamber. He lost track of time; it seemed like the hour was progressing very slowly.

On the outside the situation was anything but serene as chaos erupted. Sirens blared and lights flashed as local police and federal agents descended upon the facility. A uniformed captain from the Westchester County Sheriff led a cadre of uniformed deputies and black-suited federal agents serving warrants and making arrests. The facility had been under investigation for many months; apparently, accused of extreme cruelty to inmates and the authorities had come to shut the place down. As the staff was arrested and processed, care was taken to be sure that each inmate was accounted for. Unfortunately, no one accounted for Gideon. He had never been officially registered; consequently, there was no record of him being interred.

The entire complex was deserted within one hour of the raid and Gideon was left inside the CNS Probe, forgotten. The one technician who tried to inform the captain was given a hard blow to the midsection, handcuffed and packed into the waiting police van.

ॐ∽ॐ

LXXIV. Coryllos

CORYLLOS HAD A REVELATION. HE HAD AN IMAGE OF Gideon Jones and as he stared at it he was struck by a vague familiarity. He pulled up the file he had discovered at Joshua Smith's apartment and found the image of the lone man. There was a striking similarity between the two, not an exact match, but close enough.

"Steps to alter number one to match number two," he commanded the computer. The console worked silently for about twenty seconds, and when finished the two images were nearly identical. There was a series of steps listed on the monitor that the computer had gone through to make the requested alteration. He noticed that anyone with a few bucks could buy a kit and go to any of the automated salons and make the alterations, at least temporarily.

All this confirmed that Joshua Smith and Gideon Jones were, almost certainly, the same person. DNA samples from each would confirm his suspicions. He checked the database, but there were no records from either individual. He looked up police records and found the case of an unsolved auto explosion shortly after the death of Rep. McCally. He did find a record of DNA recovered at the scene and was able to access the result, which, presumably, gave him Smith's DNA. However that still left him lacking Jones. He was surprised that Jones was not in the police database, having been arrested recently.

He looked up public records of the arrest and found that Jones had disappeared and authorities were unaware of his whereabouts, but that a discreet search was underway. I guess I can wait, he thought. It's been more than seven years. A little longer won't make a difference. With any luck, Smith/Jones was already dead and he'd have one less task to deal with.

As he finished his research, he closed the file on Smith and opened his favorite file of images. Over the many years, he had kept records of most of his projects, ranging from simple individual performances to those carried out on massive grand scales. As he reviewed his achievements, the soaring operas of Wagner started to play in the background.

Memories of thousands of years waltzed through his mind. In the beginning he was just like all the others, but the chief saw something in him and put him on this path. The first few times were sad and woeful as he orchestrated sibling rivalries that led to tragedy, mother against father, always allowing nature to surface and burying the enemy within. The projects became mundane and regular and his initial sorrow was replaced by workman-like efficiency and eventually a sense of pride, although a hint of sadness was always present. For thousands of years they flourished. He was particularly fond of the artistry of Rome. Crucifixion was the pinnacle; the suffering, lingering, agony; cries for mercy were music that rivaled the greatest operas, followed by death and eternal torment.

He thought that they had achieved final victory when he nailed the final spike and thrust the sword into the side of that accursed Galilean, Jesus. The false claims of his resurrection were just that; lies brought forth by desperate souls anxious to feel justified in their folly.

The wars and pestilence that he engineered were his symphonies. Oh, how ingenious mankind could be as they found new ways to carry out his work. And he was always present, ready to give a word of encouragement to the human artists that brought his genius to reality. Humanity living close together in filth brought the Black Death. The passage of time coupled with ever growing human ingenuity brought forth wonderful, new weapons and mankind's perverse need to declare their superiority increased his own efficiency. Wars could be fought from a distance and millions could be killed. The chief nearly triumphed when he raised up that Hitler from the rubble and the gutter, but just missed.

Finally, after Nagasaki, he was sure they had finally reached the end. Humankind could never have the restraint it needed and surely would finally end it all. But, he was fooled again and such weapons were outlawed and destroyed. Wars disappeared and he felt lost; his sense of purpose faded away, sadness and loneliness percolated to the surface. His greatest fears started to rise; that he would be cast into the pit, his years of faithful service a vague memory, replaced by endless pain and suffering with only one hope and consolation. But, it was not yet his time.

A new way appeared; the chief gave them what they wanted, lulled them into a state of apparent bliss. No more wars, but instead of millions, now they could claim billions. It's true that it wasn't as much fun, but his work was easier and the deep inner feeling of sadness gradually diminished. Instead of massive symphonies he now composed short concertos; each a masterpiece, smaller, but more refined. The sweet perfection he achieved with the disposition of that vermin, Crash, was one such a work of art. The terror frozen into the victim's face was all the payment he could ever want.

He looked through the remaining images, death and destruction, testimony to a life well spent in service to his master. But there was a lone image that was different, a figure of tragedy and a source of sorrow that plagued him always. He quickly shut it off and the image faded from the monitor and from his thoughts. He took a break and lay down, took several pills and let his mind soar in a totally different direction.

෨ᢀᢀ

LXXV. Beauty

BEAUTY'S OPULENT CELL WAS BECOMING A WAKING nightmare. The jewels, finery, gourmet food all were meaningless. All that she cared about was the poor, hideous beast; a thing that didn't seem to care that he was ugly, but only wanted what was best for others. She envied this monster, who seemed to possess nothing but compassion for others.

Breakfast was waiting for her when she awoke and she didn't even look at it. She had no desire to eat, to dress in fancy clothes, or admire luxurious jewelry. All she wished was that the beast would return and bring his caring and compassionate love to her. However, the curtain was pulled back to reveal only the ten children playing together. Once again the parents sat nearby; it all seemed to be joyful and loving. Today, for the first time, the children ran up to the window and she could see their faces.

As they approached, seemingly oblivious to her presence she saw deep red eyes and devilish grins that exuded evil and malice. All the children were carrying objects, one a club, another a rake, another with a rope. Each had his own weapon and the ten were slowly forming a circle around the unsuspecting parents. As the adults chatted amongst themselves, ignorant of the little devils that seemed to be preparing to attack, Beauty saw a light in the distance. The children saw it also and backed away from their parents and went back to play.

They all got up and left before the beast appeared. Beauty waited anxiously for its arrival. In a few minutes he was standing at the window, peering inside, but apparently unable to see her trapped inside. The brute stood up as tall as he could and pushed on the window as if he were trying to escape to a new world; trying to get away from something. From her side of the window, Beauty banged on the glass, but all for naught. After a few minutes the monster went away, the curtain closed, and Beauty was left alone; fearful of what the next spectacle would be.

❧

LXXVI. Trapped and Forgotten

GIDEON LAY IN THE CNS PROBE WAITING. HE WAS NO great judge of time, but he was sure an hour had come and gone. He called out, "I'm still here; is there anyone out there?" He was answered with silence.

"Hello, can I get out now?" More silence.

Out of the frying pan into the fire, he thought. He tried to get up, but he couldn't move. The bath he was in grew colder as night fell with the power cut off. "This is the end," he said out loud. But then he decided that surely there was someone that knew he was there and he would be found. This is the twenty-second century; people are not buried alive, not left to die horribly, and it was at that moment that the realization came to him. That was precisely what was intended; that he be buried alive, to suffer and die a horrible death.

This truth washed over him and he saw the figure of Aaron Diblonski laughing as he sat by his huge fire, admiring his flowers and thinking how one who had the audacity to challenge his empire was in such torment. Gideon felt his face flush and the anger and hatred boil up inside. He moved his arms up against the top of his stone cold casket to no avail. He screamed at the top of his lungs and only silence replied. Finally, after several exhausting hours he gave up and fell into a fitful sleep.

He awoke to a warm feeling. The sun was shining down on his prison and the concrete box began to heat up. He felt the need to urinate and now realized his survival was going to be a very complicated matter. He was able to bring some of the water up to his head so that he could drink it and he took as much as he could hold. As time passed, if he lasted very long, the water would become contaminated and undrinkable. He moved his head from side to side and felt two small holes on either side. Air would not be a problem as these were two outlets that allowed some air in and out. He tried to move his arms and legs back and forth, but he was very confined and limited. He did squeeze and relax his muscles as much as possible to try to keep his blood circulating. Everything he did was with the intention that someone would eventually realize he was missing and would come searching. But, who was he kidding. Beauty was nearly dead, he had no family, the police, who were likely owned by Diblonski had put him in this hellhole; no doubt, he was completely alone and forgotten.

Might as well forget about rescue, he thought; *no one is going to miss me and everyone thinks I'm a killer anyway.*

"Is this it, God?" he said out loud. "Are you testing me like Job, allowing Satan to do his worst. But, I'm not Job. I never have given you any regard. I've read your story, but I don't think that I believe it. Is that it then? I'm a pawn in some cosmic battle of the wills between you and Satan/ Diblonski. Why me? Why me?"

Gideon went silent as his thoughts drifted back to times past, his triumphs as a boy and young man, the adventures around the ITP, battling the minions of Diblonski, the demon, Richard Cosby, Miss Jameson, Deborah, Little Bit, David, Ruth Rising, and finally, Beauty. He started to cry, not because of the pain he was starting to feel, nor because of his impending death. No, he cried for Beauty, the first person he had ever loved in that special way, now lost to him forever. In his sorrow, he saw her face as if she were lying beside him. His crying stopped and he was sure that he heard her voice.

"Gideon, Gideon, I know how you suffer, but in the end we will be together for eternity. You must believe that all that happens will be for good. Trust in the powers from above. You helped show them to me and now you must believe in Him."

He stopped his whimpering and lay still. His pain was being replaced by numbness and he completely lost track of time. He drifted in and out of consciousness, his body grew used to the altering cycles of near freezing cold at night and stifling heat during the days. He soon ran out of drinkable water and resigned himself to the inevitable end; the freedom and peace of death rapidly becoming a welcome prospect.

But, God's plans are never so simple and he was not ready to bring this particular lost soul home. Gideon heard a loud BOOM and thought he heard tapping on the outside of his prison. Then a drip followed by another and another. Water was dribbling in through the air holes as rain pelted down on his casket and he, like Hezekiah, was granted an extension to his life. The water soon began to flow and he drank deeply, the stream let up and he relaxed for a moment; the flow resumed and he drank again. He squeezed the muscles in his arms and legs as if to say it's time for the blood to start circulating again.

And so he lived on and the water brought renewed hope; logic told him that if God went to such great lengths to sustain him then surely He would rescue him. His thoughts drifted to God, his memories of the Bible he had learned, the Book that had saved his life on more than one occasion. For the first time in his life he offered a prayer, but not one asking for life, for God had already granted this, nor for revenge on his enemies, because Gideon believed that vengeance would come from God. No, like Solomon, he prayed for wisdom. He prayed that when he was free he would have the wisdom to choose the proper path, to be worthy of the second chance that God had given him and with this prayer he fell into a peaceful sleep, trusting in a God he had never known, but one, Gideon was sure, knew him.

He awoke with the expected warmth of the coming day. Although he wouldn't say that he felt refreshed, the hope of the previous day remained and he was sure that he would be delivered. He couldn't say when, but he knew it was as sure as Ruth Rising being out in front. The day dragged on into night. He resumed his attempts to exercise his confined legs and arms, doing what little he could to maintain his circulation and to have some function when the time finally arrived. He noticed that despite great effort on his part there was little feeling with each contraction of his legs or arms. Still, he kept at it, consciously tensing and relaxing his ankles, then his calves, then thighs, abdomen and arms. He grew thirsty again and hoped for a second rainfall.

The night became day and still no rescue. His thoughts started to wander again, back to God and Beauty, but the two faded away replaced by the vision of Richard Cosby, holding Joshua hostage until Cosby's own evil was revealed and he was finally exposed as the demon that he was until poor Jameson dispatched him permanently to some other place. Poor Ms. Jameson; who wasn't really poor, but with her simple faith was the richest person Joshua or Gideon had ever known. He knew she was with the God she had searched for all her life. If there was a God out there, if all he asked was for a child-like faith, then it was certain that Jameson was there, in the front row of all the saints, singing praises to the Savior she had sought and finally discovered and embraced with her dying breath.

Jameson disappeared and the demonic form of Richard Cosby reappeared and with him his boss, Aaron Diblonski. But, they seemed more than visions. He felt a shiver as they appeared, the elegant image of Diblonski slowly morphing into a caricature of Satan, sunken red eyes, yellow teeth, hairless, dressed in black. The demons laughed and tormented Gideon, poking at him, screaming that he was doomed, that it was only a matter of time until he would be with them for eternity, suffering, as he was now, only a thousandfold worse. Gideon closed his eyes and screamed out, "No . . . No! God, make it stop!"

At that point the images faded and he felt a sharp stabbing pain in his chest and he found it almost impossible to breathe.

He consciously tried to take slow deliberate breaths, but the pain was intense and worse with each inspiration. He lost track of all time as he continued to think about each breath, but after a few minutes he passed out.

He remained unconscious for hours and when he finally came to he still had pain in his chest, although somewhat diminished, his breathing remained labored and he couldn't feel the rest of his body. Mercifully, with the numbness the pain lessened as he resumed concentrating on his breathing, slowly in and out. "Stay awake," he said to himself, over and over and again. "If you pass out again you won't wake up." He was sure of this.

He hung on like this for hours, until a sense of peace came over him and he stopped thinking about breathing and he relaxed. *The end at last,* he thought. But at that very moment, a light shined in and a wave of fresh air enveloped him as he closed his eyes, shielding them from the bright sun. He felt his body being gently elevated out of his living tomb. He heard some muffled voices saying, "carefully . . . gently . . . bring that shower and bring the scanner . . . we're not a moment too soon, look at that . . ." and he passed out.

కురా

LXXVII. Survivor

HE AWOKE HOURS LATER AND HEARD A SLIGHT ROAR. HE looked up to see an attendant in a bright white uniform bending over him.

"How long," Gideon whispered.

"I suppose you are wondering how long you were in that box. As best as we can tell, two weeks. You've lost about thirty pounds; you've got bilateral pneumonia, a pulmonary embolus, kidney failure, multiple skin ulcers, among other things. All in all you're quite a mess, but you seem to be recovering quite nicely. You'll be up and about in no time," the attendant said with a very cheerful manner.

Gideon closed his eyes for a moment, then tried to sit up. "I'm starving, what do you have that's fresh?"

"Just be patient, Mr. Smith, start with something light and easy to digest."

"Smith? You mean Jones, don't you?"

"Gideon Jones is dead, died in that box back there. Now you have your old identity, Joshua Smith, and once you're better, you'll have your old face, eyes, everything. Oh, and we found this for you." He held out a watch, a book, and some goggles. "Your personal effects from that house of torture. You must have some incredible will to live, that's for sure. What did you think about, locked up all that time?"

Joshua closed his eyes, but didn't say a word. He wasn't sure himself what he had thought about, but as he lay there he realized that, despite all his suffering, he felt blessed. He opened his eyes and looked around. "Where am I?" He heard a dull roar outside; the room he was in was small and there weren't any windows.

"You're in a jet; property of Mr. O'Donnel. It's sort of a flying hospital, at least for the moment. In a short time we'll arrive at our destination and you will get some much deserved R and R. Mr. O'Donnel is up in front. I'll let him know that you're up. I'm sure he wants to talk to you."

The attendant left Joshua alone, leaving the little hospital room through the door at the front. Joshua sat up and looked around. The room was white, the sheets and blankets on his bed were white and he was dressed in loose fitting white pants and shirt. With some difficulty he managed to pull himself up and hang his legs over the edge of the bed as the familiar face of Mr. O'Donnel came through the door.

"Mr. Smith, you are looking quite well for someone who has been buried and forgotten for so long," O'Donnel remarked. Joshua was still achy and stiff all over and could barely move to greet his benefactor. "No need to stand up, my boy," O'Donnel said as he walked over to Joshua and put his arm on his shoulder and sat down. "You're safe and on the mend now. Please, tell me what happened, starting with your incident with David Sanders."

Joshua suddenly felt much better, much of the soreness melting away with O'Donnel's touch as he told his story, not leaving out any details.

When he finished, Joshua had a few questions of his own. The first being how he had been found. O'Donnel recounted the whole story.

"You really owe your life to Brian Sivestre, that reporter friend of yours. He started looking for you as soon as you were arrested. He was looking for an interview, figuring that with the history you two had he could get a real exclusive. Anyway, he checked the police station and no one knew a thing. As a matter of fact, he checked every police database for all of New York, New Jersey, and Connecticut, but found nothing. Finally, he tracked down the driver that was supposed to have taken you to Central New York Station and, under considerable pressure, was told that he received instructions to take you to that Westchester facility for psychiatric evaluation before you were questioned. He wouldn't say where those instructions came from and it's very possible that he really didn't know. Anyway, it took some time to find even this bit of information."

"Sivestre drove up to Westchester and found the place deserted, shut down and emptied out, apparently the culmination of a two-year investigation into abuses at that facility. He ran into stone walls and closed doors at every turn. The seized records were sealed due to pending litigation and he thought that it was hopeless. But he thought he got a break when someone gave him an anonymous tip that lead him to the list of inmates at the complex. Unfortunately, your name wasn't on that list."

"At this point he was about to give up, figuring that you were at the bottom of New York Harbor or somewhere similar and, it turned out, he wasn't far off, but he went back to Westchester one more time. He was snooping around and he came across some personal effects, specifically, your watch, Bible, and those goggles I gave you. He immediately recognized your watch. It seems that your unique taste in timepieces has some benefit. He also saw my name written on the strap of these goggles. He found my number and I met him with some of my crew. It was at that point that we found you and, now, here you are. We're flying to Bali. A few weeks lying on the beach will do you some good."

O'Donnel patted Joshua on the shoulder as he rose to leave and Joshua was left alone to ponder his good fortune.

After O'Donnel left Joshua felt much stronger. He ate some real food and was able to get himself up to the bathroom. The flight to Bali would last only about two hours, although he had no intention of staying there for weeks. As soon as he was strong enough he intended to return to New York, clear his name, and find out who had left him to die.

As he stood in the bathroom washing his hands there was a loud boom and the small restroom began to shake. The shaking was quickly followed by the sudden ejection of the bathroom from the jet and, through a window in the ceiling, he saw the plane explode. The bathroom/escape pod plummeted to the Earth as Joshua hung on. A parachute deployed and he found himself settled down in the middle of the ocean. The pod started to take on water; he grabbed his bag, which contained his few possessions along with a few essentials, kicked the door open, threw a flotation device into the water and jumped off as it sank.

This has been a bad few weeks, he thought as he looked around to see only open sea all around. The sun was high in the sky as he started to paddle, not knowing if there was a best way to go. He looked up and said out loud, "God, if you're up there; I'm in your hands, again."

෯ඁ

LXXVII. Lost

JOSHUA FELT THE COOL WATER WASHING OVER HIS FEET and legs. He let out a groan as he pulled himself forward, trying to keep sand from filling his mouth. His whole body ached as he stopped and lay still under the warm sun. After his recent ordeal, the warmth was like a soothing balm that penetrated to his bones loosening the stiff joints and muscles until he felt a new wave of strength that allowed him to pull himself a little further out of the surf. God had helped him alright. He had paddled for hours until night fell. The darkness brought a strong wind followed by thunder and lightning and a violent storm that carried him up and over monstrous waves. He spent the night holding on for dear life and spitting sea water out of his mouth until with the dawn he was deposited on this beach.

He lay still on the sand for a few more minutes until he felt a sharp pull on his left ear. He reached his hand up and tried to swat the annoyance away and felt a second stronger tug and heard a loud "Squawk!" He opened his eyes and saw a bright green bird with a huge yellow orange beak standing at his side pulling on his ear.

"Go way," Joshua shouted. The bird just hopped to his right side and pulled on his right ear. Joshua pulled himself up to sitting and the bird hopped on his shoulder and pulled on his ear especially hard. At this Joshua turned his head and looked out into the water and saw a huge wave approaching the shore. He forgot all the aches and pains and pulled himself up and headed towards a grove of trees as the huge wave crashed into shore. Joshua pulled himself up on a low lying branch and held on as water crashed all around. The green bird perched firmly on his shoulder, sharp claws digging into Joshua's skin.

The wave passed and Joshua sat down with his back against the tree. The bird hopped down into his lap. "Why don't you just fly away?" Joshua asked out loud. He put out his hand and his new companion hopped onto his finger. Joshua studied the handsome bird and saw that one of its wings seemed crooked, out of joint.

"This might hurt a bit," he remarked as he gave a gentle tug on the wing. He felt a pop and the wing became straight and immediately the bird started vigorous flapping, creating a cool breeze. Joshua studied this unusual bird. It stood about thirty centimeters tall, had bright green feathers that seemed more like fur, and had a huge orange-yellow beak that curved forward and created a backward C.

"I guess I'll call you 'Gimpy,' in honor of your wing," Joshua said continuing to stare at his new found friend. "I don't know why you've decided to join me, but I do appreciate your help. I don't suppose you can tell me where I am or how I got here." Joshua looked into Gimpy's eyes half expecting to hear an answer.

"Squawk . . . Squawk," Gimpy screamed with enough decibels to rupture an eardrum.

"Well, you certainly are loud," Joshua exclaimed rubbing his ear. He slowly stood up, Gimpy holding tight to his shoulder. "I suppose I should scout around." There was a pack around Joshua's waist containing some food and nutritional supplements in pill form, his watch and Mr. O'Donnel's goggles. His Bible hadn't survived the ordeal. "There must be some fresh water around." The two got up and slowly walked between the trees as Joshua put his watch on his left wrist and checked to see that it was still running. The time was 2:36 somewhere in the world.

The air was warm and heavy with humidity and Joshua was soon drenched with sweat and took his shirt off. He was protected from the sun by the canopy of trees overhead and there seemed to be a natural path as if he were expected and someone had come before him to prepare for his arrival. Some of the trees were laden with bananas and there were palm trees with coconuts. *At least I won't starve,* he thought as he continued his exploration. There were a variety of brightly colored birds, types of parrots he judged by the shape of their bills. He also managed to spy an occasional brightly-colored lizard.

A tropical paradise, he thought; I didn't think such places still existed anywhere on this old planet. Maybe I've been transported to Eden, like David, but, then, there should be an Eve somewhere. As all these speculations ran through his head, he heard a slight roar, the sound of rushing water. He quickened his pace and soon was greeted by a waterfall cascading down a cliff about twenty meters high. He pulled off his clothes, laid them on a large rock at the edge of the pond and eased himself into the pool. He lay on his back as Gimpy flew onto a branch. Joshua lay in the cool, clear water, floating on his back for several minutes and then slowly paddled over to the falls and let the water caress his head.

"I could stay here forever," he said out loud looking up to the sky as if addressing God. He climbed onto a large rock at the water's edge and let the sun warm his aching body; its gentle rays helping to melt away weeks of brutality. He lay there until he was dry which was when Gimpy decided it was time to get going and he flew down and landed on his bare shoulder and pulled on his right ear and gave a loud squawk.

"OK, I'm not deaf. I'm moving, I'm moving," Joshua said rubbing his ear. He pulled on his clothes and started to walk with the bright green bird perched on his right shoulder. As he walked along under the trees he felt a sudden tug on his ear and there was a loud squawk. This continued for about thirty seconds, the tugging getting stronger and the squawking getting louder. "What do you want," Joshua said to his companion. He stopped and looked at the trail ahead of him. The grass was disrupted, there was a pile of palm leaves just ahead, but there was no palm tree nearby. Joshua proceeded slowly, cautiously. He pushed the palm leaves away with his foot and exposed a deep pit, deep enough that he could barely see the bottom. He threw a stone in and heard a soft thud. "Thanks, buddy," he said. "You're useful to have around. Of course, this means we're not alone here. That hole in the ground may have been naturally made, but I don't think that it covered itself with those palm branches. Looks like we'll need to be extra careful. So much for paradise."

They continued on their way, much more slowly and carefully, Gimpy perched on Joshua's shoulder, his head turning from side to side vigilant to any possible threats. Joshua heard a rustling in the bushes to his right, but Gimpy didn't move and Joshua understood that there was nothing of concern. As they continued on, Gimpy started to squawk; up ahead was another pile of palm leaves, brown and dry. They bent down and uncovered another deep pit.

"Let's go that way," Joshua said pointing to the right. They turned and continued on. The trees thinned and the sunshine came through, making the pleasant stroll uncomfortably hot. As they entered a cleared area, Joshua thought there was something very artificial about it. The brush had been removed from an area of about one hundred meters radius from a central area where there was a collection of trees and bushes. Joshua pointed to the area and they turned once again to walk through the clearing.

"Squawk . . . Squawk," Gimpy started with great excitement. The green bird flew off of Joshua's shoulder and circled overhead.

"Must be something serious," Joshua said out loud. He proceeded very slowly. He picked up a long fallen branch and carefully probed the ground before taking each step. As he drew closer to the cluster of trees his pole went through the surface into another more shallow pit. Once again he bent down, only this time he uncovered a long low trench, with sharp, metal spikes at the bottom. The trench was about five feet across. Joshua started to jump it, but heard a loud squawk and decided a more careful approach was necessary.

"I'll go around," he said to Gimpy, who continued to fly overhead acting as warning system and tour guide. In this tedious manner, Joshua made his way to the trees and found what he had expected. Hidden among the trees and brush was a shelter, long poles and palm leaves woven together to create a hut of surprising sturdiness. He maintained his vigilance, slowly walking around the outside inspecting each wall, the few windows and the ground around the perimeter. He finally made it back to the door and, standing well away, lodged his pole in a small opening and pried it open. As it opened a large stone fell to the ground just inside.

"Paranoia or justified caution, I just don't know." He walked up to the entrance and tried to see inside. He grabbed his trusty pole one more time and bent down close to the ground and waved the pole inside the door. Nothing happened. He started to get up slowly, paused for a moment, and then quickly scooted inside. The door snapped shut and a wooden platform collapsed at the entrance revealing another pit with sharp metal stakes at the bottom.

"Well I guess I get an A in obstacle course," he said as he looked around the room. The windows were shut, leaving the single room illuminated by a shadowy light that passed through cracks in the walls and ceiling. He saw a central area with a ring of stones and charred logs, a makeshift bed of palm leaves, and a work area with what appeared to be desk or table. This really demands closer inspection. As his eyes grew accustomed to the dim light, he took careful stock of the room, looking for other booby traps. None being found, he opened the windows and sat down at the work area. What he saw left him amazed.

There were several "Green Dots" and a variety of fine tools and a small, powerful flashlight, which still worked. The "Dots were still active and there was a transformer also that would display holograms of what they contained. He activated the first one.

"Record of being marooned in the Solomon Islands, as recorded by Amos Pierson." Joshua sat down. *So this is what happened to Amos Pierson*, he thought. I wonder if he's still alive. He continued to read.

"It was a great mistake, selling to the enemy. The evil will grow and will destroy us all. I can do nothing more. I am left here with nothing; no hope, only inevitable death. I will try to continue in my research, to build upon what I know to create something new and perhaps to atone for the evil that will be unleashed in my name." —June 2152

"My study is progressing, but time grows short. The demons close in and I'm afraid they will wear down my defenses and it will soon be the end. Before they get to me I will try to finish; to build the perfect companion. I have all the tools and I have solved the greatest dilemma. The immense potential of this matrix configuration will allow the creation of an artificial being with human characteristics that will be perceived as human, rather than merely humanoid." —September 2152

"They are all around, constantly tormenting me, the whooping and howling gives me no peace. The demons are penetrating my skull and I am seeing the gates of hell open up before me, beckoning me to an eternity of pain. There is no hope for me and I fear for mankind. We are all destined for the fiery pits of eternal pain and solitude. What can I do? What can I do?" —December 2152

"They've broken through and I am being devoured by madness; by the evil and despair they bring. If only I could find a way to repent, to ask God to forgive, but it is too late . . . such horror . . ."

No date and that's the last entry. *He wasn't big on words,* Joshua thought. The next file was very technical containing a vast number of mathematical equations and computations, picomatrix configurations, and a large number of images of his artificial human, all shown as young men, naked, smooth light brown skin, about fifteen years old or so. Joshua sat back and thought about the possibilities such a creation would have presented, both good and bad. Wouldn't it have been remarkable if he had actually succeeded. He closed his eyes and before long the afternoon sun faded to dusk and he was fast asleep. Gimpy assumed a vigil perched on a pole running across the ceiling, always on the lookout for danger.

A loud screech filled the room and Joshua sat straight up, roused from what had been a very peaceful slumber. The room was cool and nearly pitch black. Gradually, he grew accustomed to the tiny bit of pale light coming from the closed windows and door and he was able to see a bit of the room. He carefully made his way to the door and slowly opened it. Moonlight provided faint illumination to the area around the hut; the screech was not repeated and the only sound was the sing-song chirping of insects and the cool breeze sifting through the trees. As soon as he opened the door Gimpy landed on his shoulder and the two ventured out of the building. Joshua fumbled with the bag that was tied around his waist and found Pierson's miniature light which was powerful enough to illuminate the entire area. He studied all the surrounding bushes and trees and as he turned to his right there was a rustling of the bushes for a brief moment and then nothing but the continued serenade of the insects.

"I guess there's nothing out here," Joshua remarked to no one in particular. As he said this he slowly walked to the right of the hut. Gimpy flew ahead and suddenly swooped down and landed on the head of the spy that was hiding in the bushes.

"Ow," screamed a voice, high pitched and loud. A young man stood up, thick dark hair being pulled by Joshua's tenacious companion. "Get him off of me," the boy shouted.

Joshua ran over and gently freed Gimpy from the tangle of hair. The bird returned to his usual perch on Joshua's shoulder and the two stood back to get a better look at the intruder. Joshua turned on his light and the boy shielded his eyes from the bright light. He was thin with a dark olive complexion, almost six feet tall, with very smooth, handsome features.

"Hello, young man," Joshua said. "Welcome, or perhaps I should say I'm sorry for intruding on your domain. You have been here for some time no doubt." He noticed the ragged shorts that the young man wore, but also noticed that his hair was very neat and clean and his finger nails and toenails were perfectly trimmed.

"My name is Joshua and this is Gimpy," Joshua said pointing to his shoulder. The boy stood motionless and remained silent. "Do you have a name? I know that you can talk. And I'll bet that you understand English perfectly."

After several minutes of silence and staring, Joshua heard a faint mumbling, and then much louder, "Jake . . . my name is Jake." His voice was a sweet tenor, but forceful and clear.

"Very pleased to meet you, Jake, or is it more properly, Jacob?"

"Jake, just Jake. Who are you and why are you here? I'm not sure I like having anyone else here."

"Well, Jake, I'm not here by choice, but this doesn't seem like such a bad place, or is it?"

"I really don't know what is considered good and what is bad."

Joshua considered this unusual response for a moment and then said, "Well, no matter, let's go inside." He reached out his hand and took Jake's hand and shook it. "Shaking hands is considered a gesture of trust and goodwill," he said. Jake smiled and grabbed Joshua's hand and gave it a long shake, nearly crushing his fingers as the three went into the hut.

Joshua's light illuminated the room as he sat on the floor with Jake while Gimpy flew up to the rafters. "Do you know if anyone else is in this place, Jake?" Joshua asked.

"I have not seen any other people like you here. There was someone here before, but he is dead. I found his body outside."

"I'd like to look at it tomorrow, when it is light. But, now have you ever seen any other people or are we the first that you've ever encountered?"

"You're the first."

"I'm looking at you and there is something very familiar about you and I've just realized what it is." Joshua activated the records left by Amos Pierson and the hologram of his proposed android appeared. It was the exact image of Jake. "Can I take a closer look at you, Jake?" Joshua asked gently.

"If you want; I have nothing to hide."

Joshua took his hand and felt along the base of Jake's neck and behind his ears. He stared into his eyes and his mouth. He took his light and inspected every centimeter of his torso and legs. "May I look at the areas that are covered?" Jake took off his shorts and Joshua continued his examination. When he had finished with the private areas, he handed the boy his shorts and the young man put them on immediately.

"I think I've figured this out," Joshua said. He ran his hand over the back of Jake's neck and felt a slight depression. He pressed this area and a spot at the base of his neck opened up revealing a glowing ring of green dots suspended by what seemed to be pure light, but what Joshua realized was a magnetic field of some sort. The dots glowed and light radiated in all directions. *So he really did it,* Joshua thought; *that Pierson made an artificial person.*

"Did you see what you needed to see?" Jake asked, totally unaware that his being was anything but ordinary.

"Yes, Jake, I saw what I needed, something extraordinary."

The days that followed were filled with discovery and wonder. Jake was innocent and naïve, but at the same time his natural curiosity was punctuated with an insight and wisdom that seemed ageless. Joshua considered the lad an unfinished work of art; one on which he would be privileged to do the final shaping and polishing; providing the finishing touches to this final masterpiece created by Amos Pierson.

The first morning after the meeting Jake showed Joshua the location of the body he had talked about. There were only skeletal remains with a decaying rope around the neck, along with a chain with the initials AP on a tag and a Green Dot adhered to the temple of the skull which was, surprisingly, still active. The contents of the Dot confirmed the body as Amos Pierson. There was much more recorded on the little device and Joshua carefully put it away for safekeeping until he had time to study its contents. He also surmised that Pierson's death was self-inflicted, suicide by hanging. He wondered if the demons that Pierson faced were real or only within.

The two buried the remains and marked the grave with a tower of stones.

"Why must the skeleton be buried?" Jake asked as the two walked along the beach under the bright tropical sun.

"Good question," answered Joshua. "I'm not sure why we buried Mr. Pierson, to tell you the truth. In olden times burying the dead was necessary for sanitation. A decaying body could spread diseases which could wipe out whole civilizations. Of course, now that is not a concern. Still, I suppose we just don't want to be reminded of death. The human race struggles, holding on to life, and when we finally die it is painful for those that are left behind. So, we hide the dead, buried underground, burnt to ashes, or broken down into constituent chemicals. All take the dearly departed out of our sight, but leave the memories of better times intact."

"Is death such a bad thing?"

"Another very good question and one that I don't think that I can accurately answer, seeing as I haven't had the pleasure of that particular experience. The real question is: what happens when we die. I'd say we've been asking ourselves that question for thousands of years. Religion thought that they had the answer. Die and we go to heaven or hell; stand before God and be judged; sentenced to an eternity of pleasure or pain. But, after all I've been through recently, I'm sure pretty there isn't any God and religion is all nonsense. We are given a finite time on this planet to do with as we see fit and when we're gone, we're gone."

"That's a very depressing thought," Jake said. He was silent for a minute. "What's the point in living then? I think I'll go with religion and take my chances with being judged."

"Be careful what you ask for. Judgment is by God's standards, at least if you trust the Bible, and no one can live up to his level of perfection."

"You mean nobody in all of history has ever been judged by God good enough to go to heaven. Hell must be awfully crowded."

"I'm sure it is, particularly with people of today. There was one person that the Bible says was good enough to meet God's standard, if you believe the myths."

"Who was that?"

"A man named Jesus Christ. He lived about two thousand or so years ago. The story is that God became man and came to live among His sinful creation. He lived a perfect life and was killed by His own creation, but in so doing took all creation's sin onto Himself. This Jesus was then raised from the dead after three days. Three days spent among the dead in Hell doing who knows what. Anyway, when Jesus came back from the dead, He gave hope to all those that believed in Him; hope that they, too, would be raised from the dead. It's hard to believe that this could be true, but there are still people in this world that do believe it. I even know some."

Jake was quiet for a while. 'I think that I'll believe it, too. It seems like the best way around death and certainly I don't see any harm in believing in Jesus."

"Now, you are sounding like Pascal. But, enough of philosophy. Come on, I'll race you to the trees." Joshua took off towards the edge of the forest, about two hundred yards away. As soon as he started he was overtaken by his young mechanical companion, who waited for him, never sweating or needing to catch his breath. Overhead flew Gimpy squawking and circling around before landing majestically on Joshua's shoulder.

That evening the three of them sat inside the small hut, Joshua finishing a meal of fresh fruit and coconut. Gimpy, as always, sat on his shoulder, sharing his feast. Joshua looked up from the food and saw a very serious look on Jake's face.

"What's on your mind?" Joshua asked.

Jake sat silently for a moment and then answered, "Tell me more about religion. After we talked for those brief moments today about God and Jesus, I realized that with all the knowledge inside me there is almost nothing about God or religion. Why is that?"

"You, my boy, are the victim of modern society. Years ago some supposedly wise men decided that religion was the cause of much of the strife in our world. God, per se, was not singled out, but of course it is impossible to separate one from the other. All religious writings and practices were eliminated from mainstream society. Believers in anything having to do with God or religion suffered ridicule, schools taught that religion and God were dangerous and both gradually faded away. You are a product of this modern thought and, therefore, there is no knowledge of God or religion within your memory cells."

"That is very upsetting, to say the least. I feel empty, incomplete somehow." He looked down at the ground, but then he popped his head up and smiled, revealing his perfectly straight, white teeth. "You seem to have a great deal of knowledge of the subject. Can't you teach me?"

Joshua reflected for just a moment and then replied, "Of course, of course, it will help pass the time. You are lucky that I was forced to become a Bible scholar a few years ago and I still remember all the highlights. Let me finish and I'll begin your first lesson." Joshua and Gimpy finished eating and then they went outside for a short while.

The night was clear and a cool breeze blew off the ocean. Joshua sat looking up at the stars. "The universe is so vast and seems to be endless; it's hard to fathom that any sort of being could be in control of such vastness. But, that is what God is supposed to be; sovereign, omnipotent, omniscient. My friend David used to say that God does things in his own way and time and we are not to judge or test him. I sometimes wish I could believe all that. After what I've been through I don't think I can ever believe that there is a God. And, even if he does exist, I can't believe that he cares about us. Certainly, if I were God, I wouldn't care about such people. From the beginning all we have ever been is disobedient. Let me tell you about Creation, as it is written in the Bible, the Book of Genesis."

Jake lay back and also looked up at the stars. "There's Regulon, so bright in the sky. There are eight planets around that star."

Joshua stopped his Bible lesson for a moment. "How can you tell that?"

"I guess it's built into my memory and my eyes can be pretty powerful telescopes."

Joshua shook his head. "Amazing," he murmured and then returned to his lesson. "In the beginning God created the Heavens and the Earth . . ." and Joshua started at the beginning and went through the Book of Genesis. Jake frequently surprised him with his insightful questions.

"Did God take Abraham up to heaven after he died? I thought he demands perfection, but Abraham and Sarah certainly were not perfect. Still Abraham surely trusted God a great deal to have been willing to sacrifice Isaac."

"You are extremely perceptive and insightful, but you've jumped way ahead to the Book of Hebrews. Your questions will be answered, just be patient."

৯৽৽৻

LXXVIII. Education

THE DAYS WERE FILLED WITH SUN, FUN AND ENDLESS LES-
sons from the Bible. Joshua was tested more than Jake, doing his best
to recount passages from each Book and explain their meaning. Jake
was a remarkable student, his mind like a sponge and his curiosity
neverending.

The Book of Genesis took almost two weeks to go through. Jake
asking a multitude of questions about Joseph, such as, "Why did his
brothers hate him so? They all had so much and what they did showed
so little regard for their father? I would never have forgiven my brothers if I was Joseph; he should have sent them back to Canaan."

Joshua did his best to explain the underlying meaning as he understood it. "Joseph's brothers were jealous. Israel favored him and this
made the other brothers angry. I suppose it's human nature. But,
Joseph understood the real meaning and importance of everything
that happened. God had His plan; the Israelites were brought to Egypt,
saved from the famine and flourished. Even though Joseph suffered
tremendously, throughout his ordeals God was preparing him for his
great purpose and in the end truly blessed him. The Bible always tells
us that God has a purpose in everything He does, although sometimes
it may not be clear."

"Did He have a purpose in bringing you or me to this place or in
making you suffer?"

"I don't really know. I'm not sure if God cares about this old planet
anymore; about me or you."

Jake had a sour look on his face as he thought about what Joshua
said. "Of course he cares; just think about your friend David. It seems
to me that God went to a great deal of trouble to prepare him to bring
His message to the Earth."

"That's true, but look what happened to him. He was a shining
light for a few years, and now his voice has been snuffed out. Maybe

enough seeds were planted to allow His word to grow; deep down I hope that's true, but I'm not sure that I believe it myself."

"You have seen so much, miraculous things, I don't know how you can still have doubts. But for me, it makes logical sense to know that God exists. Just what you have told me of the Bible, your friend David's experience, and all that you have seen, none of this could have happened apart from the hand of God."

Joshua was, once again, amazed by Jake's insight and incredible gift that allowed the boy to take a jumble of complex, unrelated events and synthesize them into logical end. He asked, "Are you sure all of this is new to you? You sure see things from a different viewpoint than even me and I know that I'm able to view such things more clearly than most people."

"It's the computer in me, I guess. Come on, I'll find you some lunch."

The lesson ended. Jake ran ahead and returned with a variety of fruit and such for Joshua's lunch. Gimpy found his own foods and Jake didn't need to eat, he received his power and energy from the light.

The Bible lessons continued day after day, Joshua did his best to recall each Book and its text; his remarkable memory served him well. Jake was an apt pupil. He absorbed the historical books of the Old Testament, shaking his head at what he called the stupidity of the Israelites. He was awed by King David's faith and confounded by his great sin.

"How could he ignore the laws of the God he so obviously loved? But, it shows that sincere repentance carries great weight with God. All in all, in the end, there is so much sadness within David."

Joshua answered, "Human nature is weak and easily succumbs to temptation. Ever since Adam and Eve ate the apple we've been slaves to human nature and weakness."

"How do you know it was an apple? Didn't the Bible only call it the Fruit of the Tree of Knowledge of Good and Evil?"

"Very perceptive; but, it was an apple because David told me. He was privileged to live in Eden, at least a Garden of Eden, and he says that it was apples which caused the Fall. So, Mr. Smart Guy, that's how I know."

"Forgive me, I won't argue with the Master again."

"Good, at least you're trainable."

The remainder of the day was spent in lazy repose. Joshua was fully recovered from his recent ordeal and Jake was content lying in the sun, quietly reflecting on all that he had recently learned. As the two of them looked up at the passing clouds, Jake remarked, "It really is amazing, this world that we live in. The warmth of the sun, food just there for the choosing, and look at you, a marvel of biological engineering. Your eyes that can see a bird swooping down from afar, your tongue that is so sensitive a tiny hair becomes a thing of great annoyance just by touching it, and your brain, so incredibly complex. With all the years of study that medical science has devoted to the human brain, still so little is known."

Joshua closed his eyes. "Enough philosophy; you're going to make my head explode. Of course humans are complex, irrational, and most of the time incredibly irritating. I wonder why we are made with so many flaws. And, do you know what I've wondered about for years? Why, if we are truly created in God's image, why do we have an appendix?"

"What?'

"An appendix. If I were in the business of creation, I would never have made humans with an appendix. It has no purpose, except to occasionally make people sick. Years ago it was a very common cause for people to need surgery. It is removed with impunity, without any side effects. So I ask you, why would an omniscient, omnipotent, inerrant God give His ultimate creation such a useless organ?"

Jake pondered this question for a while, but remained silent.

"I guess you're stumped, too. Out of everything that I've seen, experienced, and thought about, it is this question that has kept me from believing in God, at least in a perfect God."

Jake finally spoke up. "Perhaps, there is a purpose that God has kept hidden from you. There are so many mysteries in this universe;

so many things around that scream the presence of God. It seems the height of human arrogance to question everything because there is one thing, in all that is so wonderful, that you don't understand."

"Good answer; believe me that is the answer that I tell myself over and over. Still, the doubt nags at me. Enough speculation; let's get back to the wisdom books."

The sun was settling low in the sky and the night air was cool as the two men and their avian companion strolled slowly beneath the trees, and Joshua began to tell his young companion about the Book of Job.

෨ஜ

LXXIX. Job

"THE BOOK OF JOB IS GOD'S ANSWER TO THE QUESTION of pain and human suffering. Job was an upright and righteous man, favored by God. God bid Satan to consider Job and Satan and God made a wager of sorts. Take away all that Job had and he would reject God. The Book is a morality play with the character of Job on trial." Thus, Joshua started to tell Jake Job's story.

When he finished Jake had a big smile on his face, something that surprised the older man. "What is it?" Joshua asked.

"God amazes me," Jake responded. "Here he is, letting Satan do his worst to God's most righteous subject; you'd think that God would show him such overt compassion and, in a way, he does; but what a unique style."

"You jump right to the Book's heart. You really astound me. That is the point exactly. One may suffer terrible things and question God and even be angry with God. After all, we can never know why, what is the ultimate purpose."

"Don't you think that God sees us in the same way we see a young child who misbehaves?" Jake asked. "Think about it. How many times will a parent scold a child and when asked why, merely answer, 'because I said so'? Isn't that what God does here? And, I think about Joseph; he understood. He suffered incredibly, but his insight led him to the truth. Man meant it for evil, but God meant it for good. Look at you; you suffered terribly for something you didn't do, yet God sustained you through your horrible ordeal and, perhaps, you are a better person because of it."

"I'll say it again, you amaze me, really," Joshua said. "If nothing else, you understand God better than most people, better than me, I think. I hope that you're right. I hope that there is a God up there smiling down upon this world. I just wish that I could be sure; I wish I had the gift of faith that seems so elusive."

Jake put his arm around his teacher and Joshua felt better. Joshua wasn't sure why, but the youthful, artificial humanoid was a great comfort, with his curiosity, insight or, sometimes, just his timely affection. He continued the lessons going through Psalms, Proverbs, Ecclesiastes, and the Song of Songs.

"Tomorrow we'll tackle the Prophets and then it will be time for Jesus," Joshua said as they sat down on the beach watching the sunset. Jake was quiet as he thought about how his companion had suffered.

"Tell me, Joshua, what was it like for you, buried and forgotten. Did you despair, did you curse God or were you always hopeful that, no matter what happened, no matter how it ended, it would be for the best?"

"I don't know. It was torment mostly, but there were vivid, brilliant moments, revelations that screamed that there must have be some purpose to it all. When I was about to die of thirst and dehydration, I was ready; I had suffered so. And then it rained, my thirst was satisfied and I was convinced that God was sustaining me for a purpose, but then it was still quite some time until I was rescued and I suffered even more. I reached a point where I didn't know if I should praise or curse God or Satan or Aaron Diblonski. To tell you the truth I still don't know."

৵৽৾

LXXX. The Gospels

THE DAYS BECAME A ROUTINE OF GATHERING FOOD AND Bible. The Old Testament was finished and Joshua started the New Testament. He did his best to recall the genealogy of Jesus and Jake seemed to be more attentive than usual. This Jesus fascinated him more than anyone else he had ever encountered. In particular the Sermon on the Mount left him awestruck.

"How could Jesus expect anyone to follow his teachings? I mean, he asked, no he commanded his listeners to 'be perfect, like their Father in Heaven.' He might as well have told them that they needed to walk to the moon."

"Well, you jump to the heart of the matter. The Bible tells us over and over that humanity is anything but perfect. And, we certainly fall far short of God's perfection. The people of the time had no idea what they wanted. They were searching for someone; the promised Messiah who they assumed would restore Israel to glory; a king like David. What they got was Jesus and he was totally unexpected. Even up to the end, his closest followers didn't understand. But, I'm getting ahead of myself."

Joshua continued to recount Jesus' life, his baptism, temptation by Satan, his ministry and his final days. When he had finished Matthew's Gospel, Joshua saw a huge smile on Jake's face.

"What's with the grin?" Joshua asked.

"Oh, nothing; I guess it's this Jesus. He's just so surprising, and so perfect. Of course one sent by God to redeem his people could only be Jesus. Look at all the prophecies in the Old Testament. He fulfills everyone and only a suffering servant who obeyed God could really be His perfect sacrificial lamb."

Joshua looked wide eyed at his protégé and felt that the student had become the master. Such insight usually took years to develop, not five minutes.

"When did you become such an expert theologian?" Joshua asked.

"You forget," Jake answered. "I am not a boy; I'm not human. I'm just a very complex computer. For me, all this input is boiled down and collated and processed and I am left with extremely logical conclusions. Based on what you've taught me from the Old Testament and from this Gospel, the conclusion is obvious."

Joshua shook his head, never realizing it was so simple as he started to go through the Gospels of Mark and Luke. Jake was an attentive student, but Joshua sensed that it all seemed very familiar to his young companion. The Gospel of John seemed to bring a change to Jake's demeanor. The usual attentiveness was replaced by a solemn expression and a hint of sadness.

"What is it, Jake?" Joshua asked.

"John tells the story in such a different way. I almost feel like I am with Jesus in his sorrow and the pain that he felt is a part of me; not the physical pain, rather the mental anguish of battling with Satan to the end. But, oh, the exultation of his triumph. I have to say, you tell it very well."

Joshua smiled at this comment. He would never have considered himself an accomplished storyteller and he chalked it up to quality material rather than any skill he might have.

"Enough for today," Joshua said. "It's time to eat, at least according to Gimpy." The bird had flown down from his perch in a nearby palm tree and was pulling at Joshua's ear. "I feel a bit tired. Please find me something and something for my feathered friend here. I'll be waiting here."

Jake disappeared and Joshua sat down against a tree with Gimpy perched on his hand. He marveled at Jake, an extraordinary student, but with such clear perception. *He really should be teaching me,* Joshua thought. Jake returned with dinner and Joshua and Gimpy enjoyed the meal.

"What's it like, to eat?" Jake asked. "Does it bring great pleasure or merely fill a basic need?"

"Both, I suppose," Joshua answered. "Of course for living beings, food is a basic necessity, like air and water. Then there are other needs, things we can live without, but not easily; clothing, companionship, shelter and such. And then there are the luxuries and indulgences. I have to say that mankind has an overabundance of these. It seems better here, peaceful, simple. I could stay here forever; I suppose I may have to."

"I wish I could eat like you," Jake said. "I tried it once, but it just made me feel like I was carrying a load of stones inside me. Certainly wasn't pleasurable."

"What is pleasurable for you, Jake?" Joshua lay on his side and watched the sun setting, the sky painting the ocean in the distance with a palette of pinks and reds.

Jake sat next to him pondering. "You have brought me pleasure. Your knowledge; your friendship; the clever way you tell the stories. You bring it all to life with great passion. It's really a shame you can't wholly accept it as true. Perhaps if you did, you would find some peace."

Joshua stared at the sunset, but didn't say a word. He had heard similar words before, always from unlikely sources, people that knew him, but didn't know him. Jake, however, was different. He had a quiet force behind his words that lent greater meaning to such observations. Joshua didn't quite understand it, but in his heart he had a feeling of gratitude. He wasn't sure why.

ॐ✄

LXXXI. Finish and Escape

THE GOSPELS COMPLETED JOSHUA WENT ON TO THE remainder of the New Testament. Jake was attentive as ever as Peter and Paul expanded and expounded upon Jesus' teachings.

"Do you think Communion actually means that Christ's body and blood are in the bread and wine? Or, is it just a symbol of Jesus' giving himself for humanity?" Jake asked.

Joshua furrowed his brow and closed his eyes. "An age old question, I'm sure, and one that I can't answer. I think Jesus meant that we are to remember him when we eat; remember all that he was and all that he did for us."

"I don't know," Jake replied. "He said that this is my blood and this is my body. I think He comes to dwell in those things and that when we eat He is present. His grace and God's mercy are imparted to us by the communion and it brings us closer to Jesus and to the Father."

"Perhaps you're right. In all honesty, I never have given it much thought. I can't say that I've truly believed any of what I've taught you; I think I have some understanding, but I don't know if I can accept it. By Paul's reckoning I am not worthy to partake in the Lord's Supper, as it is sometimes called."

"That's sad, really. The world you describe is so mixed up, so dangerous; a bit of God's grace would go a long way towards eliminating some of the strife."

Joshua sighed and looked up at the blue sky. "Of course, you're right. I suppose if we could find a way for sixty billion people to come to the table the world would be a much saner place.

"Let's eat and then we'll go on to the last book: Revelation."

At the mention of food, Gimpy miraculously appeared and the three of them went off together and found some bananas, coconut, and mangoes. The night was cooler than usual and the moon was hidden by dark, thick clouds which blew in from the northwest. Joshua heard thunder in the distance as the wind grew stronger.

"I hope that this hut is well built," Joshua said. "It looks like quite a storm brewing. Let's get inside."

The three pulled bamboo covering over the windows and latched the door closed. Gimpy assumed his usual vigil in the rafters as Joshua and Jake stayed in the middle of the hut, away from any windows or doors. The storm moved over the island about thirty minutes later, bringing thunder, lightning, heavy rain and powerful wind. Rain was blown almost horizontal and pounded against the walls, pouring in through every crack as the walls shook, but held up.

Throughout the storm, Joshua told John's account of the Revelation of Jesus Christ.

"Who is worthy . . . the lamb is worthy . . . the mark of the Beast . . . New Jerusalem . . ." All presented with the raging storm as back drop to the raging battle of Revelation.

When Joshua finished, Jake breathed a deep sigh as the storm also abated. "God is so powerful and so good, it is such a shameful pity that He is rejected by so many today. Even you reject Him; it is so sad for you and for all the billions in the past and all those who are still living."

Joshua saw such sadness in Jake, his eyes seemed to be filling with tears and he shook his head as if he could feel the pain of all those billions. *I wonder*, Joshua thought, but with this thought there was a whooping outside and a rustling on the roof.

"Stay here," Jake whispered. "I'll go out and see what's happening."

Joshua remained seated as Gimpy flew down from the ceiling and settled on Joshua's shoulder. Jake silently went to the door and slipped outside. The bamboo roof started to shake violently as did the windows. Joshua thought of the final words of Amos Pierson, the horror. He was starting to realize what Pierson meant as Gimpy pulled on his ear and the shaking stopped, only to be replaced by powerful blasts that punched holes in the roof and walls. Joshua saw black faces with red eyes starting to come through the walls as intense fear and dread of eternal doom filled his mind as he sat paralyzed by a vision of eternal damnation. The demons were moving closer as Joshua didn't notice the increasingly sharp tugs and bites on his ear. Finally Gimpy flew right at the closest evil fiend, but flew right through the ethereal body.

At that moment the door flew open and Jake burst into the room. He shouted loudly; words Joshua didn't understand, followed by a loud: "NO . . . Begone!" The young man grabbed Joshua around the waist and lifted him over his shoulder and carried him out of building. As they reached the edge of the clearing, the hut burst into flames and was completely devoured and in just a few minutes was a pile of black ash and glowing embers. The sickening smell of burning sulfur filled the air.

"This island is no longer safe," Joshua concluded. "Now I know what happened to Pierson. If we stay it will happen to us, well at least to me."

Jake nodded in agreement as Gimpy flew down and settled on Joshua's shoulder.

"Tomorrow do we start building an Ark?" Jake asked somewhat facetiously.

"An ark for three, I suppose," Joshua said. "Noah had a lot more time. I think you startled them, Jake. Next time it won't be so easy. This would be a good time for some divine intervention." Joshua closed his eyes for a moment. "A little prayer never hurts," he remarked.

Jake and Gimpy both did the same.

꧁꧂

LXXXII. Final Escape

THE FOLLOWING MORNING WAS FILLED WITH BRIGHT sunshine and a warm gentle breeze blowing off the ocean from the west. Joshua surveyed the damage from the storm and thought about the events of the past night. There were numerous palm fronds littering the ground along with coconuts and bananas scattered among them. The hut, of course, was gone; even the pile of ash was washed away. Joshua had saved his personal effects and Amos Pierson's record and notes.

"Time to start building, Joshua?" Jake called out as he ran along the beach.

"Certainly is," Joshua answered. "I think this island is demon central for some reason. Come on over here. I have a couple of ideas that may help us escape this God forsaken place."

Jake quickly complied and Joshua stared into Jakes eyes. "Inside you, Jake, is the information we need to find out where we are and how far we are from civilization. You are, after all, just a very complex computer, if you don't mind my saying so."

"I don't mind," Jake replied quietly.

"Oh, that doesn't mean I think any less of you; it's just that inside you has to be data that will allow us to locate ourselves and any nearby islands. We should be able to map out tides and currents that will aid us. All we need to do is figure out how to get away. I guess we need to build a boat and build it quickly. I think that Chesterton was right."

"What do you mean, 'Chesterton was right'?"

"You need to tap into those memory banks, lad. GK Chesterton, when asked what was the single book he would want to have if he were stranded on a desert island, answered, 'Why, *A Practical Guide to Shipbuilding*, of course.' That is what we need now, or else a whale to swallow us and deposit us on a neighboring island that is inhabited by some civilized beings, free from demons, preferably."

Jake gave a short chuckle and then smiled at his companion. "How do you do it?" Jake asked.

"Do what?"

"Not despair; turn tragedy, misery, and danger into a joke."

Joshua didn't answer right away. "I guess it's a choice, really. Either you make the best you can of any situation, deal with misfortune as best as you can, or give up and live out your days hiding, either under your bed or behind a wall of artificial pleasures that can never provide true contentment. Of course, reducing everything to a joke will only get you so far. The really difficult thing is knowing when to act and when to take a time out and let everything pass. That's the difference sometimes, between inconvenience and suffering; or life and death. Now, let's figure out where we are and how we're going to get wherever it is we're going."

Jake easily utilized his vast database to determine their position, which was in the western Pacific Ocean, close to the Solomon Islands. Joshua was able to figure out that they were about one hundred fifty kilometers from the nearest land and that it should be an inhabited island. Now all they had to do was figure out how to get there. Some sort of raft, he decided, something they could build quickly, because their uninvited guests would surely be back and may not be so forgiving this time. Even with such obvious necessity, something didn't sit right with Joshua. Amos Pierson would have done all these same things, yet he was dead. Joshua decided that some insurance was necessary.

"Jake," he said, "it seems that the best way for us to get out of here will be to build a raft of some sort. What do you have in that limitless brain of yours that can help."

Jake thought for a moment and then announced that he'd found a good set of plans for a simple, strong raft with a sail and rudder that should be adequate to navigate the open seas to the next island. He immediately went to work gathering branches and such things that would be necessary for the construction. Joshua let the young "man" do all the work while he sat at the bottom of a tree and tried to figure out why he felt so uneasy.

Certainly leaving seemed to be the obvious thing to do and he had one advantage that Pierson lacked, that being a strong artificial human to do all the hard work. It was true that there were no signs that Pierson had ever attempted to escape and it was likely that he had suffered his fate before he realized the necessity. Still something didn't sit right with him and over the years he had learned that when he felt like this it was best to pay attention and try to find some resolution. So he sat under the tree thinking, but for all his thoughts he was stumped. Logic said leave now or else suffer a terrible fate. Perhaps it was just curiosity or stubbornness, but he decided that they should stay a bit longer; that paradoxically staying close to this known danger was the prudent thing. Out on the ocean, Joshua believed was something unknown, but more perilous.

"Keep working, Jake," Joshua called out. "I'm going to take Gimpy and attend to some other business." And he left; Gimpy, as always, riding shotgun on his shoulder. The two walked into the dense forest, between the trees until they reached an area that was more open, shaded above by a canopy of leaves and branches allowing a few stray rays of sunlight to peek through and bring a colorful array of green, yellow, white, and blue to the woods.

Joshua walked slowly between the trees looking up at the vibrant ceiling. He had walked this way before and felt at peace and almost confessed the presence of God in this particular place. He was hoping for a bit of revelation to help him with the latest predicament. "Think," he said out loud. "What do I have that Amos Pierson lacked? What does one need to battle the demonic forces of evil?"

A warm breeze blew from an open area up ahead as he thought about demons, Richard Cosby, and finally the Bible. The Bible recounted several encounters with demons, particularly by Jesus; a number of miracles included the casting out of demons and he even gave this power to his disciples. His eyes lit up and huge grin filled his face as the answer popped into his head. Jesus was the answer. *Fine,* he thought, but where does one find Jesus on a forlorn island. The Cross, perhaps; it worked with vampires? It is the symbol of Jesus' sacrifice. But it's only a symbol. He needed the power of God, not a symbol. He wished he had a Bible, and as he gave the matter more consideration, he realized he needed some help. He started to kneel, to offer a prayer of supplication to a God he barely believed existed.

"Dear God, I know that I have not been a faithful follower of You or Your commandments, but despite my shortcomings, You have blessed me all these years. Now I face a crisis and I don't see any answer. Please, show me the way . . ."

"JOSHUA . . . JOSHUA," Jake was calling from back towards the beach.

Joshua stood up as Jake came running. "I've finished the raft," Jake exclaimed, surprisingly out of breath. "Come and see."

Joshua still felt a bit uneasy as he turned around and walked back to the beach with Jake. He looked up at the blue sky and decided that he would continue his entreaty later.

Jake ran ahead, and when Joshua and Gimpy arrived they beheld a truly remarkable feat; a large, truly spectacular raft that looked more than sea worthy; more than comfortable. Joshua thought that it was downright luxurious, at least as far as rafts went.

There was a double layer of neatly trimmed logs forming the base with a railing around the entire perimeter. There were three keels for stability, a mast in the middle, and two benches on either side. The whole thing was about ten by ten meters, lashed together by a series of vines with some sort of cement like material between the floor boards.

"This looks very impressive," Joshua commented as Jake stood by his masterpiece with a huge smile on his face.

"I discovered that there is a great deal of information inside my head and I was able to work pretty fast. All we have to do is load it up and drag it down to the beach. I also made these." He held up two paddles and what appeared to be a sail. "Whenever you're ready we can leave."

"I'm still not sure," Joshua replied, his voice revealing doubt. "I think we're in great danger if we stay or if we leave. Just be prepared; as with so many things, when the time comes the right path will be clear."

They spent the rest of the day in more leisurely pursuits, and after dinner, they braced for the onslaught that Joshua knew was to come. Joshua packed up everything he wished to take away and they had managed to get the raft onto the beach, ready to push off at a moment's notice.

That night as the setting sun started to fill the western sky with vibrant pinks and reds, clouds started to roll in from the north and the sky quickly darkened. They made their way to a grove of trees and lashed everything together in preparation for another stormy night. As the wind started to roar, Joshua sensed that all the howling was more than wind rushing through the trees. He peeked between the trees and saw irregular black shadows creeping towards them.

Great, he thought, a raging storm, demons all around; what more can happen? At that moment there was a bright flash of lightning, followed by the expected crash of thunder and then a second flash, this one followed by the smell of burning leaves. Joshua looked up to see two of the trees ablaze as smoke started to fill the area. Joshua grabbed his possessions and turned to Jake, who was fast asleep.

Joshua shook him and said, "I think we should go."

Jake looked around and sprang to his feet, literally pushing one of the trees down, and led them away. Gimpy's claws dug deeply into Joshua's shoulder as he clung to his adopted master with all his strength, lest he blow away in the storm. As they left the trees were consumed by flames despite the rain and wind battering them.

"Maybe the demons won't like the rain, maybe nature's power will overwhelm them," Jake cried loudly, trying to shout above the roar of the storm.

As Jake said this, Joshua had a revelation. *Power,* he thought, *is the solution;* but not nature's power, God's power as in God's word. How does God create anything? By speaking, How did Jesus raise Lazarus from the dead? By calling his name. Their shield would be the power-ful word of God. As they walked, Joshua started to quote passages from the Bible.

"In the beginning was God and the Word was with God and the Word was God . . . God so loved the world that he sent his only begot-ten son . . . It is finished . . ."

The demonic black shadows started to move closer and tried to block their path, but with each word from Joshua's mouth, they fell back. Jake was just ahead leading the way and Joshua could hear him saying, "Begone . . . back to the fiery pit . . ." and some words that Joshua didn't understand.

Joshua kept up this monologue as they made their way to the beach and climbed aboard Jake's magnificent raft. They pushed off into the teeth of the storm, Joshua continuing his biblical speech "Faith of a mustard seed . . . Follow me and I will make you fishers of men . . ."

Jake hoisted the sail despite the strong wind and they blasted out into the storm. Joshua turned around and saw a number of black shad-owy figures lined up on the rapidly receding island.

"I guess we're safe," they both said at the same moment. Joshua stopped his quotations as Jake expertly steered the raft, doing his best to negotiate the huge waves which drenched them every few seconds. Joshua finally noticed Gimpy's claws in his shoulder and carefully pried the courageous bird free and placed his companion into a solid cage that Jake had built into the deck. A cage designed to withstand wind, rain, and waves.

As soon as Gimpy was safely stored away, Joshua looked up to see a wall of water heading towards them, and above it a line of black figures seemingly pulling the huge wave to greater height as it sped towards the unfortunate vessel.

"I think we're in trouble," Jake said in a calm voice that belied their desperate situation.

Joshua closed his eyes and started up his biblical soliloquy; trusting in the power of God to deliver them. As the wave approached, Joshua raised his voice and started to quote the Sermon on the Mount:

"Blessed are the meek, for they shall inherit the Earth . . ."

As the massive wall of water approached them, the two braced for the worst, lashing themselves to the sturdy raft as best as they could. Joshua closed his eyes as he continued to speak while Jake remained remarkably calm. As the wave was about to crash into them, Jake surreptitiously turned his head from one side to the other, and at that moment, the wave seemed to break into two halves, parting to allow the raft to pass unharmed. As soon as they passed through the tidal wave the waters calmed and the wind diminished.

Joshua saw the wave disappear along with the demons that seemed to sink into the ocean, leaving a bubbling, steaming vortex of water in their wake.

Back to hell, Joshua thought and he shuddered as he thought of that place.

"Looks like we made it," Jake said.

Joshua knocked on the deck with his knuckles after Jake spoke. "An old superstition," he remarked.

The storm faded into the distance as the night became clear, the sky punctuated with a billion points of light. Joshua settled against the mast and trusted his young friend to guide them to safety. The following morning as the sun warmed his damp clothes, he awoke with the thud of the raft as it ran aground on the beach of a nearby, inhabited island. Two days later, after surprisingly minimal fuss and very few questions, he found himself back in New Jersey. Once he and his companions were safe, he took a chance and checked all the messages that had built up for both Joshua Smith and Gideon Jones. One stood out.

જ્જ્જ્

LXXXIII. Joshua's Dilemma

JOSHUA STOOD AT THE HUGE DOORWAY TO DIBLONSKI'S mansion. In his previous visit at Diblonski's Manhattan penthouse, the entry had looked imposing, but now this identical front entrance seemed old and worn. He was quickly ushered into the study. The grand home seemed tired with a sense of death replacing the sinister atmosphere that he remembered. In the study he found Aaron Diblonski alone, laying on a recliner looking like his home, old and decaying. The deep tan was replaced by a yellowish hue, the robust frame was thin and cachectic, his cheeks sunken, and the eyes were dark brown crevices with dull murky pools at their base. He wore a satin robe and he did not rise as Joshua approached.

"Thank you for coming, Mr. Jones," Diblonski greeted him.

"It's really Smith," Joshua responded. "Joshua Smith."

"Smith . . . Jones, it doesn't really matter as long as it is you. I need your help. I think you know more about me than you let on, and assuming you know the truth about me, then you will understand what I am about to tell you." The old man waved his servant away and a weak cough came from his throat. "As you no doubt can surmise, I am reaching the end of my days. I'm sure that you thought that I was truly immortal, existing since the dawn of man, and two weeks ago you would have been correct. But, everything has changed. The essence that has invigorated me for all these years is being drained, taken away, leaving me weak and impotent. I'm sure that you know of what I speak."

"I have an idea, but I don't see the reason."

"Patience, young man, that is why you are here; to share my suffering, to inform you of the beginning of the end which is rapidly approaching. I know that you have read the Bible, that accursed book that speaks of me in such unflattering terms and I suspected from our first meeting that you knew my true nature. I have lived all these years for two purposes; the first is to do everything in my power to undermine the authority of the one who put me here, to be a thorn in the side of God, our Creator, to remind him of his failure. That is my great joy. Every human that turns away from God and embraces all that I have to offer is a triumph for me and is a painful reminder to this God; a reminder of what a dismal failure He is.

"This ties closely to my second purpose, to give mankind all that he wants: wealth, sex, drugs, whatever he thinks he needs and wants in this world. All for one goal, to make humanity turn its back on this accursed God, who asks so much and gives so little in return. Towards this end, I believe I have succeeded But, now there is a crisis at hand, for me, for you, for all humanity."

Joshua looked at the dying man. "I don't see any crisis, only the end of all that is evil in this world."

"Don't be so quick to jump to conclusions, that has never been your style. Do you know Randy Peskew? Of course you don't, how could you? Anyway, he is a brilliant researcher that works for my company, rather, used to work for me. But, it seems that he has decided that he is bigger than Diblonski Ltd, bigger than the governments of the world, and maybe, bigger than God. He has made a discovery that will change everything; all that you and I know will be gone. He has discovered a matrix within the Green Dot that allows integration of the dot into cellular nuclei, in particular human cells. This matrix essentially integrates the external dot into the anatomical and physiological composition of an individual. Furthermore, coupling this with externally produced input will allow control of any individual or collection of individuals from an external source. Do you grasp the implications of this, Mr. Smith?"

Joshua answered immediately. "I think I do, Mr. Diblonski, and I agree it is a potentially disastrous scenario for all of mankind, giving you the potential to control the actions of the 99.9 percent of the solar population that utilizes the dot."

"Aye, but there's the rub, you see. Mr. Peskew has no intention of putting this incredible power into my hands; no, he has realized the enormous potential and power and he will keep it for himself, perhaps to supplant me and rise to the top of Diblonski Ltd or, more likely, to use this power to remake the world in his own image. You see, he has disappeared, vanished to who knows where and taken with him all the means to implement such a scheme. If he is successful, the spirit that has inhabited me for all these thousands of years will be gone; gone from me and gone from the Earth forever."

"You say that like it is a bad thing."

"You surprise and disappoint me, Mr. Smith. I thought you were much more insightful, but I will explain. You see the death of Satan as a good thing for this world. From your perspective, you are probably correct. But, if Mr. Peskew carries out his plan, sixty billion souls will become passionless robots, doing the bidding of Randy Peskew and humanity as we know it will be gone. Our Mr. Peskew believes such a thing is the ultimate purpose of scientific research and will usher in a utopian age for mankind. But, of course, he is seriously in error. Now do you see, or do I need to spell it out even further for you?"

Joshua was silent for a moment and then a faint smile came to his face. "Oh, I understand now," he said softly. "This has never been your desire. You depend on the free choices that men make, choosing you and the evil that you promise and rejecting the murky promise of salvation offered by God."

"You are truly perceptive," Diblonski said weakly, his voice growing more raspy. "Of everyone that I have met, you are the only one that I ever thought could understand and be able to see the dilemma, and perhaps see a way to stop such madness. As you can see, I can do nothing."

"What about your other research people; surely there is someone else in your organization capable of figuring out what this Mr. Peskew has done and find a way to prevent it. Or, surely such a vast organization as yours can find one maverick scientist, and in your own inimitable way, to which I certainly can attest, put a stop to him."

"We've tried all these things and more. There were two other researchers who were helping Peskew, but they have proved to be clueless, having less grasp of the situation than me. And, I have put my best people to the task of finding him, without a single lead. So, my dear Mr. Smith, I turn to you; you being a rare individual who seems to have bested me in every way. You have a remarkable gift, Joshua Smith; I am asking you to help the enemy, and at the same time help yourself and all humanity."

Diblonski started to cough and held a handkerchief over his mouth; Joshua could see streaks of blood on it when the coughing stopped.

They both were silent for a time and then Joshua started to speak. "You have put me into an impossible position, sir; I hope you realize that. You give me two choices, both leading to ruin. I can help you, try to find a way to halt the plans of Mr. Peskew, which would leave Satan free to roam the world, to choose another body to inhabit, or to restore yours to its previous robust state. Either way, if I do this I would have to live with the knowledge that I could have eliminated Satan from the world, but chose not to. On the other hand, I can leave Peskew alone, allow him to complete his work and carry out his plan, which would be the end of you and the end of humanity. Not much to choose from. I never should have left the track. Mr. Diblonski. I thank you for ruining a perfectly good day; rather a perfectly good life. Good day."

"Will you tell me what you will do?" Diblonski asked.

"I won't need to tell. Just look in the mirror and it will become apparent. Once again, good day."

Joshua quickly got up and found his way out of the house. The long walk home would, he hoped, clear his head and provide a third alternative.

Aaron Diblonski, perhaps for the first time in his life, was baffled by the final words spoken by Joshua. He stood up and looked in the mirror; an old man, gray and wrinkled, stared back. He picked up a book and threw it, smashing the mirror into a million bits of sharp glass.

❧❧

LXXXIV. Deborah's Task

DR. DEBORAH TENNYSON SAT AT HER COMPUTER CON-sole staring at the numbers and symbols that filled the monitor. Since the failed triumph of the ITP seven years ago she had been much in demand. Her unique math skills and insight had brought endless assignments her way. These, combined with her duties as mother to two young children, kept her busy from early morning until late at night. With David frequently gone she often found herself alone rais-ing David Jr. and Little Debbie. They were good kids, however, and made the job of mother much more of a joy than a burden. Both chil-dren were blessed with the good fortune to have their parents' best qualities, intelligence, curiosity, insight, and remarkable problem-solving ability. David Jr. was much more mechanically-minded and Deborah could tell before he was out of diapers that he would become an engineer of some sort as he was constantly building things, but never haphazard and always with the greatest attention to detail. Little Debbie, on the other hand, was much more abstract in her thoughts, dreaming of things that could be or should be, but always planning how to make such dreams come true. She was only five, but Deborah saw such remarkable thoughts from her daughter that made amaze-ment a daily occurrence; almost mundane.

Her children, at present, had drifted to the back her thoughts as she stared at the latest equations generated by her computer. She had accepted an assignment that had her modifying the existing equa-tions for super-excited photons. These entities had, up until now, been used strictly as weapons, able to carry incredible power within a very small package. They were the energy vehicle intrinsic to laser photons and plasma photons, both extremely powerful explosives. The hope was that the vast energy stored within a super excited photon could somehow be controlled, managed in such a way that the orderly and controlled release of the stored energy would allow the somewhat cumbersome battery packs that were utilized today to be replaced by something smaller and more durable. Deborah had been fiddling with magnetic gradients coupled with controlled release of electrons, which on paper seemed to offer some promise of success. Her equations, however, had not translated into a practical model.

Consequently, she was back at her computer modifying her work to try to make it fit into the currently available materials and resources. Her engineering friends told her that unless she could discover an alloy or substance that could be utilized at temperatures greater than three thousand degrees Celsius, she would need to modify her work. That had been the latest message she had received and that was what she was staring at now. She wished she had more knowledge of metallurgy as she stared at the equations. *It's not my equations that are the problem,* she thought; *it's the available resources.* Somewhere, there must be a substance that can store photons at a super high level without generating too much heat when they are released. She sent a quick message to Dr. Troistan, her chemist consultant and then put her computer to sleep. "Enough work for now," she said to herself. "Time for dinner. I wonder where the kids are?"

She found her two children quietly playing in their room, careful not to make any unnecessary noise. They knew that their mother did important work for the government and they certainly didn't want to run afoul of any official government business. David Jr. was at his computer console playing one of the latest games, while Little Debbie was reading.

I envy them Deborah thought as she called them for dinner; so innocent, still unaware of all the difficulties that planet Earth faced. Perhaps their faith would serve them and they would live to see God's final triumph. She also had faith and it was this faith that allowed her to go on, even while her companion lay in a hospital bed, unknowing and unaware. It was only her faith that kept her from complete and utter despair. But, why did it have to take so long?

"Come on Mommy, I'm starving." Her son's pleading brought her back to reality and they sat down to pray and eat.

જ્જ

LXXXV. Amos Pierson

AMOS PIERSON WAS BORN IN 2120 TO MANNY AND SUSAN Pierson of Wichita, Kansas. His childhood was nondescript, he had been an indifferent student and followed high school by matriculating at the University of Nebraska where he majored in Chemical Engineering. He became enamored with, what he called, the perfection of the subatomic world. He impressed his professors with his ingenuity and insight into the complexities of subatomic interaction. He graduated near the top of his class and promptly gave up any meaningful endeavors to spend time fiddling in his parents' basement.

Manny and Susan repeatedly tried to make him look for a job, but Amos resisted, every day going into the basement for hours building a variety of gadgets that left his parents confused. They worried that he never went out, ate poorly and sporadically, and seemed to completely neglect himself. One day, he emerged hours before his usual time of 9:00 p.m. and showed them an image of what looked like a string of beads.

"This," he said, "is the future; something that will help you move to a big house on Royal Street in the fanciest part of town. This is the building block for what I have named the picomatrix, magnified about ten trillion times. He spoke softly to the computer and the beads seemed to move, to dance and rearrange themselves. When they had finished there was a long chain.

"When this matrix is bound to silicon atoms it will be the most powerful processing apparatus in history. Computers that are now hand held will be the size of a penny." His parents just shook their heads, worried about his health, not understanding.

Of course, his prediction came true. The picotechnology he developed was incredibly powerful, elegant, and eventually, inexpensive. The simple digital switching of individual atoms strung in series allowed the tiny silicon wafers to hold vast amounts of information that previously would have required a computer the size of a refrigerator. The ubiquitous Green Dot was the most conspicuous offspring of this technology and it made Pierson and his parents fabulously wealthy. Pierson founded Picotechnology Inc, eventually sold it to his distributor, Diblonski Ltd., and then retired at the age of twenty-eight. He continued to tinker with his picomatrix and to try different configurations of the series of chips to try to improve their efficiency and storage capacity. He always worked alone and never took much interest in having any companionship or friends. Rumors of unusual proclivities towards young teenage boys were never proven and remained only rumors.

Finally, after the annual meeting with the board of Diblonski Ltd., he accepted an invitation from CEO, Aaron Diblonski, to go on a prolonged cruise aboard the Diblonski luxury yacht. On that cruise, Pierson apparently had too much to drink or took too much of one of the available recreational drugs and disappeared, presumably falling overboard. The yacht had been cruising the Pacific Ocean, near the Solomon Islands, when he was lost. An exhaustive search failed to yield any clue and he was declared dead.

His legacy continued, however, as microelectrical engineers found new aspects of his picochips that always amazed and more frequently confounded.

ॐॐ

LXXXVI. Joshua and Deborah

DEBORAH PEERED THROUGH THE DOOR MONITOR AND saw a familiar face standing outside. She hesitated for a moment, thinking about everything she had heard; but reason triumphed and she opened the door.

"Well, good morning, Joshua, or is it Gideon?" she asked, somewhat facetiously.

"It's Joshua, for now and forevermore. Gideon is dead and buried," he answered, his tone much more serious than she ever remembered. "I need some information and some help; something, I think, that only you can provide."

Deborah thought about all that he had done for her in the past, delivering her son, standing up to the most powerful man in the government, working diligently to help bring David home safely all those years ago. "You've always been more than an angel to me. Of course I'll help in any way that I can. But, first, tell me what happened to David. Tell me you had nothing to do with his current condition."

Joshua stood silently, staring Deborah straight in the eye, a look of anguish on her face. "I was a fool, really. David preached with such strength and vivid, powerful words that really moved me; but then I saw him leaving the casino floor with two bimbos and I was overwhelmed with such anger, thinking about you and your children. I should have never let such a thing happen."

Now it was Deborah's turn to be silent. "Did you ask him what he was doing with those girls?"

"I didn't need to ask; I'd seen it all before."

"The old Joshua would have been much more perceptive. You know the story of Fyodor and how he had such a profound influence on David before his death."

"Yes, I do remember him."

"Well, as part of David's ministry he decided to carry on in the spirit of Fyodor. It's true, he was bringing those two women to his room, but just to talk, to try to show them that there is much more to this world than meaningless one night stands. Most of the time he failed and the women just laughed, but once in a while his words brought true repentance and rebirth to a lost soul. I'm surprised he didn't tell you this himself."

"I never gave him a chance," Joshua replied softly, shaking his head. "You're right, Gideon was much less perceptive than Joshua. I'm glad he's gone."

Joshua and Deborah sat quietly for a few minutes, each lost in thought. A tear rolled down Joshua's cheek as he realized what a fool he had been and that everything could have been so different if he had been a little more patient. *What's done is done,* he thought and he changed the subject to his real purpose.

"Tell me, then, is there anything left of the ITP? That is, can it still be utilized?"

Deborah's eyes lit up as she answered, "Of course the ITP still exists. It's even still used regularly; to send messages to Alpha Base One, where we still have people. It seems that the power above is gracious enough to allow our miniature modules, launched from specially designed astroplanes, to pass through to their destination. There aren't any ITP vessels in service; the only one that even exists is in the Smithsonian. Why do you ask?"

Joshua ignored her question for the moment. "Has an ITP probe ever been focused on the Earth?" he asked.

A very unusual question, she thought. "As far as I am aware, no. Why do you ask?" she queried again.

Joshua still didn't answer, but asked another question. "What do you know about Hell?"

"A place of eternal torment, pain, neverending fire, separation from God. Why are you asking all this?" Deborah was starting to feel uncomfortable; "I know that you wouldn't be asking if you didn't have a good reason."

Joshua didn't say a word, seemingly lost in thought, and then he answered her questions. "I have a problem, rather, all of mankind has a problem that has been unceremoniously dumped into my lap and I see only one solution." Joshua recounted his meeting with the dying Aaron Diblonski and his big dilemma.

"So, you see, I have a choice. Allow all that is evil in our known realm to die and allow mankind to perish with him, or thwart the plans of this Randy Peskew, a new and greater evil, and allow Satan to continue to dominate our world. What do you think?"

"I think I wish you'd left me out of this. There must be another alternative."

"So do I. I've done nothing but think about this over and over for hours and I can't think of a third alternative. But, the evil you know is better than the unknown. The first order of business is to stop this crazy Peskew person. The problem, however, is how. The most powerful organization in the solar system has been unsuccessful. There is one thing I thought of that could stop him and perhaps would even help rid this world of Satan's evil; something that is crazy, even crazier than breaking into Senator Leavitt's office. Find a way to bring Amos Pierson back from the dead and hope that he knows how to stop this madness. And, if I'm lucky, I could learn something that will bring down Diblonski's evil empire, also."

Now it was Deborah's turn to be silent. "Amos Pierson disappeared and presumably is dead."

"You are absolutely right and he is definitely dead. The fact that he is dead, and knowing what there is to know about him, I don't think he went to Heaven. No, he's in Hell, which is why I was asking about the ITP and planet Earth."

"It's never been tried; portals exist in space not on planet surfaces. The enormous energy output from an ITP portal could never stay hidden if it were emanating from anywhere on the planets' surface."

"What about from the ocean or the ocean's floor. If you think about it, the depths of the oceans are more of a mystery than the depths of our solar system. For whatever reason, lack of need, lack of interest, whatever, we've focused our attention on expanding out into space; all very appropriate given mankind's circumstances. But, Hell is universally described as beneath the Earth's surface, a place of eternal torment. Satan was cast out of Heaven into the fiery pit, which is under the Earth's surface. Hades of Greek mythology is called the underworld. There is no doubt in my mind that somewhere on this planet there is a portal that will allow entry into Hell. The only way that I can see out from between this rock and hard place that I've been wedged is through the Gates of Hell."

Deborah was speechless, but her expression spoke volumes; a mixture of fear and worry overwhelmed her. Joshua grabbed her by the arm and helped her into a chair.

"This is too much," she said softly. "David's lying in a coma of some sort, all of mankind teeters on the brink of annihilation or worse, and the only solution is to find a way into the one place that promises nothing but torment and pain? What's the point? Evil has been in the world since the dawn of mankind; let it continue, it doesn't really matter."

Joshua looked into her eyes. The doubt faded away, replaced by same look of defiance he had seen years ago when she stared down Adrian Leavitt. "I know that this is an incredible longshot, but, to me, it's worth the risk. Think about it; all your life you drift from moment to moment, never really making a difference, while all around you evil flourishes. Once in a great while you jump into the foray, find yourself beaten down and retreat as quickly as you can, back to existing, but never really changing anything. Think about what the world would be like with all the people controlled by some central computer; automatons, doing as they're told, without a free moment or thought. Would it be any different than the world we live in today; maybe it would be better, no violence, no crime, everybody would be happy. Maybe Randy Peskew is offering this world a chance at true Utopia." He closed his eyes for a moment. "Intellectually, such a world has some appeal, but my heart says no, mankind achieves greatness when it is free; free to struggle. And, now here I am given a chance to rid the world of all the evil that has plagued it throughout history. That's just it, however; a chance. If I can do what I'm thinking is possible, I might be able to stop

Mr. Peskew and eliminate Aaron Diblonski. Such a thing is worth the risk. Unfortunately, this is much more of a poker game than a horse race. I need the odds in my favor. Now, tell me, is it possible to scan the Earth's surface for some sort of entry to an interdimensional plane that exists beneath the Earth."

Deborah's expression changed dramatically as her moment of uncertainty vanished, replaced by the challenge of this new problem. "The lunar surface has the most powerful ITP probe in existence. I could modify it to probe the Earth. If there is such a portal, it would have to be of much different character than the deep space portals. Even from the floors of the ocean portal energy output such as we see in space would be detected with the most rudimentary equipment. Just thinking about it for this brief moment suggests that we are looking for a narrow corridor. I still make regular trips to the moon to research and modify the ITP. Although we've no plans for any manned flights, the ITP is still useful for interstellar communications. But, even if we find the portal, how are we supposed to utilize it? We would need someone to fly the ship."

"I have someone that is quite capable of flying, in a sense. He's waiting outside; I picked him up on my last little adventure."

Deborah looked into her outside surveillance monitor and saw Gimpy in the waiting taxi.

"That's a bird."

"You haven't lost that keen perception." He went to the door and waved. Gimpy flew straight to the door and landed on Joshua's shoulder. "Allow me to present Gimpy, an individual to whom I owe a great debt and is a really good flyer."

"Pleased to meet you," Deborah said with a little trepidation in her voice.

"SQUAWK," said Gimpy, as he flew around the room and then returned to Joshua's shoulder.

"This is your crew?" Deborah asked.

"Gimpy saved my life on several occasions; He's like an early warning system, although his way of getting my attention could be improved." Joshua pointed to his scratched up ear. He decided to keep Jake a secret for now.

"Well," Deborah answered, keeping her eye on the bright green bird, "I'm jetting up to the lunar spaceport in two days. I'll find some way to justify scanning the Earth's surface. I really hate going up there; now more than ever with David being in such a state. But seriously; who's going to fly?"

"That's a minor detail I haven't worked out yet. In this world I'm not sure if there's anyone that I can really trust."

"I know someone who can do the job and can be trusted. He's flying around up there somewhere. I'll contact him to meet me on the moon."

After this serious discussion, the two sat and laughed and cried for a while, reminiscing about their past adventures, until it was time for Joshua to leave and Deborah went searching for her kids.

෨෧

LXXXVII. Lost in Thought

THAT NIGHT DEBORAH LAY IN BED THINKING ABOUT THE problem Joshua had presented. A full moon shined through her window and she got up and looked into the night sky. The bright harvest moon drowned out the stars and she thought she could almost see the bustling activity that she was sure was there. *All that activity,* she thought. That's a big problem. The peace of the previous moments gave way to consternation.

"It will never work," she said out loud. "There's no way that I'll be able to scan the Earth's surface undetected." Any activity utilizing the ITP scanner would be monitored in a dozen different ways. Even if she could distract the technicians her movements would immediately be noticed by security. This task would require a completely new approach.

I need to start with the math theory, she thought, *and then find a way to prove it and apply it, and I need to work fast.* Instead of going back to bed she sat down to her computer and started to work; starting with the physical, electromagnetic, gravitational, and geothermal characteristics of the planet. Perhaps by working backwards the area that was most likely to harbor some sort of portal would become apparent. Knowing where to focus would make the job much simpler and less likely to draw unwanted attention. She had never been very interested in Earth science and reading the detailed characteristics was nearly impossible for her, but the mathematic representations of the atmosphere and various fields that shrouded the planet were absorbed into her extraordinary mind like a dry sponge soaking up spilled grape juice. There were several areas where aberrations of the various electromagnetic fields were apparent, mostly over oceans or on sparsely inhabited mountain or desert regions. These were all collated and stored as she started the next step which was the pure math of interdimensional physics; *the fun part,* she thought.

"Start with space-time representation and topography," she said and her high powered computer went to work. Numbers and symbols danced across the monitor; values at regular intervals across the globe popped up and Deborah applied the standard ITP formulas to the actual measured values. She assumed that any interdimensional portal originating from the Earth's surface would be very small and the energy output would be much less than that found in the deep space portals she was used to scanning. Large energy outputs would have been detected long ago and there were no such reports in any of the available archives. She concentrated her study on each of the known areas of energy aberration. She sat back as the computer applied her formulas to each of the measured values, and in less than two minutes, she had her answer. There were fifteen areas that represented possible ITP portals, predicted size varied from 0.6 meters to ten meters in diameter. All but one were in areas with harsh environments; six from ocean floors, three from desert regions, four from polar regions and two from high mountaintops. The other one was just off a group of islands in the western Pacific; the Solomon Islands according to her computer. *That's unusual,* she thought, *why that one that seems different than the rest?*

"At least this will help a little," she said to herself. At least I know where to look. She felt better as she climbed back into bed to try to catch a couple of hours sleep before David and Debbie woke up.

❧❦

LXXXVIII. Randy Peskew

RANDY PESKEW SAT AT HIS MONITOR STARING AT THE extreme magnification of the picochip. Every hidden switch or possible keyhole was scanned and he was rapidly producing a map of sorts of the chips surface. A final key would soon be produced that would unlock all the mysteries Amos Peirson had managed to pack into this molecular marvel. *It would be a better world,* he mused. No greed, no frustration, perfect satisfaction for everyone. Never again would a young boy suffer ridicule at the hands of his "friends"; never again would those who were seen as different be hated and left out; never again would a young woman's life be snuffed out crushing the hopes of all the loved ones left behind. No, it would be a better place for all, and in a short time, it would all be brought to complete fruition.

His name would be revered, he would be the new messiah, showing all the world the path to perfect harmony with their fellow man. He smiled as he thought of those days long ago when he was the one that was the object of mockery and cruelty. Now he would be in charge and no twelve-year-old boy would ever suffer again, no one would be better than anyone else and everyone would be content to play whatever role they were given; the meek would finally inherit the Earth.

He turned back to his work. He had finished the analysis of the picomatrix, properly delineating all the pertinent functions and systems. Now he was faced with the task of teaching the picochips to recognize all the varied biological fields. An assimilation on the massive scale he was anticipating required that the chips be semi-autonomous, each would have to monitor their individual's cellular electric potentials and interpret them properly to allow for picomatrix integration. He set to work teaching his prototype all the biology it would need to know. As the picochip "learned " the new knowledge, he had a feeling that he thought must be similar to the pride felt by a father as his young son first learned how to walk or ride bicycle. If the chip faltered Peskew scolded himself, never his sometimes reticent student. Each success was accompanied by encouragement as he advanced step by step through the learning process. As he progressed, he was repeatedly amazed that the picochip seemed to assimilate the information autonomously, bypassing the input Peskew provided. *Brilliant*, he thought, as his work progressed.

၏‑ၐ

LXXXIX. On the Moon

DEBORAH, DAVID JR., AND LITTLE DEBBIE JETTED UP TO the moon two days later, just as planned. Little Bit also went, his whole demeanor uplifted when he heard the word "moon" and the general's name. Deborah had an idea of a plan that would allow a few minutes scan of the Earth's surface, which she had calculated would be adequate to get a reading from the Earth's surface. General Moosewood met her as she exited her shuttle.

"Hello, my dear, and look at those big kids," he remarked. "They do grow quickly. Let me help you with your bag."

"Thank you, General," she replied. "I'm glad you could get here on such short notice."

"It wasn't any problem; actually, I was on my way when I received your message. Now what can I do for you."

"In a minute, General," she said.

"I understand." And they went inside the terminal, which was a cavernous building with a huge transparent roof made of corundum, very hard and very durable. Deborah stopped to notify the Lunar Center director of her arrival and to receive her final itinerary.

"I've got about two hours until my first meeting, sir. Let me drop off these bags and kids and then we can talk." She deposited both her bag and the two children in one of the Lunar complex guest quarters, activated the automated babysitter and left to meet the general at the base coffee house. As she sat down, she activated a device on her wrist.

"One can never be too careful," she said.

"So," the general started, "what's it all about?"

She told him the whole story and her plans. The general sipped on a cup of black coffee as he listened closely to the story of Joshua, Gideon, Satan, and everything else. When she finished, he didn't know whether to laugh or cry.

"That is quite a remarkable tale and this Joshua fellow is either the bravest man alive or the biggest fool."

"I once called him 'peculiar' and that hasn't changed. He's the most perceptive, keen individual I've ever met. And, he's searching, searching for meaning and purpose in his life. He may be a fool, but he is already a hero to me and now he may be a savior for all of mankind."

"Well, I'll look forward to meeting him. One other thing; how are you going to scan the Earth's surface undetected?"

"You know, General, when all else fails try charm and sex appeal. It's never been my strong suit, but it may work in this case. It's a good thing David's in a coma; he probably wouldn't approve."

৵৽৻

XC. Charming

THE FOLLOWING DAY DEBORAH AND HER KIDS WOKE UP A little earlier than usual. They stayed in the standard living units available to personnel assigned to the lunar base. Spartan, but functional, Deborah slept with Little Bit in one unit, while the children slept in an adjoining room. Each room had a bed, hygiene center, a food synthesizer, and an entertainment system. Deborah told her kids that it was like staying in a budget motel without a swimming pool.

Still the children liked the occasional trips to the lunar surface. The spectacular view of the Earth and the fun they had bouncing to great heights in the low gravity rooms were a great treat. This trip was a bit more somber as there was serious business at hand. Deborah's idea required assistance from David Jr. to intercept the scanning data when it became available.

Little Debbie would be free to play. The general stopped by their quarters before he left for an excursion to Titan, one of Saturn's moons.

"Can I go with Uncle General, Mommy?" Little Debbie asked. "I love riding in space. Maybe we can go by the portal?"

The general looked at Deborah and smiled. "It's OK with me; nothing better than having some company on a space run."

Little Bit jumped up and barked as if to ask if he could go, too.

"That little dog," the general observed, "always wants to go. I guess he's reliving his glory days when he was the big celebrity flying about the galaxy. It's Ok, you can go, too. Don't worry, Mama, I'll take good care of both of them and I'm sure that Little Bit will take care of me."

The three made their way to the hangar and in ten minutes were on their way to Titan, by way of the infamous ITP portal. The general had an illegal ITP sensor installed on his vessel. Having former Chief Engineer Scully as his partner had many benefits; in this case an ITP sensor which allowed him to launch message pods through the

ITP, usually to the outpost at Alpha Base One, but there were the well heeled dreamers who hired him to send messages through the portal directed to God.

Deborah watched for a few minutes and then started her usual survey of the ITP equipment and data. She left David Jr. in his quarters, ostensibly playing on his computer. She stopped by the main control center and talked with Colonel J.M. Murdoch, who briefed her on summary data from the various scanners and also reported on the new portals which had been catalogued. He was an efficient administrator and nothing he presented was new or surprising. Deborah sat down at the console to run through her own survey of the data and Murdoch left her alone.

She took a break after this and had a cup of tea in the cafeteria, waited until it was 11:35 a.m. lunar time (corresponding to eastern standard time on Earth), and then made her way to the ITP sensor station where she would do her usual first-hand observations of incoming data. This was mostly routine, but in the past she had noted slight fluctuations in the incoming signals that when interpreted in context of the current protocol led to improved efficiency in ITP transmissions as the procedures were refined. The sensor station was manned by Captain Zechariah "Zeke" Willard, a career military man of about fifty who was always the epitome of military competence, but also had a bit of a crush on the petite physicist.

"Here for our annual physical, Doctor?" Zeke asked a bit facetiously.

"A bit of close physical examination is always good for the soul, don't you think, Captain Zeke?" Deborah replied with a soft lilt in her voice.

Zeke perked up a bit when she called him by his nickname; in the past it had always been Captain Willard and always in a very professional tone.

"I would certainly have no objection to any close scrutiny, particularly by someone with such lofty credentials and pretty eyes. Perhaps we could discuss it later when I'm off duty," he proposed.

"Oh, I'm sure that I'll be much too tired later. It would be best to carry out any intense diagnostics now," and she put her hand on his shoulder.

"Ma'am, don't you think that such actions are more appropriate for off duty time."

"Oh, now, when I'm in the mood for scrutinizing, I don't like anything to interfere or postpone my actions," and she put her other hand on his opposite shoulder and spun him around. She took a quick glance at the clock and saw that it was now 11:49 a.m.

Zeke turned off the surveillance and wrapped his arms around her and gave her a big kiss. She fell back against his console and her arm reached behind and she turned a big knob on the console exactly ninety degrees. Almost simultaneously she took off her glasses and laid them down on the edge of the console. At that moment a loud alarm sounded in the station and lights started flashing. Deborah suddenly pulled her arms away and knocked her glasses to the floor.

"My glasses," she screamed feeling around for her wayward accessory. Zeke bent down to pick them up from the floor just as she kicked them into the corner.

"Captain," spoke a voice over the speaker, "is everything under control in there? Your ITP sensor is offline and we are not getting any readings."

Zeke quickly picked up the black rimmed eyewear and handed them to Deborah, then looked at the console and saw that the ITP monitor direction had been rotated one hundred eighty degrees. He quickly turned the knob back and then called to the security monitors.

"Everything's OK, just a little accident."

He reactivated the surveillance system as a uniformed security guard opened the door.

"It was all my fault, sergeant," Deborah said to the guard. "I lost my balance and fell against the console and then my glasses went flying. Next thing I know, the Captain here is trying to find my glasses and all these alarms went off. I'm really sorry."

The security guard looked at Zeke and then back at Deborah, very sternly. Before he could speak, Zeke said, "That's exactly what happened, just a big misunderstanding. I'm sure no harm was done. Here, let me run a quick diagnostic."

He pushed a button and in less than ten seconds the monitor displayed big blue "READY" sign.

"See," Zeke explained, "everything is in order. Just a brief interruption, like we sometimes get from solar flares. Don't worry, I'll fill out an incident report and deliver it to the colonel later."

The guard's expression didn't change as he turned around and marched out of the room.

"I guess I should have been more careful," Deborah said. She sat down at the console and finished her required functions. "I guess we can meet later, perhaps at about eight o'clock in the canteen."

"Eight o'clock it is," Zeke replied with a note of anticipation in his voice.

Back in his quarters, David Jr. took the recording disc from his computer and placed it into his mother's. He then went back to his games; his system acted flawlessly through the whole episode as the readings from the Earth's surface made it to David Jr's computer and nowhere else. The boy sat at his computer and patiently waited for his mother to return, hoping that everything went well on her end and they had all the information she needed.

ᐁ∘ᐃ

XCI. The Portal

THE GENERAL, LITTLE DEBBIE, AND LITTLE BIT CONTINUED on their excursion into space. After they were underway, Little Debbie climbed into the general's lap and pretended like she was driving.

"I wish I could really fly a ship like my Daddy did," she remarked.

"Your Father was the best pilot I ever saw, fearless, resourceful, with just enough contempt for this life to be a step above his rivals. It's sad that he's in such a state now," the general answered.

"Oh, don't be sad, Uncle. He'll get better. God wants him to continue to talk to the people that don't believe. Daddy has to get better to continue God's work."

"I hope you're right, baby girl."

As they flew along, the general pointed out the sites. "That's Mars on the right and Jupiter will be next. It's hard to miss; it has a big red spot and it is really big. I'll fly close so you can get a good look. Once we pass Jupiter, it's only a short bit more until we reach the portal. Of course, if you just look at the portal there's nothing to see. But, the computer will show it on this monitor."

"I've seen pictures of what the portal looks like. Mommy looks at them all the time."

"I'm sure she does. Your Mommy discovered that they were out here and she showed us how we could use them. I think your Mommy is the smartest person in the world."

"So do I."

They'd been gone about three hours and the general made a turn as they passed Jupiter and headed towards the portal. He received a radio message from an Astropilot patrolling the area; a routine inquiry into the nature of his business. The general was well known to the Corps, frequently sending message units through the portal. Of course all such utilization required proper authorization. Standing orders were that no unauthorized ITP use was allowed. Any such attempts were immediately terminated using all available means.

"I'm going to find Little Bit," Little Debbie stated.

The general responded glibly, "I'm surprised that little dog isn't up here pestering me to let him drive."

Little Debbie left the flight deck and went down below to the cargo area where she knew Little Bit would be. She kneeled down and whispered to the little white dog.

"Now you know what to do. Daddy needs our help and you're the only one that can deliver this message." She tucked a Green dot into the dog's collar and then opened the door to one of the message pods that were used to send supplies and messages through the portals. She gave Little Bit a kiss as the dog hopped in and gave a little bark as if to say, "Don't worry, I know what I'm doing."

As soon as he was inside, Little Bit hit the console with his paw and it lit up. Although it was not designed for manned transport, there were controls. In the cargo area the little girl activated the launch mechanism, set it for ten seconds, with a twenty-second delay, and then quickly returned to the flight deck.

"Did you find that little dog?" the general asked.

"He was sleeping in the cargo area; he does a lot of that these days. I guess he's getting old." She tapped the general on the shoulder and pointed outside the window. "What's that star over there?" she asked innocently.

The general looked out the window. "There are so many stars out there. I don't think all of them have names." At that moment there was an alarm that sounded and he turned back to the console. "What the . . ." Before he could say anything more the message pod was launched and Little Bit was on his way.

"Good-bye, good luck," Little Debbie whispered just loud enough for the general to hear.

"What's going on?" he asked, a hint of anger and worry in his voice.

"I'm sending Little Bit to see God and to ask him to help my Daddy."

The general's anger melted away as he looked at the young child and saw such hope and trust. Instead of scolding her, he hugged her and said, "I'm sure that God will bring your Daddy back to you. And, if anyone can deliver your message, it's that dog. He really is remarkable."

੨৽৽৻

XCII. Surprise

DEBORAH RETURNED TO HER QUARTERS AS QUICKLY AS possible, but tried to walk in a nonchalant way so as not to draw undo attention. David Jr. carefully saved the data he had collected and even integrated it into his mother's ITP algorithm. He didn't quite understand all the numbers and symbols, but after he finished he realized something was unusual.

When Deborah returned and saw the data and the ITP result she shook her head and then laughed. "This is going to be quite a different ride for Joshua," she said out loud.

"What's different, Mommy?" David Jr. asked.

She looked up from the monitor when she heard the question, looking a bit confused as if she had forgotten that her son was in the room. She laughed again and then told her son what she found amusing.

"This portal is very different from the deep space portals. I guess I laughed because the mathematics is so elementary. You know your mother is a bit strange, finding comedy in math formulas. Anyway, it will be fairly simple to send Joshua through this portal. He won't need any special equipment, just a ship small enough to fit through a space that is ten by ten meters."

"I don't get it," her son stated. "It doesn't seem very funny to me."

"Maybe when your older," she said. "Come on, let's get lunch, and as a reward, I'll let you have ice cream for dessert."

ॐ∾⌘

XCIII. Little Bit

LITTLE BIT SAT AT THE HELM OF HIS MINIATURE SPACE vessel, driving like a real pro. All the lights were green and everything appeared ready for an uneventful passage through the portal. Back on General Moosewood's vessel things were anything but calm. The Astrocorps patrol had picked up the unauthorized launch of the message pod and calls were coming in demanding permit numbers and explanations.

The general's first response was silence, but as the requests became more threatening, he answered that the launch was due to equipment malfunction and that attempts to retrieve the wayward pod had not been successful.

"Is the pod carrying anything?" a voice asked over the speaker.

"Nothing illegal, just standard supply packs that are routinely kept on board each pod. I don't think you should have any cause for alarm," the general reassured the disembodied voice.

There was silence for a minute and then the voice returned. "General, a routine scan reveals that there is a living organism aboard that pod. Do you have any knowledge of this?"

The general didn't reply immediately and the voice returned. "General, did you copy my last transmission? Please respond."

Finally, the general answered, "It seems that there is a dog on that pod. I don't know how it happened but we did have a dog on board, but now we can't find him. Do you think you can disable the pod without hurting the little critter. He's very special to the little girl I have with me."

Little Debbie jumped in, "Please don't hurt my doggy. He's always bad, but I love him anyway."

By now Little Bit was getting closer to the portal, with Portal Entry in less than two minutes.

"We'll see what we can do to stop him without causing any harm."

From their distant vantage point the general and the little girl watched as flashes of light shot out from the Astroplane that was now visible. The plane was several hundred thousand kilometers away and the message pod was very small. A direct hit would be very difficult from that distance. On board Little Bit could see the flashes of light all around, but none seemed to cause any disruption to his flight. The portal loomed large on his monitor and all the lights remained green.

"Vibration initiation in five seconds," said the computer on the general's vessel. They watched as Little Bit approached the portal, flashes of light still bursting around the little ship. Little Debbie bit her lip as she saw the portal on the monitor and Little Bit moving closer. As soon as he reached the interface, there was a flash and he was gone.

On board Little Bit barked and scurried down from his pilot's chair and then back into the chair as bright white light filled the cabin. The light was blinding and then all the lights, all the power and everything else went black. The little dog sat there in the darkness for a few minutes and then a faint white light appeared in the distance.

Little Bit gave a short bark as if to announce to everyone that he had come home. The light grew brighter and brighter and seemed to move closer. Little Bit jumped down from his seat and the door to the little cabin opened and he ran out into the still darkness as the light approached. He gave another short bark and then started to run; like a spry young westie the old dog raced towards the light and as the brightness became overwhelming he launched into the air and landed in the arms of a man. The man had a dark olive complexion and he caught the little white dog in midair and held him close to his chest so that all that was visible were two black eyes and a black nose; everything else shrouded by the intense white light.

The man held Little Bit up and stared into the dog's eyes and nodded his head as if to say, "Welcome home, old friend, welcome home and thank you; thank you for a job well done." He put him down and they ran together like old friends until they stopped and Little Bit barked at the man who finally spoke as if answering a question.

"You know everything will be OK. In the end, everything will be as it is meant to be. Now, our Father is waiting."

Little Bit stood up on his hind legs; the man scooped him up and the two went off together, the light fading as they moved into the distance.

A short time later a message was sent back from Alpha Base One. A message pod had been received, empty, without any message, instructions or supplies. They asked if there was some error.

❧⟨

XCIV. Home

AFTER THE EXCITEMENT WITH LITTLE BIT THE GENERAL proceeded on to Titan and finished his business. Little Debbie sat at the controls with the old pilot, but didn't seem interested in the flight.

"It's sad to lose an old friend, isn't it?" the general remarked as he left orbit around Titan. "You grow up with someone and then, one day, they're gone. That little dog has been through more in his life than ten astropilots. I'm sure he's happier now than he's ever been."

The little girl looked up at her "uncle" and smiled. "Oh, General, I can't be sad, not for Little Bit. He was old and I knew he didn't have much time left anyway. I'm happy that he got a few moments doing what he loved and now, more than anything, I envy him. He's in his final home and there's nothing better." She looked out at the stars as they whizzed by and put her nose up to the window. "He's out there somewhere, running like a puppy, probably pulling at Jesus' robe and wanting to play." She continued to look out into space and the general half expected to see a little space vessel shooting out of nowhere with a little white dog at the helm.

He looked at his console and saw that they were approaching the lunar landing site. He activated the radio and sent a message informing Deborah that they would be landing shortly as he slowed his vessel and the moon loomed large in the window.

Deborah and David Jr. met them as they landed and they both immediately noted the absence of their little westie. The general talked to Deborah privately while Little Debbie told her brother everything that had happened.

Deborah knelt down and hugged her daughter. "That was a wonderful thing you did, for both your father and Little Bit. I'm sure that our brave little westie delivered your message. Now we just have to trust in God." Deborah wiped a tear away as they said, "goodbye," to the general.

"He's leaving already, Mommy?" the little girl asked.

"He's got some important business to attend to, but don't worry, we'll see him again and maybe your father will be better by then. Come on you two, let's get ready for the trip home tomorrow."

Deborah sent her regrets to Zeke, explaining about the tragic events surrounding Little Bit and how she needed to stay and comfort her children. She promised that they would get together on her next visit as she and the children went back to their quarters for a well-deserved rest.

The general visited her later in the day and she told him of the plan she and Joshua had devised. He offered his help as pilot and then left to pursue a few other projects that had been left unfinished. They agreed on an appropriate signal that would be sent when everything was in place for Joshua's flight.

Back on Earth, Joshua, Jake, and Gimpy were laying low, staying at Deborah's double-quad home, out of sight and out of trouble. Joshua spent the time studying everything he could find on Hell, Hades, the underworld, demons, Satan, and such. He turned to books, avoided computer searches, mostly due to his own mild paranoia about government monitoring such activity. He was particularly wary of the alliance that existed between the government and Aaron Diblonski. He worried that Diblonski might have particular interest in anyone that displayed an unusual curiosity about such things.

Luckily, he was able to find what he needed in a variety of second-hand bookstores. Dante's Inferno, Paradise Lost, The Prince, Dr. Faustus, Greek, and Roman Mythology all were useful resources along with his Bible.

Jake took the time to actually read the Bible and realized how impressive Joshua's instruction had been as the actual book varied little from Joshua's teaching. Gimpy spent his time sitting with Joshua, perched on his shoulder, pretending to read.

Deborah and her children were only gone a few days, but it was more than enough time for Joshua to finish his preparation. When she returned and announced that Joshua's plan was mathematically feasible and that arrangements had been made to get them to the portal Joshua gave a weak smile and then disappeared into his room. He remained locked away for several hours leaving his companions confused. Jake, however, of all people, was the first to observe what a tremendous strain everything had been on his mentor.

"Look at all he's been through over the past few weeks. Attempts to murder him by that devilish Diblonski, love found and lost, accusations of attempted murder, being buried alive, almost blown up, lost on a demonic island and now the prospect of waltzing into Satan's backyard to try to save the Creation that Satan hates. I think he deserves some time alone," Jake observed.

Deborah initially agreed, but after another hour knocked on the door, but there was no reply. She found the door unlocked and let herself in.

She found him lying on the bed, staring at the ceiling, lost in thought. She sat down beside him and the sudden movement brought him back to reality. He looked at her and offered a weak smile.

"It's hard," she said quietly.

"What's hard?" he answered, already with some inkling of her meaning, but wanting to be sure.

She lay back and stared up at the ceiling and said, "It's hard to have the future of mankind on your shoulders; to know that every action you take, every little step has the potential for catastrophe for yourself and for those that depend on you."

Joshua closed his eyes and grabbed Deborah's hand in his own. "You used to think that I was, I believe, strange was the word you used. I think that my peculiarities are going to get me killed or worse. Who do I think I am, anyway? March into the bowels of Hell and walk up to the head honcho and casually ask, 'I'm from the Earth up above; I have an order to place'." He shook his head. "I don't think strange is the proper word, crazy . . . insane, those are more appropriate."

Deborah squeezed his hand and stared into his eyes. "You have been given wonderful gifts and from what I've seen, you have given more of yourself than any person I've ever met. I couldn't blame you if you said, 'to Hell with the whole affair,' and went back to the track."

Joshua smiled at her comment. "A good play on words for someone for whom words are such a challenge. What do you think I've been thinking about all this time? I'm not anybody special; I've been lucky I guess and look where it's brought me; smack dab in the middle of a cosmic tug of war and I don't know if I'm doing this crazy thing for God or Satan or both. You know, before David met you, before the ITP, when I was a horseplayer and David was the top pilot, we shared one thing. We both thought that this world was all there was. Live, die, it didn't matter. David was given a sharp punch in the soul that revealed the truth; that showed him there was absolute truth and that our actions do make a difference to ourselves, to other people and to a God that still cares. Now, for whatever reason, this God has chosen me, set me on this path that could lead to the end of evil in this world or to the end of mankind. I know what I have to do and there really isn't a choice."

Deborah interrupted. "Of course you have a choice. No one is forcing you to do this. It's possible things could work out on their own."

Joshua closed his eyes and thought for a moment. "I almost have a sense of how Jesus must have felt after Peter's great confession and in Gethsemane before he was arrested. God has given me a choice; choose his way, follow this path he has laid before me or give up, let mankind perish or give Satan his final triumph. I know what I have to do." He put his arms around her and gave her a light kiss on her cheek. "I'm glad we had this time together. Now let's get ready to go."

They came out of the room together and went over all the details for the voyage into the underworld. General Moosewood was ready to go at anytime. Joshua was hopeless as navigator, but Jake proved more than able to perform the task, going through dozens of simulations perfectly. Deborah gave Joshua a parting gift, a small metal object that she said contained some superexcited photons that might be useful at some point. Two days later, Joshua, Jake, and Gimpy took the great plunge into the depths of the Earth; into the unknown world of torment, Hell.

ॐ

XCV. Entrance

JOSHUA, JAKE, AND GIMPY WERE RELEASED FROM GENeral Moosewood's vessel like a stone from a slingshot, set on a perfect trajectory to intercept the portal that would carry them to the great unknown. With Jake at the controls, the small shuttle hit the entrance dead center at a speed of .0001c; slow by interplanetary standards but plenty fast for flight within the atmosphere. Once through the portal they raced through a black tunnel heading at very high velocity; passing through a nothingness that Joshua started to think would result in a crashing disintegration of their vessel.

As they progressed, the black void became ringed by flames which grew increasingly bright, going from blue to red to orange to nearly white. The inferno started to fill the tunnel as they continued at breakneck speed through the blazing void. It became oppressively hot inside as Joshua had a vision of a large pig roasting on a spit. Suddenly, however, they slowed and abruptly stopped, the fire melted away, they hovered for a moment and then settled down into a very soft surface. Joshua looked at the inside and outside elapsed time monitors and saw that time had stopped.

"A very interesting ride," Jake remarked with an air of indifference.

"That's the understatement of the year," Joshua said as he continued looking at all the monitors. Unfortunately, there were no readings, no data, nothing. He looked outside the small window and saw that they had landed on what appeared to be a vast pillow; outside was illuminated by a faint glow, just enough to see the outline of the surrounding area, which seemed empty. "Let's go," Joshua said to no one in particular. "Bring anything that you can carry and that you think you may need."

Joshua picked up a bag with all of his essentials, some food for himself and for Gimpy, his special goggles, his new Bible, and a few other essentials. He had an idea that he may not need food or water, being outside time and space, but he put a water generator in his bag just to be on the safe side. Finally, as an afterthought, he put in his deck of playing cards and ten pennies. "In case we get bored," he said. Gimpy flew onto his shoulder and they opened the door.

As soon as the door opened Gimpy pulled at Joshua's ear, repeatedly.

"I know it's probably not safe; you don't have to remind me."

After the three exited their vessel and walked a short distance, they heard a sudden sucking sound as if a giant were drinking through a straw. They turned to see their vessel sink into the soft, pillowy ground and disappear from site.

"This could be a long trip," Jake said.

"You have a real talent for understatement today," Joshua remarked. Gimpy let loose with a loud squawk as if to say he agreed.

"The light seems to be coming from that direction," Joshua said, pointing to a spot in the distance. "There's nothing else around so that's a good place to start."

There really was nothing else to be seen. It appeared that they had set down in a vast empty space, no demons, no fire and brimstone, no lost souls, nothing but the mushy, soft surface they stood upon and the faint glow in the distance. The air seemed thick and heavy, but the temperature was comfortable, around twenty-five degrees Celsius.

The three started walking towards the light, the soft surfaces slowing their progress as with each step their feet seemed to sink into a soft mattress. Of course, Joshua realized the one thing that did not matter was time. As they grew closer to the glowing light, the air seemed to be warmer and a breeze started to come from the distance bringing a faint smell, unrecognizable to Joshua, but definitely unpleasant. The glow became a light and the breeze became a strong wind as they reached the source.

Their path was blocked by a shallow pit that extended as far as they could see in either direction and emanated a light that shifted with every moment. Joshua stared into the pit but all he could see was a billion points of light, each moving, shifting with each moment.

"What do you think?" he asked rhetorically.

Jake started down the shallow slope. "We don't have a choice, do we?"

Joshua followed as Gimpy took this opportunity to fly ahead. The air seemed heavier and it was now uncomfortably hot, Joshua sweating as he removed his shirt, leaving a sleeveless, white undershirt. The heat did not disturb Jake who went first on the lookout for any signs of danger.

As Jake reached the bottom he immediately saw the source of the lights. Large scorpion-like insects with luminescent tails scurried around on the ground. They immediately crawled up Jake's legs and started to cover his body. Gimpy flew down and picked one off, but they kept coming. Joshua waited at the edge, trying to think of an answer to this first barrier. But, as soon as the first scorpion reached Jakes eyes, it retreated, followed by all the rest. As Jake walked out among them a path cleared and he was able to walk unharmed.

Joshua started to follow, but a scorpion started to crawl over his foot and he backed off.

"They don't seem to be afraid of me," he called.

Jake turned around. "Hold on, I'm coming back." Like the Red Sea the path cleared for Jake as he approached. "Stay close to me and I think you'll be OK." Gimpy landed on Joshua's shoulder, ready to pick off any scorpion that ventured too close.

"These scorpions were probably all lawyers and politicians in their previous lives," Joshua remarked as Gimpy flew down and picked up one of the fluorescent beasts in his beak. Joshua looked at the vicious creature and noted. "Look at this thing; why it even looks like it's wearing a black suit with red suspenders, so similar to some of the shysters I've met." Gimpy tossed it away with a shake of his head and the little scorpion lay motionless on the hard ground as hundreds of its companions gathered around and appeared to devour it. Joshua threw his pennies to the ground, towards a clear area about ten meters away.

They landed with a light clinking which resulted in all the numerous vermin rushing towards the noise.

"Definitely lawyers and politicians," Joshua observed.

The three proceeded across the valley of scorpions, Joshua staying as close as possible to Jake. As they reached the end a shadow came across them as they walked up the slight incline and out of the valley and came face to face with a black wall. The air was still uncomfortably hot as they stared at the solid barrier that seemed to stretch to infinity in each direction.

Joshua took out a coin. "Heads we go left, tails we go right." He tossed it in the air and it landed on the ground propped up against the base of the wall. "We can't go straight up," he said. He threw it again and it landed heads up. They turned to the left and started to walk. Joshua wondered what he had gotten himself into, his mind wandered back to the track and better times as he walked slowly, silently. The image of Beauty came into his head and he picked up the pace.

"Keep your eyes open for anything that looks like a door," he commanded. Gimpy flew up to the top of the wall, but came back and sat on Joshua's shoulder, shaking his head back and forth

"I guess it's safe, at least for now," he stated, his ear untouched by the diminutive bodyguard.

The wall was solid and smooth, not even a seam to suggest a door. It seemed to extend for kilometers, straight; no corners or curves. As they walked they started to hear a high-pitched whine coming from nowhere and everywhere, growing louder and louder. Gimpy started to screech in his very own loud way as ahead of them they saw a gray figure making his way towards them. The loud whine faded away as the shadowy figure approached.

It appeared to be a man, very tall, dressed in a light gray robe that emanated a faint light. His face was also gray, a shade darker, with empty black sockets where his eyes should have been, dark gray teeth within a mouth without lips, a pair of flat holes for a nose, and tiny gray buds for ears. His hands were bony thin and the robe covered his feet. He seemed to float just above the ground as he quickly and smoothly moved towards them.

He hovered before them addressing no one in particular, seeming to look to the distance rather than at their faces. "Nothing is as it seems, believe nothing and nobody and you will find your way," he said in a voice that was a high-pitched whine. "You have been informed and I will say nothing else."

Joshua came forward a bit and started to speak, "Who are you, how do we find our way, where . . ." As he spoke, Gimpy flew towards the shadowy figure and tried to land on its head, but flew right through it as if it were a hologram. The figure turned and receded as quickly as it had appeared.

Joshua turned to Jake. "What do you suppose that meant . . . a riddle perhaps?"

"That's what I was thinking. A bit of advice from our unseen host."

"Hmm, nothing is as it seems; I wonder." Joshua turned to the wall and put out his arm; it passed straight through the wall. As a team both he and Jake turned and walked through the wall and into the outskirts of Hell. Gimpy was left on the other side and when he tried to fly through the wall he smashed into what to him was a solid structure. Joshua reached his arm through and pulled the bird inside by its feet, despite loud squawks of protest.

❦

XCVI. Inside the Wall

INSIDE THE SKY WAS DARK WITH A FAINT RED GLOW and it was warm, not uncomfortably hot, but heavy and humid. The ground was hard and there were what seemed to be black rocks and boulders strewn along the way. The three stood in the same place for a while and their eyes grew accustomed to the faint light. There were no plants or animals, no clouds, no sun. Joshua felt like he had landed on a lifeless moon somewhere billions of kilometers from Earth. He looked at his watch; the time had not changed since they had arrived or else it was broken.

"Well, we need to get going somewhere," Joshua said. He took a small object from his bag and set it down at the base of the virtual wall, pushed a button, and a red light shot out in a straight line. "This pointer will project this straight line for at least ten kilometers and it will project from this wall at a right angle so as to lead us towards the center of this God forsaken place."

Jake looked at Joshua and remarked. "This place may be frightening and spooky, but it is not God forsaken. He is present here as much as anywhere, maybe more. May be that is a message we can deliver to those that are here. Perhaps, there is hope. At least I believe that to be true."

Joshua smiled at the lad. "Yes, you're certainly right. There must be hope or we are as lost as every last soul that is suffering in this place. Now let's go."

They followed the light beam which passed between all the black shadowy rocks. Gimpy stayed glued to Joshua's shoulder, his claws digging into his companion's flesh. As they walked along, the rocks and boulders seemed to move with them; when they stopped these shadowy figures also stopped.

Joshua kept walking, but turned to Jake and said, "I think we're being followed."

Without turning his head or breaking stride, Jake replied, "Oh, I've known it for some time."

Joshua thought for a moment. "Just keep going. We'll find out about them soon enough, but I don't think they are anything to worry about. Probably sentinels. I think we'll be OK as long as we continue on this path."

The three continued following the red beam as the black shapes shadowed their steps. There was nothing else to be seen, the landscape remained a vast emptiness, the seemingly shapeless black emissaries started to form a corridor for the three voyagers to follow. Partly to overcome boredom and partly to get a clearer view of the terrain, Joshua donned the goggles he had been given by Mr. O'Donnel. The picture of the land changed dramatically.

With the goggles on the light became bright red, the vast empty landscape was really filled with a multitude of black creatures with deep red eyes, short and squat, with long arms. Besides the ones that they could see around them there were also creatures throughout the land, all very similar in appearance, positioned at regular interval, sentries keeping watch and awaiting new arrivals. Joshua, however, felt more than a twinge of concern. After all, why would such an army be necessary? After all, hell was a place that was only visited by the newly dead? As they walked Joshua received his answer.

With his goggles on, he started to see the creatures becoming aroused in the distance; starting to whoop and dance. Four of them were carrying a new soul, sentenced to an eternity in Hell. As the new arrival passed from the real world into this dark spiritual world, the demons celebrated; a multitude gathering around the lost soul as he was transported to his final resting place. The face of the recently deceased, as the demons danced and celebrated their arrival, betrayed a fear and terror that left Joshua overwhelmed with pity for all the condemned. Joshua watched sadly until the doomed one was out of sight, carried to the depths of Hell and a destiny of eternal torment.

"We're lucky that we aren't dead," Joshua said to his companions. Gimpy gave his usual squawk, but Jake was silent, his face revealed a sorrow that made Joshua stop as a tear formed at the corner of his young friend's eye.

"It is so, terribly sad, such a thing and so easily prevented." He turned to Joshua. "You taught me that God made it so easy to avoid such torture; just believe in Him and His word and He'll take care of you. Why didn't that person believe it?"

"That's the problem with the world today. Nobody hears those words anymore. Religion, the Bible, God; they've all been wiped away from the civilized world, replaced by very brief moments of pleasure and self-indulgence. If people could see this place; well, churches would be packed every day."

They continued to follow the red beam, but it seemed that they were reaching the end. Ahead of them the demonic escorts seemed to be gathering in their path, presenting a formidable blockade. Gimpy tried to fly over them, but a number of them rose and sent him heading back to the safety of Joshua's shoulder. Jake and Joshua stopped about twenty meters from the whooping, writhing wall of black demons.

Any ideas?" Jake asked. Joshua didn't say a word, but reached into his pocket and took out his Bible.

"This has worked before," he said as he started to read. "The Lord is my shepherd, I shall not want . . . Yea though I walk through the valley of the shadow of Death, I shall fear no evil for thou art with me." As he read, the three walked forward and the demons parted. They passed into a new realm, brighter with yellow sky, warmer and heavy with thick air. Once again the landscape was barren; devoid of plants, animals, and at least for the moment, demons. Joshua put on his goggles, but there was no change with or without them. The red beam could be seen however and they continued to follow it, downward, deeper into the bowels of the underworld.

❧❧

XCVII. Next Level

THE GOING WAS EASY AND THEY MOVED FAIRLY QUICKLY. Joshua was sweating with the warmer air and he took his undershirt off. Gimpy tried to perch on his bare shoulder, but Joshua pushed him off as the bird's sharp claws dug into his skin. As a compromise, Gimpy perched on Joshua's head as they continued on their way. At times Gimpy would fly on ahead and scout around, returning after several minutes to his perch on top of his partners head. One time, however, he didn't return and in the distance they heard his loud squawk.

Jake and Joshua ran at top speed towards the loud noise, Jake racing ahead. Joshua arrived and started to bend over to catch his breath when he looked up to see what appeared to be three large birds chasing his brave companion. Gimpy dived and weaved and seemed to be eluding the three larger birds. As Joshua looked closer, he realized that these flying creatures were not typical birds at all. They did have wings, but without feathers. The heads were those of old women with long gray, scraggly hair, deeply wrinkled faces, yellowish skin, and nearly toothless.

The proverbial toothless hag, but with wings, Joshua thought. Jake spoke up. "Harpies, I'd say, from Greek mythology. I'd say we should try to help Gimpy, but it looks like he has the situation under control."

Indeed, the green parrot had his three pursuers completely turned around and it appeared he was chasing them. He abandoned the pursuit and landed on Joshua's head as the three harpies hovered overhead, panting from the exertion.

The one in the middle, after catching her breath, started to talk. "You are not of this place, go back. Only the dead are allowed here. If you come any further you will never be allowed to leave. You have been warned, leave now or face an eternity of pain and suffering."

Joshua looked at Jake and said, "We must be getting close to something. Are you worried?"

Jake's expression never changed. "I have nothing to fear; after all I'm only a machine. You and Gimpy are living and are most vulnerable."

Without hesitation, Joshua said, "Mankind is looking at its end if we give up now. Besides, where would we go? We can't get out the way we came. We have no choice but to continue and pray that we find success. One thing I'm convinced; if we find the way to locate Pierson we will also find the way out."

The harpies continued to hover above them. When they saw that the three intruders intended to proceed, they became angry and flew at the three, baring their sharp claws. As they swooped down, Joshua ducked, but Jake, with lightning speed that surprised Joshua, grasped two of the old hags around their necks and held them. Gimpy chased the other until she was exhausted.

Joshua stood up and addressed the leader of the harpies. "Tell me, my dear, what can we expect as we journey farther into this place and how do we find our quarry, a dead soul named Amos Pierson?"

Jake loosened his grip slightly to allow the old witch to speak. "The greatest dangers wait ahead, beauty, beasts, and fire. The hounds of Hell guard the gate to the innermost places and there is the one filled with sorrow and hate. She is the evil one's possession, a temptress and tormentor. She will be the end of one of you. Beyond her is the valley of fire; the resting place for the eternally damned. An endless search you will find, but only one has the key and only one can show the way."

Joshua shook his head. "Can't anyone speak plainly here?" he asked rhetorically. He motioned to Jake, who loosened his grip and let the beasts free. The three harpies slowly disappeared as Joshua, Jake, and Gimpy continued on their way, passing into the next level, a land of bright red light, hotter still and filled with thorns and brambles, but also flowers of bright colors. There was no obvious path and it was clear the passage would be difficult.

XCVIII. Temptation and Loss

JOSHUA PUT HIS SHIRT ON, PREFERRING TO ENDURE THE heat rather than be tortured by the dense thicket of thorns that blocked their way. Even Jake saw the task ahead as daunting; despite his artificial nature he still could feel the pain of a sharp thorn in his flesh.

"It would be helpful to have a machete," Jake said. "Or, maybe we could set fire to the whole place and burn our way to an open path."

Joshua smiled at his companion as he put on his special goggles. As he expected the goggles revealed a path through the undergrowth of brambles. "Follow me," he said as he started to weave his way between the thorny bushes, Gimpy now perched on his shoulder. Jake followed closely.

"Those goggles really are amazing," Jake remarked, making small talk as they slowly made their way. "I've looked at them closely and they're nothing but tinted glass. There isn't any mechanism, no nano or picochip to power them. No, nothing but cheap glass. Still, if they can find the safe path, I'll take it. I wonder, however, if the path that we are taking is really obscure or if it is within you to see the proper way, rather than those 'magical' goggles."

"Well, there must be something to them; without them all I saw was a wall of thorns and before I saw life among the lifeless. Of course, Mr. O'Donnel saw clearly without any such aid and he intimated that all I had to do was to train my mind and I wouldn't need these anymore. I guess my mind is still an apprentice, because without these cheap things I'd be pulling brambles and splinters from every square centimeter of my body."

Joshua stopped when he finished these words.

"What's wrong?" Jake asked.

"I don't see the path anymore. All there is ahead is thorns; the clear path has vanished." He turned around and saw the same thing behind him. "It seems that we have somehow been led into a trap; I guess we're on our own. Still, it doesn't make sense, I wonder what happened to the 'magic'?"

Jake answered immediately. "The magic is real or else we wouldn't be here; but, someone has decided that it was too easy and has closed the easy road and is forcing us to take the more difficult path."

A metaphor for life, Joshua thought as he inched his way forward through the sharp underbrush. "Gimpy, fly up and see how far we have to go."

The bird flew up and into the distance, Joshua keeping him in sight. He had learned to judge fairly well how far away Gimpy was as he flew. Gimpy seemed to be about half a kilometer away when he turned around and returned.

"Not too far," Joshua said. "Well, let's get going." The three inched their way along, Joshua crying out in pain with each bramble that pierced his skin. As they were making progress the thicket seemed to grow around them and close them in. Joshua stopped, unable to get through the dense branches and thorns. "We're stuck," he said matter-of-factly. The thicket had even grown overhead trapping Gimpy also. "I'm open to ideas," Joshua said. Jake was still, but Joshua saw a look of determination and resolution on his face.

Enough of this, let's go." Jake took his right hand and pulled on the fingers of his left hand. Like a glove, his skin came off, exposing the mechanical hand underneath, Using only this left hand, he pulled and pushed his way through, thorny branches being hurled in all directions, and in a few minutes they safely emerged into a clear area filled with bright red light. A short distance ahead they saw a lone figure, dressed in a crimson gown. The air was even heavier and a foul stench of smoke and sulphur filled their nostrils.

"We must be getting close," Joshua remarked. "At least judging by the smell."

The three approached the lone figure, a beautiful woman with deep blue eyes, bright red hair and smooth alabaster skin. As they approached, she held up her hand, motioning for them to stop. Joshua could clearly see her face, which was as despondent as it was beautiful. Around her neck was a striking gold chain with a jeweled pendant hanging against her white skin. The pendant was shaped like a butterfly with bright emeralds and rubies on its head. As they advanced a figure shrouded in black materialized and approached her.

They stopped as the black individual reached her side and they heard her speak, a loud clear voice, powerful with authority, but also edged with sadness. "This is the final place; your final stop before entering eternity. Come forward and let me see your face so that you may be judged. All who are to rest in this domain shall receive justice." The doomed ones head bowed and then fell to his knees. The judge pointed and shapeless demons appeared and ushered the doomed departed one to his final resting place, vanishing behind the beautiful judge to places unseen.

"Come forward; there is nothing to fear. We are all to be judged and be held accountable."

Her voice was a haunting call and Joshua felt himself being drawn towards her. Gimpy flew from his head straight towards her taking dead aim at her eyes. As he drew close, she raised her hand and the bird froze in midair and started to plunge towards the ground. Only the quick actions of Jake saved the fearless bird from being smashed into a billion pieces as Jake caught him and gently cradled the bird in his arms. Gimpy had been transformed into a glass-like statue, wings spread and a very angry look on his face. Jake carefully placed him on the ground.

Joshua, as if in a trance, continued to advance. Before his eyes, he saw his whole life, things that he had never seen before. His parents on a ship, putting a baby in a small probe and sending it out into space, an older boy staying behind and their ship exploding under the attack of an unseen assailant. The baby landing on Earth, growing from infancy to childhood to adulthood, and with each moment commandments broken, the bad overwhelming any good. As Joshua grew remorseful over a life filled with sin, he felt a sharp blow to his head and crumbled to the ground.

Jake reached behind his left ear and then placed something in Joshua's hand, before walking forward to face the beautiful judge and his final judgment.

❧∽❦

XCIX. Alone

JOSHUA SLOWLY SAT UP, RUBBING HIS HEAD. HE LOOKED at his hand, happy to see that there wasn't any bleeding, but also noted the five picochips glowing in his palm. He quickly put them in his pocket, immediately guessing what they were, fully aware of their great value. As he got up on his feet he looked to the beautiful judge and was immediately overwhelmed by a blinding light. Her red gown had become bright white and she was kneeling at the feet of Jake who had his hand on her head. He started to run towards his young companion but was stopped by the light which had become more intense; brighter than the sun, now emanating from Jake. Joshua noticed that the oppressive heaviness and fetid smell were gone, replaced by a cool breeze and the smell of freshly baked cookies. Jake seemed bigger, more imposing as the hopeless expression that had adorned the beautiful judge of the damned was gone, replaced by serenity and peace. The light intensity increased and Joshua had to shield his eyes. It then quickly faded and he looked up to see that both Jake and the judge were gone and he was alone.

Gimpy remained a lifeless statue and Joshua saw a clear path that led to a glowing light that he was sure was a distant fire. The air grew hot and heavy again and the smell of cookies faded away. "I guess I'm on my own," he said out loud. "At least the path is marked . . . follow the yellow brick road," he murmured as he picked up Gimpy and started on his way.

The light in the distance gradually grew bigger and the air became hotter. He took off his shirt and wrapped it around Gimpy as he walked. The terrain was flat without obstacles and he made good time. Despite being outside time and space, he was sweating and thirsty. *There probably isn't a water fountain for kilometers,* he thought as the fires in the distance moved closer. He took out his water generator and made himself a drink, not ice water, but refreshing enough.

After walking for a few kilometers, the air became a little cooler and he thought he heard the sound of running water. He looked ahead and saw the fires reflecting off a flowing river. He quickened his pace and came to the edge of a rushing river, about thirty meters wide. On the opposite side he could see three large dogs pacing back and forth and beyond them a black gate. *One problem at a time,* he thought. The river glowed red as it reflected the fires that were still far in the distance.

He walked to the edge and knelt down and put his hand into the water. It felt cool and refreshing; he started to take a drink when reason overcame thirst and he sat down at the water's rim to think. Surely the water wasn't put there just for him. It must be a barrier of some sort, keeping something out or preventing something's escape. Mythology spoke of a ferry across the river Styx, guided by Charon, if he remembered correctly. He looked up and down, but there was no sign of a boat or a courier. He continued to ponder the problem for a few minutes and then a smile came to his face. He reached into his pocket and pulled out the goggles. As he put them on he saw the shadowy figure of a long boat and a lone oarsmen moving slowly in his direction.

As the boat approached he saw the expressionless face of Charon, his eyes blank, white spheres and his body gaunt, with white hair. "A penny to cross," he said in a voice that was raspy.

"How much for a round trip?" Joshua asked glibly. "I'll be coming back this way shortly."

"A penny to cross," Charon repeated.

Joshua reached into his pockets and pulled out all that he had, his deck of cards, the web of picochips that was all that remained of Jake, his Bible, and no money. *I shouldn't have wasted all that change on those vermin,* he thought as he realized he could be in trouble. But, he looked at his possessions and then at the boatsman, and had an idea. Forgive me, Jake, as he pulled one of the picochips from the array that was in his pocket. It's about the size of a penny and it looks like Charon can't see anyway. *This should get me across.* He walked up the edge and put the round chip into the outstretched hand and climbed into the ship and sat down in the bow. His courier pushed away from the shore and in just a few moments, deposited Joshua on the opposite shore where he stood face to face with three large dogs, with black, short fur and what seemed to be very unpleasant dispositions.

Charon quickly pushed the ferry away. Joshua set Gimpy down as he sat down at the river's edge and pulled out his Bible and started to read from the Book of Psalms, Psalm 23 to be exact. *It worked before,* he thought, *perhaps it will work again.* The three hounds came closer, growling, their eyes glowing red and baring sharp yellow fangs.

Joshua rolled over on to his back and then got up on all fours and crawled towards the hounds. The three dogs looked confused as Joshua barked and then lay down. The dogs came closer and sniffed him from top to bottom as Joshua got up on his hands and knees again and sniffed the other dogs and scratched their backs and then their tummies. Before long the four of them were acting as if they were long lost buddies and Joshua felt comfortable enough to get up on his feet. The hounds followed him docilely as Joshua descended deeper into the bowels of Hell, approaching a huge black gate. As he approached, the gate swung open and he walked into a vast country which was black underfoot with deep red filling the sky. His trepidation grew as the three hounds stayed behind and the gate closed behind him.

৯৩৬

C. Inside Hell

JOSHUA SAW WHAT APPEARED TO BE THE FIRST SEM-
blance of a shelter up ahead as he walked into downtown Hell. There
was the proverbial fire shooting up beyond the low buildings and there
was a definite scent of sulphur and burning rubber filling the air. *It's
good that I'm outside time and space and breathing isn't really necessary*, he
thought, *because the air here is caustic and stifling*. He consciously tried
to not breath, trying to avoid even a tiny whiff of the stench that was
all around.

As he walked on, carrying his Bible, he was met by a tall, black
figure walking fully upright, muscled with red piercing eyes and long
sharp fingernails. He was clothed in blackness, androgenous, but a
very imposing figure.

"You are not of the dead, Joshua Smith. You have no right to be in
this place," the demon spoke, although his lips did not move.

Joshua walked up to this frightening emissary and responded, "I
come seeking one that has died and is now in this place. You will bring
him to me." Joshua decided the forceful direct approach may be best
and figured the worst that could happen was that this demon would
say no.

Raucous laughter filled the air from all directions as the demon
turned and walked away. Joshua stayed right behind and continued
his dialogue.

"You seem to be in charge here. You must have billions of inmates.
Surely you have the authority to release one of them, or, do you have
to get permission from the big boss? You are just a peon, is that it?
Well then, let me talk to someone who can really make a decision, not
some lowly flunky. What's your name anyway. Demon?" *I'm taking a
big chance*, he thought. This big lout probably could crush me with one
hand.

The imposing figure seemed to grow taller and, as they reached what turned out to be a series of gazebos, turned to Joshua, towering over him. "My name is Krono, keeper of the denizens of Hell. That book you carry is not wanted here." Joshua's Bible burst into flames and in an instant was nothing but a pile of ash. Krono turned and started to walk away, but then stopped and turned towards Joshua. "You may look for the one you seek among all the inhabitants of this place and if you find him you will both be free to leave. However, you will only be able to make one choice and no matter who or what you choose you must leave, and be content to live with your chosen one until it is time for you return to this place."

Joshua thought over these terms and realized he wasn't in much of a position to bargain. *Maybe I can get a little more help,* he thought. "Where do the inhabitants live?"

Krono moved aside and Joshua looked out over an endless sea of black boxes, stretching as far as Joshua could see and each surrounded by flames. He heard soft whimpers and blood curdling screams while black demonic figures patrolled overhead screeching their ear piercing cries, their red eyes glowing against the black sky.

"You are free to go out among the people, look at them, study them and when you are ready we will know and the one you choose will be released to you and you will be free to leave."

"But, what . . ." Joshua started to protest, but Krono was gone as Joshua thought of the impossible task that lay ahead. *At least I've got all the time in the world,* he thought. He stooped down and scooped the ash that had been his Bible into his hands and put it in his pocket. *It may have some usefulness later,* he thought. As he passed the gazebos he saw a series of striking images, incredibly vivid paintings, photographs and holograms all suspended in midair and each displaying great tragedies from Earth's past. Cain murdering Abel, people perishing in the Flood, great wars, ancient Rome with crucifixion upon crucifixion leading to the Crucifixion, plagues, epidemics, mass murders all in excruciating detail. In each image the specter of Death could be seen, cloaked, his face hidden. Along with the multitudes that had perished the faces of the perpetrators were clearly seen, a hall of fame of evil in all its dubious glory. As he passed this gruesome display, Joshua was struck by a face that seemed to be present in almost every representation; the same man over and over, wielding a knife, a rope, disease, automatic weapons and every other means known throughout history that could bring death. The same man standing over the prostrate body of a beautiful woman, a bloody knife in his hand and a look of sadness on his face, appearing again as a Babylonian, later as a Roman soldier, and then a general riding at the front of his troops; be it in a chariot or a tank, a bishop during the Inquisition, and many others, always at the scene of death and destruction, but with the passage of time the look of sadness disaapeared, replaced by looks of satisfaction, triumph and exultation. As Joshua exited the macabre gallery, he wondered about this ageless agent of death, who this man was and if he was still out in the world. Joshua made his way to the edge of a short slope and looked out over an endless sea of black boxes. As soon as he reached the first black box he realized just how daunting this task was going to be.

The air was oppressively hot and Joshua had to be careful to avoid the frequent flames that shot up from the ground. The pungent smell of burning sulphur filled the his nostrils; luckily there was a faint hiss before a fire flared up so he was able to avoid being burned, although these flares made his chore more tedious. He reached the first box and saw that the top was cloudy, but he could see inside, a sight which horrified him and made him jump back. Inside he saw a human figure, hairless, naked, being slowly consumed by what seemed to be a liquid fire, wide swaths of skin dissolved before his eyes leaving the underlying muscles exposed and the lost soul writhing in pain. The dead one slowly melted away; muscle and organs dissolving until it was only a skeleton which became dust and then the whole process reversed and the body reformed; seemingly causing as much agony and suffering during its regeneration as it had experienced with decay.

There was no clear way to identify the poor individual, the eyes were empty black sockets, the gender indiscernible; indeed, there were no distinguishing marks of any kind on the body. He went on to the next box and found that, although the body was different, still it was impossible to identify that individual. As he studied each of the lost, demons flew overhead delivering new arrivals. It was easy to identify each new guest; although stripped naked, their faces and bodies were easily distinguishable, maintaining the appearance from their moment of death. Joshua felt sad for them as they were lowered into their boxes of doom and he pitied them as they screamed, but he was helpless. Then two demons flew up close to him with a smaller bundle. Joshua heard a faint whimpering as he saw the black monsters lower their charge into the waiting resting place. He stopped his work as a child, a young girl no more than ten was gently placed into her awaiting torture chamber. He was able to clearly see her face, a face full of inno-cence and trust. He watched as the lid was closed and flames started to creep over her petite frame.

Joshua sat down on the hard, jagged rocks that separated each box. The soft cries of the child filled his ears and he started to cry, feeling completely lost and helpless. It finally dawned on him that this was a truly hopeless task. Overhead the screaming of various demons grew louder as Joshua closed his eyes to contemplate the impossible mission he faced. Hopelessness overwhelmed him as he continued to weep, not for himself, but for all of humankind that was condemned to eter-nal suffering. He wept for lost children and for the rest of humanity destined to bear such a cruel fate and he cursed Satan. "Oh God, Lord . . . if you are truly good; how can You allow Your creation to suffer so?" And he wept. The crushing despair gradually faded, replaced by weariness. He moved away from the sea of the damned and lay down to rest. After a short time he returned to his search.

There must be some way, he thought. If such a place as this exists, which it obviously does, then, there is no question that Satan is real. Of course, he knew this to be true because he had seen his demons both here and on the Earth's surface and he was pretty sure that he had seen the Evil One himself. If Satan is real then God must also be real and if He is truly God, then He is in control and surely will provide a solu-tion to this insurmountable problem.

After a few minutes, though, no great revelation came to him and he resumed the tedious quest to find Pierson. Peering through the cloudy glass like covers he easily studied each individual. He gradually became unaffected by the litany of screams and whimpers that emanated from each eternally damned soul, and after a while he was able to recognize distinguishing characteristics of each individual. He learned that he had to study each box at the moment their bodies had completely regenerated to get an accurate examination. Still, it was exhausting and his work progressed very slowly. He really wasn't even sure what he was looking for, assuming that when he found the right one he would somehow jump up and announce his presence. He searched for hours and hours, day after day; examining thousands of living tombs without any hint of success.

Although he knew that time didn't matter, the limitations placed on him by Krono worried him. All his life he had utilized his special God given skills to make an endless series of "right" choices. Now, with the fate of mankind depending on his next decision, he was understandably hesitant to make any choice. As his searching continued the demons flying overhead became more familiar and, to break up the monotony, he even tried to talk to them. In particular there was one pudgy little black monster who seemed especially interested in Joshua's predicament.

"You up there," Joshua called. "Come down here and give me a hand."

The fat demon looked confused; no one had ever spoken to him before. He flew closer, but did not land. He was hovering at eye level as Joshua spoke to him. "You must know all these lost souls pretty well. I'll bet you're the one that makes sure the big furnace or whatever is under here, is actually working. Help me find the right one and I'll get you a better job."

The demon looked at Joshua with his red squinty eyes, almost seemed embarrassed, but then flew away, back to patrolling the sky. Joshua closed his eyes, and even though he wasn't sure what he believed, whispered a brief prayer of thanks. From that moment,

Joshua took every opportunity to address the plump little evil spirit as he continued his search, more for show, not really expecting any success. His new "friend" frequently hovered close and Joshua would talk to it like he was talking to a second cousin from a foreign land, never sure if he was understood, but confident that their distant relationship was enough of a bond. The time passed slowly (figuratively). Each time, however, the demon stayed longer. The other wraiths flying overhead seemed oblivious or indifferent to the meetings.

One time Joshua felt the demon, which he had named Pudgy, brush against his shoulder. Pudgy's foot was like a horses hoof, hard and rounded, uncloven. Finally, Pudgy spoke, "What are you looking for?"

"A person," Joshua replied.

"These are all dead persons; isn't one of them good enough?"

"I'm looking for one particular person."

"Good luck, they all look alike to me. Only the big shots know who's who."

The conversation was getting interesting. "Who knows and how do they know?" Joshua asked.

"I think that Krono keeps it all in his head. He can find any one individual in an instant. Once in a while the bigshots have special jobs for some of these dead folks. It gets them out of their box for a time. Of course it's always so sad when they have to go back in."

"Do you see Krono very often or know where he keeps a list?"

"Oh, he doesn't have any sort of list. I told you, he has it in his head. I don't see him much. He spends most of his time playing cards with some of the other bigshots." Pudgy said this with a note of envy and disgust.

At the mention of cards Joshua felt a glimmer of hope. He reached into his pocket and pulled out his deck of cards. "Does he play with cards like these?"

Pudgy took the cards from Joshua, who reluctantly gave them up. Pudgy turned them over and over and looked at each one individually and then handed them back.

"That's what they play with. Either Krono or Death almost always win; I think they cheat."

Joshua thought about this for a while and realized that there was a better way to find Pierson, a much easier way than searching through each God-foresaken box. He only hoped that demonic nature was not much different than human nature.

"Come on, Pudgy, I'm going back to find Krono and, with any luck, I'll have my man very soon." The fat little demon hovered overhead, confused, but curious and more than a little worried by Joshua's confidence.

శ్రీంళ

CI. For Keeps

JOSHUA WAS WHISTLING AS HE RETURNED TO THE EDGE of the sea of glass coffins. Krono and some of the other demons were waiting, almost as it if they expected his return.

"You have made your choice?" the demon asked as Joshua walked up the short embankment and stood by Krono who continued to speak. "You have been very quick in your search; I hope that you choose wisely. We have never had a living being join us in our eternal festivities. Your presence has been very entertaining."

Joshua took a step back and looked up at his adversary. "Oh, I'm tired of the search," he remarked trying to sound carefree. It's time to take a break and relax. One thing I've figured out about this place. Time doesn't matter; so, two days, two months, two millennia, it just doesn't matter." He sat down and took out his deck of cards and started to lay them out in the array that would be expected for a game of solitaire. Krono and the other demons looked on with great interest.

"You enjoy playing cards, Mr. Smith?" the black figure asked.

Joshua nodded as he continued to flip through the cards, clumsily. "It's all the entertainment I could carry here. Not too many things that amuse me can fit in my pocket." He continued to play the game, deliberately putting a red five on a red six.

Krono looked on and pointed out the mistake.

"Forgive me," Joshua remarked. "Cards, although OK to pass the time, have never been my strong suit. I was much better at horses."

"Oh, you are forgiven, but do you only play solitaire? I mean, there are other games."

"I've played bridge once in a while and poker, but not very well."

"Well, that's quite a coincidence. We play poker sometimes to pass the time as you call it. There isn't much to do here. Our guests don't require much attention. Perhaps you would like to join us?"

"I don't really know," Joshua said with an air of innocence about him. "I don't have any money or anything of much value."

"That's OK. We'll just play for fun," Krono responded, a sly smile creeping onto his thin black lips.

"Sure, I'll give it a try." He scooped up his cards and followed the head demon to a table set up a short distance away. A few other larger, more important looking demons joined them.

"We usually play straight poker, five card draw," Krono explained with his powerful voice.

Through all this banter, Pudgy hovered overhead, but remained in the background, trying to stay out of the way, but also trying to capture every word that was spoken. When he saw what was happening he tried to warn Joshua. "Don't do it, you can't . . ."

"Silence, insignificant troll. Get back to work," one of the larger demons snarled.

Pudgy receded into the background, but didn't leave.

Joshua sat down at the table with Krono and four other large demons, three looked just like Krono, but the fourth was cloaked and only his bony hands were visible. Chips were given to each player and everyone anted up.

"Five card draw it is, boys," Joshua said almost cheerfully. He shuffled the cards, rather ineptly and dealt them out.

Joshua slowly fanned out his cards, just enough to see what had been dealt. His adversaries were a little less cautious and Krono was downright gregarious, saying, "Ok, now it's finally time for some action; you. Bones," he said, pointing to the cloaked figure, "try not to be so loud," and the head demon let out a big laugh as he looked at his cards carelessly. Joshua exposed a pair of Kings, along with the five of spades, four of clubs and two of diamonds. He started the betting with twenty dollars. The chips, he learned, were designated as one, five, ten, and twenty dollars, with a limit of two hundred.

Krono called, as did Death. Joshua called his bony competitor, while the others folded. The draw brought Joshua another King and a pair of sixes, a full house. Joshua checked. Krono bet one hundred and Death called. Joshua raised one hundred and Krono raised another hundred as Death folded. Joshua also folded, giving the pot to his rival, but also laying the groundwork for his ultimate plan.

The play went back and forth and Joshua continued to lose. As the game dragged on, Joshua was soon down to only a few chips. "It looks like I'm the big loser, so far," he said.

Krono looked over at him and said, "Soon, it will be time to pay up. You owe quite a bit. What do you have to settle your debt?"

Joshua emptied his pockets; which now contained his goggles, Deborah's superexcited photons, the ashes that had been his Bible, and the four remaining chips that had been Jake's. When the demons saw the chips and the goggles, they became silent and then seemed excited. Joshua realized that these demons recognized the special importance of these items.

"I'll tell you what, fellas. Let's play a few more hands; I offer myself along with these paltry trinkets as the stakes. That ought to more than cover my debt. But, what do you have of value to put up?"

Krono offered women, Joshua's freedom, and valuables, but Joshua refused them all.

"Here's the deal, demons. I'll put up myself, these goggles, and these four life-giving chips and my friend here"; he hoisted the frozen form of Gimpy onto the table, "against your giving me what I came for. The return of one Amos Pierson, but not any Amos Pierson, because I'm sure that you have several here. No, it has to be the Amos Pierson that discovered the picochip technology and I want him fully intact and functional."

Krono looked at Joshua and his possessions and then at his fellow demons. Joshua noticed a look of concern on his face, one that he quickly exploited. "A real gambler, a pro, wouldn't have to think for even a second. You have billions of souls here, I'm only asking for one. What does it matter to you if one person leaves. Your boss, he'll never know the difference. I certainly won't say anything"; Joshua looked at Pudgy. "You won't say anything, will you?" Pudgy smiled, but remained afraid to speak. Joshua thought that he had one thing in his favor. Krono, for all his bluster, was not a very good player. As a matter of fact, Death was the only one that really understood the game. Still, poker was not the races; there was much more luck with cards.

Finally, Krono spoke. "OK, you've got a game. Only," and he gave a devious smile, "it will just be you against Bones, here. Five card draw, stakes will be you and your affects against the return of the Arthur Pierson you are seeking. Each of you will be given two thousand dollars in chips and play will go until one of you has lost all. Agreed?"

Joshua's expression never changed as he answered, "As you've said, except it's Amos Pierson; but, give me a few minutes break and then we'll start." Krono agreed.

Joshua got up and took a short walk; Pudgy trailing a few steps behind. He had exactly what he wanted, at least what he thought he wanted. But, it was dawning on him that the stakes were terribly high. He had never cared a bit about the money he had won and even when he was matching wits with the likes of Richard Cosby or Adrian Leavitt, he really had very little to lose. But now he faced an eternity of suffering and the possibility that he was giving the enemy the means to create life. Perhaps, the stakes were too high. He thought about Deborah and her kids, David, Bessie, and Beauty. Their lives, their happiness were worth the risk. He shook his head as if he were shaking the doubt from his mind. *What's done is done,* he thought. *Let's get on with it.*

Pudgy sensed his anguish and hovered overhead and offered a smile, but was afraid to do anything more. He saw Joshua put his head down for a moment and then turn and return to the game.

"OK, Bones, deal," he stated resolutely. They each threw in their ante and the game commenced. Joshua carefully peeled his cards back revealing a whole lot of nothing. He looked over at his rival; only the bony hands were visible, his face remained cloaked by the traditional garment. "Check," Joshua stated softly.

"Fifty," was the hushed, raspy reply.

Joshua threw his cards down. *A long way to go,* he thought. But, for the first time in his life, his hands shook as he shuffled the cards and dealt the next hand. He picked up his cards and gingerly exposed them, trying to reveal only enough for his eyes. This was a better hand, queen of diamonds, queen of hearts and the rest diamonds.

His rival opened the betting with fifty. Joshua paused for a moment, looked at his cards again and called. He took three cards in the draw, while Death took one.

"One hundred," said Death.

Joshua looked at his draw, which had brought him another queen. "One hundred," he quietly spoke, "plus two hundred more." The stakes had quickly escalated, but Joshua saw a slight tremor in the bony hand and felt more confident as he was called. He lay down his three queens and was inwardly elated when his opponent tossed his cards with a raspy grunt.

The play went back and forth for a few hands as no one seemed to get any decent cards. Joshua's confidence was building and with it his eloquence.

"You know," he addressed his cloaked adversary, "you really have an unfair advantage, not showing your face. I mean your facial expression could be your downfall. If you really want to be fair you'll pull that cloak down and let me see what you're really made of."

"As you wish," said the soft croaky voice. The bony arms reached up and pulled the hood from his head, revealing a barren skull with large spiders, scorpions, and a variety of disgusting insects crawling in and out of the various orifices. Joshua was indifferent to the horrid display and said, "Deal."

Death picked up the cards and started shuffling with a dexterity he had not previously demonstrated. Joshua watched diligently for anything unusual as the ruffling of the cards replaced the silence. For a brief moment the cards disappeared from view and Joshua suspected something was about to happen. When he fanned open his cards he was greeted by four fives. He had just over two thousand dollars in chips and started with one hundred. Death called and raised fifty and Joshua called. Joshua took one card and his opponent three. The betting resumed and Joshua bet one hundred. Just to be sure he peeked at the cards again and confirmed that the four fives were still there.

After this first bet Death spoke, softly saying, "Let's end this duel," and he pushed all his chips into the center. Joshua looked at his cards again and quietly called. Death, with the slight tremor in his hands lay down his cards revealing four eights. He started to pull in the chips when Joshua stopped him.

"Whoa, Tex," he said in a fake southern accent. "Read 'em and weep." He put his hand down revealing four queens and before any of them could do anything he stood up and grabbed his valuables. *Paul Newman would have been proud,* Joshua thought. "Now, I believe you owe me one Amos Pierson," he said addressing Krono.

The demon's eyes glowed a deeper red and he shot a fierce glance at the forlorn figure of Death; defeated by a mere mortal. The cloak had been replaced and he was slowly walking away.

"A deal is a deal and the wager is to be honored. The one you seek will be delivered to you and will be with you when you leave this place. However, it is up to you to find the way out. I will only tell you one thing. You must follow the rules to exit with Mr. Pierson, and I trust that you know the rules. Neither myself or anyone of this place will assist you." He gave a sharp look at Pudgy. "You are free to go."

"When can I expect Mr. Pierson to arrive?"

"Don't worry, he'll be with you. Good-bye, Mr. Smith." A blaze of flame shot up from the ground enveloping all the demons and surrounding Joshua, who stood by unfazed by the heat and the demons. He picked up his belongings and Gimpy and looked around. In one direction was the endless graveyard of lost souls, while behind was the presumed path out, back the way he came. He had to follow the rules, but no one had told him the rules.

"Think . . . think," he said to himself. "How does one get out of Hell." He sat down and tried to recall every story he had ever heard about Hell, Hades, the underworld, the fiery pit, and such. The air seemed hotter and flames were moving closer. I'm going to be forced to make a move very soon he thought. There was a narrow corridor between walls of fire, but he remained wary. He put on his goggles and saw that his caution was justified. The corridor lead to a deep pit; definitely not the way to go. He looked around and saw that the fiery red curtain had a small blue area that was invisible to his unaided eyes. It was a very small corridor, but passable if he crawled.

He picked up Gimpy, put the cards, the ashes of his Bible, Deborah's supercharged photons, and Jake's chips into his pocket, and crawled to the deep blue exit.

ठ≈ढ़

CII. Escape

THE WAY WAS CLOSE AS THE REAL FLAMES LICKED AT his arms and legs. He had become accommodated to the heat and the superficial burns he suffered were ignored. Indeed, he had been through so much pain the last few weeks that he felt like any true comfort would almost be more disturbing. The safe passage seemed to go on forever; he wondered when Pierson would be delivered to him and he worried that his safe corridor would collapse at any moment. He was tempted to look behind, but he remembered his Greek mythology, Orpheus in particular, so kept his eyes forward. The goggles and the flames kept him focused.

After what seemed to be a couple of hours of crawling, he emerged from his fiery tunnel to three growling hounds. He hoped that they remembered. The dogs moved closer and Joshua realized that his previous antics would not be helpful. It was apparent that they were much less receptive to bodies leaving than to those arriving. The three growled and circled around. Joshua put Gimpy down and reached into his pocket hoping for a miracle. He felt the picochips and his cards and then the ashes of his Bible. *It's worked before,* he thought, *maybe it will work now.* He pulled the charred remains of the sacred book from his pocket and sprinkled some down in front of his feet.

The dogs came forward and sniffed the blackened paper and then took a few steps back. Joshua put a bit more out and in this way, slowly made his way to the river. He placed the last remnants of his Bible in a small pile next to the edge of the river as he stared ahead across the water. He expected Charon to appear, but after waiting for several minutes he realized that the boatsman only carried things one way across the water. He knelt down and put his finger into the water; it was cool and the current wasn't too swift.

He looked across the river with his goggles and saw a point where the water had a greenish hue, definitely separate from the black appearance of the rest of the river. He inched his way over to the edge, keeping a wary eye on the hounds, but they were still mesmerized by the charred remains of the Bible. Once he reached the spot he eased his way into the river, still keeping his eyes focused ahead, across the water. The greenish hue revealed a shallow area, very narrow, but passable and he inched his way across, fighting the swift current, holding Gimpy aloft. As he reached the opposite shore a strong wind came up and blew all the blackened portions of the Bible across the water where they coalesced in front of a very surprised Joshua and reconstructed themselves into the Bible he had lost. He stooped down to pick it up and as his ear came close to the ground he started to hear a roar. From both sides there was a wall of water heading towards him and he could see Charon in his boat pointing in his direction. Joshua didn't hesitate as he picked up the Bible and Gimpy and started to run away from the river towards what he presumed was the way out. The goggles revealed a distant light and he headed in that direction.

The waters closed in as Joshua stumbled frequently over the very rough terrain. He kept his eyes focused on the distant light as he ran. The air was becoming intolerably hot and sweat poured down from his forehead and the goggles slid down around his neck. The distant light disappeared and he scrambled to pull them back on, all the time running as fast as he could to stay ahead of the raging waters and angry boatsman chasing him. He managed to get them back over his eyes just in time to see a wall of flame flare up in his path. He abruptly stopped and nearly dropped Gimpy as he saw the flame shooting up from a deep chasm. As he stopped the frozen form of Gimpy banged into his face and the goggles were thrown off, landing on the edge of the ravine. He carefully put Gimpy down as the flames shot up on one side and the waters approached from the other.

Not much of a choice, he thought as he bent down to retrieve his extraordinary eyewear. As he went to grab them, however, his hand brushed against some pebbles and he saw his goggles slide over the edge into the abyss. He stood at the edge and watched them disappear, thinking, for a moment, that he should jump in after them. But, he remembered what O'Donnel had said, hearing the older man's words as if he were standing in front of Joshua.

"We see and hear what we have been trained to see and hear . . . I have already learned to see where others are blind."

The words resonated in Joshua's head as he looked out over the chasm and saw a narrow bridge that started just to his right, the distant light also faintly appeared on the other side. "OK, here I go." He picked up Gimpy and started across the bridge which seemed to be suspended in the air without any support. Joshua heard the water reach the edge of the gulch, but he kept his eyes focused straight ahead. He reached the far side safely and walked on. He could clearly see the light in the distance. He looked at his watch and saw that the hands remained stuck at 2:22, which meant that time hadn't started yet and that he had a ways to go. He fully expected more obstacles as he walked on.

ॐ

CIII. Most Dangerous

THE LIGHT IN THE DISTANCE GREW CLOSER AS JOSHUA continued his escape. The land became more civilized, smoother, with patches of grass. The light was very bright as he passed through what seemed to be a park. There were no signs of any living creatures as he approached the light and walked towards a low building. He approached slowly. Light emanated from a lone window; the inside was obscured by a curtain.

A final tormented soul, perhaps, but one who is special as it appeared to be a more spacious prison. He stood at the window, staring, trying to find a crack to see inside. As he was scrutinizing the various folds of fabric the curtain drew back revealing an elegantly appointed room, filled with jewels, fine food, linens and a woman, sleeping face down on the bed. He banged on the window, but she didn't move. Her chest heaved up and down as she slept and after a time she turned and Joshua let out a loud gasp, for there was Beauty, or at least the exact image of Beauty. Joshua couldn't believe his eyes and could do nothing but stare at the lovely figure that was now starting to rise from the bed.

The first thing that she did was approach the window and smile. She put her hand up and Joshua did the same opposite her. *This must be some sort of trap,* he thought. This cannot be his Beauty; even though his head said leave, his heart said stay. He looked around for a door or any entrance, but there was none. There were plenty of rocks around, perhaps he could smash the window and free her. *Chivalry lives on,* he thought; *nothing like rescuing a damsel in distress.* He picked up a medium-sized stone, large enough to shatter the glass, but small enough to easily throw.

He stood back and motioned for her to do the same. His arm cocked, he suddenly relaxed. *Something isn't right,* he thought. He sat down to think, but kept his eyes fixed straight ahead. He thought about Satan, he tried to remember everything he could about the evil one, every word the Bible used to describe the Prince of Darkness. He was called the Evil One, Accuser, Father of all Lies, Spirit of the Air, Ruler of the Earth. He hates God's Creation, will not bow down to man, hates mankind, Father of all Lies, Father of all Lies. This description resonated over and over again in Joshua's head. He put the stone down and went back to the window. Beauty was smiling at him, but when she saw that Joshua had no intention of smashing the window, that he was going to walk away, she grew angry.

She gave him the most hideous look and threw herself on the bed, got up, tore her silken gown and with each act of anger, her face changed. The smooth white skin became gray and rough, her hair fell to the ground, the finely manicured nails grew long and curled into claws; her deep thoughtful eyes boiled red. Beauty had become the Beast; a hideous beast that, for a brief moment, resembled Aaron Diblonski. Anger twisted the monstrous face into an unrecognizable mask as it approached the window and, with a single blow, shattered the glass. Joshua picked up Gimpy and raced away as fast as he could, but the beast was faster and quickly started to close the gap between them.

This is the end, I guess, Joshua mused. He stopped and sat down, pulled out his Bible and started to read, randomly opening the book, landing, not on Psalm 23; this time it was Isaiah 43. He skipped the first part and went straight to, " . . . when you walk through the fire you shall not be burned and the flame shall not consume you. For I am the Lord your God . . ." The monster stopped for a moment. Joshua kept reading, but also reached into his pocket. He pulled out the chips that Jake had left for him along with Deborah's superexcited photons and held them in his left hand as he continued to read from the Bible. The beast, his eyes blazing, claws extended and mouth gaping started to advance. Joshua continued to sit and read, thinking it ironic that someone that only cared to consume fresh food was about to become the freshest of meals for Satan's demon. As the monster reached out with his arms Joshua pushed the switch on the superexcited photons which activated instantly and released a blinding white light. The vicious monster stopped and stood straight up almost falling backwards, putting his hands over his eyes. Joshua jumped up and struck the beast on the wrist with his Bible and slapped the four remaining chips onto the scaly skin of its forearm. The chips glowed with an even brighter white light as the towering servant to Satan let out a deafening roar before staggering back, falling to the ground and bursting into white hot flames. In a matter of moments there was only a pile of ash.

Joshua stood up, wiped the dust from his feet, picked up Gimpy, his Bible and what he saw was one of the chips which had survived the attack and still glowed with power. He put it in his pocket and looked ahead. A long stairway lay ahead, carved into a steep stone hill and continuing upward as far as he could see. There was a faint light and patch of blue; the way out he presumed. He walked on, always keeping his eyes focused on what was ahead. He reached the stairs and started the long climb, stopping every so often to listen for any pursuit. It was a tiring climb, but there were no more obstacles, and as he went higher the air became cooler and less fetid.

He looked at his watch, still 2:22 and no movement. "Can't get any sort of break," he said out loud. "I hope Krono has kept his promise." He stopped again and thought he heard a light thud behind him. He smiled and continued on his way, humming Beethoven's Ninth Symphony as he went. He felt a cool sea breeze and in a few minutes he found himself back on the same island he had been stranded on before. He looked at his watch, which now said 2:23, but kept looking forward until the faint thud changed to the sound of footsteps in the sand. He turned around and was greeted by Amos Pierson.

৯৩

CIV. Life and Death

"AMOS PIERSON, I PRESUME," JOSHUA REMARKED AS HE shook hands with the obviously perplexed man. "Welcome back to the land of the living." Pierson appeared to be about forty, blonde hair, fair complexion, dressed in loose fitting, bright red shirt and pants, and barefoot. He stared at the ground as Joshua walked towards him; the rope burn on his neck and scars on his wrists and forearms were obvious. He had a confused look on his face and squinted in the bright sun when he looked up.

"How is it I'm back here, on this island of evil? We need to leave now," he screamed emphatically.

"Oh, we shall be leaving very shortly, Mr. Pierson; but, tell me, what do you remember?"

Pierson closed his eyes silently then shook his head as a tear rolled down his cheek. "The most horrible dream one can imagine is all I remember. It seemed like it would never end; I kept trying to wake up and, now, I finally have. Back here where the nightmare started. Please take me away from here."

With these words a faint drone became a louder roar and General Moosewood descended from the clouds and lightly set his transport down on the beach. The hatch opened and the two men scrambled inside. In a flash they were airborne and docking with Moosewood's larger vessel. The general whispered something in Joshua's ear and then went back to the controls as Joshua excused himself. He went into the hygiene center and looked in the mirror.

"Now you are a site for sore eyes," he said to his reflection, a colossal understatement. Staring back at him was a face covered with soot, almost all the hair gone, his skin a mosaic of red and gray, hands with burned areas on the knuckles and palms, all in all, medals of honor for an ordeal that no one should ever had experienced. He bowed his head for a moment and a tear came to his eye as he thought about Gimpy and Jake. He felt in his pocket; the one chip remaining along with his Bible and the deck of cards. He started to step into the hygiene center when he heard a loud squawk. In a flash he jumped out of the small room and smiled as Gimpy flew and landed on his shoulder and gave a playful tug on his ear. Joshua laughed and stroked his fur like feathers as Gimpy squawked and flapped his wings with joy. "You aren't a cat, but you certainly have nine lives," Joshua exclaimed as the bird flew joyfully around the small room.

Joshua looked over at Pierson and explained, "This is Gimpy, one of my companions and one who was extremely helpful in resurrecting you from the dead."

Pierson gave a faint smile and held out his hand, which the parrot immediately tried to bite, and he said, "Thank you for your help; I guess I'm happy to be here. But, could you please explain why you went to so much trouble?"

Joshua gave a brief scolding to Gimpy and told him to mind his manners and then turned to Pierson. "Let me get cleaned up and then I'll explain. In the meantime, make yourself comfortable; I'll only be a minute."

Joshua disappeared into the hygiene center and in about one minute emerged looking fresh and clean. He sat down and picked up an apple and some cheese. "Excuse me for a moment, Mr. Pierson, but I feel like I haven't eaten in a year." He devoured the fruit and the cheese and washed it down with a bottle of water.

"Now let me tell you our problem." Joshua explained the whole situation, leaving out the parts concerning the possible demise of Diblonski. Pierson sat silently and smiled when Joshua finished.

"So, you want me to stop this renegade geek from making the entire world's population into mindless zombies. If you ask me it may not be such a bad idea. Maybe it would take the wind out of Aaron Diblonski's sails and would go a long way towards wiping out the tremendous sorrow of our frail human condition."

"Please, Mr. Pierson, this is serious business. We went to great trouble to bring you here; don't you have any thoughts?" Joshua pleaded.

"Oh, the problem has a simple solution. Just turn the 'dots' off before your Mr. Peskew can initiate his plan. Of course, you really have to turn off the picochips inside which isn't that hard to do. You just need the right 'key.' "

"And where does one find the 'key?' "

"Well, that's the thing, isn't it. What's it worth to you? The 'key' is in here," he said, pointing to his head. "So, tell me, what's in it for me?"

Joshua's voice rose a bit and his neck turned a bright crimson, "Believe me, sir, the benefit to humanity should be payment enough. However, I'm sure that if you cannot find it within you to help with what you've said is a fairly simple task, I'm sure that I can find a way to send you straight back to your never ending nightmare, only, I'm positive that the accommodations you return to would be even more unpleasant than those you've recently escaped. But, in the spirit of fair play, if you help us, I can tell you something that will guarantee you will never have to return to that God forsaken place. It will only require a few minor actions on your part. Is that acceptable to you?"

Pierson stood up and offered Joshua his hand. "We have a deal, young man." He disappeared into the hygiene center as Joshua went up to the flight deck to speak with the general.

❧❧

CV. Peskew

RANDY PESKEW SAT AT THE COMPUTER CONSOLE IN HIS makeshift workshop. He had one final problem to solve before he would be ready to launch the plan. The coordination of the dot assimilation required simultaneously beaming the command signal off the high orbital satellite array above the Earth. This was necessary to have the near instantaneous initiation that he thought necessary.

One final computation was necessary to make the system failsafe. This was really a backup system, but he would only get one shot at this and he couldn't afford even a minor slip-up. As the numbers and symbols danced across the screen he felt a sharp pain and grabbed his right side. *I shouldn't have made such spicy food for lunch,* he thought, *stupid synthesizer, it's supposed to look out for such things.*

The room seemed to move up and down and a queasy feeling rose from his stomach; He felt lunch and breakfast rising into his throat. He jumped up and put his hand over his mouth as the day's meals landed in the waste receptacle. The pain in his stomach was still there and he winced as he stood up and tried to take a deep breath.

He felt the nausea again and pulled the waste can to his mouth and filled it with bitter yellow green fluid. He winced as he turned to the console, glanced at the figures and said, with a groan, "save." He took a deep breath, which made him scream and called out, "Medical emergency." A hologram appeared, life size, and started to talk.

"Please state the nature of your emergency," the female figure said.

"I need a health care agent, severe abdominal pain."

"One moment while a scan is initiated, thank you."

A yellow beam came from the computer and probed Peskew's body. In thirty seconds the hologram spoke again. "Our scan indicates that your pains are indicative of peritonitis and additional tests will be necessary. Please proceed to the nearest health care facility equipped with advanced diagnostic and surgical services, thank you"

"I'm too sick, please send an ambulance."

"Your request has been noted, an emergency vehicle has been dispatched and will arrive in two minutes. Have a nice day and thank you for using Diblonski Healthcare."

Peskew sat back and waited; the pain was less as long as he stayed still. In five minutes there was a knock on the door and he was whisked away in the ambulance. His plans would have to wait.

ॐ∙ॐ

CVI. The Right Key

PIERSON FIRED UP HIS OLD COMPUTER; JOSHUA HAD managed to get it from the Diblonski R&D department by telling Mr. Diblonski it would be essential to the success of his plan. Pierson examined the current picochip and Green Dot schematics, noting with some pride that there hadn't been any changes from the original design he had introduced years ago. He quickly scanned through hundreds of pages of new research into the elemental composition and physical properties of the picochips and picomatrix. The numerous keys that unlocked the many hidden "compartments" were listed in a summary paper. He noted that there were no published studies of the integration of the picomatrix with living animal cells, the aspect of the matrix that Peskew was exploiting to carry out his plan.

Joshua sat patiently in the room, keeping his eye on Pierson and assisting him as much as he could. Pierson spent several hours going through all the recent studies and finally raised his head from the computer monitor.

"I haven't been able to find anything that says our adversary has discovered the cellular assimilation module," he announced. "I don't think you should have any concerns."

Joshua stared at him with a very somber look on his face. "Mr. Pierson, there is no question or doubt as to Randy Peskew's intentions. Besides the unshakable truth of my source there is also the psychological history of this man. He has been a victim all his life; a victim of this 'perfect' society that makes anyone that is unusual an outcast, or even worse, an object of ridicule. Given such a powerful tool, one that he sees as a solution to the flawed 'human condition,' Mr. Peskew will, without a doubt, implement his plan on a global scale. And, as far as all your published studies are concerned, what man possessing such great potential power, would publish it in some technical journal for all the world to see?"

"OK. OK. I get the picture," Pierson said. "Well, to initiate his plan he will need to utilize the satellite system that is in the highest orbit around the Earth. The activation sequence will need to be transmitted to each satellite and a pretimed initiation implemented to allow simultaneous integration."

"Which means?"

"He needs to do a lot of planning and a lot of ground work to carry out his scheme. The act of turning off the Green Dots, however, need not be so elaborate. Since there is no need that it be done as a coordinated, simultaneous event, we can use existing planet based communication."

"Won't the wearers complain and bring their Green Dots to be fixed?"

"I'm sure they will, but it won't make a difference. Once they're off, they stay off, until the command is given to reactivate. And, I'm the only one that knows that command. Furthermore, to anticipate your next objection, all the 'Dots' will be off, new, used, bought, unbought. The world will actually have to go back to speaking to each other."

Joshua smiled for the first time in a long time. "Well, then, let's turn them off."

"Give me a minute to put in the proper command and then we'll be ready."

He put a series of symbols into the computer, hit some keys and, finally, gave the activate command. Nothing happened.

꙳

CVII. At the Hospital

THE BLARING OF THE SIREN FADED AWAY AS THE AMBU-lance rolled up to the ER entrance. Randy Peskew's stretcher rolled from the ambulance into the acute care Emergency Center. He passed through a body scanner en route to a room where he sat for about ten minutes. A portable physiologic monitor was connected to his finger and a variety of numbers started to appear on the screen.

He looked at the figures some of which he recognized: pulse, blood pressure, oxygen level, while others were more obscure. A red flashing light appeared that read emergency scan result, MD notified and almost at once a live nurse, dressed in blue with her hair covered by an orange cap, came into the room.

She looked at the monitor and the computerized diagnostics and then walked out of the room without saying a word. Two minutes later she returned and spoke to the very worried patient.

"Good afternoon, Mr. . .", she glanced at his bracelet, "Pierson. I'm Miss Hoabit, your nurse. Your scan indicates that you are one of the rare individuals we see with acute appendicitis. Treatment has been initiated and, if you are typical, you will be out of here and back home in twelve hours. Do you have any questions?"

Peskew, who had checked in under an assumed name, choosing Pierson instead of Peskew for safety reasons, was impressed by the efficiency of the medical system, but the delay of twelve hours worried him. He was almost ready to begin his grand scheme and bring a new order to this dying world. The orbiting satellites would soon be properly aligned. Every second wasted increased the risk, although he was confident that his plans remained undiscovered, he still was anxious to get on with it. The pain in his side wasn't any better, even though he had supposedly started therapy. He started to feel warm and light-headed, and at that moment his nurse returned.

"I've just received this message from Dr. Barnes, one of our surgeons. It seems that you are in need of a surgical procedure to remove your appendix; a very rare event these days. Your scan revealed that rupture is imminent and the prudent thing to do is remove the nasty little beast immediately. So, I need you to sign these papers or at least give your verbal OK."

Peskew felt the room spinning around and the pain in his side was worse.

"Of course, anything that will make this pain go away," he gasped. "You have my permission. Where is the surgeon?"

"Oh, Dr Barnes?" the nurse asked incredulously. "Of course, he's not here. He's in Philadelphia. But don't worry. He'll be overseeing every step of the way. Here comes your 'surgeon' now."

A yellow-gray machine with flashing lights and various hooks and needles for appendages motored into the room. A light beam shot out from one of its "eyes" and then it spoke, in a robot-like tone. "Diagnosis . . . acute Appendicitis . . . recommended therapy . . . immediate surgery . . . consent confirmed by voice match . . . patient's legal counsel notified . . . operation will commence immediately."

The machine rolled towards Peskew who started to object. "I'm feeling better, really; can't I see a live doctor . . ."

A panel on the machine lowered down over Peskew's abdomen and the sick man felt his abdomen become numb. A screen came down from the ceiling and he watched the entire spectacle. A small tube entered his abdomen and what appeared to be a tiny robot rolled over his intestines and found the offending organ. With incredible skill and dexterity, the little man lifted the normal intestines away from the appendix, which was black with yellowish wormlike material on its surface. A beam of light shot out and the appendix was then picked up by the little robot and sucked into an opening as if the little surgeon was swallowing it. The robot rolled back to the tube and went inside and the tube was withdrawn, leaving a neat red line where the incision had been.

The machine spoke again. "Operation is complete. Pathological analysis indicates that the preoperative diagnosis is confirmed as Acute Appendicitis, Common. No findings of malignancy or unusual infectious agents."

The surgical machine withdrew, continuing its commentary, "Thank you for using Surgibot Therapeutics, a subsidiary of Diblonski Ltd. It has been a pleasure serving you. Have a nice day."

❦

CVIII. What's Wrong

PIERSON SCREAMED AT THE MONITOR. "YOU'RE SUPPOSED to be off. Now go."

Joshua was not amused as the smile faded away from his face. He pushed Pierson away from the monitor and read the message that had appeared: "Command not accepted, improper code sequence."

"What does improper code sequence mean, Pierson? Are you going to be able to shut these things down or what?"

Pierson shook his head and input a few symbols and then a question, "Has the picomatrix enabler been altered?"

The monitor answered, "Yes."

"Present new configuration."

"Please logon," answered the computer.

Pierson typed in his password. "A simple oversight on my part. This should only take a minute."

"Password incorrect. Have you forgotten your password, Mr. Pierson?"

"I'm sure that's my logon info; someone has been playing my part."

Joshua, feeling some consternation, asked, "Are you going to be able to turn these blasted things off? Or do I need to form some sort of Plan B?"

"Give me some time alone, please, so I can figure this out," Pierson answered softly. "We should have some time, anyway. Our adversary will need to wait until the satellites are properly aligned. They just passed proper alignment and nothing happened, so, he will have to wait at least twelve hours more. Besides, for all we know he could be days away from implementation."

"OK, keep at it. Call me if you figure anything out or need any help. I'm going to work on Plan B."

"What's Plan B consist of?"

"Don't ask; I'm not sure myself. But, I'm going to need some help. Come to think of it, if you need to hack into your system I know someone that can help. Give me a moment."

Joshua went into another room and made a call. "Can you come over now? It's a bit of an emergency . . . Let me talk with her . . . We're in a bit of sticky situation . . . no, it'll be safe . . . put him in a taxi and send him over. Thanks."

He went back into the room to see Pierson hunched over the console, a few beads of sweat appeared on his forehead as the same message appeared, "password incorrect."

"Who would have had the chance or desire to get into your system?" Joshua asked.

"Lot's of people, but probably one of Diblonski's henchmen."

"He plays things pretty close, if you know what I mean. You can be sure that it was either Diblonski himself, or his number one hatchet man, Masur. Maybe that will help. Anyway, the best hacker I've ever seen is on his way over, should be here in a few minutes. Oh, and don't be put off by his size. He's very sharp. In the meantime, I'm going to try to figure out where Mr. Peskew is hiding and what can be done to stop him or at least delay him. I'm really surprised he hasn't already initiated his plan. From the information Diblonski gave me, he should have finished his work by now. I'm going to check local police records and such to see if there is any public document that may help me find him."

Joshua went into the next room and accessed the municipal database encompassing the entire east coast. He searched for anything pertaining to Randy Peskew, putting in all the characteristics and features he knew about Peskew. Nothing was returned. Of course, Diblonski's people would have done all this and more, and had come up empty. He thought for a moment and then put in a new name, Randy Pierson. In less than thirty seconds he received a single sentence: "Mr. Randy Pierson was taken to Rockaway Hospital by ambulance #54 yesterday, October 24, 2163, severe abdominal pain." Joshua contemplated this new information for about thirty seconds; there could be another Randy Pierson out there, but he had no other ideas and as he thought about it he decided this had to be Peskew.

Great, Joshua thought, *he was in the hospital, maybe he had an accident and is permanently incapacitated.* Joshua called into the next room, "I'm going to Rockaway Hospital. Your help should be arriving any minute. Oh, and one other thing, you are to leave this helper alone, do you understand. When he arrives you'll understand what I'm saying. If you do anything unsavory I guarantee that you will be back roasting in Hell by nightfall."

Pierson responded with a grunt as Joshua quietly closed the door. One minute later the bell rang and Pierson opened the door to find a boy, very robust looking, but also very young.

"Hello, Mr. Pierson, Joshua asked me to come give you a hand. I'm David Sanders, junior that is. My mom said that time is of the essence, so let's get to it. First tell me about the person that stole your identity."

The two went into the other room and David Jr. listened closely to everything Pierson could tell him about Diblonski and his henchman, Masur.

ও০৯

CIX. Rockaway Hospital

JOSHUA TOOK A CAB TO ROCKAWAY HOSPITAL, WHICH was about fifty kilometers away. He prepared by quickly purchasing a white coat and a handheld medical scanner. Looking the part was easy, but fooling the security systems would take some finesse and luck. *I need a bag like that one we used to smuggle Little Bit into Senator Leavitt's office.* He actually had that bag at his old apartment, a place he hadn't been in months, but it was in Oceanside, too far away. He opted to just to bring a small briefcase and bravado.

He looked up a few other items in the local ambulance and police log, stuffed a few additional items into his bag, and headed to the hospital. He went in through the front entrance and stopped at the information kiosk. The hospital was a brand new brick and concrete building, fully automated; the pinnacle of efficiency. He stopped at the kiosk and entered a name. He typed in Louis Farregi. The monitor said that no such patient existed. He typed the same name again and received the same message. He did the same thing two more times, with the same result. After the fourth attempt he received a message, "Please wait while an attendant is called to assist you." *Step one accomplished*, he thought.

In less than a minute, a young woman in a white uniform, blonde with creamy white skin and a very prominent chest, appeared and tapped him on the shoulder. "May I help you, sir?"

Joshua turned around and, with tears in his eyes, put his arms on the woman's shoulders and started to wail loudly. "He's here . . . and it's all my fault. My boy is dead, I know it . . . but this damn computer says he doesn't exist," Joshua sobbed.

"Now, Now, I'm sure everything's alright. Now, tell me what happened . . . tell me your name," the woman said.

"Jacob Farrego," Joshua said. "My son, Louis, was thrown off his ATV and they brought him here, but this damn computer says he's not here. I put it in four times. Maybe you can try it. Machines never seem to like me. I remember one time this coffee maker kept . . ."

The woman interrupted Joshua's story. "Let me try; what's his name?"

"Louis, Louis Farrego"

The woman typed the name in and the information appeared on the screen: "Louis Farrego, ATV accident, admitted to ICU."

"He's on the fourth floor, ICU," the young woman said. "You seem upset; I'll take you there if you want."

"Thank you, thank you very much, Miss . . ."

"Haverly, Judy Haverly, and it's my pleasure. After all, that's why I'm here. Follow me."

Joshua followed his escort to the elevator and they rode up to the fourth floor. On the way, Joshua made a point to study the hospital map which was posted in the elevator. On the fourth floor he walked a little behind Miss Haverly and ducked into a stairwell at his first opportunity. *Crude, but effective,* he thought as he headed to the fifth floor, the post surgical floor, where he expected Peskew might be if he were hospitalized with abdominal pain.

❧

CX. Back Door

DAVID SANDERS JR. SAT AT THE CONSOLE LOOKING AT THE monitor full of unsuccessful logins. He typed a few commands and the picomatrix interface materialized on the monitor. It appeared all that was necessary was to find the proper path either to the password archive or the level three cache which usually led to the "sink" where access routes were often "dumped" by the central processor.

"Matrix configuration on screen," he commanded. Immediately a green array of lines and squares appeared. "Front door configuration." The voice input appeared in red as did the monitor. "Back door configuration." Nothing happened. He tapped some of the keys on the console and still nothing happened.

"This console has quite a few layers of security," he said rhetorically.

Pierson sat back, suddenly feeling very inadequate, but also somewhat awed by this seven year old boy manipulating this complex apparatus like it was a box of crayons. "How do you learn such things at your age?" he asked, not really expecting an answer.

"Oh, my Mom is the smartest woman in the world; I guess I get it from her," David Jr. answered.

"I'm sure she is," Pierson answered, not really believing. "I suppose your Dad is a genius, too?"

"Oh, no. He was an astropilot, then he worked for God, only now he's sick. I don't think he'll ever wake up. He was shot and now all he does is sleep."

"Who's your Dad?"

"David Sanders; used to be Major David Sanders of the Astropilot Corps, but then he went through the ITP and saw God, and now he's God's messenger in this solar system."

"Who's your mother?"

"Her name is Deborah Tennyson; she's famous, I think. I think she's the smartest person in the world. She invented the ITP."

"Never heard of your mother, but I've been gone for a while. Anyway, are you making any progress?" He moved his chair closer to the boy and started to put his arm on his shoulder, but remembered Joshua's words and the torment he had escaped and moved his chair away.

"This computer is tough," David Jr. observed. "Usually there's a back door that either bypasses the need for a password or a side door that will lead to a list of acceptable access codes. So far, all I see is the front door. I may have to build a back door. That takes time."

"Can't you just guess the new password?" Pierson asked.

"That's possible, but if I didn't get it on the first five tries we'd be out of luck until it was reset by the owner, which in this case is one Aaron Diblonski. From what I've heard he wouldn't be very helpful."

Pierson let out a long sigh, stood up and walked around the room, sat down, and let out another sigh. Finally, he said, "Start building kid, but make it snappy. We probably have less than ten hours."

David Jr. set to work laying the foundation for a back door into the computer. A series of commands opened a new sector of the pico-matrix and when this flashed on the screen the young master grinned and immediately put his computerized foot in the door and built a stop; this prevented the security system from recognizing the tampering and shutting down the entire system. Pierson, the architect of the picotechnology was suddenly acutely aware of his substantial inadequacies, but was also amazed at the advances that had been made in a few short years and even more impressed by the diminutive wizard seated next to him.

"I've got to be very careful now," David Jr. remarked. "If the security software figures out what's going on it'll be over." Pierson thought it was like breaking into a bank vault and that he was in the presence of a master safecracker. The work progressed very slowly as Pierson watched the clock, less than nine hours left. He put his arms on the boys shoulder and said, "You are a true genius. I wouldn't be surprised if you discover something better than the picomatirx when you're older."

The boy smiled, but didn't take his eyes off the monitor.

∂∞∂

CXI. Dr. Smith

JOSHUA OPENED HIS BAG AND PULLED OUT HIS WHITE coat and scanner. *At least I look the part,* he thought. He was a little worried that he didn't have an ID badge; he would have to work quickly. He tried to access the charts on the monitor, but he realized he didn't have appropriate login or passwords. There were several nurses at the workstation, glancing at the monitors and talking about everything but the patients.

"I was at the Hard Rock . . ." one said.

"Four drinks too many . . ." said another.

Joshua approached the station and addressed the first nurse he saw. "Excuse me, Miss, but there is a problem with Mr.Randy Pierson. Are you his nurse?"

An older nurse seated on the opposite side of the station turned her head. "I'm Miss Konrad, Mr. Pierson's nurse; may I help you Dr . . ."

"Smith, Dr. Smith. I'm covering today and I received word that Mr. Pierson was not doing well. I know that it's unusual, but I decided to come see for myself."

"I'm sure he's fine," Miss Konrad stated. "I was in there not more than ten minutes ago. He was sitting up looking like he was ready to go. As a matter of fact he told me that he needed to be released because he had a pressing deadline to meet in less than ten hours."

Joshua answered, "I don't know, Nurse; the readings I saw suggest that he is relapsing. That's why I came to check for myself."

"Relapsing from appendicitis? What's he doing? Growing another appendix?"

"I meant that his infection may be returning. I wanted to check him before I ordered another round of Immunocide."

"Well, then let's go see him; after you, Doctor."

Joshua thought he detected a slight hint of sarcasm in her voice, which he swiftly returned. "Ladies first, Msss. Konrad. I insist." And he followed her down the hall to Peskew's room.

Peskew was sitting in a chair, dressed and ready to leave. He stood up as soon as Joshua and Miss Konrad walked in.

"It's about time someone showed up. I feel fine; I need to get out of here."

Joshua approached him, put on some gloves and stared at his scanner. He hadn't used such a thing in years and his was antiquated by current standards. He stared at the normal readout, printed it out, and turned it over. "According to this, you have residual intra-abdominal infection that may require additional surgery. You need to stay for more tests."

Peskew's face grew red and he paced back and forth. "I don't care about more tests," he said loudly. "I have vital business for Mr. Diblonski and I need to get it done in the next few hours. Just let me sign myself out. If I start feeling sick I'll be back in twelve hours."

At the mention of Aaron Diblonski the nurse became more attentive. She turned to Joshua and said, "If he's working for Diblonski and he says he needs to leave, I think we should let him." Her eyes were full of fear.

"Very well," Joshua responded. "If you could give us your address and number; so that we can contact you if necessary."

"Don't worry, Doc. If I need you, I'll call."

Joshua persisted. "At least give me your number so that I, or one of the very efficient nurses here, can check on you tomorrow."

"OK, OK; 12-299-800-7654. Now, I really need to get going."

"Certainly. Nurse please bring the discharge forms and Mr. Pierson can be on his way. Have a nice day and be sure to call; especially if you get any pain where your appendix used to be."

Joshua left the room and exited the hospital in a hurry. Luckily, there was only security getting in; anyone could exit unnoticed. He was a bit troubled by Peskew's comment; that he was working for

Diblonski. After a little thought, Joshua decided that it was just a bluff to get his way. It was true that Peskew had worked for Diblonski, but Joshua was positive that this current venture was not under the purview of Diblonski Ltd. He was also sure that Peskew planned to activate his key and implement his plan at the next opportunity which was less than ten hours away. He placed a call to the real Pierson.

"How's it going," he asked.

Pierson's hologram appeared shaking his head. "The kid's working away, but we'll never get done in time. There's a ton of security that he's having to circumnavigate and, it seems, one wrong move and we're sunk."

"Well, keep at it," Joshua replied. "I'm pretty sure that Peskew will be ready to initiate his plan at the next opportunity. Tell David that I'll cook him a real meal if he fixes everything."

Joshua looked up at the blue sky over Long Island as he hailed a taxi to take him back to the city. He shook his head as he thought of the fate of humanity resting on the fingertips of a seven-year-old boy. The scenario had an eerie familiarity as he thought about Little Bit and his encounter with Richard Cosby. Seven years ago the hope for mankind rested on the paws of a little white dog, one who had performed brilliantly. The irony was not lost as Joshua thought about all the humble individuals that rose to outshine the powerbrokers of the day. Little Bit, Jameson, and now David Jr. along with so many others that gave all they had for their fellow man.

❧❦

CXII. Race to the Wire

PESKEW RACED BACK TO HIS LAB IN RECORD TIME. "ON," he commanded the computer. "Activate countdown chronometer and display." A digital timer appeared in the upper left hand corner of the large center monitor and started counting down from 9:28:00. "Final simulation array on screen," he said. The series of commands, uploads, and satellite array appeared and he started the test as the clock ticked away.

Across town, David Sanders Jr. picked away at the security on Pierson's computer. Joshua walked through the door and tapped Pierson on the shoulder and they went into the adjacent room.

"How's it looking?" he asked.

"The kid's pretty bright, that I've got to say, and careful," Pierson answered. "How much time?"

"Less than nine and a half hours."

"At the rate he's working I don't think he'll make it. Of course, he could break in at any moment and then we'd be done, or he could hit a steel wall and we'd be back to square one. What about Plan B?"

"Plan B has come and gone, I think. Peskew is out of the hospital, somewhere in the city, I think. He gave me his 'number,' which turns out to be Grace's Escort Service. So, at the moment all we've got is a seven-year-old whiz kid. Let's see how he's doing."

The two quietly went back to the adjacent room and saw David Jr. rapidly punching keys and talking to the computer.

"I think I've found the way in. Look at this."

Joshua and Pierson looked at the schematic on the screen. Joshua recognized the central processor and saw that progress had been made within two circuits.

"I'm not detecting any more security so all I need to do is activate the program and we should be in business." He turned to Pierson.

"What's the application we need to startup?"

"Picomatrix shutoff/one/universal."

"OK, let's give it a shot." David Jr. spoke to the computer. "Activate application, Picomatrixshutoff/one/universal." A message immediately appeared on the screen.

"Application not found."

Pierson's eyes grew wide and he jumped to the console, pushing the boy aside. "It has to be here." He punched in a series of commands and a new message appeared on the screen.

"Application permanently deleted, July 26, 2163, 2:09:16, by Randy Peskew."

"Now we know what happened," Joshua said. "That Peskew seems to know his stuff." He sat back in his chair and said, "I'm certainly open to ideas."

Pierson answered, "Maybe we should just let this Peskew do his thing, then when the deed is done, we can find a way to be the ones in control."

Joshua gave Pierson a dirty look and the other man returned a very sheepish grin. "Just kidding, really." He thought for a moment. "I guess I can rebuild the application, but that will take some time, about eighteen hours, I think."

Joshua replied, "I don't see any other choices at the moment. Perhaps the two of you can work out some shortcuts. I'm going to try Plan C."

"We have a Plan C?" David Jr. asked.

"Not yet, but we will."

Joshua left as the man and the boy sat hunched down over the computer. On his way out he stopped and had the food synthesizer prepare some snacks and a meal for his two companions.

"Come on," he said to Gimpy, who had been sitting patiently on his perch. "Maybe together we can figure out something to do."

Meanwhile, the first simulation proceeded flawlessly and Peskew started on the simulation of coordinating the satellites which was necessary for simultaneous delivery of the software key and activation command. His monitor displayed the array of satellites high above the Earth's surface as the clock in the corner read 7:05:12. He didn't foresee any problems and would be ready in plenty of time.

At that moment, in the posh surroundings that Aaron Diblonski called home, the business tycoon sat alone in his most comfortable chair, close to the huge fire that blazed away night and day. He held a leather-bound book in his emaciated hand, barely strong enough to turn the page. The room was dark and decaying; the rare plants that filled the solarium were becoming as dried and withered as their owner, testament to the festering death that filled the mansion. The lights illuminating the numerous works of art had dimmed as if they were also dying with their owner.

Diblonski looked at the cover of the book, the title carved into the leather, its gold embossing faded to brown. *A Christmas Carol* by Charles Dickens, a story of hope for a man whose candle was about to go out. He closed the book and closed his eyes and silently cursed the one who had brought him to this point. He sat there, helpless, anticipating the end he had dreaded for thousands of years.

Joshua left Pierson and David Jr. to their work and hit the street. Find Peskew was all that was in his head; find him and stop him. Don't worry about Diblonski, he would get his when the time was right. *Perhaps a little help,* he thought. He whispered, "Aldous, voice only," and in seconds the young pastor came over the old-style phone Joshua was using.

"The Lord is my Shepherd . . ." Joshua said and Aldous immediately recognized his caller.

"It's been a while, what happened?" Aldous said softly. He had always been careful when communicating with Joshua. He wasn't sure why. "What can I do for you?"

"I need to find someone, find him very quickly. I know his name and that's about it."

"It's a big city. Who is it?"

"A certain Randy Peskew, a scientist/engineer who is plotting a worldwide revolution of sorts. Can you help?"

"Peskew? He's the big problem?"

"Do you know him?"

"Certainly; he was seeing Martha before her tragedy. He seemed like a very nice man, very polite and respectful; not someone I'd expect to want to destroy humanity."

"That explains a great deal. All the more reason to find him. If we can stop him I think he can be saved along with the rest of the world. If he succeeds, it will be the end of mankind and not just because he controls everyone. No, the Earth as a living planet will cease."

These last comments confused Aldous; he made a mental note to ask Joshua at a later time what he meant. For now, he changed the subject. "What do we do if we find him?"

"Merely detain for a period of time."

"Any other information that might be helpful?"

"He's working on a modification of picochips and picomatrix. Perhaps Barnabas can help."

Aldous was startled by Joshua's mentioning the old engineer, but didn't change his demeanor. "Meet me under the Brooklyn Bridge, along the river, and I'll see what I can do."

Ten minutes later Joshua was there and found Aldous, his friend and former nemesis, waiting with Barnabas.

"Let's go back to the church," Aldous said. "Is time a problem?"

"Yes, a bit; we've only got a few hours," Joshua looked at his watch. "Six hours and thirty-six minutes to be exact."

Barnabas hadn't said a word, he stood nearby, shaking his head and looking down at the ground. Joshua sensed his apprehension.

"Don't worry, Barnabas. I know that the evil one's arms are long, but we are not fighting him. What we are searching for is an adversary; an adversary against everything that we know, good, evil, and indifferent. Let's go and I'll fill you in."

The three quickly made their way to the safety of the church as Joshua told the two men everything that had happened.

❧❧

CXIII. Photo Finish

PIERSON AND DAVID JR. POUNDED AWAY ON DUELING consoles, hitting every step in a dance of computers. Utilizing a new, more efficient language that David Jr. had developed, the work and commands were zipping along. Still, despite their speed, the clock ticked down, now under six hours. The application was taking some shape, but still not enough to restore the picochip shutoff.

The young boy looked at the system configuration, magnified a trillion times in the schematic and noticed something very familiar.

"This looks just like the system for one of my games, Interdimensional Warriors. Maybe we can save some time by modifying that game to do this job."

Pierson looked at the game's system diagram and agreed that it was very similar to the picomatrix they were working on. "OK, why don't you work from that angle and I'll keep slogging away at the stepwise building. Maybe one of us will get the key into the lock and turn these suckers off."

The two went back to work each lost in his own intense concentration.

Across town Randy Peskew had finished his final simulation and everything was perfect. The satellite system would be in alignment in just a few hours and he was ready. All that remained was to activate his transmitter and hit the upload button. Everything was in readiness; the computer would launch the upload at the exact moment that would allow rapid synchronized communication between the satellite array and simultaneous activation. Once activated the assimilation process would proceed over about five days and would be irreversible. Every Green Dot would receive the new commands and everyone that owned one would be effected, as long as the dot was in direct contact with the individual. Peskew was shaking in anticipation as he envisioned a world free from violence and cruelty. He hit the first activation key and sat back to wait.

Barnabas sat in a pew shaking his head, while Aldous went to Martha's room to look for any clue that might be helpful. Joshua looked at Barnabas and saw the forlorn look on the old engineer's face.

"Don't be so glum, Barnabas," he said. "None of us is sporting a Green Dot, so we'll be safe. Maybe Pierson will get them all turned off or maybe the whole thing just won't work."

Barnabas slowly looked up. "Oh, it'll work, alright, of that I have no doubt. These are brilliant people, very thorough and careful in their work. And, it doesn't matter that you or me or Aldous won't be immediately affected. Once the population has been altered it will only be a matter of time."

"If that's the case, then let's do something. Help me find this madman, help me stop him. Think; tell me, how can we find a needle in this haystack. What does he need to finish his task that will tell us where he is?"

"What does he need? A little computer and a transmitter set to the proper frequency. He can probably find everything he needs in public databases. He could even use a simple global communicator, one put out by any company that utilizes this particular satellite system."

"There's no special power booster or such that he would need to send his message?"

"No, nothing. I'm sorry; I'm not being much help,"the old man said, still shaking his head.

At that moment Aldous returned holding a Green Dot on his finger. "This is Martha's," he said. "It may have something about Peskew on it. I feel funny opening it up; I mean, it's like her diary."

Joshua took the dot and put it on his finger. He looked at it and addressed the little device like it was an old friend. "You, my boy, may hold the key to the salvation of mankind. Now, show me what you're made of."

A hologram appeared and they searched for Randy Peskew. There were over one hundred entries about him. Joshua zeroed in on addresses. A list of twenty appeared, all with some link to Peskew in conjunction with Martha. One immediately jumped out at Joshua.

David Jr. and Pierson continued to hammer away frantically on their keyboards. Junior, in particular, was making great headway. Interdimensional Warriors was melded to Pierson's picomatrix system with the result that he was only two steps away from finishing the alteration of the application that would allow them to implement a global system shutdown. The clock in the corner continued to count down, now under ninety minutes. Pierson abandoned his work as the boy was so close to breaking in.

"What would happen if you tried this?" Pierson asked and he pushed a key on the board, one he thought would immediately activate his system.

"Don't . . ." Junior screamed. Too late. He looked at the monitor as a big red X appeared indicating that a security breach was sensed and that the matrix was shutting down.

Pierson turned away, a faint sheepish smile on his face. The boy looked at him, then quickly turned his head as Pierson now looked ashamed.

"I guess I can't do anything right," Pierson he cried and started to slap the side of his head and bang his head against the wall. "I should be back in Hell. I don't deserve a second chance." The clock was counting down and they were back to square one. David Jr. jumped up and put his arm around the older man, who finally calmed down and composed himself. "Any other ideas, kid?" he asked.

Junior sat back down at his console and said, "Give me ten minutes to reboot this thing and maybe I can get it back fairly quickly; unless the system learns from our mistake and I have to find a new way in. I think it'll work better if I go at it alone."

"Perhaps you're right. I'll try a different approach over here."

They each went back to work.

Aldous and Joshua looked at the clock, less than twenty minutes to go. They pulled up to the building at Madison and Fifty-Eighth Street. It was a tall building, an old mix of concrete and glass. The front door was bolted and it appeared abandoned.

"Are you sure that Peskew is here?" Aldous asked.

"No, but it makes no sense for Martha to have this address associated with him. She grew up here and there was something peculiar about the way she had it entered in her 'diary.' I hope that Peskew is here. It's a tall building and, at least in his mind, it's a sort of tribute to her memory. He's probably on the top floor. How do we get in?"

"Oh, I have my ways," Aldous commented as he fiddled with the lock. In less than thirty seconds the door was open and they entered the cavernous lobby which was dark and deserted. "I doubt the elevators are working; here's the stairs; we better move."

The clock ticked down under fifteen minutes as they raced up the stairs. Aldous and Gimpy went on ahead, being younger and not suffering the ill effects of Joshua's recent ordeals. The building was eighty stories and they still would have to find their quarry on the top floor. Joshua didn't think they'd make it in time.

As they raced up the stairs Aldous called down to his companion, "Do we know what room Martha lived in?"

Joshua shouted that he didn't have a clue; they'd have to go room to room.

Meanwhile, Peskew was making final preparations to upload the key to activating the Green Dot assimilation. On one monitor the satellite tracker counted down the minutes while another monitor showed the Green Dot key and two backup systems poised to be launched. Peskew's hands shook slightly as he gave the final command and activated his plan. Everything was a go and the program would upload at the precise moment. In the lower right hand corner of the monitor was a red abort icon, blinking on and off. Once the activation started nothing in the universe could stop it. He stared at the clock as it approached five minutes. He thought he should just sit back and relax, but the tension was too much and he stayed perched on the edge of his chair.

David Jr. and Pierson looked at the countdown and shook their heads almost simultaneously. Pierson's melancholy had passed for the moment and a faint smile appeared on his face as he thought about what would happen if Peskew succeeded. The world would be different, that was for sure, but he wasn't so sure that it would be worse than it was at present. Perhaps, if he played his cards right, he could be a world leader, maybe along with or even in place of this Randy Peskew. Of one thing he was certain, if Peskew succeeded, he would never be subject to the fires of Hell again.

The clock was down to three minutes and David Jr. realized two things. First, this Mr. Pierson had given up trying to get inside this system, and second, no matter what they did, they were going to run out of time. He continued to work anyway, but at the same time he took off his Green Dot.

Aldous and Gimpy reached the top floor and burst into the hallway. The dim light concealed the history of the old building. The hall went in two directions and Aldous turned to the right and raced down the hall. Gimpy flew ahead and stopped at the last room and flew at the door bumping it with his wing. Inside Peskew heard the bump, but didn't budge from his chair. The clock was down to thirty seconds. Aldous reached the room and banged on the door. He saw a faint light from beneath that confirmed the bird had found their quarry. Peskew didn't make a sound or move as Joshua finally arrived and the two men tried to break down the door. Together they rammed the door with their shoulders and it sprang open as they crashed to the floor. At that moment the clock reached zero and the activation key was launched.

Joshua ran to the console and saw the counter reading negative ten seconds. He grabbed Peskew by the throat and screamed, "Stop this madness."

Peskew shook his head and pointed to the screen. The image of the program joining with the satellite computer was complete and the disturbed scientist just sat there grinning from ear to ear. Joshua realized it was hopeless and fell back to the floor as Gimpy landed on his shoulder and Aldous sat down beside him. They all remained silent as they watched the key upload to the satellite and prepare to assimilate.

At that moment, one hundred fifty million kilometers away a spot on the sun became active, more active than it had ever been. A powerful flare was discharged from the surface of the sun carrying an electromagnetic wave and supercharged particles at a velocity of one half lightspeed heading straight for the Earth. On the Lunar surface, the powerful flare was detected ten minutes later, leaving only enough time to activate safety mechanisms in their immediate area. A few minutes later the solar flare reached the Earth's atmosphere and all the satellites in that portion of the uppermost orbits were enveloped by the blast. In particular, one satellite at the center received the greatest blast and was disabled. Communications on the Earth were blacked out as the satellites were disrupted.

Peskew stared at the console in disbelief as an error message secondary to power failure was received. Joshua breathed a sigh of relief as he took out Martha's diary.

❧

CXIV. Recovery

JOSEPH FLYNN SAT AT HIS CONSOLE AT THE SATELLITE Tracking Center in Denver, Colorado. He stared at the satellite system on his screen and noted the effects of the sudden solar flare and isolated the damage to a single satellite. The system redundancy prevented a prolonged blackout as most people experienced only a two-three minute disruption of service. He noted that the one affected satellite was completely offline and its stored memory completly wiped out. He initiated a total restart and reuploaded the basic system and then had the satellite reestablish telemetry with the rest of the array. The "key" uploaded by Peskew had been erased and any initiation would require a new upload.

Back in New York, Joshua and Aldous shut down Peskew's system; the computer engineer still in a state of shock over the unexpected occurrence. In a way Joshua pitied the man whose spirit seemed completely broken; he had the look of a man who had lost his best friend, favorite dog and all his possessions in one single blow. The Book of Job and his teaching of Jake raced through his head as he sat down next to the broken man.

"This is all for the best," Joshua said as he put his arm around Peskew, who pushed it away.

Peskew turned his head away and Joshua saw tears in his eyes. He stood up and put Martha's Green Dot on the table and he, Aldous, and Gimpy left the room, leaving Peskew alone as a hologram of Martha appeared. She was dressed in her finest church outfit as she started to speak.

"Dearest Randy; I hope you find this message and hope that my passing beyond this world has not left you in despair. It is best for me, as it is for anyone that knows the Truth, to leave the sorrows of this world and move on to the glory that God has promised. To be in the company of God and His Son is all the purpose that anyone could ever hope."

Tears flowed from his red, swollen eyes as the image of Martha sat next to him. Even as a hologram, the radiance of her presence overwhelmed him. He moved closer to the lifeless image as she continued to speak.

"The brief time we spent together showed me that there is love in this world; love that filled my heart nearly as much as the love I feel from Jesus. I am grateful for our time together, although brief; it was enough. I know that you will feel empty and alone. Please, please do not suffer alone in silence. The world is full of caring souls; people who will come to you and provide wondrous spiritual comfort and solace and want nothing in return."

Peskew closed his eyes and almost felt the warm body of Martha next to him as she continued speaking.

"Our church is filled with such people. We are all searching for that special thing that gives us meaning and provides a sense of purpose. Please, don't let my passage cause you to despair. Come to the church, look for these people, sit with Aldous and let him tell you the Gospel; good news that saved me from oblivion and now lets me look forward to an eternity of joy and happiness.

"I know that despair can lead you to hopelessness and with the great power at your finger tips this presents a great danger to yourself and to this world. But, as evil as the world seems, it is a gift from our Creator. When Adam and Eve sinned and ate the fruit from the Tree of Knowledge of Good and Evil, their eyes were opened by this Knowledge. But, such knowledge without wisdom has blinded us. All around we see the line between good and evil blur and now all that is good we call evil and all that is evil we embrace. Even Solomon, who knew the importance of wisdom, could not avoid this fate and descended into the depravity that is inherent to humanity.

"Please remember that the great knowledge you possess is nothing without wisdom; the wisdom to choose the right path. And, should you consider any actions that I know you would later regret, please stop, open the Bible and read the Gospels, and learn about One who suffered; suffered more than all of us and all for us. It is in Him that you will find peace, And, remember, although I am leaving you now, a place is being prepared for us to be together forever in Paradise. I love you and I will be waiting for you."

Peskew sat back for a few minutes and relived every minute he had spent with her and then stood up and found the others in the adjoining room. He had a big smile on his face as he greeted them.

"Thank you," he said as Aldous wrapped his arms around him. They sat down together as Peskew thought about what he had done and what had almost happened. "It's lucky that solar flare blew by," he said softly as the full implication of his actions hit him. He started crying uncontrollably as Aldous sat with him.

"Luck had nothing to do with it," Joshua remarked to Gimpy as he removed the memory chips from Peskew's computer and destroyed them along with a backup system he found. He left Peskew with Aldous as he started down the stairs with Gimpy on his shoulder. He needed to get back to Pierson and David Jr.; although they had not been successful there was one task that Pierson needed to accomplish. He made it to the street and decided to walk back to Pierson's apartment. He started down Fifth Avenue humming Beethoven's Ninth Symphony.

After what was a leisurely stroll, he arrived and found David Jr. feverishly at work. Pierson was sitting nearby, but his console was blank.

"Why all the fuss David?" Joshua asked.

"The young lad looked up briefly then went back to pounding away at his keyboard. "We haven't solved the problem yet; even though this deadline passed, the next one is coming."

"Oh, I think we're safe," Joshua remarked. "And, I think that Mr. Pierson here can help us make it permanent." Joshua sat down at Pierson's console, turned on the computer and when it was active, activated the picomatrix program and entered some symbols. He was immediately brought to the Green Dot picomatrix application. "Ok, Pierson, you're in. Now I want you to enter a key that permanently blocks the biologic assimilation function that is built in to the picomatrix. Once it is entered you will then send it out over the available wireless system so that every Green Dot in the world is safe. Then you will create a modification to the matrix that the manufacturer can then utilize to eliminate this function from all future Green Dots. Do you think that you can do this?"

"I certainly can, but I don't think I want to," Pierson responded with a note of defiance.

"Very well, but you know what the future holds for you. You're safe right now, but you won't live forever. Of all people you should fear what awaits you when you die. I have the 'key' that will save you from having to return to torment and pain. I only ask this one small task. Do it and I promise I will give you the means to be free for eternity."

Pierson's defiance melted away at the thought of returning to the cruel fires of Hell. His face grew ashen and he sheepishly sat down at the console. David Jr. and Joshua stood behind him as he entered a few commands and then a few more. In less than five minutes he was done.

"It's really simple if you know what you're doing," he said as he stood up and went into the bedroom.

"Are you really going to tell him how to avoid Hell?" David Jr. asked.

"Of course, but it's no secret. You know it as well as me," Joshua answered. He went into the bedroom, pulling the Bible out from his pocket as he walked through the door. He closed the door.

He was in the room only a minute and then David Jr. heard Pierson scream, "Get Out!" and Joshua came out of the room closing the door behind him. David saw Pierson sitting in the bed holding his head in his hands. David noted that Joshua didn't have his Bible anymore.

"Some people are afraid of the truth, even when they know that it is the only truth," Joshua remarked. "Come on, I'll take you home."

"What's he going to do?" the boy asked.

"Truly, God only knows. Mr. Pierson has a great deal to consider; I pray that he does it quickly," Joshua said, a hint of sadness in his voice.

"I think you have a great deal to consider, too, Joshua."

"You're very bright and perceptive. Yes, I have much to consider, too. I also have some unfinished business."

The two climbed into a taxi as David Jr. tried to figure out what remained to be finished. In an hour, they were at Deborah's apartment in Wildwood. David Jr. ran into the house as Joshua paid the cab and slowly walked up to their apartment. Deborah was waiting at the door and welcomed him with a glass of ice water.

"Your favorite as I recall," she said as they sat down together on the sofa.

"This soft couch is like a bit of heaven," he commented. He sat back and closed his eyes. "You won't believe what happened."

"Well, I heard a bit of rambling from Jr., but tell me the rest . . . from the beginning."

Joshua recounted the entire tale from the moment he arrived in the underworld until he stepped out of the taxi in front of Deborah's apartment. When he finished, Deborah breathed a sigh of relief.

"Just hearing such a story is exhausting," she remarked. "You should be knighted or given the key to the city or something. Do you think it strange what happened to Jake?"

"Strange? No, not strange; more of a miracle. You know what is miraculous? When I had my final encounter with Amos Pierson, I thanked him for his creation of Jake. I mean Jake exactly matched the prototype in the schematic I found on that island. Do you know what he told me?"

"What?"

"He never made any prototype. He was playing with the design and theory, but that's as far as he got. That's why I call it miraculous. Divine intervention is always welcome. As I think back on my 'teaching' it's very apparent that the student provided much more education than the teacher. Perhaps I was really on the road to Emmaus."

"Well, I'm glad it all turned out for the best."

"It turned out, I'm still not sure it's for the best. How's David?"

"Still the same; locked in with no change; although he seems to be happy. He's always got a smile on his face. And, from what I've been able to find out, your Beauty is also the same. I'm afraid we'll have to accept that they'll never be better."

"I'm not so sure," Joshua said as he reached into his pocket and pulled out the single active chip that had been part of Jake. "This comes from Jake and I suspect directly from Heaven. I think it can be used to restore David."

"It's yours," Deborah answered. "If it has any sort of power, use it to help Beauty. You've given so much of yourself. The two of you deserve some happiness."

"Listen, I've given this a great deal of thought and you know that I'm usually right. David has a family, his work is very important, more important than anything I will ever do. It's best that we try it on him. Besides, for all we know it may not do anything or it may remain active enough to use a second time, but one thing I'm sure about is that this is meant for David."

Deborah realized that there was no point in arguing further. She started to feel a sense of elation and anticipation. She called her kids and the four of them headed to the hospital. When they arrived, Joshua stopped at the entrance and put the glowing chip into Deborah's hand.

"Take this," he said, "and put it behind his ear. I'm leaving you to attend to some unfinished business. You don't need me for this and I'd rather let you be alone with David and your children. I'll stop by later."

"But . . ." Deborah started to object, but Joshua was gone. She stared at the dime-sized bit of silvery metal. It emanated a reddish golden glow and she thought she felt a slight vibration as it rested in her palm. She clenched her fist around, put her arms around her two children and went up to David's room.

❧

CXV. Joshua

JOSHUA COULDN'T BEAR TO STAY WHILE DEBORAH WENT to see David. In his mind he knew that he had done the proper thing, but his heart told him otherwise. He feared that at the last moment he would snatch the bit of life out of Deborah's hand and use it for his own selfish purpose. And he did have unfinished business to attend. His first stop was the police station and a meeting with the head of homicide, someone named Ryan.

He called the police station as he was walking and made sure that Lt. Ryan was available. His primary intent was to clear his name, even if suspicions aimed at Gideon Jones died with the presumed demise of Mr. Jones at the Westchester facility. He also had some strong suspicions regarding the series of events and the police could be very helpful in confirming or refuting these. The autumn day was warm and sunny as he walked the few kilometers to the station. He felt at peace for the first time in a long time; finally seeing a way to end the years of unease he had experienced waiting for the long arm of Diblonski to reach out and crush him. He hoped that it was Diblonski who would finally be crushed making the world free from his subtle, but very treacherous tyranny.

He walked into the main entrance of the police station and confronted the security scanner.

"Please stand on the two foot prints to receive security clearance," a voice ordered. Joshua looked around and saw two black footprints on the floor. He stood there as directed and a silent light proceeded to scan him from head to toe. The process was repeated two more timed and then a uniformed sergeant approached him.

"There seems to be a problem with the scanner, Mr . . ." the policeman said.

"Smith, Joshua Smith. What seems to be the problem?" Joshua asked.

"The scan is not making positive identification. It seems we have conflicting results that are ID'ing you as two different people. One Joshua Smith and the other, a Gideon Jones. This Jones is wanted for questioning in a double attempted murder."

"Your scanner is very accurate, Sergeant. That's why I'm here; to clear up the exact misunderstanding that your very efficient equipment has detected. I have an appointment with a Lt. Ryan, the Head of your Homicide Division."

"Just a moment," the sergeant said. He turned his head and spoke softly into his communicator. "He's expecting you; follow me."

He allowed Joshua to pass through the security entrance and they walked down a brightly lit corridor to one of the interrogation rooms.

"At least the scanner told me you're not carrying any weapons," the sergeant remarked.

Joshua nodded his head as they reached the windowless interrogation room. Lt. Ryan was waiting for him. He stood up and offered his hand as Joshua took it and received a very strong handshake. The room was well lit and cool with very obvious recording equipment and, Joshua was sure, more discreet physiologic scanners. He sat down opposite Ryan in a very comfortable leather-like chair.

"I'm glad to meet you, Mr. Smith, or is it Jones," Ryan began.

"Joshua Smith, Lieutenant. Gideon Jones is dead. He died up in Westchester County. He died of neglect," Joshua stated.

"It's interesting that you should know that, Smith; no one knows that except myself and a very few others. I presume you have a story to tell; I'm listening."

"Of course, that's why I'm here. I want to clear Mr. Jones name and possibly help you find the real murderers. You see, I am Gideon Jones. Rather I was Gideon Jones. It's a long story, but let's just say that you have very remarkable scanning equipment. That's how I know that Gideon Jones 'died' in Westchester. I lived through two weeks of hell and the remains you found were left to convince you that Jones was dead; to call off the dogs so to speak."

Ryan didn't look surprised in the least. "The dogs, as you so eloquently stated, have been called off for a long time. We've known for weeks that you had nothing to do with those assaults or any of the other murders."

It was Joshua's turn to be intrigued. "How can you be so sure?"

Lt. Ryan played his hand for a few moments, trying to build some suspense.

Joshua sensed it immediately. "You're looking at an old horse-player and someone who has literally cheated Death. You don't need to build to the moment. Just tell me."

Ryan smiled and said coolly, "No pollen."

Now Joshua's interest was piqued; "Did you say 'pollen'?"

"That's right, no pollen. The murder weapon, the victims, Representative McCally and one other murder victim named Crash all had one thing in common. A particular, identical, and unidentifiable pollen. And, you didn't have any on your person, at least according to the spectral analysis done at the scene. So, Mr.Smith or Jones, you were eliminated as a suspect fairly quickly."

Ryan continued, "We're pretty sure that Crash committed the two assaults; the ones perpetrated on David Sanders and Beauty. We still don't know who killed Crash and McCally."

It was Joshua's turn to smile. He sat back in his chair and stated, "That's very interesting, Lieutenant. I think I may be able to help. Give me an hour and then come to this address. You'll find your murderers there. I need to go first, however. They'll be expecting me. If the police show up, you'll find nothing. Trust me; do as I ask and you'll get your men."

Ryan looked a bit perplexed and voiced his disapproval, but in the end realized that Joshua was right. Joshua stood up and discreetly exited police headquarters and started out for the mansion of Aaron Diblonski.

❧❦

CXVI. Deborah and David

DEBORAH AND THE CHILDREN WENT UP TO DAVID'S room at the hospital. There were the usual nurses milling about and David lay in his bed unchanged from their visit the day before. He had a look of serenity on his face and Deborah felt a sense of peace within the room despite the interruptions caused by the beeping of various monitoring devices. The lights were dim and the curtains were tightly closed preventing any sunlight from entering.

"Could you leave us alone for a few minutes?" she asked the nurses. The two nurses that were in attendance checked all the monitors and then left the room. Deborah closed the door behind them and locked it. She leaned over David and gave him a kiss on his lips as Little Debbie and David Jr. climbed onto the bed. Deborah pulled the glowing silver disc from her pocket and held it up to the light; it seemed to glow more brightly.

"Perhaps we should give Daddy a bit of room," she said to her children. They both moved to her side as she said a brief prayer and put the chip behind his left ear.

David and Ruth remained by the edge of the water, but David couldn't stay seated and got up and walked along the shore. He had felt uneasy ever since he saw Joshua in apparent trouble. He would sit at Ruth's side for a short time, but, after a few minutes, he would jump up and peer into the water, pace around a bit more and then sit down again.

Ruth finally stood up and started to slowly walk away, remarking, "It is not time for us to be together. You have so much unfinished work. There will be time enough later on."

David realized she was right as he watched her slowly fade into the distance, until all he could see was her pink gown. A bright, white light appeared and he found himself standing face to face with the man.

"It is not time for you to be with us; Ruth is right. But, David, it is not good for you to let her leave you this way. Go after her; there is still a brief time remaining for you to be together."

David stared into the eyes of the man and then turned and ran after Ruth. As he ran the light became brighter and brighter as if the sun had come to that place. He caught Ruth and put his arms around her and kissed her.

Deborah and the children watched as the little disc glowed brighter and brighter. The light became blinding as it filled the room. A rushing noise like a strong wind swirled around the hospital room and Deborah heard faint pounding on the door which seemed very far away. The light grew so intense she had to close her eyes, but even with her eyes closed, she was able to see the light envelope David. She leaned over the bed and called his name.

"David, David," she said softly as the noise lessened and the light started to fade.

David, as he kissed Ruth, heard his name softly spoken. He looked into Ruth's eyes and saw Deborah staring back at him speaking softly, "David, I love you."

He opened his eyes and said, "I love you, too," as he wrapped his arms around her. The two children leapt on the bed, whooping and hollering with delight as David hugged the three of them and held them tightly.

Tears of joy streamed down Deborah's cheeks as she looked down at the little metal disc that lay on the bed, lifeless. Her happiness was interrupted by thoughts of Beauty destined to exist in a purgatory of bare existence and Joshua who had given everything for Deborah and her family, as well as so many others. David looked at her and sensed her uneasiness, looked into her eyes as she whispered one word into her ear: "Joshua"; he understood immediately, but only held her more tightly.

At that moment, the nurses burst into the room and stood back dumbfounded by the miraculous rebirth of the patient they had long given up as lost.

"Sometimes, a little faith can do what all the science and medicine and technology in the world can never hope to achieve; isn't that right, kids," Deborah exclaimed.

"YEAH," they screamed as they continued to hug and kiss their father.

෨ଡ଼ୡ

CXVII. Joshua and Aaron

JOSHUA STOOD AT THE GATE OUTSIDE AARON DIBLON-ski's huge mansion. He had considered that catching Diblonski completely by surprise might have been effective, but in the end decided that a direct meeting, completely up front, would be most appropriate. He pushed the button on the stone post and waited for a response.

"May I help you?" queried a disembodied voice.

"Joshua Smith to see Mr. Diblonski," he responded.

Nothing happened for about two minutes, and then the gate swung open and Joshua was greeted by a man in a black suit driving a small enclosed cart. The man didn't say a word as Joshua climbed into the cart and he was quickly whisked away to the mansion. The grounds were an immaculate landscape of bright green plants and a great variety of colored flowers, brightly blooming in defiance of the autumn weather. He was deposited at the front door which opened automatically as he walked up the brick stairs.

Mr. Diblonski was standing in the foyer and greeted Joshua himself.

"Welcome, Mr. Smith. I've been expecting you for quite sometime. I thought that I would have been your first stop after your recent success. Well, no matter; I'm pleased to see you now."

"You're looking quite well, sir," Joshua remarked. Indeed, the man that had appeared to be at death's door only a short time ago now looked to be in perfect health with an appearance of youth and vigor that belied his well-known extreme age.

"Thank you for noticing, Mr. Smith. Please come into the study." Diblonski motioned with his hand and Joshua felt a slight shiver run up his spine, feeling like a fly being ushered into the spider's lair. The two sat down in the dimly lit study as the huge fire blazed away, illuminating shelves of books and a variety of unusual flowers.

"I see that your fine watch has survived all your travails," Diblonski observed, pointing to Joshua's wrist.

"Yes, this is one very tough antique; a real tribute to Swiss quality and humanity's ingenuity," Joshua answered. He looked up as a door opened and closed and he saw Mr. Masur come in. "It seems you were expecting me," Joshua said.

"As I said before; we have been expecting you for quite a bit of time. It does make one wonder what you have been doing with yourself," Diblonski's voice seemed a bit more forceful.

Mustering his best poker face Joshua calmly answered, "I suppose it would have been proper for me to come to you first, but I do have other friends who worry about me. I thought that I should see them first and let them know that I had survived a very arduous experience."

"Very well," Diblonski accepted this explanation. "I must congratulate you on the splendid outcome of your little endeavor. I dare say that even Mr. Masur here could not have done it any better." Diblonski gestured towards his underling, who seemed to wince at the mention of his name.

Diblonski continued, "Although I am not completely privy to your methods, the elimination of Mr. Peskew's diabolical plan has breathed new life and vigor into Diblonski Ltd. and I am truly grateful. As part of my gratitude, I am prepared to offer you a very high position in my organization. Your resourcefulness, ingenuity and extraordinary powers of deduction have been and will be invaluable to us."

Joshua listened with great interest. "Exactly what are you offering?"

Diblonski did not waste any words. "You will be number two man in the organization, replacing Mr. Masur, who has reached the limit of his usefulness." As he spoke these words, five black-suited "executives" came into the room. Masur stood silently, but Joshua noticed a trembling of his lips and sweat starting to bead on his forehead.

"A very generous offer, sir," Joshua stated. "But, before you offer me something you may later regret, there are a few things that you should know about me. You have been searching for me for more than seven years, although you don't know it. One Richard Cosby, I believe, worked for you in a very vital role; one that helped you maintain a very special sense of order. This order, although still largely maintained, was disrupted somewhat by Mr. Cosby's untimely demise. Of course, I was there and I can tell you truly that his destruction was entirely due to his own hypocrisy and inability to properly judge the people around him. But, part of the blame for his downfall rests with you or Mr. Masur here as I'm sure one of you assisted with his training. After all, playing the role of evangelist does not come naturally to demons."

At that moment, another door opened and Coryllos came in from the foyer. Mr. Diblonski revealed a brief look of surprise when he walked in, but Masur didn't move. Joshua recognized the face immediately; he had seen it in almost every image of death displayed in the grisly hall of fame that was displayed in Hell. Coryllos raised his weapon and pointed it at Joshua.

Joshua maintained his calm demeanor. "Careful, sir; you wouldn't want to assassinate your boss's new right-hand man."

Diblonski gave a faint gesture and Coryllos lowered his weapon.

"It seems that we have all the major players here," Joshua observed. "Everyone that wants me dead," he turned his head to Coryllos and Masur, "or alive," he said looking a Diblonski. "Now, let me tell you what I want."

"We are all at your disposal, Mr. Smith," Diblonski said calmly.

"Good," Joshua started. "Let's make everything as crystal clear as possible. I would like to know who is responsible for trying to blow me up, both in the limousine and on the jet plane, and who arranged my little internment at that Westchester facility and I would like that party brought to me for punishment. As your second in command, I would require complete control of day-to-day operations and a direct line to you." He gestured towards Diblonski. "And, finally, I would like restoration of Miss Beauty to her previous picturesque form; something that I'm sure lies within your powers."

Diblonski sat down and poured himself a glass of wine. "Would you like to join me, perhaps, to toast the start of what I'm sure will be a long and profitable relationship."

"No, thank you. I'll remain as I am."

"As you wish. To begin; the failed attempts on your life and your unfortunate incarceration were completely the idea and were executed by Mr. Masur here. He was the architect and the engineer. He will be put at your disposal. I'll even grant you the services of Mr. Coryllos, a most capable assassin. Your request for operational control will be easy to grant, with the elimination of the current number two man. As to the young lady; her restoration, as you called it, is possible, but not immediately. Once you are established in the organization she will be allowed to recover. As a gesture of good faith . . ." He nodded his head and the five "executives" started to descend upon Masur.

"Why you . . . After all I've done . . ." Masur reached into his coat and pulled out a weapon and aimed at Diblonski. Before the five security guards could react, there was a flash and a short "Blip" and Masur fell to the ground. Coryllos replaced his weapon as quickly as he had fired.

"Mr. Coryllos is very good at what he does as you can see, Mr. Smith."

"Yes, I can see. I imagine the two of you have seen much together. Mr. Coryllos, I recently had an encounter with your boss. Oh, not the big boss here, no, your more immediate superior; the one so affectionately known as the 'Grim Reaper.' We played cards together, and I'm happy to report that he lost." Joshua stared at Coryllos and shook his head. "Poor Coryllos, a truly lost soul. A shell of a man, who lives in fear; afraid of living, but terrified of dying. You are a man with the tenacity of a bloodhound and the power of a pit bull. I suppose that you will continue as always, living but not alive; a few moments of euphoria coming courtesy of the latest mind altering substance. What is it now, wine, opium, cocaine; no, I suspect it's the latest modern ingestable, Valustet, rapid onset, long lasting, easily reversed, few side effects. I look at you and I can see that you have been at evil's side for thousands of years. Tell me, did Adam and Eve cry when they were driven out? Or, were they defiant? Did Jesus utter any words to you before you nailed Him to the Cross? Did all those millions of Jewish cries fill your heart with joy or your eyes with tears?"

Coryllos started to pace back and forth as Joshua spoke and finally stopped and shook his head. He raised his weapon and pointed it at Joshua. "It wasn't my fault. I didn't have a choice; surely you can see I didn't have a choice."

Joshua remained outwardly calm. "Of course I can see that, but what I see really doesn't matter. I don't have any power to stop your suffering. I cannot ease your pain. There is only one who can do that, and although he is always here, you refuse to see him. But, only two little words can free you, give you everlasting peace and final rest."

Coryllos lowered his weapon and continued to shake his head. Joshua sensed his desperation, walked across the room to his side and put his arm around him. He noticed a striking gold chain around the distressed man's neck with diamonds and emeralds on a pendant hanging from the chain. He remembered a very similar piece of jewelry adorning a much different person in a much different place. Joshua spoke softly to Coryllos.

"Did he promise that you would be united together, that he was protecting her so that at some vague time in the future you could be together for eternity? I know how you must have suffered, but I can tell you that she's not there. He doesn't control her anymore; she's free from torment and, finally, at peace. If you want to be with her you must listen to me."

He whispered in Coryllos' ear and a faint smile appeared on the assassin's face. Coryllos mouthed a few words silently and then looked up at Diblonski. He looked at Joshua and then Diblonski and then raised his weapon. Before he could make another move a silent flash appeared and Coryllos crumbled to the floor. Joshua crouched down and cradled his head.

"I'm sorry," Joshua said softly.

Coryllos raised his finger to his lips as if to silence Joshua's words. "Thank you," he whispered in a barely audible voice and a smile appeared on his face, a smile of final peace, before he died.

Joshua gently laid the dead man on the floor and then sat down opposite Diblonski. "It seems that your hired help is having serious health issues. But, I'm sure it's no worry to you. There are billions more to come to your aid." Joshua looked around the room. "These are some very impressive flowers you have here."

Diblonski nodded his head as if to say thank you, but remained silent as Joshua continued to speak.

"They do release a lot of pollen, however. Look at the dust on this lamp."

Diblonski responded, "Yes, it requires a great deal of diligence by my cleaning staff."

"I don't suppose that you are aware that this pollen sticks to all sorts of surfaces, clothing, skin, even weapons. It looks like it comes from this particular plant. It's really very beautiful." Joshua held up a pot containing a plant adorned with bright orange and red flowers. There was a thick dusting of pollen on the soil and along the edge of the pot. Joshua continued, "I'll bet that if the police arrived right now and tested the pollen from this 'one of a kind' plant it would match the pollen found at the murder scenes of Rep. McCally, Crash, and the assaults on David Sanders and Beauty. Do you think that I'm right?"

Diblonski remained composed as he answered, "You are extremely perceptive, Mr. Smith, a talent I find very admirable and one that will be very useful in my organization. I offer you the world. I offer you kings and presidents that will bow to you, power that you cannot imagine. You have already shown me remarkable fortitude and resolve. If you join me I will give you an eternity of wealth and power unimaginable."

"Until . . ." Joshua interjected, "Until someone new comes along to take my place and then I spend the rest of eternity roasting alone on a spit in Hell. No, Mr. Diblonski, what you offer is not enough. I don't think you have anything that I want. This," he held up a small transmitting device, "has everything on it. Perhaps not enough to send you to jail, but enough to bring Diblonski Ltd. to its knees."

"But," Diblonski interrupted, "you forget about Beauty. If she dies now or later she will belong to me and she will suffer the worst cruelty and pain one could imagine. Are you going to let that happen to one who is so innocent."

"I certainly know that what you say is possible, but I put my faith in God. If He is truly just, He will free her. I know that even if she is lost to me, God will free her." And Joshua activated the transmitter.

At that moment, Diblonski nodded his head.

❧

CXVIII. Final Confrontation

LT. RYAN AND HIS MEN WERE STATIONED AT STRATEGIC points around the Diblonski mansion. They quietly deactivated all the security systems and then waited. He figured they could be inside the building in less than thirty seconds once the signal was received. After some thought, he decided that they needed to be closer. He sent word to his men and they moved closer to the building. The security personnel they encountered were quickly disabled before they could put up any fight. *Thank you neural disrupters,* Ryan thought as his two hundred officers silently entered the home through every window and door. Once inside, they waited.

The wait wasn't long as Joshua's signal sounded loud and clear in Ryan's earpiece. They immediately cut all the power to the house throwing it into darkness.

In the study, Joshua noticed the gesture from Diblonski and threw himself down to the floor as the lights went out and flashes emanated from every corner of the room. There were screams from police and Diblonski security forces as Joshua crawled under a nearby table, reaching up to the end table and pulling the incriminating plant to the floor and cradling it to his chest. He looked up to see silent flashes going back and forth. After what seemed to be an eternity, but in reality was less than two minutes, the flashes stopped and the lights came on.

He felt a hand tap him on the shoulder and looked up to see the smiling face of Lt. Ryan. The lieutenant offered his hand and helped Joshua to his feet.

"Are you OK?" Ryan asked.

Joshua looked around and saw blood on his right shoulder. He lifted the plant and felt pain shoot down his arm. "I guess I've been shot," he said with an air of indifference. "Here's some evidence for your murder investigation." He held the plant out and Ryan took it and carefully handed it to a uniformed officer.

Joshua looked around the room. Two of Diblonski's security people lay dead and the other three were in custody along with Diblonski, who trembled uncontrollably as if he had a neurologic disorder; his face suddenly lined with wrinkles; the tan replaced by a rough grayish hue. His hair was white and scraggly and Joshua realized that there were very few days remaining for Aaron Diblonski.

Ryan called an ambulance and Joshua was taken to a nearby hospital, treated and released. He wondered how Deborah had made out as he walked up the stairs to the apartment he hadn't lived in for months. He lay down in his bed and passed into a deep, peaceful sleep, dreamless and untroubled for the first time in years.

಄಄಄

CXIX. Media Response

THE ASSAULT ON THE DIBLONSKI RESIDENCE WAS INItially met with anger by the various media outlets. Such an unwarranted invasion of personal property was to be condemned was the initial consensus. However, as the facts were revealed and details of Diblonski's numerous misdeeds came to light the tone changed considerably. The report filed by Brian Sivestre was typical:

"Details of a vast conspiracy by the Diblonski Ltd. empire have been trickling out of the Northeast Police headquarters over the past several days. The conglomerate apparently was deeply involved in everything from bribery of government officials to murder. The Senate has called for an immediate investigation into all aspects of the Diblonski corporation with dismantling of the conglomerate the ultimatel goal.

It, of course, was inevitable anyway with the demise of the top two executives within the Diblonski organization. Abraham Masur was found dead at the Diblonski mansion in New Jersey, allegedly murdered by one of the chief executives own bodyguards, while Aaron Diblonski himself succumbed shortly after being taken into custody. Preliminary reports state that the well known tycoon suffered a massive stroke on his way to police headquarters and died a few hours later. The investigation remains ongoing . . ."

The whole nasty affair was fodder for the various media outlets for weeks as truth melded with hyperbole until no one was sure what had really happened.

಄ೲ

CXX. Dinner with David

JOSHUA WAS GLAD THAT DAVID HAD BEEN RESTORED BY the gift from Jake and as soon as they both had enough time to recover he invited his friend for dinner. David arrived alone looking as fit and healthy as ever. He even remembered to bring some fresh food, arriving at the apartment with a bag filled with fresh bread, wine and cheese.

"Where's Little Bit?" Joshua asked.

"Home," David answered. "Not home with Deborah, but his final home."

Joshua understood as he ushered David into his home and put the food items away. When he returned he looked into David's eye and then down at his own feet.

"I'm sorry for my lack of trust," he said. "Perhaps if I had taken the time to listen, none of this would have happened."

David put his arm on his friend's shoulder. "None of this was by your design or mine. It was all part of a grander scheme. Just look at what you did. Because of you, evil has been vanquished and the word of God has an even greater chance to flourish. No, this was all for the good."

Joshua poured a glass of wine for David and ice water for himself and they sat down on Joshua's very comfortable sofas.

"Of course, you missed most of it; slept right through the whole thing, while I was being starved, chased by demons, matching wits with all sorts of evil beings, even literally cheating Death. I think I've had enough adventure for ten lifetimes. If you are talking to God anytime soon, tell Him thank you for the ride, but it's time for me to get off."

David smiled as Joshua made these remarks. "For someone who long ago dropped out of 'polite' society, you certainly seem to have a knack for jumping in where you don't belong. Isn't it time you went back to the track?"

"Soon, very soon. I've got a lot of unfinished business. I'm going back to New York tomorrow to stay with Beauty and to find out what happened to Mr. O'Donnel. You know that O'Donnel said something when I first met him. He said the best way to hide is to be in plain sight, a place where no one expects to find you. It worked for me and as I think about it, it worked for him."

"What do you mean?"

"I mean that nothing that I did had anything to do with me. Everything was orchestrated by God. Start with O'Donnel's name, Gerald O'Donnel, i.e. God. Those goggles; they were nothing but plain glass, but they allowed me to see things that I was blinded to, all because of my faith in them. Even now, I can walk down the street and see things that I never saw before, without any such 'goggles.' And then there was Jake, my so-called student. Only he did much more teaching than I did. He opened my eyes to the real truth in the Bible. Oh, I always had this intellectual understanding of it, but only after my sessions with Jake did I really grasp its true nature and value. It's a bit of what you experienced, a personal encounter with God's son; only I didn't realize it at the time."

"Now do you believe the truth?"

"I believe that God is there and that he does care for us and I believe that he has used me for some great purpose; I even had the purpose behind creating us with an appendix explained."

"But . . ."

"But, even with Satan deposed and the world free, at least for a while, there is still tremendous evil. I can't get the images of Hell out of my mind, that sweet innocent child sentenced to endless pain, seemingly for no reason; it's going to drive me mad. And, another thing; what about Beauty? If she dies, what becomes of her? An eternity of torment all because of an untimely, unfortunate event? If that is God's justice then I don't want to be part of it. Besides, suppose she dies tomorrow and I have said that I accept God and Jesus and I'm ready to be trundled off to Heaven. What becomes of her? If I keep myself as I am and I die, then I get sent to Hell. That gives me a chance to rescue her. Isn't her future worth the risk?"

David thought about Joshua's words for a minute and then remarked, "Your logic is always impeccable, but you've made a fatal error. You judge God on your level. He has one thing that you or I can never have nor completely understand: besides justice, He has infinite mercy. If you pray and God agrees that your prayers are for the good and for His glory, then He will answer them; in a way that glorifies Him, but will also satisfy you. And, perhaps God has a plan, a plan hidden from us to redeem those lost souls suffering in Hell. I have to believe this; I have to have faith in God's mercy and His grace."

"I hope you're right," Joshua answered. "I've done nothing but pray for Beauty since the whole incident started. I also pray for all those suffering in Hell and in this world." At that point there was a bell and dinner was ready. Joshua turned on Berlioz and they sat down to pasta with eggplant with three cheeses and a salad, washed down with a fine red wine. Dinner conversation found David filling in Joshua on his adventure in the twilight world he had visited as they talked about family, the weather, and left God alone for a while.

After dinner, conversation turned to more specifics about Joshua's plans.

Joshua answered, "I'm going up to New York tomorrow. I haven't seen Beauty in weeks and I just want to be with her. And, like I said before, check on Mr. O'Donnel and I also need to check in on Amos Pierson. I'm not sure about him. He seemed a bit overwhelmed by all the events and a little ambivalent about God and almost angry about being back in the world. I'm worried that he will dismiss all that I told him and that the realities of Hell will fade from his memory. I don't think that he was what would be considered an upright individual before, he seems depressed and I don't think he copes well with this crazy, mixed up Earth. Anyway, I think I have some obligation to help; to try to save him from himself."

David stopped him. "You have presented the Gospel to such lost individuals over and over, with some success. I wish you would truly, finally believe your own words."

Joshua sat back and closed his eyes. "Jessie Sorino said almost the exact same thing to me years ago. On a purely intellectual level nothing makes more sense or is as clear as the Gospel of Jesus Christ. I wish I could dismiss the doubts that continue to plague me. All my recent experiences scream of God's presence and his constant intervention into this world. I really should be standing on rooftops shouting His name and imploring people to stop and repent. Who knows, perhaps that's what I'll be doing next week."

He sat up straight and opened his eyes. "Tomorrow, however, I'll be sitting at Beauty's bedside. And the next day and the next; as long as it takes. If by some miracle she can be restored then, perhaps, I can be at peace. I was worried that I may have some trouble getting to see her or staying with her, since I'm not family and all. But, she has no family and is under the government's authority. I'm sure whoever is in charge will be happy to let someone else be responsible. Then, I hope that after everything is resolved, I'll find my way back to the track. I hope all this adventure hasn't dulled my instincts. How about you, what will you do?"

"I'll spend some time with the family and then return to work. I think I'll try out west a bit. The East has had a good start and Aldous is making good headway in New York."

"Looking for a new dog?" Joshua asked.

"Little Bit will be hard to top. Maybe I'll take a walk through the market one day and see if any little white dog tries to steal my food. If he can beat me like Little Bit did then that'll be the one. Until then I think I'll stay solo. Maybe I'll get a cat."

Joshua wrinkled his nose at this suggestion, but didn't comment. They shook hands and David slowly walked away. Joshua was left with the sense that he would never see his friend again.

෬∞ණ

CXXI. Ride To New York

AT NINE O'CLOCK IN THE MORNING JOSHUA CLIMBED into a taxi and started on the short ride into New York City. He flipped on the news as the cab pulled onto the turnpike. He saw the familiar face of Brian Sivestre, who immediately appeared as a hologram in the adjacent seat.

". . . in a stunning chain of events the Diblonski empire has suffered an unprecedented collapse. Government agents swooped down on Diblonski Ltd. headquarters in New York City today and seized thousands of documents that allegedly detail corruption that touches the highest levels of the government as well as the Diblonski hierarchy. Charges of bribery, securities fraud, and even murder have been whispered about just hours after the murder of Diblonski president, Abe Masur, and the incapacitating stroke and final demise suffered by Aaron Diblonski.

"Congressional and United Nations leaders are saying that only a breakup of the conglomerate will prevent a reoccurrence of such criminal behavior. Recently appointed interim CEO Peter Simmons held a press conference just a short time ago and promised full cooperation with government officials." The image of Sivestre faded as Simmons appeared with a very grim look on his face.

"We've practiced our business in the shadows for too long," Simmons stated. "It's time for openness and time for Diblonski Ltd. to clear the air regarding many of its business practices." Simmons image faded away.

"Diblonski stock plummeted on the Global Stock Exchange today, falling by more than forty points, a loss of sixty percent," an unseen voice announced.

Sivestre reappeared and continued his report. "In a related story, Amos Pierson, the developer of the picochip and founder of picotechnologies, miraculously reappeared today. Picotechnologies, which is best known for the ubiquitous Green Dot, was sold to Diblonski Ltd. over fifteen years ago. Pierson disappeared shortly after this sale and was presumed dead. However, his return was brief as tragedy occurred when he fatally plummeted from a pedestrian overpass above the Major Deegan Expressway. Eyewitnesses say he appeared distraught as he crossed the overpass, but reports were mixed as to whether this was a horrible accident or a suicide. There were unconfirmed reports that there was a handwritten note in his pocket which said, 'God Forgive Me.' "

An old image of Pierson appeared and then faded replaced by a young woman in a white jacket.

"Bellevue New York Hospital spokeswoman, Dr. Lisa Trestco, said the massive injuries that Pierson suffered made resuscitation impossible. Just how and when Mr. Pierson returned from his prolonged absence was not immediately known. A police investigation is ongoing.

"Finally, we have some sad news, also from New York Hospital. The lovely young lady known only as Beauty is reportedly nearing death. Miss Beauty, who captured the hearts of all of New York with her special vitality while dating the now deceased Gideon Jones was brutally assaulted several weeks ago."

The enchanting image of Beauty appeared and Joshua closed his eyes as the report continued.

"She has been in a state of complete neural disruption since the assault, but reports from those close to her say she is not expected to survive the week. Apparently, her organ systems are weakening and supportive measures are proving inadequate. Once again, Dr. Trestco."

"The tragic figure of Beauty has been such a valiant fighter since the incident that brought her to us. Unfortunately, the human body can only withstand so much and she is starting to fade. At this point only a miracle can prevent the inevitable outcome."

Joshua opened his eyes to see the hologram of Dr. Trestco fade away. He recognized her as one he had been acquainted with during his time in medical school. He was about to ask the taxi to speed up, but noted that he was less than two minutes from his hotel. He instructed the cab to reroute to New York Hospital as quickly as possible. When he arrived, he had no difficulty getting in to see Beauty. Somehow, his name appeared on the very short list of allowed visitors. He arrived in her room and found her lying peacefully in her hospital bed. He noted that her blood pressure read 80/55 and her pulse was 120. All the physiologic parameters were depressed, exactly what one would expect in someone who was fading out of existence. He sat down beside her and held her hand.

Dr. Trestco came in and smiled at him. She did not recognize Joshua.

"She's been my personal project," the doctor remarked. "Are you a relative?"

"Very close friend," Joshua said softly. "Very close."

"I'm glad she has a friend to be with her when she is so ill. It seems that she was all alone in this world."

Joshua looked up with tears in his eyes and whispered, "Aren't we all, Doctor, aren't we all."

❧❧

CXXII. Beauty and the Beast

BEAUTY AWOKE TO ANOTHER DAY IN HER SPLENDID cage. Breakfast was waiting for her, but she didn't even give it a glance as she walked to the window. She waited for the curtain to be drawn, hoping that the monster would return. The past several days had been an endless replay of children happily playing and their parents chatting among themselves, casting only an occasional glance at their offspring at play. The violent ugliness of previous days seemed to be forgotten; indeed it was as if it had all been a nightmare that had never occurred.

The view from the window was crystal clear, illuminated by a bright sun that filled the blue cloudless sky. The children laughed and sang and Beauty was starting to think that it was impossible that such ugliness as she had witnessed could have come from such darling youngsters. As they played the blue sky filled with clouds; they all stopped and sat on the ground to a picnic lunch.

Beauty saw a light starting to approach from the distant horizon. As it grew larger and moved closer, she was sure it was her beastly monster. The families also saw its approach and quickly packed up their belongings and hid. The monstrous eyes and mouth of the ugly beast became clear as it moved closer and closer. Beauty watched as the families started to gather large stones and sharp long sticks; quickly returning to the safe cover of the surrounding trees and shrubs before the ugly brute arrived.

Beauty stood up as the monster drew closer and shouted at the window, "STOP, GO AWAY . . . NO, GO BACK."

The beast couldn't hear and made his way right past the waiting mob. Beauty gasped as she could see their faces as they stood up and surrounded their pray. The clean, bright attractive men, women and children were gone, replaced by hideous figures with small wide set eyes, pig-like snouts, long sharp teeth and coarse hairy bodies. The only difference between the men, women and children was their size.

The gracious monster was surrounded by these demons from Hell and they set upon him unmercifully, beating him repeatedly with their sharp rods, pelting him with stones and whipping him nonstop for an interminable period of time. Beauty pounded on the window, to no avail, she screamed and cried and finally took a large silver platter from her table and hurled it at the window.

A bright light filled her room as the horrific assailants scattered in the face of this newcomer interfering with their sport. Beauty rushed from the safety of her prison to save the beaten, bleeding figure. She found him nailed, with huge spikes, to one of the posts; nails piercing his hands and feet. Bloody fluid was pouring from deep gash in his right chest, his face was swollen and bruised and, free of her cage, she could see he was no longer a beast. Indeed, the beast was now a man, dark olive skin, dark hair, and gentle blue eyes that stared clearly back at her as she, with miraculous strength, lay the post down on the ground and freed his hands and feet.

Blood poured from the open wounds drenching her in a crimson bath as she cradled the dying man in her arms. She looked down at the kind, piercing blue eyes that stared at her, revealing a love that filled her heart and soul with a peace she had never known.

He started to slowly close his eyes and she screamed, "NO, don't leave me. I'll be lost without you." And, she laid her head on his shoulder and cried.

Finally, he found the strength to speak. "Thank you, thank you for your kindness. Even though my life passes away for a time, I shall return and always be with you. In your grief and in your happiness, if you look, I'll be with you forever." And he closed his eyes. She sat with his lifeless body in her lap as the playground faded away and the day turned to night. After many hours she finally passed into a deep and surprisingly peaceful sleep.

❧

CXXIII. Miracle

JOSHUA SAT AT BEAUTY'S BEDSIDE WATCHING THE MONOT-
ony of the monitors, holding her still hands, occasionally dozing, but
never leaving. He arranged for his meals to be brought to her room.
He spoke to her of everything and nothing, recounted his adventures
or the day's news and events. Her failing body never stirred, never
responded, but lay motionless on the bed. Occasionally, the monitor
indicated a change; a rise in heart rate or blood pressure, rapid breathing followed by calm. Joshua took hope in these brief moments, but
then she would return to her previous state, but with a slightly lower
blood pressure or episodes of low heart rates. Joshua realized she was
fading away.

He sat down on the bed and wrapped his arms around her, half
expecting her to return the affection. "Oh, Beauty, what's to become
of me and you. You can't leave me now; how will I be able to follow?"
And tears welled up in Joshua's eyes as he laid his head across her
chest.

He sat up when a nurse came in to turn on the lights and bring his
dinner. The sudden brilliance of the bright overhead lights caused him
to close his eyes.

"I'm sorry I disturbed you, sir," she said.

He looked up at the young, attractive woman and smiled. "Quite
alright, miss; I guess I dozed off for a while. Let's see what they've
whipped up for me this evening."

He uncovered the tray to see a glass of ice water, sliced apples and
melon, a block of applewood cheese, and a fancy concoction of cake
and cream and strawberries for dessert.

"Fit for a king," he remarked as the nurse left the room.

While he sat at his table eating, a uniformed janitor came in with a
broom and a cart with various cleaning supplies.

"Do you mind if I clean while you eat, sir?" he asked.

Joshua waved his hand, gesturing to say go ahead. The man was very efficient, cleaning the windows and blinds, wiping down all the surfaces with a sweet smelling cleaner that had a scent like fresh baked cookies. The janitor whistled as he worked, a piece Joshua recognized as sacred music by Vivaldi. Joshua didn't pay him much attention as he stared at Beauty, listening to the rhythmic beating of the monitors blending in with the very clear tones of Vivaldi.

As the man mopped the floor he reached around the bed to reach a spot in corner and accidentally knocked over a pitcher that was on the tray table over Beauty's bed. The pitcher spilled all its contents over her, drenching her from her shoulders to her feet. Monitors started beeping louder and then ceased.

"I'm terribly sorry, sir, to be so clumsy. Let me clean her up." He pulled out a towel and wiped her feet. "This is soaked; I'll get another." And he left the room, leaving Joshua alone trying to mop up the mess.

As he worked he felt a slight movement. He stopped for a moment and looked at Beauty; she remained still. He went back to cleaning and felt her move her arm. He stopped again and looked at her face. There was some twitching of her eyes and nose, and then she opened her eyes. The monitors came back to life and starting beeping and chiming and Joshua was sure that they were playing the Hallelujah Chorus as a bevy of nurses stormed the room.

"What did you do?" one of the older nurses asked with a touch of irritation in her voice.

"What did I do, you ask. I did nothing but try to clean her up and now she's awake. It was your janitor that spilled that pitcher of water on her."

Joshua picked up the wet sheet which had a slight cream-colored stain and sniffed it. "That pitcher had water in it" he remarked, "but this smells like white wine."

"Impossible, we don't serve wine in this hospital."

"See for yourself." He handed the stained sheet to the older nurse as Beauty started to sit up and stretch.

One of the younger nurses turned to Joshua and said, "This hospital has a fully automated cleaning system. We don't have any janitors."

At this comment, Joshua stopped, smiled, and ran out into the hall calling, "Has anyone seen a man dressed like a janitor?" He raced down the hall, but no one had seen the mysterious man. He did, however, find the cart with cleaning supplies near a stairwell. He raced into the stairway, called up and down, but there was no trace of the man. Joshua returned to the cart and found a note pinned on it.

"Blessed are they which are persecuted for righteousness sake; for theirs is the Kingdom of Heaven." It was signed, G. O'Donnel. *That answers that question*, Joshua thought. He put the note into his pocket and quickly walked back to Beauty's room.

For Beauty the wonderful nightmare came to an end. The darkness that had engulfed her faded away as the slain "beast" she embraced started to glow, grew brighter and brighter until she was engulfed in a white light brighter than the sun. The light slowly faded away, receding into the sky, until she found herself in a bed; she sat up and found herself in a brightly-lit hospital room, surrounded by a group of strangers all with the most incredulous looks on their faces, smiling and pointing at her.

Joshua came through the door and saw her sitting up, looking as beautiful as ever. She saw the slightly built man come in the door; there was something very familiar about him.

"Gideon?" she asked.

"Close," Joshua responded and he sat down on the bed as the nurses laughed and cheered.

ও∾ô

CCXXIV. Later

WEEKS LATER, AS BOTH JOSHUA AND BEAUTY REGAINED their strength, thanks to expert care provided by Dr. Trestco, they found their way to Aldous' church in Brooklyn on a bright, sunny Sunday morning. Beauty was full of enthusiasm and new found faith in God's power and goodness. Joshua's doubts continued to nag, but not enough to keep him away. They were joined by Dr. Trestco, still very unconvinced, but with an open mind and curiosity spurred on by the numerous unexplainable events.

The church was full as the three found seats near the front. A small orchestra played Bach as Aldous stood for the Call to Worship. Before he could say a word, a lone figure stumbled into the front of the sanctuary, dressed in a white shirt and dark pants and looking very embarrassed. Aldous paused as Joshua got up from his seat and took the confused visitor by the hand and led him to a seat next to him and Beauty.

Joshua whispered to Beauty, "This is Randy Peskew, my dear. A very good friend." Beauty nodded hello and the three sat back to participate in the worship of God.

After the service, Peskew, Joshua, and Beauty met Aldous in the front of the church. Seated next to the front pews was Adam. Peskew had only met him that one time, but it seemed to him that the unfortunate boy was less active and had lost weight.

Aldous commented, "Ever since Martha left us, Adam has been fading away. He eats very little and cries and wails uncontrollably much of the time. He's quiet during worship services; I think the preaching reminds him of Martha and calms him down."

Peskew looked sadly at Adam and then asked, "May I take him out for a walk, to the park perhaps? I think it would do him some good; perhaps remind him of better times."

"A very good idea," Aldous replied. "Perhaps Joshua and Beauty would like to go?"

"We'd love to," Beauty answered.

The three walked slowly to the park and stopped just inside the large green metal gate at a large grassy area. It was a warm, sunny day with a light breeze. Joshua lay down in the grass as Beauty sat beside him, Joshua resting his head in her lap. Peskew wheeled Adam a bit farther and then raised the canopy over the chair to shield both Adam and himself from the sun. Peskew reached into his pocket and pulled a small dime-sized Green Dot out and, after looking around, placed it on Adam in front of the boy's left ear.

He murmured some words, audible only to himself. "Dear Lord, I know that I have been the worst of sinners and I deserve nothing, but this boy loves you and he deserves all your grace and mercy. He cannot ask for himself, so I'm asking for him. Please take this tiny man made device and use it to rebuild him; to rejuvenate him; to bring him back to those of us that have grown to love him. I know that by myself I can do nothing, but for the sake of my dear Martha who is with you at this moment and for the sake of Adam, please use this instrument of evil for good." He paused for a moment and then added, "In Jesus name I pray, amen."

There was a loud moan which brought Joshua and Beauty running. They saw Peskew standing over the chair and they saw the green dot glowing brightly. What they saw next filled them with amazement.

Adam's contorted face started to become untwisted. His arms fell to his side, and his spastic fingers straightened and then clenched into a fist. The acne on his face cleared and his legs extended long and straight. The Green Dot stopped glowing and fell to the ground.

Adam, his eyes shining brightly in the sun, turned to his companions and in a clear voice said, "I'm thirsty and I think I want to get up."

Joshua and Beauty ran to him and undid the strap that held him, and the young man stood up tall and then ran across the field jumping with a joy Joshua had never seen before. Beauty ran with him as Joshua stood next to Randy, who explained.

"When you destroyed the biological assimilation program I managed to save one chip that still had the active key. I wasn't sure that it would do anything for poor Adam, but I thought it was worth it to try. It's good to see that some good has come from all this."

Joshua nodded his head in agreement, but he was also sure that he could smell the distinct odor of freshly baked cookies, for just a moment, before the breeze came up and the pleasant scent faded away.

ༀ

CXXV. Pulitzer Prize

BRIAN SIVESTRE WAS ONE OF THE FIRST PEOPLE TO VISIT the newly united Beauty and Joshua. He felt personally responsible for their good fortune, having rescued Joshua and being the only reporter to interview Beauty. He spent several hours interviewing Joshua, asking question after question about his amazing ordeal. For the first time in eons, he did not need to add any embellishment, the remarkable tale being unbelievable already. From start to finish the "Trials of Joshua Smith" was the most widely read serial in over fifty years and won the Pulitzer Prize for Sivestre.

Starting with his friendship with David Sanders, moving on to his previously unseen role in the initial ITP voyage, his exposition of Senator Adrian Leavitt, his chance encounter with the slain Rep. Dennis McCally, Gideon Jones, Amos Pierson, and Aaron Diblonski, the story captivated audiences from Earth to Alpha Base One. It spawned a series of Senate investigations and kept Joshua busy testifying for several months. He was celebrated as a great American hero and efforts were initiated to draft him to run for political office. In the end he politely declined all offers. He wished he could simply return to the track.

After all the excitement, he and Beauty settled down together with a real lifetime marriage contract. They both were still drained from their ordeals and found a secluded spot in upstate New York to recover. They shielded themselves from the prying eyes of the media and tried to lead a normal life, which they did for many years until the next crisis descended upon humanity.

Acknowledgments

Very special thanks to Gianna Carini, Charles Gelber, and Duncan Long for their assistance in bringing Joshua and Aaron to publication.